OTHER BOOKS BY TODD WALTON

Inside Moves

Forgotten Impulses

Louie & Women

NIGHT TRAIN

A novel by
Todd Walton

MERCURY
HOUSE®

Mercury House, Incorporated
San Francisco

This is a work of fiction. Names, characters, places, and incidents are either the product of the author's imagination or are used fictitiously. Any resemblance to actual events, locales, or persons, living or dead, is entirely coincidental.

Published in the United States by
Mercury House
300 Montgomery Street
San Francisco, California

Distributed to the trade by
Kampmann & Company, Inc.
New York, New York

Manufactured in the United States of America.

Library of Congress Cataloging in Publication Data

Walton, Todd.
Night train.

I. Title.
PS3573.A474N5 1986 813.54 86-7905
ISBN 0-916515-13-3

for my wife, my love, my muse,
my best friend, Julie

NIGHT TRAIN

the earth spun us into darkness

1

No matter how far down you get, you gotta get up. You can't let the worst failure keep you from trying. I'm talking about being in the gutter. Not some middle-nothing depression. No. I'm talking about the *tangible* gutter, the concrete, the real stink dungeon. I'm talking about life hovering barely an inch above death. But even there you have to try.

I'm not a saint. Far from it. I'm a man, my skin happens to be white. I make art, so I haven't made much money so far. I've lived on the road, and I've stayed in one place. I've had things, and I've had no things. Got so hungry I'd put anything in my mouth—any drug, any smoke, any food, anyone—to quell the hunger. I've made mobiles out of garbage, painted my colors anywhere I could find a blank space, and written songs that made shit sound beautiful. To me, if nobody else. You gotta start somewhere, right? Here goes.

It's a hot and muggy September night, and the air tastes of death. I'm driving a stolen caddy down a bad stretch of Sunset Boulevard at two in the morning. I'm stoned out of my mind, singing my head off, when I see this young white woman running along carrying this little baby. She looks real good in her black miniskirt, white sequin blouse, and high-heeled cowboy boots. I pull over, open the door, she gets in, and off we go.

Now I'm rolling along with a woman and a very small baby. I thought I was ready for anything. You have to be or you don't pull over, you don't even slow down. I *thought* I was ready for anything, but I'm not ready for Lily. She pulls a gun on me and says, "Listen, boss, I appreciate the lift, but I ain't fuckin' you."

"Roger," I say. "I read you. Wilco, over and out. Ten four. Aloha. Whatever."

She isn't sure if I'm joking or psycho. To clear things up I add, "Now read this, lady. You put the gun away or this train stops. I put up with plenty, but not with guns."

She puts the gun away and pulls a knife. She does it for show and tell, but knives don't freak me like guns. I can see she needs the strength with her baby and all, so I just nod and we drive for ten minutes without either of us saying anything.

Finally I say, "Where are we going in my stolen car?"

Her baby starts crying. "Perfect," she says, shaking her head and rolling her eyes. She unbuttons her blouse and lets her child suckle. She looks at me looking her over, closes her eyes, and says, "I will kill you if you try anything."

"I got the message, lady," I say, looking away. "I'm not into force as an aphrodisiac. You know what I mean? It doesn't turn me on."

"Lucky for you," she says, her eyes steel.

"Lucky for me," I say, nodding.

"I need out of state," she says, shooting me a quick glance. "I can make it worth your while."

"I'll take you anywhere we can pay for gas to get to," I say, "though currently I am without funds."

"The car is hot," she says, calmly. "Interstates would be death."

"I know the back roads from here to Sacramento," I say.

"I've got a credit card," she says, nodding. "It'll probably be good until tomorrow night or maybe even the day after."

"We got assets to burn," I laugh. I like the way this gal talks.

"There's a couple people after me," she says, shrugging.

"Who?"

"The police and . . . some other people," she says, sighing. "But that's *way* too long a story."

"No jealous old men?" I say. She's got a body, this one. Long legs. Great face.

"No," she says, grimacing. "They're all gone now. And they only liked me because I can sing."

"You sing?" I say, smiling at her. "So do I."

"Sure you do," she says, looking out the window. She turns to me and says very sincerely, "I truly do wish it would rain. Don't you?"

Her baby falls asleep. She buttons up her blouse and resettles herself. She brushes her honey brown hair out of her eyes and shows me how beautiful she is. Not glamorous. Quietly beautiful. And sad. She has the saddest smile, the saddest frown. But she is so lovely her sorrow makes her even more beautiful.

She begins to sing. No warning. She just starts in singing a lovely tune I've never heard before, and she sings it so high and pretty, the tears run down my cheeks in rivers. She paints pictures in my mind. She kills off all my old vows. If she can sing like that, there has to be a God, and maybe hope. When she finishes, she puts her knife away and we stop for gas.

2

When we're fueled and moving again, I say, "I like Highway One."

"Oregon," she says, almost whispering.

"There's some bad spots along the way," I tell her, "but it beats the desert."

"I know places we can crash in Santa Cruz and Frisco," she says, sighing. She leans her head against the window and says, "When will I *ever* get to sleep?"

"Tired," I say, nodding. "I know how you feel."

"Yeah," she says, nodding with me. "Wish I could get somewhere and just *be* there."

"I know what you mean," I say, changing lanes. "When you're running you want to stop, and when you been stopped too long you want to run. I'd like to beat that someday. Or put a beat to it, or something."

"You write songs?" she asks, staring curiously at me. "You talk like you do."

"Yes," I say, nodding. "I sing pretty good, too. But not like you. I'm primarily a lyricist, but I love a good rhythm track."

"Sometimes I wish I didn't know music," she says, checking her baby asleep on the seat between us.

"Then you wouldn't feel this big record town pulling you?" I ask, smiling at her.

"You got it," she says, closing her eyes. "I've come close, so close."

"It's when you get close it gets dangerous," I say, remembering the feeling. "They'll rob you, kill you if they have to."

"They beat me up good," she says simply. "More than once."

"I wrote a song a long time ago that made the charts," I say, hoping it's true.

I haven't spoken of it in seven or eight years because it seems like such a lie, but I want to tell her and remind myself that I haven't always been down so low. I remember the power pulsing through me, the top of my head lifting off when I heard that song spilling out of a random radio. It made the charts for one incredible week. I made some money, but my sudden friends and overnight lovers gobbled it up before I could get out of my hole of an apartment. God, I hated that place. The little rooms of death.

"Which song?" she asks, trying to seem uninterested, but I can hear the tremble in her voice.

"Might be before your time," I say, hoping it is.

"I'm thirty-two," she says, shaking her head. "Can you believe it?"

"Never would have guessed," I say, trying to seem shocked. "I wouldn't have guessed a day over twenty-something. You're just a big girl."

"My name's Lily," she says, extending her hand. "And I'm a lady."

"Charlie," I say, giving her a shake.

It's nice. It breaks the ice. I let my shoulders down and smile out into the night. We're in the middle of nowhere and it's time to make our move.

"Oregon," she says, frowning to herself. She looks at me and asks, "You ever been there? I hear it's greener than anything. I love the color green. I just love it."

"I got some stuff stashed near here," I say. "Okay we get it?"

"How hot *is* this car?" she asks.

"Very hot," I say. "Blazing. Men with guns, etcetera."

"You do anything else when you took it?" she asks, picking up her baby.

"You mean kill somebody?" I say, grimacing at her.

"I didn't necessarily mean that," she says, looking away quickly.

"I'm not a killer," I say, my voice trembling. "I'm an artist. If I kill somebody, I might as well kill myself."

"You can get over it," she says, staring steadily at me, her voice a gruff whisper.

I hear death in her. I do. But I know she's a sweet songbird. I heard her sing. Oh God, what a voice. I can feel myself falling for her. I'm such a sucker for the multi-talented. But I'm scared, too. My shoulders tighten and I check my mirrors. The road is clear, but I'm not so sure I want to travel with her for much longer.

She senses all this. She watches me turning to stone. It seems to please her. She rolls down the window and sticks her head out into the wind. Her hair blows all sexy. Her butt is sensational. The kid wiggles its fingers and gurgles happily. I look at Lily and see how small she is, how slender and small. I want to see her naked, but I don't think I ever will.

"Be nice to breathe some good air again," she says, looking at me looking at her. "Which song was yours?"

" 'Hey Baby,' " I say. "A few people did it."

Her eyes widen. She doesn't say anything for a minute. She frowns and says, "Wait a minute. *You* wrote 'Hey Baby'? That's like a classic. You should be rich forever off that. I mean, you hear that in grocery stores. I heard it over in Italy, the only time I went anywhere." She shivers and glares at me. " 'Hey Baby'? Come on, man. I been to town. I'm thirty-two, remember? I can *sing*. That's a great song!"

"Well, I did," I say softly, not sure whether to believe it myself. It seems absurd. It seems like some drug-induced memory. Except I *remember* writing it. I remember how it crawled out of me when I was dying, and how when I sang it just right, and my voice held up on the high notes, it made my body tingle. It made me feel useful to the world.

"They keep the money from you?" she asks, putting a hand over her mouth at the thought of it.

"No," I say. "I signed my rights over to a man so they wouldn't kill me."

"Drugs?" she asks, breathlessly.

"Everything," I say. "And I mean everything down to nothing. Except for this, what you see, they got everything."

"Doesn't matter," she says, reaching out and touching my arm. "God talked through you."

And now she sings my song. She sings it and I hear it truly for the first time. She sings it high and sweet and pure. Now her voice turns all sultry and bluesy, and blows me away, blows me out of my body. I don't take a breath until she finishes.

Hey Baby, how you been?
Haven't seen you in a while.
Hey Baby, come on in.
Give your old daddy a smile.

Hey Baby, you're lookin' good,
Or I should say you're lookin' fine.
Say Baby, don't tell me you're in love.
Oh, I wish you were still mine.

Wish you hadn't believed those lies.
I swear none of them were true.
Wish you hadn't believed those lies.
I never stopped loving you.

I've been trying to get along,
But it's hard without you.
I've been trying to keep myself strong.
I been fightin' those blues.

Say Baby, won't you come again?
You know you made my day?
Hey Baby, why don't we be friends?
Then I can love you anyway.

Then you'll learn that all you heard were lies.
I swear none of them were true.
Wish you hadn't believed those lies.
I never stopped loving you,
Loving you.

3

Abandoned cars clog the streets around the ghetto of three-story buildings. If you haven't been to hell, you don't know this place. You can't imagine.

"Looks familiar," says Lily, as we pull into the alley behind the place. "Can we wait here? The baby fusses. I should stay."

"If you want," I say, "but I could use the cover."

"That bad?" she asks.

"No," I lie. "Only fairly bad occasionally."

"Think they'll hit the car?" she asks, looking around.

"Some pretty desperate people around here," I say. "But we'll be okay if we get in and out fast."

We lock up good and she comes with me. I figure the baby gives us an edge. We resemble a family. That usually makes the super-paranoids less suspicious.

Jackie's home. He doesn't remember me at first, but after his brain warms up a little, he unlocks the door, and lets us in. The stench is overwhelming. The toilet stopped working a long time ago. He goes in plastic buckets and pisses in the sink. There's garbage everywhere. The upholstery is all but gone off his couch. Newspapers and aluminum cans are scattered everywhere. The carpet is disintegrating. Under the garbage we can see patches of grease-stained concrete. The roaches are crawling all over the place and the fleas are hopping and hungry.

"Hey," says Jackie, smiling dreamily at us. "I just fixed. God."

He goes back to the couch and sits between two piles of fast-food containers. The television is on. The only color is blue.

Captain Kirk looks out at Jackie and says, "Do the best you can, Bones."

Jackie is big and round. His head is shaved, his cheeks are puffy, his chin dissolves into his chest. He's wearing a white tee shirt that only half-covers his huge stomach. He's got on blue sweatpants, tight on his giant legs. He has one sock on, a red one, and how he cares enough to keep going I couldn't say. His life is over, but he's still alive.

"He a friend of yours?" asks Lily.

"No," I say. "Friend is a gross exaggeration. And I do mean gross."

"Then what are we doing here?" she asks, glaring at me. She hugs her baby to her and wrinkles her nose at the smell.

"I have to pick something up," I say, feeling stupid for bringing her along.

"Okay," she says, her voice softening. "Get it and let's go."

She stays in the living room while I hurry down the hall to the one bedroom. The door is open and there's somebody asleep or dead on the bed. I tiptoe into the room and go to the closet. I hold my breath and pray my stuff is there, but it isn't. There's just rags and old newspapers.

Jackie is unconscious when I get back to the living room. Lily's still by the door, tense and ready to go. Her baby's waking up and doesn't like the smell of the place any better than its mama does.

"You get it?" she asks, her voice trembling.

"No," I say. "One more try."

I shake Jackie awake. He grimaces and says, "What the fuck, man?"

"Where are my tools, Jackie? My tools. Tools. I had two big red toolboxes here."

"No, man," he whines. "She never brought them. I swear to God."

He's lying, but I know it won't do any good to force it out of him. We don't have time.

"What do you need tools for?" Lily asks.

"I'm a carpenter," I say. "It's how I eat."

"We'll stop at a hardware store," she whispers, nodding rapidly. "I have a card. Remember?"

"What?" says Jackie, perking up. "You got a card?"

"No," I say. "No, no . . ."

He's on his feet and coming at me before I can set myself. He knocks me down and tries to sit on me, but I roll away and get up just as he does. I kick him hard in the gut. It's like kicking a sack of flour. It hurts me more than it hurts him. He backs me into a corner and I can see he's gonna hit me, so I jam a knee into his nuts and push him away. He pukes and I have to dance fast to dodge his spew.

Lily's already out the door, moving down the hallway, her baby whimpering. Jackie sits down in his own mess and gives me a dead look. I feel sorry for him, but there's no time.

I catch up to Lily outside. We're almost to the car. "Sorry about that," I say. "I didn't . . ." Suddenly I feel something big and murderous coming for us. The back of my neck is on fire! Lily sees me turn and turns with me. There's a big guy charging at us with a four-foot length of pipe. *Big* guy. Thick pipe. I get ready to dodge him. Lily shifts her baby from one arm to the other, pulls a revolver out of her pocket, and fires before I know she's doing it! The bullets fly into him! Into him! The bullets go into him and he dies! The man falls horribly and dies!

"Oh, my god," I say, looking away. "Oh, my god, no." I feel numb and dizzy, like I'm gonna puke.

Lily grabs my arm and shakes me, saying, "Move, Charlie. There's more coming."

We run and get in the car. I'll have to puke later. She tells me to drive straight ahead, though I'm not sure the alley goes through. But it does. Hallelujah. Twenty minutes later, we're almost to the coast. Malibu under a new moon.

"You want to tell me about things?" I ask, my body still shaking. "Friend of yours? Ex-husband? Bill collector? Your doctor, what?"

"I saw Pearl's Corvette," she says, her hands trembling as she holds her baby. The kid's been crying since the gun went off, freaked out of its little mind.

"Who's Pearl?" I ask. "Is that a company name, or . . ."

"She's the main person that's after me," says Lily, closing her eyes and breathing a sigh of temporary relief. "She's well-connected."

"You think they know this car now?"

"Yeah," she says wearily. "If it was hot before, I guess it's double-hot now."

"What did you take from her?" I whisper. I've never felt so cold in all my life. That man died so fast. No transition whatsoever.

"I can't tell you," she says, looking away from me.

"Lily," I say, speaking her name for the first time, "you *have* to tell me. It could keep us alive. We don't have any choice but to trust each other now."

"You wouldn't understand," she says, shaking her head. "Besides, we gotta stop and get some diapers for my baby."

"Nice way to dodge the issue," I say, glaring at her.

"You got any money?" she asks, her jaw trembling. She is very beautiful, and the trembling jaw has always worked on me.

"No," I say softening. "Not even a dollar."

"I have a little," she says, rummaging in her pocket.

"Is that what you took from Pearl?" I ask, imagining it is.

"Among other things," she says, coming up with a handful of cash.

4

My eyes are drooping as the sun comes up, but I'm afraid to stop somewhere and go to sleep. I think she might bump me good and take the keys. Then I'll be no place with nothing, as opposed to no place with a stolen car. Still, I haven't slept in two days and I'm fading fast. So I say, "Lily, I have to rest. Can I trust you?"

"I never do anybody bad unless they do me first," she says, looking me in the eye. "Besides, I owe you. They were right around the corner when you stopped for us. And I don't know how to drive anyway." She shrugs a couple times and says, "I just never learned."

"Wow," I say, shaking my head. "Can't imagine living around here and not knowing how to drive."

"No?" she says, frowning at me. "Most of the people I know don't know how to drive. But we make terrific passengers."

So I drive us to a little beach south of Santa Barbara and we park with the surfers. Lily carries her baby down to the sand. I climb in the backseat and go to sleep. A few hours later, she shakes me awake and says, "I'm sorry, but I'm getting nervous. I'd like to use that card before it goes bad."

"Sure," I say, yawning. "Be nice to do some shopping."

"You sleep okay?" she asks, her voice almost tender.

"Yeah," I say, getting out of the car to stretch. "I was dreaming about your baby, but I didn't know her name."

"His," she says, smiling at her little boy. He's sitting happy on the front seat, playing with his fingers. "Doesn't have a name yet. Gonna wait until a good one comes along. He's only ten months."

"Where's papa?" I ask, hoping she won't tell me.

"Don't know," she says, smiling ever so slightly.

"Why do they want your baby?" I ask, looking at her.

"Who said anything about that?" she asks, the steel coming back into her voice.

"Just a guess," I say, shrugging. "The way you . . . hover."

"Was I being obvious about it?" she asks, her voice shaky. "I'd really like to know how you knew."

"Just the way you hold him," I say. "Like you're afraid somebody might try to grab him from you."

"You're pretty perceptive, Charlie," she says, her eyes narrowing. "How do you know so much about holding babies?"

"I *don't,*" I say, raising my hands in surrender. "I'm sorry I brought it up."

"No," she says, pointing a finger at me, her face red with anger. "You asked why they want my baby, I'll tell you. Because I'm nothing to them. I'm not even a person. I'm just a lowlife. You know what I'm talking about? I'm talkin' about being nothing, Charlie. Except I have a baby, a perfect little white baby. And that's still something. Do you know what I'm saying? I *made* that baby. But I'm nothing to them. Except I have this baby."

"He's a beauty," I say, looking in at the boy. "Nice eyes. Your eyes, I think. He certainly has your lungs. That dude can scream."

"Yeah, he can," she says, proudly, her jaw trembling again. "You shoulda seen him crawling around on the sand. Looked like a sumo wrestler or something. Cracked me up. He'll be walking soon, pretty little thing."

She nurses him before we leave the beach. She's a tender mother, though she doesn't usually give in to his crying unless he's in dire straits. She reminds me of a gazelle I saw a special on. They have to give birth to their baby and get it up and running all in an hour, or the lions have an easy kill. I like watching him drink from her breast. It makes me feel good to see that greedy little life.

We park the caddy in the lot next to the old Mission Santa Barbara, squeezing it in between two Winnebagos and halfway under a big mulberry bush. It feels safe to leave it there for a few hours. I once knew a guy who drove a stolen car for ten years without ever being stopped. When they finally pulled him over one day, there was no record the car even existed.

The old car we're driving belonged to a drug dealer. He was having sex on a regular basis with my cousin. She was letting me sleep on her couch until I got the money to get a room somewhere. I had to leave every time he came over to bang her. I hated the guy, hated that he was doing my cousin, so I took his car. I had no plan, no goal. I was thinking I might just drive it into the ocean and quit fooling myself. Then I found a joint in the glove compartment, lit up, got high, and was just about to turn around and take the car back to my cousin's, when I saw Lily. Call it fate, call it stupidity, here I am. If he catches me, I'm dead, but I was almost dead anyway, so what difference does it make?

We take a bus downtown and go into a big discount department store. Lily buys herself some nice blouses, a couple skirts, and a pair of slacks. She buys me some clothes, too. I agree with her taste for the most part, but I have to draw the line at some of the more radical outfits. I let her talk me into some sleeveless shirts, because I can see she likes the looks of my arms.

Now we go to a shoe store and she goes a little crazy when we get in among all that leather. Her face turns red and her hands start to shake. Shoe freak. I have to take her aside and calm her down. Even so, she buys two pairs of high heels, a pair of tennis shoes, and two pairs of sandals. She buys me a pair of soft suede boots, a pair of pointy black Italian things, and a pair of French dress sandals. Her taste in socks is esoteric, but I don't quibble. I like her style.

Next we hit a hardware store, and I go a little nuts myself. When the man runs a check on Lily's card, we hold our breaths and get ready to run, but the charge is approved. Lily signs and we walk out of there with two big blue toolboxes, one full of hand tools, the other loaded with electrics. I'm happy. New tools always make me happy.

We find a grocery store that takes plastic, buy a deluxe ice chest and fill it with gourmet goodies. The only problem is we now have too much stuff to carry on the bus. So Lily goes back into the grocery store and pouts until the checker gives her a hundred dollars on her card so we can take a taxi back up to the mission.

It takes a while to get the car packed. I'm feeling exposed. I want to get going, but Lily wants to put on our new clothes and go see what everybody finds so fascinating about the mission. I tell her we're too close to Los Angeles to be playing tourist, but she wins out and we go in. It's a nice place, cool and quiet. Lily says it makes her want to sing. She wants to hear her voice bouncing off the tile walls. I tell her to go ahead, not thinking she will, but she sings a few lines of my song and all the tourists and the nuns and a couple priests gawk at us like we're insane, and maybe we are. Lily smiles at them and bows slightly.

An old man comes up to her and says she has a lovely voice. He sees the baby in her arms and tells her to go out on the patio and dip the boy's feet in the fountain. He says some people believe the water is holy. Lily asks him if he believes it and he says yes.

"What did it ever do for you?" she asks, genuinely curious.

"It made me happy," he says, nodding, "and my warts went away."

So, we go out onto the patio. The sunlight is dancing on the glossy bricks. The fountain is splishing and splashing, sending silver spray into the air. Her boy likes it. He makes all sorts of talking sounds and holds out his hands to show he wants it. She takes him close and holds him up to the basin. He splashes his hands in the water and shrieks with delight. Now she dips him in, all the way. He comes out smiling, unafraid, gurgling with delight, begging her to dip him again, but it's time to go.

As we're getting in the car, she says, "We should have taken a dip ourselves."

"Next holy water we come to," I say, smiling at her.

For a second I think she might laugh, but she catches herself. She isn't ready to get too friendly too fast, and I have to respect her for that.

5

"Where are we gonna stay tonight?" asks Lily. She's in the backseat changing the kid's diapers again. Little guy has the runs and he's going through diapers like old Custer going through the last of his bullets.

"I know a guy in San Simeon," I tell her. "Lives near the castle. Very out-of-the-way. We can get some rest."

"I hope he's better off than that other guy," she says, leaning forward, her face closer to mine than it's ever been. "Who was that guy, anyway?"

"Jackie?" I say, not wanting to talk about him, but knowing I'll have to. "He's a friend of a woman I used to work for."

"What did you do for her?"

"Anything she told me to," I say, wishing I could forget.

"That's the same kind of gig I had with Pearl," she says, nodding. "It stinks, huh?"

"No fun being a slave," I say, wondering how similar our lives have been.

"No, but sometimes it's better than being hungry," she says. "Not usually, but sometimes."

"Speaking of hunger," I say, clearing my throat, "I haven't eaten anything in a long time."

"Let's have a picnic," she says, kissing her boy. "On the beach."

We stop north of Morro Bay and I hold the baby for the first time. Little guy seems to like me okay, so after we eat, Lily takes off running along the sand, getting a little freedom. She runs clear out of sight. I don't panic until the kid starts crying. I've held my share of babies, but never without the mother close by. He begins to stink a little, so I carry him up to the car and take a shot at changing him.

He seems to like that more than anything, the little pervert. I lay him out on a blanket on the hood of the car, pull off his soiled diaper and wipe him with one of those antiseptic towelettes. I powder him, put a fresh Pamper under him and tape him up good and tight. Now I pick him up and hold him high in the air. He *loves* that. He giggles and gurgles and looks sad every time I stop. Crazy thing, life. Half a day before his mama was jumping into a stranger's car on Sunset, now that stranger is holding him, changing him, making him laugh.

She's waiting for us on the beach. I offer the baby to her, but she shakes her head and says, "Any trouble?"

"No, you got him liking a change."

"Clean him good?"

"Think so," I say. "I never had a kid."

"I had one other," she tells me, pushing her bare feet through the sand. "Gave it away. Never should have."

"Might be okay."

"Doesn't matter," she says, looking at me, her face full of worry. "She was mine. My only daughter. I can't have kids anymore."

"I'm sorry," I say.

"Me, too," she says softly. "They say I blew the transmission having this one."

I don't say anything. A man shouldn't talk about what he doesn't know about.

"Makes me especially sad," she says, looking out at the waves, "because I just started having this dream about a farm in the hills, green hills, and a river and a big garden and so many flowers you couldn't even try to count them all. It would be a perfect place to have another kid or two."

"Who knows . . ." I start to say.

"Yeah," she says, taking over, "I guess somebody might figure out a way for me to have another one before my hormones give out."

"Sure," I say, bouncing the boy. "They do things now that were considered impossible ten years ago. They can switch a man back on easy now."

"Little tube," she says, grinning at me. "In comparison, I mean."

"I know what you mean," I say, liking the banter.

We stop for milkshakes in San Simeon and I call my friend Jerry. He's home and sounds glad to hear I'm in town. He asks us to pick up some food and a couple movies since he's way back in the hills and doesn't like to come to town if he can avoid it.

We're about to head inland. Lily touches my arm and asks if we can stay and watch the sun color the clouds. Those are her words. She says she doesn't like to think of the sun ever going away. So we drive out onto a bluff overlooking the ocean and wait for darkness.

We have one of those edge-of-the-world sunsets, and I have a strange thought. I see the world as a petri dish, one of those glass discs where they grow bacteria for scientific experiments. I see human culture as this bacteria somebody put on the dish to see what would happen. And I see that we've spread all over the whole dish except out where there's too much water and no land. And I see that we're either gonna eat all the gel and starve, or we're gonna pollute all the gel so we can't eat it, or we're gonna radiate ourselves to death, or maybe somehow we're gonna stop being a cancer or whatever we are and change ourselves into something else.

I don't usually think about things like that. I usually just think about my own life. But that's what I'm thinking as we stand on that bluff watching the golden clouds and the sea and the sky and the shadowy gulls. I hold the boy and think about miracles. I listen to the pounding waves and feel like swimming out until somebody from the future picks me up.

Now I look at Lily. For a moment I feel like I've known her for a thousand years. She looks at me, her tired girlish face reflecting the soft light. Now she says in a whisper, "Seems like we've been together longer than eighteen hours or however long it's been."

"How long does it seem?" I ask, holding my breath.

"At least a week," she says, frowning at me. "I've never trusted a man with my child 'til I've known him for at least a couple of weeks."

"Well," I say, giving her baby back to her, "I'll take that as a compliment."

"I shouldn't trust you," she says, turning away and moving toward the car.

"Why not?" I ask, following after her.

"I don't know you," she says, speaking so softly I can barely hear her.

"I wouldn't ever hurt you," I say. "I like you too much."

She spins around, sets herself like a cornered cat, and snarls at me, saying, "Don't talk shit like that to me!"

"I'm sorry," I say, backing away, remembering her gun.

"You don't know what you might do," she says, holding her baby close. "You never know."

"I know I never would intentionally hurt you," I say, meaning it.

"Look, I don't know you," she says, calming down a little. "You helped me out and I appreciate it. That's why I bought you the tools, okay? But don't go making promises to me."

"But . . ."

"*Listen* to me," she says urgently. "You think I wanted to kill that guy? I *never* wanted to kill anybody. It makes me sick. It makes me want to die that I did that, but I knew him. I knew what he was gonna do."

"Who was he?" I ask, my heart pounding.

"He was Pearl's man," she says, shuddering. "He was a monster. He would have beat you to death, and then he would have broken all my bones and left me alive so Pearl could have the last shot."

"God, Lily, why would . . ."

"*Listen* to me, Charlie," she says, her eyes wild. "These people are crazy. They don't know what a promise is. They don't know anything except how to kill, how to take, how to rape, how to get things and keep things with guns and clubs and murder. And they will chase me until they get me. That's the only promise I can make."

"We'll just have to outrun them," I say, wanting to hold her, but afraid to go near.

"Don't be stupid," she says, shaking her head. "If you have a brain, get the hell out of here."

"No brain," I say, smiling at her.

She takes a step toward me, shoves the baby into my arms, and runs back toward the sea, to the edge of the bluff. I turn to watch her, and when she goes over the edge I run after her, but she's okay, walking slowly down the stony slope to the water's edge. She gets down there and wades out into the shallow surf. She folds her arms and looks out at the last of the light.

I decide to leave her alone. I carry the boy back to the car, feed him some baby crackers and listen to a ball game. Something about the announcer's patter pleases the kid. He listens wide-eyed, as if he understands.

Breaking ball. Outside corner. Tricky hop. Two and one. Full count. Slider. Hooking foul. Three up, three down. Deep drive. Double play depth. Two out. Bottom of the ninth. Down by one. Full count. Here's the pitch.

6

I know Jerry from way back. I met him in the living room of an old Victorian in the Haight Ashbury. We were both on acid. I thought there were green flames coming out of his head. I told him so and he started laughing. Little red bubbles poured out of his mouth. When I told him about the bubbles, he stopped laughing and howled like a wolf. He had fangs. That day or night, I don't remember which because the sky was purple, he gave me to his sister. She took me to bed and we made love in front of Jerry. He said we looked like insects. After that he called me Mantis.

Then the three of us hitchhiked to Big Sur, and Jerry's sister ran off with a black guy who said he was from Jamaica, but I'm pretty sure he was from Oakland. Jerry and I hiked a couple miles up the Big Sur to a waterfall. We dropped acid and fasted for seven days. I chose the fasting. He chose the seven days. I had a pretty good time, but Jerry freaked out on the last day. I had a hell of a time getting him out of the woods. Something had snapped in him. He was hallucinating long after the acid was gone.

We got a ride to San Simeon in the back of a pickup truck with a bunch of political activists going to L.A. for some election or protest or something. I got Jerry settled near the castle, and I went on down to Hollywood. He never left. He's been here close to twenty years, but I don't think he ever really made it all the way back from that last trip.

He lives in an old caretaker's cottage about four miles north of the castle. He grows marijuana and sells the buds to a dealer who visits him once a year disguised as a cowboy. The guy leaves his sharkskin suit in the closet, leaves his El Dorado in the garage, rents an old pickup truck, and drives up to Jerry's mid-October. He trades a suitcase full of small bills for a hundred ounces of Jerry's one-hit killer weed. Then he changes clothes and deals the pot for a hundred times more.

As we drive up to his house, and our headlights illuminate the scene, it looks like a still from some low-budget horror movie. The Night of the Living Dead Volkswagons. There must be twenty old bugs and vans surrounding his place. All the cars are pointing toward the house. I imagine it looks like a strange flower from the air, his cottage at the center, the vehicles radiating out like petals, catching the rusting rays of the sun.

"This guy have a girlfriend?" asks Lily, giving me a worried look.

"Don't know," I say. "I haven't been here in three years."

"Lonely out here," she says, shaking her head. "I'd want neighbors, wouldn't you?"

"He likes to be alone," I explain. "Just a few little ideas can keep him busy for months."

Jerry comes out on his front porch as I cut the lights, but I turn them back on to make sure it's him. He stands in the glare, posing a few different ways, imitating a fashion model. He's wearing a long white robe. His gray hair hangs down to his waist. His face is so changed, so emaciated, I'm not sure if it's Jerry or some replacement hermit.

"Welcome!" he shouts, his voice booming over the empty hills.

We get out of the car. He seems to float over to us. I hug him and there's almost nothing to hang onto. He bows to Lily and kisses the baby's hand. Lily shoots me a questioning look in the faint light of the open car door. I nod to reassure her, but the truth is, I don't know what Jerry's like anymore.

We carry the groceries and our stuff inside, and I lock the car up, though it's probably unnecessary. We're way out in the boonies. Jerry pulls a mattress into the living room for us and I help him make it up with clean sheets and big fluffy pillows. He shows Lily the little kitchen and demonstrates how to light the burners on the gas stove. After the quick tour, we sit on the couch in front of the fire. He offers us food, drink, or pot.

Lily says she's staying clear of everything that might be harmful to her baby, even sugar, until she stops breastfeeding him. "But the day I stop," she says, smiling at me, "I don't know what I might do. For now, I'll have some milk."

I have a couple hits and Jerry has a cup of tea. He keeps smiling nervously at Lily and peering at the baby. The more stoned I get the weirder he seems to be acting, so I say, "Jerry, what the hell you so interested in? You never seen a baby before?"

"She's a mother," he says in amazement, his voice hushed. "She's sacrificing herself for her child. She's sacrificing her own immediate desires for the health of her child. I think that's incredible."

"I don't want him retarded," she says simply. "They proved it'll do that sometimes. Not worth the risk."

"No," says Jerry, nodding, "that's exactly right. He needs the best brain he can possibly have. That's what my parents never understood. They tried to give me lots of *things,* you know, but they didn't feel they had any control over the quality of my brain."

"You still working on those engines?" I ask, looking around. The room is moving. The walls have a pulse. Lily is too lovely, too sweet. I am overwhelmed with a desire to kiss her.

"I look at the pieces now," says Jerry, frowning at me. "I have pieces from the engines spread out on the ground, and every day I go out and look at them. It's a puzzle. But I don't put it together because I don't have a vision of what the pieces make."

"Don't they just make engines?" Lily asks, standing her child up on her lap so he can work his legs.

"Ah," says Jerry, shrugging, "that's what I thought. But now that doesn't seem possible. There *has* to be something greater than the sum of its parts. The sum is an engine. There has to be something more, if life has any meaning, which it may not, but if it does I keep feeling that the answer is right here in the pieces, and I keep waiting to have a vision in which they coalesce. I sometimes think it's going to be a robot of some sort, but I guess it could be another of those jokes I never get. I watch the tube and I hear the audience laughing, but I never get the jokes."

"I'm tired, Jerry," says Lily, smiling at him. "How about we all get some sleep and talk some more in the morning?"

"Yes, you sleep," he says, reaching out and petting the baby's head. "I have to go to my plants. I have to do my weeding at night."

"In the morning, then, Jer," I say.

"Sleep well," he says, getting up and going to the door. He holds up his hands like a prophet and intones, "In the light of the new sun we will eat pancakes together."

"Okay," says Lily, waving to him. "We'll see you in the morning."

She gives me the baby and goes into the bathroom. I lie down, holding the boy on my chest. My mind is wild with thoughts. I can feel his little heart thumping, and for a moment I can't tell his heart from mine.

Now Lily comes in. She's wearing a thin cotton nightgown. I can see her body, shadow-like underneath. I like what I see. It's a sweet perfect dream. She takes the baby from me and puts him down on a thick quilt beside the mattress. Now she lies on her side facing me, puts her hand on my chest, and kisses me. I didn't think I'd ever get this excited again. I feel twenty.

"You don't have to do this," I say, pulling back a little.

"I want to," she says, pulling me closer, her eyes searching my face. "I said I'd make it worth your while, and I will."

I want to tell her she doesn't owe me anything. I want to tell her I care about her and her baby, but I can't speak. She watches me, her eyes searching my face, her hand still on my chest. She whispers, "Is it because I killed that man?"

"No," I say.

"Then what? You seem to like me pretty well."

"I . . . I don't want you to think I stopped for you because . . ."

She kisses me softly and says, "Nothing wrong with wanting sex."

"Maybe I did," I say, my heart pounding, "but now . . ."

"What?" she asks, kissing my cheeks, kissing my forehead.

"I don't know," I say, groping for the right words. "I guess I just want to be with you."

She frowns at me and takes her hand away. "You don't want . . ."

"I think you're beautiful," I say, touching her face. "I think you're about the most beautiful thing I've ever seen, and I'd love to . . . you know, but . . ."

"You're a shy thing, aren't you?" she says, pressing herself against me, running her hand over my bulge.

"Not really," I say, kissing her. "I guess I just want you to like me."

I stand up and take off my clothes, letting her get a good look at me before I turn off the light and lie down beside her again. I take her in my arms and pull her on top of me. We kiss slowly for a long time. She sits up, straddles me, lifts her nightgown over her head, and drops it beside me.

I can barely see her in the darkness, but I can feel her body and it's soft and delicious. She leans down and kisses my throat, her breasts brushing my chest. I pull her down beside me, kissing her mouth, her breasts, tasting sweet drops of milk. I kiss her tummy and the insides of her thighs, and touch my tongue to her pleasure and lick her until she spasms into orgasm and pushes my head away.

"Damn you!" she says. "Damn you! That felt too good! How'd you get me going so fast? How'd you do that? Damn! I don't like that, Charlie. I don't know you."

"I just loved you," I say, kissing her tummy again and again.

"Damn you," she says again, only there's pleasure in her voice now.

I crawl over her, kiss her lips, and start in, but she reaches down and takes hold of me and says, "That's a nice big thing, honey, but you gotta go slow with that, okay? I'm outta practice, so be nice. We'll do fine. Just go slow. We'll do fine."

So I go slower than I ever have until I'm in her all the way and she says go. I pick up the pace. She hooks her legs around me and gently kicks my butt as I move in and out of her. It's too much pleasure. It's better than any music. I never want to stop. I never want it to end. But I can't hold back. I get my hands under her butt, lift her up, and come and come and come and she's moaning with me.

7

"This puts a whole new light on things," says Lily, pressing her forehead against my shoulder.

"Yeah," I say, watching the day come on. "I guess it does."

"You *guess?*" she says, going up on her elbow and glaring at me. "I don't know about you, but that's never happened to me."

"I didn't know," I whisper, taking her in my arms. "I didn't know what you were thinking. I just . . ."

"Well, ask me," she says, pressing against me. "From now on when you want to know what I'm thinking, just ask me. I'll always try to tell you."

"What *are* you thinking?" I ask.

"I'm thinking I've never made love until you, though I've probably gone down with a thousand men."

"That's nice of you to say," I tell her, kissing her.

"I'm not saying it to be nice," she says, stretching her arms skyward. "It's just an amazing thing. I never thought I could enjoy it like that, and have all these feelings."

"What did you think it would be like?"

"The usual," she says, laying her head on my chest. "I haven't had much that somebody wasn't paying for." She closes her eyes. "If it bothers you to talk about this, I'll shut up. I just wanted to tell you how different it was, how good you made me feel. You're strong, Charlie, but you're tender, too. That's a real good combination."

"I'm as amazed as you are," I say. "It was the last thing I expected."

"Me, too," she says, smiling at me. "I guess things aren't as bad as I thought.

Her baby wakes up and she gets up to change him. She brings him to bed and lies in my arms while she nurses him. Nothing so sweet and satisfying has ever happened to me before.

Jerry comes home an hour or so later and we have that big pancake breakfast he promised. In the light of day he seems unnaturally aged and grotesquely tired.

"How far to your plants?" I ask him.

"The first one is about a mile from here," he says, seeming very sad. "I have thirty plants this year. It's too many. I get too tired."

"How do you water them?" asks Lily, giving her baby a piece of pancake. He squishes it in his hand so it gooshes out between his fingers.

"Drip system," says Jerry, almost whispering. "I tap into a spring on the ridge above them. They're growing in the poison oak, impossible to spot from the air. I can't find them myself sometimes. They're safe, but I worry about them. I have dreams about going to visit them and finding them gone. I'd like to have them all live with me here, but it wouldn't be safe."

"You need a lady," says Lily. She says it quietly, gently.

"A woman?" says Jerry, grimacing.

"A woman," says Lily, nodding. "You know, a female companion."

"You're insane," he mutters, getting up from the table, glancing around wildly and stalking out the door.

"*I'm* insane?" Lily asks, looking at me as she puts another piece of pancake into her baby's mouth.

"You scared him," I say. "He's been alone for twenty years. He just . . . he can't imagine it."

"Didn't mean to scare him," she says, picking up the boy. "Let's go talk to him."

Jerry's outside, squatting beside a long rectangle of engine parts. No piece touches another, but they're all nearly touching. It looks like a shattered metallic jigsaw puzzle. Jerry gestures out over the parts and talks to himself.

We squat down beside him. He glances at the baby and says, "You look out over these hills where that newspaper guy built his castle, and you think about the Indians and before them maybe nothing human, just bison and elephants and big trees, and you're talking about hundreds of millions of years life has been going on here. Now, you look at these pieces and you realize this stuff has only been here a split second, and it's already obsolete when, a split second ago, it was a revolution that changed everything. In twenty minutes it won't even be remembered. I spent eighteen years of my almost nothing life trying to make sense of it, trying to make these little metal turds go! And for what? I thought it was for something beyond me, and you come here and say I need a woman. And of course you're right, if I was someone else, but I'm me. It's too late."

"I'm sorry," says Lily, looking steadily at him. "I didn't mean to offend you, Jerry. I just meant you shouldn't be alone so much. People aren't supposed to be alone all the time. It's not healthy."

Jerry groans and shakes his head. He looks at me and says, "You were there, Charlie, when I saw those grids of different colored energy. Remember? I saw that death was nothing more than one energy field collapsing into another. The color changes. That's all. Death is when you change into something else you can't ever recognize or remember as yourself. And that would be okay if I believed God was physics, but I always thought I was gonna be reborn. That I would get another chance."

"And you saw something that made you stop believing that?" asks Lily, an urgency in her voice. "What was it?"

Jerry licks his lips and nods. "I saw the essential molecules. They don't have emotions. They don't care. That's it. They don't care. I get the joke, but it doesn't make me laugh."

"But at least it's not painful," she says, looking down at her baby. He paws at her shirt, trying to get to her breast.

"Except I don't *want* to be a different color and not

remember who I am!" he shouts. "I want to be a human again. I want a fresh start and to *know* it's a fresh start!"

"You can," I say. "But you do it *before* you die. You do it this time, Jer."

The baby starts to cry. Jerry stands up suddenly and walks away. Lily hands the baby to me and says, "He's gonna kill himself."

"No," I say, patting the baby's butt. "I don't think so. He's just letting off steam."

"You some sort of suicide expert?" she asks, glaring at me.

"No," I say, "but he *wants* to live. He just said so."

"He said he wanted to start over," she says, sighing. "There's a difference."

We go inside. Jerry's rummaging around in his room. I put the baby on the bed and sit down on the couch. I pick up a three-year-old sports section from the Los Angeles Times. And suddenly I realize that *I'm* the person who brought it here, three years before. The magnitude of his isolation and loneliness hits me in the gut. I wonder if my call was the first one since my last call, three years before.

Jerry comes out of his room. He's taken off his robe and put on jeans, hightop tennis shoes, and a swami somebody tee shirt. He has his hair in a ponytail and a red bandana around his forehead.

"Are you going somewhere, Jer?" I ask, getting up.

"Yes," he says, his hands trembling.

"Where?" asks Lily.

"Down the road," he says solemnly.

"You need a ride?" I ask.

"No," he says tersely, "I got one."

"This is pretty weird, Jer," I say. "Why don't we talk this out? We just got here. Let's have a visit. What do you say?"

"No," he says. He looks at Lily and says, "I have a name for your son."

"What is it?" she asks, smiling at him.

"Brother," he says. "Brother."

"Brother Jackson," says Lily, smiling. "Sounds like a preacher, if you know what I mean. Might make a good nickname. I don't know, I'll have to think about it."

"Well, that's what I'd call him," says Jerry, "because then he'll grow up thinking of himself as a brother instead of as an unconnected thing. And he'll always have friends because people will like somebody named Brother, and then he won't ever have to be alone."

"I'll think about it," says Lily, looking at her boy, trying out the name in her head.

Jerry goes out the door and I follow him. He heads east, moving fast up the steep sloping hill. I can't decide what to do. Lily comes up beside me and says, "He's going to die, Charlie. You gonna try to stop him?"

"How do you know?" I ask, not wanting to let myself believe it.

"Just a feeling," she says, nodding. "You recognize those clothes?"

"Jesus," I say, the back of my neck tingling. "That's what he was wearing that day in the woods when he flipped out."

"I'll bet he's got a couple tabs with him," she says, sadly. "Wants to take a last wild ride. Guess you can't blame him, huh?"

"Shit," I say, taking off after him.

"Don't get lost," she shouts, calling after me.

I nearly do. There's no way I can keep up with him, and when he sees me following him, he dodges into the high brush and poison oak. I hunt for an hour, hoping to find him sitting somewhere, off in a trance, but he's vanished. I call for him, but my voice sounds stupid and weak. I can't even get it to echo.

When I get back to the cabin, Lily's making sandwiches and the baby's napping. She puts her arms around me and kisses me. I tell her I lost him, and she says he might come back.

"Might have a good trip, you never know," she says, shrugging hopefully. "He might get past all the scary things and fly into that universal joy stuff and come back ready to try again."

"I don't know," I say. "Seems to me it just expands whatever you're feeling."

"No, that's what pot does," she says, kissing me again. "Acid blows you into new territory. At least the acid I took did."

"I never understood what I saw," I admit.

"You weren't supposed to," she says, pressing against me.

"What was I supposed to do?"

"You're supposed to make love with me," she says, her voice all breathy and sexy.

"What if Jerry comes back?" I say, taking her in my arms.

"He won't," she says, leading me to the mattress, moving the boy onto his quilt. "He'll be gone a while. I guarantee it."

I lie on my back, put my knees up behind her and she lets herself down on me, easing me into her. And now she gets going, her face so red and pretty, her eyes closed, her mouth open, breathing hard as she rides me and rides me until she groans and hunches forward wanting to pull off of me, but I grab her, lift myself up on my toes and rock in and out of her until I explode.

She gives me this sweet incredulous look and says, "I gotta rewrite some songs. Seriously."

8

I think we should leave, but Lily wants to stay. She says we should take advantage of the refuge to get rested up. So we settle into the silence. I write some lyrics, play with the baby, eat too much junk, and flip through a stack of old rock 'n roll magazines while Lily makes a thorough search of the house. She comes up with a big pile of coins and ten ounces of good pot. I'm for leaving it no matter what happens, but she says we oughta wait and see how we feel about things in the morning.

We make love again that night, though it feels strange to be making love in Jerry's house, not knowing if we'll ever see him again. He and I weren't especially close friends, but we shared such powerful experiences, I think I must see him as a part of myself. I can't stop thinking about him. Lily is so eager for sex, so praiseful of my body, but I keep thinking I hear Jerry coming back, and that keeps me from losing myself in our lovemaking.

In the morning, we see buzzards circling the ridge a couple miles away, so I figure we'll be taking the money and the dope after all. I fill a wine bottle with water, tie a bag of bread to my belt, find a pick and shovel, kiss Lily good-bye, and set off hiking as fast as I can make my old body go. It takes me an hour to get to the ridge and another half hour to find the body.

It's down in the poison oak, curled up around a marijuana plant so big I thought it was a tree at first. I can't see how he killed himself, but he's definitely dead and in need of burying. Takes me three hours to dig a good deep grave. I put him in the ground, tell him I hope he'll rest easy, take a few minutes rest myself, and fill in the hole. I spend another hour rolling big rocks on top of the grave, in case dogs come by and want to dig.

On my way back down the dry hills, I keep thinking to myself that I must be at some turning point in my life. So many overwhelming things are happening to me so fast. The cabin comes into view, but the car is gone.

I go inside the house, hoping for a note. The place is in shambles. A serious ransacking has gone on. I can't believe Lily did it. She already searched the place. It smells of desperation, and that usually means drugs. It occurs to me it might be the bogus cowboy who buys Jerry's pot, except it isn't October yet. I don't want to let myself think that Lily might have just loaded the car and left.

I go outside again, hoping the car has rematerialized. It hasn't. I look for tracks in the dust, but there's nothing clear. Somebody else has come, and Lily is gone. That's all I know. The question is, should I wait to see if she comes back or should I get the hell out of here? It's twelve miles to the coast. I have absolutely nothing, not even a stolen car.

I go back inside and crawl around until I come up with a couple dollars in change. I take an old knapsack and go out to Jerry's toolshed and scavenge a few rusty old tools. I go back inside, and as I'm rummaging in the refrigerator for something to eat, I hear a vehicle coming up the road. My hopes rise, but fall because it doesn't sound like our car.

I run into Jerry's bedroom and peek out the window. A six-wheel pickup truck, followed by the caddy, pulls up to the house. It doesn't look good. I don't want to try to sneak out. There's no cover. And I know if they see me, I'm dead. But I know they'll be coming inside. So I go into the bathroom where I noticed a little square of the ceiling had been cut out to allow access to the crawl space above. A piece of plywood is covering the hole. I stand on the toilet, push the plywood out of the way, and climb up. I slide the plywood back into place just as whoever they are come through the door.

Old two-by-six rafters run the length of the building. All

sorts of old boards are tacked to the bottomsides of the rafters to make the ceiling. I have to stay on those rafters or I'll fall through the thin wood. So I squat, my heart pounding, trying to hear what's going on below. It's dusty and I'm having old movie fantasies of sneezing and giving myself away.

Whoever they are, they gather in the living room. I'm too curious to stay where I am, so I inch along the rafters until I'm almost above them. I can make out three men's voices.

"Somebody went through here before us, I'd bet that," says one of the men. "You said he left money and dope just lying around. This place was cleaned out."

"Yeah, but where is he?" asks another man. "Maybe he packed up and went on a trip."

"No," says a third voice, a deep powerful voice. "He's in the hills somewhere, right around here. He can't leave here. The man's terrified of everything. That's how come I could cut the deal with him. You see what I'm saying? I'm trying to teach you guys something. You find the weakness, then you exploit it."

"Why doesn't he come down?" asks the first voice.

"The call may have freaked him," says the man who thinks he has a deal with Jerry.

"We shouldn't have wrecked the place," says the second voice.

First voice replies, "But what about that caddy? Pissed me off him dealing with somebody else. That's a dealer's car, I'd bet money."

"*I'm* the one he's been doing business with," says the third voice, the deep powerful voice. "Twelve years now and steady money. Best pot in the whole goddamn state, and no hassle getting it, either."

"Well, let's go find the plants," says the first guy.

He sounds like your typical hothead. Second guy sounds like a life insurance salesman. Third guy is definitely the boss, and he's all shook up about his meal ticket being in jeopardy.

"No," says the boss. "First of all, we'd be lucky to find *one* of them. He's got 'em scattered all over the place. Second of all, they may not be ready to harvest. It's a couple weeks early, but I thought it being a dry year they might be ready, you know, prices sky high and everything, so I thought I'd give it a try. We spend a few thou on this trip, might pay off big. But we can't rush the guy. He knows. He's a wizard with plants. I shoulda waited. This was stupid. That shit we smoked was *dipped* in something. We never should have wrecked the place."

"I can find 'em," says the hothead. "Shit, I gotta nose for that stuff."

"Maybe we oughta just wait for him," says the salesman.

"No," says the boss. "I know this guy. He won't come back as long as we're here."

"Shit," says the hothead, "he's fuckin' with us, I just know it."

"I don't think so," says the boss, his voice trembling. "I thought so, but that's because that shit you scored is paranoid dope. That's why I like Jerry's dope. You can still think."

Salesman says, "Maybe we oughta straighten up a little."

"Fuck that," says Hothead.

"No," says the boss, "that's a good idea. Let's put it back as best we can, and I'll leave him a note and some cash. He understands about bad pot. He breeds that paranoia right out of it."

"I'm not cleaning this shit up," says Hothead. "I'm not a goddamn maid."

"We wrecked it, we clean it up," says the boss. "I'm trying to teach you, you dumb fuck. Make a mess, clean it up. Never run unless you absolutely *have* to. And don't get smart with me, okay? It's not the time. Now is the time to do what I say. Unless you want to go back where I found you. Remember how that was? It stunk, right? You said it was like being in scum all the time. Well, the way you stay out of the scum is by cleaning up your messes. You following this?"

"Jesus," says Hothead, "what about the car? I still think it's the one they're looking for. Why don't we make a call? They said it was a big old caddy. You *wanted* to take it to them."

"No," says the boss. "I don't want anybody knowing about

this place. They can find their own goddamn car. I panicked on that bad shit, but I'm straight now."

"Maybe this guy's got a girlfriend," says Salesman, nervously. "Maybe they . . ."

"No," says the boss, moving around, starting to pick things up. "This guy isn't into ladies. I told you he was scared of everything. He only has *one* friend. A guy in Los Angeles. Nobody else. He told me. Could be his car. They're probably up there watching us, scared shitless, waiting for us to leave. For Christ's sake, the guy doesn't even have a gun. But he's kept me in silk shirts, see? I'm not gonna fuck up my entire operation by calling somebody about a goddamn stolen car. You got that? They'd want in on this action, and I can't afford that. They got plenty of their own dope anyway."

"I thought you said they knew about this operation," says Hothead, a tremble in his voice. "You said they knew. I don't like to think we're crossing those guys. They're very well connected."

The boss hesitates before replying, "They *don't* know. Got that? This is my private enterprise. Got that?"

"Then let's go find these guys," says Hothead, trying to change the subject. "I can find 'em."

"No," says the boss. "Just help us clean up, okay?"

"I'm not picking this shit up!" screams Hothead.

A deadly silence falls. I hold my breath.

"You pick it up or you're finished," says the boss. "I mean it. Nobody is gonna want to touch you."

"Now wait a minute," says the Salesman, "couldn't we just . . ."

"Shut up!" says the boss. "Jimmy's gotta learn to clean up his messes."

"I'm outta here," says Jimmy. "I don't need this shit."

"You go out that door and . . ."

BOOM!! The house rocks with the explosion and I nearly lose my balance. Smoke from the blast drifts up through the cracks in the ceiling and stings my nose.

"Oh my god," whispers Salesman. "Oh, god, did you have to do that?"

"You scared, Sal?" asks the boss.

"No, no, I'm fine," says Sal. "It just seemed so . . . I don't know. I'm fine."

"You sure?"

"Yeah, yeah, I'm fine. I just didn't think . . ."

"You didn't think what?"

"Well . . . he was just pissed off. He's got a temper. I didn't think he was really gonna leave."

"Doesn't matter," says the boss, coldly. "He wouldn't clean up his mess. He thought this was some bullshit movie where nobody does any work. But this ain't a movie, Sally. This is the real thing. Besides, he was gonna pull something. I know he was. He was gonna blow my operation here and I couldn't allow that. If he'd had his way, I could have lost this whole operation."

"You're right," says Sal, laughing nervously. "Yeah, I see that now. You're right. Sure."

"You're scared, aren't you Sal? It's okay to be a little shook. Tell me the truth. Tell me you're scared."

"No, I'm fine. I am. I'm fine."

"I don't think I can trust you if you can't cop to being scared. It was Jimmy brought you in, right?"

"Of course you can trust me!" says Sal, hysterically. "You can! Really. I'm fine. I am."

"I don't know," says the boss, speaking very quietly.

"No. Really. Please. I'm a little nervous, that's all. It's natural. I didn't think you'd actually *shoot* him. But, I think it's great. I do. Absolutely *had* to be done. I'll get over it. I'll be fine. No! Please! No!!"

BOOM! BOOM! It's all I can do to keep from screaming and falling. My whole body is shaking. My legs are aching from squatting for so long. I want to cough or groan or something. I take a slow deep breath and try to calm my pounding heart.

I can hear the boss grunting as he drags the bodies around. I can't imagine what he's doing. I only hope he doesn't take too long. I feel sick and shaky. But there's nothing to do but wait. A few minutes later, I hear him go out. The truck engine rumbles to life and he drives away. I inch back along the rafters, and lower myself down onto the toilet. It's the last thing I want to do, but I have to see how he's left things.

It's a god-awful mess. The guy I think must be Jimmy is sprawled on the couch, shot through the heart. The boss has left a big gun in his hand. He looks like a young urban cowboy. His eyes are mean, but that could just be death. I decide Sal must be the middle-aged guy. He's lying in front of the fireplace, a gun in his hand, too. His pale blue suit is soaked with blood. His face is expressionless. One eye is open, the other closed.

I guess the boss wants to suggest a gunfight, but since I know what happened, the suggestion is absurd. Still, I suppose it might fool somebody, if anybody cares. I can't think clearly in the presence of the bodies, so I go outside and walk over to the caddy. I wonder where they started to take it to. My fingerprints are in there, along with Lily's. So I take off my shirt and start wiping away the evidence, trying to formulate a plan.

I'm exhausted, hungry, terrified the boss or somebody else will find me here, and I'm worried about Lily and the baby. I pray to God they got away safely. I guess I get lost in my worry, because I don't hear Lily calling to me until she's fifty yards away, coming down the hillside. I run to her and hold her, making sure not to crush the baby, but afraid to let her go. I tell her my story and she tells me hers.

She says the phone rang, and she sensed something wasn't right about that, so she hauled our things out of the cottage into the high brush, strapped the baby to her chest and went looking for me. She hunted for two hours. As she was hiking back down the hill, she saw the truck and our car roll in. She ducked down behind a bush and waited. Then she heard shots and prayed I was still up on the ridge burying Jerry. When she saw me come out of the house after the boss drove away, she figured I must have things temporarily under control.

"What do we do now?" she asks, kissing my cheek.

"We get rid of this car," I say, "and hope one of Jerry's vans has some life yet, or the potential of it anyway. I know next to nothing about engines."

"I know a little," says Lily. "Not much, but a little."

"I thought you said you didn't know how to drive," I say.

"I don't," she says, "but I hung out with a guy who knew cars. Older guy. They're pretty simple, really. I just know a few things, that's all."

"If we could just get this caddy to Salinas," I say, shaking my head, "we could park it in the barrio, and day after tomorrow it'd be a burgundy lowrider with new license plates and black velvet upholstery. Nobody'd ever be able to find it then."

"We could risk it," she says, handing me the boy. "We've made it this far."

"No," I say, bouncing the kid, "I have a very bad feeling about this car now. Very bad. Those guys knew about this car."

"They did?" she says, going pale. "Shit, Charlie, we gotta get out of here!"

"Yeah," I say, "but how? This car was hot before, it's molten now."

"Jerry must have had wheels," says Lily, shielding her eyes and glancing anxiously at the bugs and vans surrounding the house.

"Maybe so," I say, "but this caddy is the big problem right now. We gotta dump it somewhere and hope nobody finds it for a while."

"Why?" she asks, irritated with me. "You said these guys were dealers. You *stole* it from a dealer. So leave it. Anybody comes around, they'll think it belongs to the dead men."

"You're pretty smart, you know that?" I say, squinting at her. "How come I didn't run into you ten years ago?"

"You were lucky," she says, looking away. "Ten years ago I was shit. I'm gonna see if I can't get one of these things running. Why don't you finish getting rid of our prints, and then we can get out of here."

"Hey, Lily," I say, taking her hand.

"Yeah," she says, giving me a sullen look.

"I'm glad we're still together. I was afraid maybe . . ."

"What?" she asks, putting my hand to her lips.

"I thought maybe you'd gone," I say, handing the boy back to her.

"No," she says, smiling sadly at me. "It never entered my mind. Probably should have, but it didn't."

"Thanks," I say. "I . . ."

"We'll talk later, Charlie," she says, solemnly. "But we gotta get out of here. Right now."

9

"I don't remember ever being able to talk so easily to anyone before," I say to Lily.

"What?" she says, shouting over the old engine.

"I say, I don't remember ever being able to talk to anybody like I can talk to you! It's amazing!"

"I feel the same way!" she yells, smiling at me.

We're driving one of Jerry's old vans, the seventeenth one Lily tried to start. Our top speed is twenty-nine miles per hour. We're leaking oil and the engine is on the verge of exploding. Our dream is to reach Santa Cruz, but we'll be happy with Monterey. We stop on the coast just south of Carmel and let the engine cool down. Besides, we need to give our ears a rest from the sputtering drone.

"So, you were like a kept man?" asks Lily, watching her baby.

He's sitting in the sand, carefully examining the little black and gray and white grains sticking to his drool-covered fingers. He sees something funny and looks up at his mama and gives her the sunniest of smiles.

"God, he's cute," I say. "How come he's so cute?"

"That's how they survive," says Lily. "You think anybody'd put up with this shit if they were ugly?"

"Oh, you'd love him if he was a troll," I say.

"You got that right," she says, laughing.

"Hey, that's a first," I tell her. "You laughed. I like it."

"Listen," she says, growing serious, "don't push this romance too fast, buddy. I like you, okay? Let's leave it at that for now."

"Well, wait a minute," I say. "You just asked me if I was a kept man. That's fairly personal, don't you think? So how come I can't comment on the fact that you laughed? Doesn't seem quite equitable. Equal. You know what I mean."

"I'm sorry," she says, touching me. "I'm a little scared of you, okay? Scared of feeling this way, whatever it is."

"Don't be," I say. "It's good to feel this way."

"How do you know what I'm feeling?" she asks, sullenly.

"Because I'm feeling it, too," I say. "It aches, but I love it."

"You write any other songs?" she asks, out of the blue.

"Lyrics mostly," I say. "When I'm not around an instrument. Wrote one yesterday for you, but it's pretty romantic so I doubt you'd want to hear it."

"No, I do," she says eagerly. "Nobody ever wrote me a song. You sure you wrote it for me?"

"I'm sure I'm sure," I say. And I kinda speak it and sing it at the same time. I sort of have the melody figured out. It's a gospel progression, but with a nice groove to it.

I'm jealous of your old lovers
I'm jealous of your old boyfriends
I'm jealous of each and every one of those guys
And I'll be jealous to the end

But I'm not jealous 'cause you were lovers
And I'm not jealous 'cause you made love
I'm not jealous that you
Felt passion and joy for them,
No, I love you for that, baby
I love you

No, I'm jealous of the time
That we were not together
I'm jealous of the time
We did not have
I'm jealous of every minute

Of every hour of every day
That we were apart
I'm jealous of the time, baby
So jealous
Of the time.

"That's a nice song, Charlie," she says, her jaw shaking in that sweet way it does. "I would cry, but I can't. There's no more tears left. I'm a tough old broad now, but I'll tell you something. That's a beautiful song. I'd like to sing it someday. Will you teach it to me?"

"Sure," I say, my heart swelling. "I'd marry you in a minute. All you have to do is say yes."

Suddenly all the sound in the world stops. The sun seems to shoot big golden rays of light all around us. We have halos and the air smells of honey. I'm exaggerating, but it's pretty incredible. A crow drifts by, now a whole fleet of gulls. I expect the earth to start singing. I'm in love with Lily. She's the only woman I've ever wanted to marry. I've asked a few in ignorance, but I never meant it until Lily.

She looks at me for a long time. I guess it doesn't matter how tough a woman gets. An offer of marriage from a decent man is a powerful thing. I take the liberty of calling myself decent. She doesn't smile or frown. She just looks at me until the roar of the illusion dies down, and she says, "Charlie, our charge card went dead on us this morning, as you know. We've got a hundred bucks left, and we don't know where we're going. Do you know what I'm talking about? I mean, sometimes I don't believe there is a God, and then other times I think there *must* be a God because of moments like this."

"I love you, Lily," I say, crawling to her and kissing her.

"I can't say that to you, Charlie," she says, pressing her cheek against mine. "I want to, but I can't. I'm sorry."

"It's okay," I whisper. "Whenever. If ever."

"I'm honored," she says, looking at her baby and smiling. "He's honored, too, I'm sure. He likes you and you make my heart beat so fast I *would* cry if I could, but I don't ever cry anymore."

"Do you mind if I say it now and then?" I ask, holding my breath and pressing my lips to her hand.

"No," she says, looking away, blushing, "you say it whenever you feel like it."

We get as far as Watsonville that night. We find a camping spot in the middle of an abandoned pear orchard. We're out of sight of the road and it feels pretty safe. We're both worn out, so we eat some tuna sandwiches and I make a bed for us in the back of the van using our clothes and a couple old blankets we took from Jerry's. I fall asleep right off the bat, but Lily rouses me an hour later to make love to her. I may be tired, but she wakes me right up. She makes me feel so damn young I can hardly believe it.

We lie in the darkness and she tells me about the last time she saw her mother.

"I was sixteen," she says, sighing deeply, "living in Santa Monica with a woman named Jan. She was paralyzed from the waist down. For room and board, I hauled her in and out of bed and pushed her around town in her old wicker wheelchair. We had a pretty good time. She didn't have lots of money, but it was more than I'd ever had. She taught me to sew, to play cards, and she got me listening to classical music. First time I heard Bach I nearly had an orgasm. We were sitting in her living room watching television. I'd been with her about a month. Before that I'd been bummin' around. I ran away from my mother when I was fourteen. Anyway, I remember Jan turned the volume down and asked me if I wouldn't rather hear some music, so I said sure, thinking I'd probably hate it."

"What did she play?"

"Oh, Charlie, she played the Brandenburgs. You ever heard them? There's one in there that makes you feel like you're flying. Then she played me Satie and then she hit me with the Brandenburgs again and everything I'd ever thought was changed. That's the moment I realized I wasn't stupid or insane."

"That sorta happened to me with Ray Charles," I tell her. "I was pure white until I heard him, but after that there was no going back. Got in touch with my black self. It was so good to find it."

"Same with me and Ella Fitzgerald," says Lily, nodding.

"But you were saying about your mother," I remind her.

"Oh, well, so my mother came to visit, and it was like I didn't even know her. She seemed so coarse and mean. I was having a decent life for the first time, so I didn't see that she'd changed, too. She was living over a bar in Oregon somewhere. She was lonely and wanted me to come up there and keep her company. But I said no. She begged me, but I said no. It felt like a choice between heaven and hell. We were down on the street in front of Jan's apartment. Mama was wearing platforms and tight white pants and a black sweater with big white buttons. She'd come all the way on a train to try to get me to come back with her. She loved me and I didn't see it. Her hair was blond and kinda wild and she was wearing red lipstick. She was sexy I think. I got her body for the most part."

"You're long and small and perfect," I say, kissing her.

"You're too nice to me," she sighs. "I don't trust it."

"I'm in love," I say. "I love to hold you. I love to think about you."

"Yeah," she says, shaking her head a little, "anyway, I remember she was standing by a stop sign, and I remember thinking how her lips matched the red of the sign. She was crying and her tears made tracks across her face. And her hands trembled. I think she wanted to reach out to me."

Lily falls silent. I wait. I would wait forever if she wanted me to.

"I should have at least said I loved her," she says softly. "I should have called her or sent her a card or something, but I never did. And then all of a sudden she was dying."

"When was that?"

"Oh, four or five years later. She got cancer. She called me and said, 'Well, Lily, your mother has cancer. That's me. I'm your mother. Remember me?' That's when I let myself get pregnant for the first time, thinking I could have the baby and take it up there and show it to her before she died. But she didn't make it, so I gave the baby up."

"What were you wearing that last day?"

"Huh?" she says, coming out of her memory. "You mean when she died?"

"No, that last day you saw her."

"I was wearing a dress I'd made myself, a cotton thing, blue. And fake pearl earrings and a fake pearl necklace. Why?"

"Just wanted to see the picture better."

"Well, it was so sad, Charlie, because we wanted to love each other. I think she patted me on the shoulder, but I'm not sure. I can just see her hands trembling, her long red fingernails, her big bamboo bracelets on her skinny wrists."

"Yeah," I say. "I think my father shook my hand once or twice after I was old enough to remember."

"We oughta touch people more," she says, kissing my cheek. "We oughta hold and hug this baby until he's pushing us away."

"Don't want to spoil him," I say, teasing her.

"I don't know," she says, her voice on the verge of song. "Maybe we do."

10

"When was the last time you talked to her?" I ask. I'm holding the baby while Lily mashes up a banana in a cup of rice.

"Juneau? About five years ago," says Lily, making little gooey balls and popping them into her baby's eager mouth.

"She might be long gone," I say. "People in this country move every *three* years."

"Not Juneau," says Lily, smiling.

"Maybe we could call her and she'll come get us?" I suggest. "This fuckin' thing could blow up at any minute."

"No," says Lily, shaking her head. "I took something from her and never paid her back. But if we show up with the baby, she won't turn us away. She loves anything young."

"How old is she?" I ask, wanting to get a picture of her.

"Not telling," says Lily, making a happy face at her baby. "Want it to be a surprise, don't we big boy? You biggest boy! Don't we?"

Somehow, through divine intervention I think, we make it over the rough roads to Santa Cruz, up the steep grade past the university, and down a long gravel driveway to an old geodesic dome house nestled in the redwoods. I try to turn the engine off, but it won't stop. It starts to whine and pop ominously. We quickly unload our stuff and stand back. The pops get louder and louder, the whining becomes a shriek, and . . . everything stops. A blessed silence falls. I lift the flap to look at the engine, and the damn thing has melted into one stinking, oozing mass of rubber and steel.

"See what I mean," says Lily, shaking her head. "Are we lucky or what?"

"I don't know," I say. "I guess it all depends on how you look at it."

"I look at it we didn't blow up on the freeway," she says, knocking on the front door. "She's probably not home. Her car's gone."

"Are we sure she still lives here?" I ask, surveying our pile of clothing, shoes, tools, and baby stuff, so picturesque here by the rusty van. "If she sold the place and somebody else comes home, then what?"

"Then we'll ask them if we can stay here," says Lily, in all seriousness. "And if they say no, we'll leave."

"Good plan," I say, nodding. "I'll carry the shoes, you can carry the tools."

"Don't worry, she's still living here," says Lily, putting her boy down on the redwood duff. "Juneau will never move from here. You'll see what I mean."

We formulate a plan while we wait. I'll get some carpentry work and deal Jerry's dope to the profs and book freaks at the university. Then we'll buy the newest vehicle we can afford and head north. If we're lucky, we can make Oregon in a week.

"Wish we could get in," says Lily, peering through the kitchen window. "Juneau's got a piano and she keeps it in tune."

"Do you see it?" I ask, hoping she does.

"No, but I can sense it in there," says Lily, bouncing her eyebrows. "I can feel it, you know?"

We hear somebody rolling down the driveway. The only sound is tires crunching gravel. A tiny electric three-wheeler comes to a stop ten feet from us. The old lady stays in it, frowning out at Lily, her wrinkled face topped by a tangle of curly white hair. When she sees the baby, her frown fades. The side panel slides open and Juneau steps out into the light.

Her body is a big surprise. It's firm and young and shapely. I can't stop gawking. She's seventy-something and the sexiest thing next to Lily I've ever seen!

"Gimme that baby," she says gruffly, striding over to the boy and picking him up. She makes a fierce face at him, bites her lower lip with her front teeth and says, "Oooh, you're cute! Who gave you permission to be so cute?" She shoots a hard glance at me, glares at Lily and says, "Who's he?"

"My husband," says Lily, not missing a beat. "Charlie. Charlie, this is Juneau."

"Pleased to meet you," I say.

"I'll bet you are," she says, turning away and going to the dome, the baby tucked snugly on her hip. "You can stay for three days and then we'll see."

"Thanks," says Lily, more submissive than I've ever seen her.

"Don't thank me," says Juneau, opening the door and carrying the baby inside. "Whatever you do, don't *thank* me."

"Is this all right?" I ask Lily.

"This is better than all right," she says, taking my hand and squeezing it. "We got us a place to stay and the world's greatest babysitter."

Juneau makes a big pot of tea and we sit around the kitchen table, sipping and talking. I let Lily do all the lying so we won't contradict each other. Juneau listens intently for about a minute and says, "What a bunch of hooey, Lily. If that's your *story,* don't torture me with the truth. We'll start from now and see what develops. I have two dance classes to teach at the university this afternoon and yoga class tonight in town, but my weekend is free except for my Sunday dance marathon and the twelve mile beach run tomorrow morning. But I'll be back before breakfast."

"You're very kind to put us up," I say.

"I love Lily," says Juneau, staring grimly at me. "We were lovers, did she tell you?"

"No," I say, trying not to show my surprise.

"She broke my heart," says Juneau, looking at the baby in Lily's arms, "but I will always love her."

"I'm sorry," says Lily, "but . . ."

"You're right," says Juneau, nodding and closing her eyes. "It's an old tape. Consider it filed."

"Can I come to class with you?" Lily asks. "Charlie can watch the baby."

"Yes," says Juneau, standing up. She turns to me and cautions, "Do anything you want, eat anything you want, but don't mess with my computer, okay?"

"I don't know computers," I say, taking the baby from Lily.

"Ah," says Juneau, smiling sadly at Lily. "He's good with kids, but afraid of technology. I could have predicted that."

So I hang out with the boy for a few hours and wish I could live at Juneau's forever. Down the sloping hill behind the house there's a pretty little creek where old redwoods are growing from the stumps of ancient trees, cut down in the time before we ever thought things could vanish. I know the boy loves water so we stay at the creek until he wears himself out. I carry him back to the house and he takes a nap.

The place is jammed with thousands of hardback novels. Her baby grand is in fine tune, too, but I don't want to wake the boy, so I sit on the couch and gorge myself on words. I feel so comfortable here, and I realize the feeling comes from my childhood.

My parents were wealthy. Until the divorce, we lived in a big house with lots of space and light. We had big art books and a huge backyard and I think a redwood tree, though it might have been a pine. I can't remember. My father was a systems designer for a multi-national, and sometimes he played catch with me and sometimes he read me stories at night, but he was always distant, aloof, scary. That was in Marin County, north of San Francisco. Everyone had cars then, and there were never any shortages.

Then my father turned forty and found himself a new mate. I was ten years old when my mother sued him for divorce. And then everything went wrong. She didn't get the house. We landed in an apartment in Berkeley. She worked as a secretary. I shared a room with my brother. My sisters slept in the same bed with my mother. My father lived alone with his lover in the big house. It made no sense, but there we were.

I did okay until my mother remarried. I was fourteen. I had my friends, my connections, my plans. I knew the streets. I knew the safe places and I knew how to get around without a car. And suddenly we were moving to Massachusetts. Her new husband was a big bossy Italian guy, a professor and a bigshot for another multi-national. I hated him. I communicated with amplified noise. He screamed at me to turn it down. It was a war and I lost. I left home at sixteen, hitchhiked back to Berkeley, and soon found my way to the low end of San Francisco, Oakland, and from there all points everywhere. I wouldn't recognize my mother if I saw her today, and she certainly wouldn't know me. Sometimes I think about calling her, but I'm pretty sure I'm better off a memory to them, them to me.

But it sure feels good, in some reassuring way, to be sitting in this spacious place, the afternoon sun slanting in, illuminating the dust, the big books all around me. So I get stoned, because I want to get so deep into the moment, I'll forget it isn't real. I get lost in the romance of my new love with Lily. I tell myself I'm getting stoned to amplify my pleasure, but I know all the while it's to escape the growing fear that something bad is going to happen, or worse, that nothing will happen at all.

11

We make love our first night at Juneau's, our first night together in a real bed, in a clean safe place, and it is sweeter and stronger than I ever dreamed love could be. I've never allowed myself to trust anyone the way I trust Lily. I stop thinking and vanish into her for a long, long time. We get out of bed, walk out into the chilly night, and hold each other until our bodies cool down enough for us to sleep.

Juneau is a nice old gal, but her loneliness is *so* tangible, I find it hard to be around her for long. She holds the baby almost constantly and never lets Lily out of her sight. She tolerates me, but that's as far as it goes.

Juneau knows people who need carpentry done. She calls them for me, tells them who I am, lets me speak to them. I land two jobs right away, carpentry being something of a lost art. She makes a few more calls and sells our pot for us to a dope fiend prof.

I borrow her electric car and buzz up into the hills to build bookshelves for a philosopher. He's got an old farmhouse on a patch of scavenged ground. He says he's gonna plant a thousand new trees and sow the soil with wildflowers. When he sees I do good work, he asks me how long it'd take me to rebuild his kitchen and add a solarium onto his bedroom. I do some quick figuring and tell him two or three months if I can get the materials.

He's a wild-looking guy. He has long brown hair and restless gray eyes. His body seems too small for his huge head. We're standing on the spot where he wants the solarium to be. He stares at the ground, calculating. He looks up at me, flashes a little smile, and says, "Let's do it. I've got the dough. I never *thought* about it, but I got it. You know how that is? I'll probably live here for life."

I tell him I'll have to talk to my wife before I can definitely say yes, though I'm tempted to grab it. I don't know if Lily wants to stay, no matter how great the opportunity. We need to think about the danger together.

At first she says definitely not. We have a little cash from the pot sale and she's for getting out as soon as we can. She says Santa Cruz feels perilously close to Los Angeles. She sees us living somewhere in extreme isolation for a couple years until Pearl gives up the search. But the money is tempting, Juneau's eager to help with the baby, and if we're real careful we might stay here as well as anywhere. Lily says she'll sleep on it, but wakes me in the middle of the night to say she wants to stay.

We get up the next morning, happy and excited, dance into the kitchen where Juneau's feeding the baby, and a call comes in. Lily stiffens, her face contorts, and she backs away. Juneau says hello. A voice asks for Lily. Juneau hangs up, looks sadly at the baby and says, "How did you know?"

"Pearl?" I ask, wanting to scream.

Lily nods and we're on the road again. We pack in a hurry, Juneau drives us to a used car lot, we pay most of our money for an old Japanese truck, and say our good-byes. Juneau kisses Lily, kisses the baby, gives me a gentle swat and tells me to take care. Two minutes later, we're chugging along old Highway One again, hoping to make Oregon in a few days.

"Fast reality change," says Lily, holding her boy up so he can peer out the window at the passing brussels sprouts.

"Beautiful day for it," I say, feeling lighthearted for some reason.

"Thanks for sticking by me," she says. "You could have had a whole new life back there. Sounded like a pretty good gig."

"You're my gig now," I say, touching her. "How am I doing?"

"So far so good," she says, letting herself smile.

"Are we gonna stop in Frisco?" I ask, wondering if the truck can make it that far.

"Only if we have to," she says, nodding. "I think we oughta drive straight on through if we can."

The sun comes hot like summer. The old road sweeps through the brussels sprout fields and curves in a long arc along the shimmering coast. There are few places I've ever seen as beautiful as this land north of Santa Cruz. We're about three miles south of the little town of Pescadero. Lily grabs my arm and says, "I'll bet she was *close* when she called. She could be right behind us!" She turns and looks back down the road. "God, I hope they don't hurt Juneau."

"Why would they?" I ask, shocked at the thought of it.

"They probably won't. Unless she gets heroic. Pearl doesn't like that."

"Juneau has that potential," I say. "She barks loud enough, it almost sounds like a bite."

"She's no dummy," says Lily, closing her eyes. "She won't try to fight Pearl."

"Listen," I say, "let's cut inland. We're sitting ducks on this road in this old thing if she *is* following us."

"You know a way?" Lily asks, swallowing nervously.

"I know a road you'll hope you never see again," I say. "The Pescadero run. The road few stomachs have conquered."

"I can make it if you can," she says, puffing her cheeks out and rolling her eyes.

We leave the coast highway and head inland, stopping at the little village of Pescadero to gas up. The news here is bad. The old truck is throwing oil. We buy twenty quarts, Lily sings a prayer to the god of old Japanese engines, and we start our climb up and over the coast range. The best we can do on the steep slope, full power, foot on the floor, is fifteen miles per hour. To take our minds off the bad road, Lily tells me how she met Juneau.

"I was twenty-two, playing with a quick grits band. We were pretty good. We ran up to Santa Cruz from L.A. now and then to play the Catalyst and a bunch of other dumpy clubs. I wore a buckskin miniskirt, sang real high and pretty, you know, and let the boys think I was built."

"Built just fine," I say, reaching over and gently touching her breasts. "Prettiest things I've ever seen."

"I doubt that," she says, blushing a little. "Anyway, one night in between sets, Juneau came up to me and asked me if I'd be interested in doing some work up at the university putting music to dance."

"Amazing how we get from one place to another," I say, smiling at her. "I remember once I was driving down old Sunset Boulevard in a stolen car and I saw this vision of loveliness running along with a baby in her arms."

"You're a romantic, you know that?" says Lily, putting her hand on my head and smoothing down my hair. "That's why you stopped, isn't it? Robin Hood? Am I right?"

"I was sent," I say, bouncing my eyebrows, "It was my destiny."

"Sure seems like it," she says. She makes a sick face and I pull over before she loses her breakfast.

When we get going again, the engine starts to whistle and groan and the baby starts screaming. God what lungs! Blow your ears out! He doesn't like the hairpin turns one bit. His temporary insanity takes Lily's mind off her stomach until we make it to where the road straightens out at the big redwoods of La Honda.

We buy some bubbly drinks at the quick stop, Lily lets the boy crawl around for a few minutes, and we burp our way up and over the last rise and down into the suburban sprawl south of San Francisco. We stop to check the oil, add several quarts, and take the decrepit surface streets into the city. Takes us two hours to get to the Haight Ashbury. On the way in, Lily finishes her story about Juneau.

"I lived with her for eight months," she says, amazed. "She was a mother to me at first, encouraged me, you know? Then one night we got high together, on wine I think it was, and she started kissing me. I didn't have anywhere else to go, Charlie. I never liked it much. I never liked the sex part with her, though it wasn't any worse than what I got from men. Just different."

"Did you ever do music for her?" I ask, feeling kind of depressed.

"No," says Lily, shrugging, "but she got me dancing. I danced three or four hours every day. Got into incredible shape. And I hung out with her professor friends, went to concerts, learned to toss a disc. It would have been paradise if she hadn't wanted to be lovers."

"What did you do?" I asked, wondering how it would have been if I'd met her back then.

"Called the ride number at the university. For almost nothing I got all the way to Santa Fe."

"So was this the first time you'd seen Juneau since then?"

"No," she says wearily. "I went to visit her after I'd been with Pearl for a few months. See, Pearl played it pretty loose with me at first, let me think I was free. So I used to go on little trips without her, and one time I went up to Santa Cruz, hoping I could patch things up with Juneau. But we had an awful time. She kept asking me to make love and I kept saying no. But, even so, I wanted to stay because I had a bad feeling about Pearl. I didn't want to go back to her."

"So why did you?" I ask. "Why do we go back, even when we know we shouldn't? That's the part I never can quite figure out."

"Well," she says, looking out at the blur of concrete, "I don't know, Charlie, but Pearl came up to get me. She met Juneau. They hated each other. We had a huge screaming fight and I was about to get the hell out when Pearl pulled an incredible swindle. Oh, Charlie, it still amazes me when I think about it."

"What did she do?" I ask, remembering a few swindles I'd been through.

"She got a very big producer to call me," says Lily, nodding slowly. "I'm talking about one of the most powerful guys there was at that time. And he said he'd heard about me from somebody else, and wanted me to make him a demo. He said he was sure I could get a contract. He said he was sure, Charlie. For which Pearl probably gave him free snort and anything else he wanted for life."

I think about the fantasies I had when I was just getting started writing songs. I dreamed about phone calls like that. I look at Lily sitting there, remembering the thrill, however false, and my heart aches for her. I want to tell her that it takes two to work a swindle, but I know she already knows that, so I ask about Pearl instead.

"She a dealer?" I say, knowing she must be at least that.

"No," says Lily, looking at me. "She's way up the line. She's big in the trade. But I didn't know that then. I was a stupid kid. Getting a call from this guy was like having God call me. So, naturally I went back with her and she gave me a new guitar and a mountain of crystal. And nothing ever happened, except I got hooked. Took me a year to get clean."

"She wanted your power," I say, remembering the hungry souls that materialized around me when my hit tune came. "She *must* want you alive."

"She'd probably like that, yeah," says Lily, her eyes narrowing. "It kills her to think of me being happy without her."

"Envy just eats people up, doesn't it?" I say.

"It's much more than that," she says, wiping her baby's drool. "She's addicted to destroying what's good."

"You believe in evil?" I ask.

"Absolutely," she says, looking wide-eyed at me. "Don't you?"

"I'm not sure," I say. "I don't see the purpose of it anymore. Maybe in the caves, to keep us sharp, but why now?"

"What do you mean?" she asks, wrinkling her brow. "There's lots of things that exist without a purpose."

"I don't know," I say, shrugging. "It's just a guess, but I always thought that evil was some sort of deep pain that turns into something else so it doesn't kill the person carrying it. Sorta like a tumor."

We pull over in a "no parking" zone so I can check the oil. Our gauge is now broken. Lily puts a hand on my arm. "I'm not talking about how evil things *get* here, Charlie," she says, shaking her head rapidly. "They're *here!*" She digs her fingernails into my arm and whispers, "Don't move."

"What?" I whisper back, frozen in my seat, my hand on the door handle.

She says nothing. I glance in my rearview mirror. An armored car has pulled up behind us. Several things go through my mind, but the first thing I say is, "Whatever you do, Lily, don't pull that gun. These guys are *heavily* armed."

"Okay," she says, taking her hand out of her pocket.

There's a gentle tap at the window. I try to stay calm. I fix a smile on my face, and roll down my window. He is entirely armored. I can barely see his eyes through his mesh visor. He's just a kid. His voice is soft, his tone apologetic. "Sir," he says, "I'm sorry, but you can't park here. This is a bus stop."

"Gosh, I'm sorry," I say. "I really am. I didn't see the . . ."

"It's my fault," says Lily, leaning across me and batting her eyelashes at him. "My baby was puking, see he's a messy little guy, and I made my brother here pull over. Do I know you? It's my fault."

"It's not that important," he says, removing his helmet and smiling at Lily. "See, the problem is there's nowhere else to park, but at the same time, we can't have people blocking the buses."

"Of course," says Lily, nodding and smiling. "We just never had it explained to us that way. That makes perfect sense, doesn't it Charlie? I sure hope you aren't gonna fine us."

"No, no," says the policeman, reddening slightly. "Just wanted to let you know."

"I don't know you, I guess," says Lily. "Coulda sworn I did. Do you think it'd be possible to get your name? I'd like to write a letter and tell somebody how helpful you were."

"No need to do that," he says, looking away, an enormous smile on his face.

"I really would like to," says Lily, her voice trembling.

I watch her in amazement.

"Uh, it's Mason," he says, bowing slightly. "Traffic division. James Mason, like the actor."

"Thank you, Jim," says Lily, giving him a dazzling smile.

"You're welcome ma'am," he says, winking at her.

I close the window, start the engine, look at Lily and say, "Oh, sis, maybe you could ask him for an escort through town." I'm pissed off. I feel demoted and cheapened.

"No," says Lily, her smile fading. "I just want to get out of here alive. We were lucky to get a nice one."

"So am I your brother now?" I say, still pissed off. "Or your husband?"

"We'll be whatever we have to be, Charlie," she says, patting my leg. "Whatever we have to be to get us through."

"And who decides what that is?" I ask, still hurt about my status change.

"We do," she says, solemnly. "We do it together."

"I don't mind being your brother," I say, softening, "but I'd prefer being your husband whenever possible."

"Okay," she says, looking away from me, nodding out her window.

The armored car rumbles past us. I get out and pour the last of our oil into the truck. We pull back into traffic. We don't talk much for the rest of the ride.

12

I wake up suddenly, not knowing where I am. Total darkness. I reach for Lily and she's there, so I know that much isn't a dream. The boy whimpers. Reality fills out. We're in a bed in a room in a place called Rock and Roll Breakfast, a Haight Ashbury hotel run by Lily's friend, Rain.

Lily stirs, touches my face and says, "Can you see if the baby's okay?"

I turn on a light and look into the crib. Little guy is lying face down, his butt up in the air, his thumb in his mouth. I turn him onto his side and cover him with his quilt. He gives a little sigh, urps up his mother's milk, and puts his face in it. I wipe up the mess and he urps again. I smell poop and figure I'd better do a complete rebuild.

When I get back to bed, I'm buzzing. So I get up and go downstairs to see if I can find some beer. Rain is sitting at the kitchen table, sipping tea, listening to music on her headphones, writing something, a letter or a poem. We share some of the last of Jerry's pot and I have a beer.

She's a tall, sexy black woman with a tight afro, big beautiful lips, and gigantic ivory teeth. Her eyes are big brown mirrors, and she has one of those big, powerful sexy smiles. She tells me she sings in a combo called Bafadu. They play no songs, only music. She was born in the Haight and says she expects to die here, though she wouldn't mind having a cottage by the sea someday.

"I was at the bottom of the deepest hole they got in this city," says Rain, closing her eyes and taking one of the longer tokes I've ever seen. Half a joint in one fell swoop.

"That's strong stuff," I say, warning her with a smile.

"That's the point," she says, laughing. "Anyway, somebody or something wanted me down, you know what I mean? Felt like a conspiracy, but it was probably just this one guy, this man full of tunes. He *wrecked* me, but he wouldn't stick around to put me back together. I was raw. I was in deep, deep pain! Nothing helped me! Nothing killed it until somebody gave me my first shot of heroin. Man, I had my free will, yeah, but it hurt too much so I numbed it. And then I met Lily."

"You mean . . . she was fixing, too?" I ask, not wanting to believe it.

"She was *there,*" says Rain, clenching her fists, the veins on her arms standing out like blue snakes on brown soil. "She was there with me, Charlie, but don't you worry, she will never go back to that shit. Never. We both left it far behind."

Silence falls. I drink my beer. She sips at tea. We get high.

"Yeah," she says, her voice low and easy, "we used to sing together. All night sometimes. We'd lie on our backs in the living room and jam along with records, jam along with just ourselves. God, Lily can sing. Got *me* singing, and now that's the main thing I do. That's what I *am* now."

"You and Lily lived together?" I ask, realizing that I'm all set to be jealous about Lily's old boyfriends, I've already sung her a song about them in which I very nobly deny my jealousy, and now it turns out her past is mostly full of women.

"God, yes," says Rain, closing her eyes and laughing. "We were sisters, didn't she tell you? We worked together."

"What was she like?" I ask, trying to imagine Lily ten years younger.

"Outrageous, wild, full of life, and *cute*?" says Rain, shaking her head. "God, the men were absolutely out of their minds about her, Charlie. And I didn't do so badly myself. We made rather good money. It was dirty work, but the pay was fine and we took a day off any time we wanted. Now, how many people can say that?"

"Why'd you give it up?" I ask, hoping she has.

"Acid," she replies, nodding slowly. "A major trip, Charlie. Most of which I couldn't possibly get into words, except to say that you shoulda seen this bird Lily turned into, a big rainbow-colored thing, and I flew on her back, and when I looked down through the clouds, from way the fuck up there, I saw New York and heard a thousand saxophones playing my note, my special one, so I knew I had to go there and get it."

"You haven't seen Lily in all these years?" I ask. "How long has it been?"

"I see Lily every night," says Rain, smiling. "And sometimes she's me and I'm her. We're bonded, man. Our souls got glued together with stuff that's never gonna break."

"She's powerful," I say, nodding, knowing the glue Rain's talking about.

"You got that right," says Rain, grinning at me. Out of nowhere she says, "Hey baby, what's about you and me making a little love? Lily won't mind, and I could sure use the ride."

"You don't think she'd mind?" I say, wanting very much to think she would. I'm trying to stay cool, but I'm having a hard time. It never entered my mind to sleep with Rain, though she is a very lovely lady.

"When you've done together what we did together," says Rain, sighing, "believe me, Charlie, a little sex with you would just be one more thing we have in common."

I can tell there's no point in lying to her, so I say, "Rain, I like you and I like your style, the whole package, you know? But the thing is, I only want to make love with Lily. I can't help it."

"You in love with her, Charlie?" she asks, frowning at me.

"Yes," I say, positively overwhelmed by feelings of loyalty.

"That's good," says Rain, giving me a curious smile. "Maybe down the road when you get over this physical ownership stuff, you'll come back and we'll have a good time together."

"I've never been loyal to anyone," I say, bowing my head. "Even to myself."

"Well, then it's a good time for you," she says, shaking her head and closing her eyes. "A time to build some trust, though I can almost guarantee you that some of the things you do now will seem incredibly stupid in retrospect, like turning down a very ready black woman with a great body and no communicable diseases. But then, you have Lily, and she *is* the best I know of."

"Sure seems like it," I say, laughing in relief.

"She doing the same for you?" asks Rain, smiling sadly at me. "Staying true, as you no doubt put it?"

"I don't think she's had a chance not to be true," I say. "I *know* she hasn't. We've been running too fast."

"You better talk that shit out," she says, shaking a finger at me. "That girl can get a man's pants off faster than anybody in history. You better talk about it, Charlie. Save you some grief down the line."

I crawl back into bed about an hour before dawn. Lily presses her warm body against mine and says, "I missed you. I kept dreaming about you. I've been awake and wanting you a couple times already." She hooks her legs around me and pulls me into position.

And now I love her with all new feelings. I've chosen her instead of another. She's my mate, not some convenient piece. She's the woman I love, the woman I give everything to. I am so profoundly thrilled to be in her, to be sharing the hot, soft, delicious, private love we have, sharing it with her alone, that when I come, I am happier than I have ever been, and she knows it.

13

"I want to get some place far away," says Lily, looking across the table at her boy.

He's in a high chair with a big plastic tray in front of him. He's drowning his muffin in a sea of milk and drool. Lily and I push ourselves away from the table, unable to stuff any more of our Rock and Roll breakfasts into our greedy little mouths. Rain's brewing coffee. We've been talking for hours about what to do next.

"You have a place in mind?" she asks, giving Lily a doleful look. "You want another waffle, Charlie? You only ate four."

"No thanks," I say, holding my stomach. "They were unbelievably good."

"I'm pretty sure I know the place," says Lily, picking at her fingernails, "but I'm not quite sure where it is. I'll know when we get there."

"You keeping secrets from me?" asks Rain, giving Lily a curious frown. "Who am *I* gonna tell?"

"Nobody bad," says Lily, smiling at her. "That's for sure."

"And please don't keep it secret from me," I say, taking her hand. "I'll need to know where to turn. Which highway to take."

Lily pulls her hand away and gives me a sullen look.

"Hey," says Rain, "it's safe in the city. Dye your hair, wear some mousy looking glasses, nobody'd know it was you. Unless you were planning to do some singing."

"I was," says Lily, sipping her chamomile tea.

"Then that's no good," says Rain. "You got that damn voice of yours. Too easy to spot."

"Doesn't matter," says Lily, taking my hand again. "I don't want to bring my boy up here anyway. I want him to have more room to run."

"Too wet in Oregon," says Rain, looking up at the ceiling and grimacing. "Dee-pressing. And boring? How you gonna help save the world up there? Remember? That's what you were gonna do with your songs. Remember?"

"Right now I'm trying not to get killed," says Lily, closing her eyes.

I put my arm around her and say, "We'll do your songs. Once we get settled and the heat dies down."

"I'll come visit you," says Rain, arching an eyebrow, her voice dry. "You send me smoke signals or something. I'll bring you a suitcase of what's happening."

"You could come with us," Lily says, hopefully.

"Why would I want to do that?" asks Rain, lifting her nose in the air. "Your old man won't even give me a tumble. So what would I *do* up there? I'm not tremendously attracted to lumberjacks."

"Charlie'll sleep with you," says Lily, smiling slightly. "Won't you, Charlie?"

"No," I say, relieved to get it out in the open. "I only sleep with you, Lily."

"See?" says Rain, giving her cheeks dimples. "The woods without sex is like music without rhythm. Nice, but after a while, what's the point?"

"I don't remember saying anything about that," says Lily, frowning at me.

"Could we talk about this in private?" I ask, feeling bad.

"I gotta make some calls," says Rain, rising slowly from her chair, giving each of us long looks. "I'll see you all in a little while. Help yourself to that coffee, Charlie."

Lily takes the boy out of his high chair and carries him upstairs. I pour myself some rocket fuel, cut it with milk, and decide I better follow her. She's changing the baby on the bed when I come in. She shoots me a hard glance, and finishes the change. I sit in a big armchair and look at the boy smiling up at his mother with so much love I can't bear to watch him.

"She ask you to sleep with her?" Lily asks, staring intently at her baby.

"Yes," I say, feeling heavy and tired. The chase is catching up with me.

"Did you want to?" she asks in a whisper.

"No, I just want you," I say, meaning it with all my heart.

"Well, that's okay for you," she says, looking at me, "but I can't promise that on my side. I'm gonna do whatever it takes to survive, Charlie. If I need a hundred bucks and I can't get it one way, I'll get it another. You understand?"

"Yes," I say, my heart about to burst, "but I'm gonna take care of us, Lily. I'm gonna make it so you never have to do anything you don't want ever again."

"Oh, really?" she sneers. "You think I want to do *this?* Run from Pearl's dog-men? You think I want that? You know what they'll do to me once they get me back there? They'll rape me every night. Only they won't call it rape. They'll call it sex. It's how they have fun."

"They aren't gonna catch you, Lily. I promise."

"That's right," she says, nodding, "but not because of you. Because if they ever get close, the last two bullets are for me and my baby. You got that?"

"Lily . . ."

"Don't say anything, Charlie. You saved my ass a couple times now, and I'm grateful. And we got something real good here when we make love. I don't know why, but we do. Nobody ever turned me on like you do. And you're good with my boy . . ." She looks away, close to crying. I go to hold her, but she puts out a hand to stop me. She says, "You're good with my boy, and that's a good thing. But I'm so far from love, Charlie, there isn't a map big enough to show you how far away I am. There's a whole part of me that's dead, Charlie. Too many people have stabbed it too many times, so I don't know if I will ever be healed enough to love you the way you want me to."

"You trying to scare me away?"

"Yeah," she says, nodding. "I want you to know the truth, Mr. Romantic. I've got some pretty strange ideas about life, and what I'm here for, and what I'm gonna do. I don't want to hurt you, because you've been good to me, and I like you. But my baby comes first. If you walked out tomorrow I'd be sad, for more than a little while. But then I'd find some other way to get along. Or not. It's *my* choice. That's the one thing I know."

"I guess I have to prove myself to you," I say, taking her in my arms. "Let's get out of here. Let's leave tonight."

"Let's fix the truck," she says, squeezing me. "Let's figure out some way to get some money."

"Maybe Rain would lend us some."

"Rain doesn't lend," says Lily, kissing me. "Rain gives."

"Did you want me to sleep with her?" I ask, bracing myself.

"No," she says, feebly trying to break away.

"You like it that I didn't?" I ask, whispering in her ear.

"Well," she says, blushing a little, "maybe I'm kind of flattered."

"Good," I say, kissing her. "That's what I was hoping for."

"Don't take this romance crap too far," she says, slipping away from me. "I'm warning you."

"Why not?"

"Because we aren't clear of the mess yet," she says, picking up her baby. "I'm going down to talk to Rain."

"I'll fix the truck," I say. "I love you."

"Good," she says, going out.

I drive the old thing to a nearby service station. A Japanese guy takes a quick look. "Throwing oil," he says, peering in at the oil-covered engine.

"Yeah, I'm aware of that," I say. "That much even *I* know."

"Oughta get an electric," he says, yawning. "No fuss, no muss."

"Look," I say, irritated, "this is what I've got, okay? What I want to know is, is it big or little? The problem."

He fools with the engine a little, and has his six-year-old son rev it while he checks various inner orifices. He approaches me, ceremoniously wiping his hands on a clean white towel. "Big," he says, nodding gravely.

"If I fed it oil whenever it needed it, how far could I get? Oregon?"

"No way to know," he says, smiling slightly. "Might go two blocks, two miles, two hundred miles. Anything is possible. But if you don't get a miracle, you won't go far."

I decide to sell it. I drive to a used car lot and they offer me next to nothing for it. I'm thinking the offer over when a wimpy little guy with rotten teeth comes up to me and says he knows a guy who'll give me quite a bit for the truck. I ask him where the guy is. He says he'll show me. I don't want to trust him, but the thought of coming back with something instead of nothing seems worth the hassle. I drive with him into the Sunset to an old apartment building. I tell him I'll wait in the truck while he gets his friend.

He goes into the building. Five minutes later, he's still in there. I beep my horn. I wait a few more minutes, and I beep my horn a few more times. Nothing. Now I'm mad. I get out of the truck and start toward the building. I'm pissed off. Right? I don't like it when somebody . . .

I stop. My neck hairs stand on end. I can *smell* those men, waiting behind a door, three or four of them with knives. I run back to the truck, get in, gun the engine, and drive away as fast as I can, feeling lucky to be alive. I get back to the used car lot. The truck is oozing oil. I consider myself lucky to walk away with three hundred dollars.

It's a ten block walk to Rock and Roll Breakfast. I rack my brains for a way to turn the money into a little bit more. I'm a block from the hotel. A city bus goes by. On the side of it there's a gigantic advertisement for the races. Four huge horses running neek and neck, ridden by four abstract jockeys. And that reminds me of Buster and Molly.

I go back to the hotel and break the bad news to Lily. She

takes it calmly, but says she could use something bubbly. We leave the baby with Rain and go a few doors down to a sandwich joint. I tell her about my friends at the racetrack. She tells me gambling is a waste of time.

"I know a guy who wants a song of mine," she says, a tremble in her voice. "It's a special song, one I've never tried to sell, but I know he'll give me plenty for it."

"How's it different from your other songs?" I ask, pretty sure I know.

She looks around the joint, leans close to me and whispers, "I've got about ten songs, Charlie, out of the thousands I've written, that came out of nowhere. I couldn't even play them at first. They were made of chords I didn't know. You know what I'm saying? They weren't like any other songs of mine. They had so much power it scared me to sing them at first."

"Jesus," I say, my body tingling again, "you can't sell *those,* Lily. Let's try our luck with the ponies first. Buster might have a sure thing for us. He sometimes does."

"There's no such thing as a sure thing," she says, smiling at me. "That's one thing I remember from my mother. But it'd be fun to see some horses run. I always did like a good horse-race."

So I make a call over to the track. After a long hold, Molly comes on, sounding gruff and bothered. I'm afraid she won't remember me, but she does. I tell her I want to bring my new wife over for a visit and a few races. She says fine, except Buster isn't doing so well. I ask what's wrong, and she says cancer.

14

I met Buster at the Oakland induction center a long time ago. We were sitting in the lobby, waiting for our names to be called. We waited all day. By the time they called us, we'd decided we should have gone to Canada.

I had a heart murmur, so they didn't take me. But they wanted Buster. He lived through a year of combat. When he was discharged, he came down to Los Angeles and hung out with me. I was making pretty good money, waiting tables in a nice Hollywood joint, hoping to sell some songs. Buster was full of jungle terror and had a duffel bag stuffed with hash.

Somehow or other, Buster ended up at the track. He sold enough dope to buy himself a mediocre racehorse, then taught himself to be a trainer. I used to go out there and bet the horses he liked. Most of the time I'd win a little. Then we'd sit around in the tack room, and he'd tell me about the jungle, and I'd tell him about the music industry, and it seemed like we were talking about the same thing.

Then he took a job near San Francisco, training a whole fleet of young horses. The man who hired him had a daughter. Buster fell in love with her and they decided to get married. I drove up for their wedding. He asked me to hold the rings, so I guess that made me best man. Molly seemed friendly enough, but we barely spoke. They asked me to come visit, but I never did.

Lily and I take a slow commuter train to the track. It feels strange to be traveling without the boy. The freedom is nice, but I miss him. Lily says she misses nursing him. We know Rain is taking good care of him, singing to him, playing with him while she works the front desk, but that doesn't keep us from worrying. It's a new experience for me, worrying about a baby.

The fifth race is over by the time we get up to the Turf Club. Molly said for us to meet them there. So we're standing by the bar, staring up at the results of the last race, waiting for things to settle down, and this little old man, a few tufts of hair clinging to his shiny skull, comes up to us and says, "The only race to bet today is number nine. Seven in nine." He smiles, and though I don't recognize him, I know it's Buster.

I can't say anything. I can't move. This isn't Buster, but it is. He's half the size he was at his wedding. His cheeks are caved in. They used to be so round and rosy. His voice was a big booming bass, now it's weak and raspy. I'm afraid to touch him. He seems like something from a nightmare.

"Yeah, it's me," he says, holding out a trembling hand.

I grab it and shake it. He grimaces with pain and I let go. "Sorry, Bus," I say, unable to look at him. "This is Lily."

"Hi," he says, smiling at her in his unmistakable way.

"Hi," she says, holding out her hand to him.

They shake hands, and he compliments Lily on her beauty. We walk through the smoke and dim light to a table overlooking the track. Molly's there, smoking a long cigarette and drinking tequila, no ice.

I don't recognize her. She's gained all the weight Buster's lost. Her blond hair is full of gray. Her face is bloated. We sit down and I order a beer. Lily orders some mineral water. We talk horses in the sixth race for a minute, and Molly says, "It's from the jungle, you know? The cancer. They dumped that defoliant shit all over him."

"God, I'm sorry Buster," I say, my stomach going queasy.

"Yeah, it's bad," he says, grimacing.

"I told him to stay in bed," says Molly, glaring at Lily. "Hurts him to walk. But he wanted to get up and meet you here. He hasn't been out of bed in two months. I hope you're honored."

"Let's go back to your place," I say to Buster. "Get you comfortable."

"No, I'm here," he says, looking down at the track. "Good to see a race, maybe win a little money in the ninth. Tired of hearing the crowd and not seeing anything."

"They say he's got three months, max," says Molly, waving to the half-naked waitress. "They radiated him, but all that did was kill his appetite."

"I got an idea," says Buster, taking a deep breath. "Let's not talk about it anymore today. Let's just do the races and hear what old Charlie and his beautiful friend Lily are up to."

"Thank you," says Lily, smiling at him.

"Well, *I* need to talk about it," says Molly, her lips quivering, a big tear rolling down her face. "They poisoned you. It's murder. It's not anything else."

"I know, honey," he says, reaching out to her. He's so tiny next to her. "But just for an hour let's get into the horses. Okay? Have some fun?"

"I can't," she says, getting up. "I'll see you all later."

Buster bows his head, so I bow mine. Lily jumps up and goes after Molly. We sit here for a couple minutes, not saying anything. When they don't come back, Buster says, "She's a sexy gal, Charlie. Great smile. Good legs. Looks strong, too."

"Yeah, she's a real good one," I say. "Best one so far."

"You need some quick cash, huh?" he asks, grimacing.

"Yeah," I say, "but I don't ever expect to get it here."

"Today you might," he says, nodding. "People talk to a dead man."

"What do you mean?" I ask. I know he's dying but I hate to think about it.

He gestures for me to come closer. I pull my chair up next to his and he whispers in my ear. His breath is dry. "There's a fix on in the ninth race. Not number seven. I was just pimping the odds. People listen to me. It's number three. King's Guardian. Big strong horse. They always beat him by forcing him outside. He hates to run in the pack. Today they're gonna let him through. He'll go off at twenty to one, maybe better. Unless he breaks a leg, he'll win."

"It's a bet then," I say, my hands getting sweaty. "I had a feeling . . ."

"Good," he whispers. He closes his eyes and says, "Charlie, I can't stay up. You help me get home?"

"Sure," I say, helping him stand.

"It's good to see you," he says, smiling at me. "I was hoping to see you one more time."

I could carry him he's so light. He leans on me as we walk through the smoky room to the elevator. The crowd is cheering the finish of the sixth race. Buster turns back to watch it on the screen above the bar. "Good," he says, closing his eyes, "that old gal needed a win."

Molly and Lily aren't in the trailer. It doesn't surprise me. The trailer is hot and smells of illness. "We'll open all the windows," says Buster, sensing my discomfort. I help him undress. He's shriveled and bent. He gets in bed and I put pillows behind him. I give him a quick rundown on what's going on. He listens with his eyes closed, straining to hear me.

"Sounds dangerous," he says, opening his eyes. "You got much to bet in the ninth race?"

"Not much," I say. "Couple hundred."

"I'll give you some," he says, licking his dry lips. "Maybe dying will be good for something."

"I'm sorry, Buster. I'm so very, very sorry this happened to you."

"You oughta be," he says, trying to smile. "Shoulda dragged my stupid ass out of that waiting room and gone to Canada with you. Couldn't have been any worse than this."

"I didn't know," I say, bowing my head. "I had an inkling, but I didn't really know."

"I know," he says weakly. "If I had any strength left, I'd blow that fuckin' place up. Can you believe those companies made trillions killing boys? Can you believe it, Charlie? I can barely piss anymore, and somebody got rich off it."

"You shouldn't have gone up there today," I say, trying not to cry. "We would have been glad to come here."

"No," he says, closing his eyes again. "I wanted to be a man when I saw you again. Not what I am now. You were my best friend. I never had one until you. If I'd known this was gonna happen so fast, I woulda spent more time with you."

"I'm sorry," I say, crying. "I'm so very sorry."

"Well, shit," he says, his eyes full of tears, "as long as you're here, how about another hit?"

"Maybe I better go make that bet first," I say, grinning at him. "I'll get lost in this circus if I get stoned."

"No," he says, shaking his head, "you gotta wait until the last minute. You don't want to scare those odds down at all. I'll tell you when to go. It's a straight line from here to the window."

We get a shoebox out from under the bed and have a few hits from an old clay pipe. He gives me three hundred dollars, lays back against the pillows, sighs and says, "Yeah, we sold all the horses. We're just hanging on here 'til I die." He swallows back his tears and smiles at a memory. "She was so beautiful, Charlie, before this, but when I got it, she started going downhill, dying with me. Then she went after the government. That woke her up, but they beat us, paid us shit for my life. Now she's just . . . I could see her going to the streets, Charlie, screaming at strangers. She's hooked on death. God, I think of her when I first met her, all full of life. She loved to fuck. Me, you, anybody. She loved to ride, and we had nothing but winners for three years. We named a filly Hey Baby. Did I tell you? She won her first two races, then broke her leg, but I couldn't bear to put her down, so we mended her. People still ride her, you know, kids."

"Thank you, Bus," I say, touching my heart. "You do me great honor."

"Yeah, but then I couldn't sleep anymore," he says, lurching forward suddenly, his eyes wide. "I was sweating. All the time. Dizzy. Then I went and they said it was in my liver. Can you imagine? Your liver full of that shit? They gave me chemo, but we couldn't seem to win anymore. I felt so clogged. Then the radiation. I *knew* that wasn't right. Now it's nothing but a long wait." He frowns at me and shakes his head. "I was nineteen, Charlie. A teenager. I didn't know anything. I wasn't a sinner. I never did anything to anybody. But they took me over there, Charlie. I remember sitting in that black jungle. It was brain torture. Thank God you missed it, Charlie. You never would have survived. But you know what? You know how fucked up we were? When those piles of shit came down, we *cheered!* Because we hated the jungle! We thought it'd be good to get rid of the leaves so we could see the enemy. But when the leaves were gone, nobody was there. That's the joke. Nobody was there but us. Did you know that for every man killed over there, five came home and killed themselves? Did you know that?"

"No," I say, trying to remember how many died over there.

"Is that it, Charlie?" asks Buster, grabbing my hand. "That's life? Three years of winning, ten years of dying? It's bad odds. It's not a race to bet on. See, with horses it's *not* luck. I'm training an athlete. The smartest, fastest horse wins. Almost every time. That's not luck. Am I right?"

"You're right, Bus," I say. "A horse-race is a hell of a lot better than war."

"I always took pride," he says, settling back against his pillows, "that I could take a horse other people said was no good, and I could get that horse feeling good enough to be proud of himself, win or not. That was my goal. To make a horse proud. Fuck the winning. Because when they're proud, Charlie, when they believe in themselves because me and Molly believe in them, they *do* win."

"I love you," I say, the tears coming fast now.

"I remember a horse named Gravy Train," says Buster, shaking his head and smiling like a little boy. "Big, slow thing. Coulda pulled a plow. But we got him sprinting. We got him *thinking* he was fast, and he started to *be* fast. And one day, at a hundred to one against him, he came down the stretch and beat a monster by a half inch. I got the photo somewhere. An unbelievable thing, Charlie. A nothing beat a champion because he thought he was something."

"And then what happened?" I ask, holding my breath.

"For eighteen races he was unbeatable," says Buster, nodding slowly.

"And then?"

"He lost," says Buster, the tears rolling down his cheeks. "He lost and never wanted to run again. So we put him out to pasture, but he didn't like that, and he died."

"I might want to make that bet now, huh?" I say, standing up.

"Yeah," says Buster, nodding, smiling. "You go out the door and go straight ahead. Go all the way straight. Don't let anybody stop you, and remember, number three in the ninth to win. Put it all down, Charlie. King's Guardian."

I get to the window. It's three minutes to post time. But the number three horse isn't King's Guardian anymore. He's been shifted to number five. There's no time to go back and confer with Buster. I check the odds. King's Guardian is going off at *thirty* to one. I have no time to check his stats. I step to the window, look the fat man in the eye and say, "All this on King's Guardian to win." He looks at me sadly, and punches up my ticket.

Time slows down. A second takes a minute. A minute is an hour. I see every detail of everything. There are these wonderful wispy clouds above the track. The afternoon sun is coming in from behind the horses, making their shadows rush ahead of them. The crowd is vibrant, noisy, expectant. This is the race of the day. The race of the millennium. Everyone on earth has bet on this race. The outcome will determine the fate of the world, possibly the universe. The bell sounds and the horses leap forward, igniting the crowd.

At the halfway point, King's Guardian is hiding in a clump of horses a few lengths behind the leader, a big gray horse called Mi Corazon. King's Guardian is a coal black beauty. I like his style. On the final turn, Mi Corazon and King's Guardian are neck and neck, flowing toward the finish on a cushion of speed! The crowd is roaring! I feel someone touch my elbow and I know it's Lily, but I don't dare turn to look at her. My soul is riding that big black horse!

And he wins! Yes, he does! By the merest fraction of an inch! I turn to Lily and she gives me a frightened look, but I grab her anyway and lift her high in the air, whooping so loud I almost pass out for lack of air. "We won!" I scream. She claps a hand over my mouth and leads me away. "What's wrong?" I protest. "We won!"

"Shut up," she says sternly. "I mean it."

I shut up.

"How much you win?" an old man asks.

"Fifty bucks," says Lily, glaring at him.

"So what?" he says, turning away in disgust.

When we're free of the crowd, I say, "What's wrong, Lily? We just won tons of money."

"Good," she says without a trace of joy. "I hate to ruin a good thing, but somebody spotted me, Charlie. I should never have come to a place like this."

"Pearl?" I ask, shaking my head. "Man, that bitch is everywhere."

"Somebody who knows her," says Lily, scowling. "He's probably calling her right now."

"We should go," I say. "I'll go cash in and we'll get outta here."

"Yeah, we'll go," she says, her eyes narrowing. "Soon as I can figure a way to get out of here without being seen. They probably have people at the gates."

"So fast?" I ask, doubting her.

"They came into a hospital and took me," she says, her eyes wild. "They do whatever they want, and they do it faster than you can imagine. It's their business, Charlie. They don't have anything else to do."

Buster's in a bad way when we get back. He starts coughing and can't stop. I find some medicine in the refrigerator, but it doesn't help. Lily tries massaging his chest. That helps for a while, but he starts again. It seems he might die from the exertion, but finally he stops and collapses into sleep.

I leave Lily in the trailer and go to get our money. The supervisor has to come to the window and approve it. They try to get me to take a voucher, but I insist on cash. Finally, they give it to me. I run back to the trailer. Molly's there, hysterical, saying she's never seen him looking so bad. She wants us to take him to the hospital. She begs us to drive them.

So that's our way out, in their old Swedish station wagon. Lily sits in back with Buster. Molly sits up front with me. When we come to the exit, Lily pretends to be looking for something on the floor in front of her. The guard recognizes Molly and waves us through. We drive on by. There are three big goons standing just past the guardhouse, watching us. I almost flip them the bird, but think better of it. You never know what might get flipped back.

15

Buster moans with pain. The rough road jostles him, no matter how slow I drive. Molly curses at the government, curses at the car manufacturers, curses at the engineers, curses at life, curses at death. Lily sings an old favorite of Buster's, and it soothes him. I watch the road for potholes and take the unavoidable bumps as gently as I can.

I carry Buster into the emergency room. They get him on a gurney and put tubes into him. Ten minutes later he's in the intensive care unit. They start to hook him up to the life support machine, but he struggles up onto his elbows and says, "Wait a minute."

The nurses ignore him.

"I'm in my right mind!" he shouts. "May I please speak to a doctor?"

The nurses ignore him again.

I step in, put a finger in a nurse's face and say, "We would like to speak to a physician. Now. Not in a while. *Now.* You got that?"

About ten minutes later, *two* doctors arrive. They're both exhausted, as usual. One of them is vaguely familiar with Buster's kind of illness. Molly starts screaming at them, and Buster uses all his precious energy trying to make her shut up. I'm shouting, too, but getting nowhere. So Lily takes one of the doctor's hands and says very firmly, "Buster would like to say something, doctor. Okay?"

Silence falls.

Buster looks at Lily and says, "Thank you." He looks at the doctors and says, "I don't want to be hooked up to that thing. I want to die."

But the doctor says they won't know how bad he is unless they can plug him in and monitor his signs.

"No," says Buster, shaking his head. "I don't need you to tell me how bad I am. People been telling me I'm bad all my life. Right now I just want to leave my body."

So they move him to the hospice section. No machines. Flowers everywhere. They put him in a spacious room. There's a skinny old lady sitting in a chair reading a big book, waiting for him. She's his hospice guide. They've got live plants in the windows, vines growing up the walls. The old lady has some cinnamon incense going.

"What is this place?" Lily whispers to me.

"Hospice," I say. "It's where they make it nicer to die."

"I never heard of it," she says, awed.

"I had a friend die in one," I say. "I used to go there all the time while he was dying."

The lady with the big book smiles at Buster and says, "Welcome. My name is Ruthie." She's cute. Curly white hair. Shiny blue eyes. There's something coquettish about her, though she's probably eighty.

Molly sits down in a chair at the foot of Buster's bed and bows her head. She's spent. Wrung out. Lily leaves the room to call Rain and see how the baby's doing. I sit beside Buster.

"You always show up at key times," he says, smiling a little at me. "Right before the army, my wedding, now. Remember that night at the track when those two guys were gonna beat the crap outta me and you showed up and made them kiss my ass?"

"Yeah," I say, though nothing like that ever happened.

"Maybe he's bad luck," says Molly, sneering at her husband. "You ever think of that?" Her face is streaked with mascara and lipstick. I want to get a washcloth and wipe it clean.

"No," says Buster, sighing. "He's my witness or something."

"Yes," says Ruthie, putting her book down. "Watching and being watched. It's such an essential need."

"Oh, Jesus," says Molly, rolling her eyes. "I need a drink."

"No," says Ruthie, smiling at her. "We're talking about things that could help save the world."

"I haven't felt positive about it ever," says Buster, staring curiously at the old lady. "I want to, but I can't."

"No," she says, "because no one helped you see the beauty of death."

"This is gross!" says Molly, standing up. "I'm having you transferred, Buster. This is sick!"

"Wait," says Buster, reaching out weakly to Molly. "I like Ruthie. She's a good friend."

"Jesus," says Molly, making a terrible face. "Thirty seconds and she's your friend? Gimme a break." She leaves.

"Sorry," says Buster, shrugging at Ruthie. "She was fine until I got sick. It's been so damn hard on her. Years and years of it."

"It's a shame," says Ruthie, sighing. "She could have learned so much."

"Well, except I got cancer," he says, trying to smile at the old lady, grimacing instead. "I just hurt, you know? All over. All the time. I'm so weak. You can't believe how weak. A pound is like a ton."

"Yes," she says, nodding. "It's a terrible test."

"Why are they testing?" asks Buster. "Don't they know yet?"

His question cuts right to my heart. I want to hug him. He's like a baby speaking his first words.

"It's the lesson of life," says Ruthie, coming to Buster's side. "You're near the end. That means you'll learn the lesson. There's nothing more to fear. And once you know the lesson, the pain stops. And then you can die."

"The pain stops?" he asks, frowning in disbelief. "*Before* I die?"

"Yes," she says, her eyes sparkling. "People who learn the lesson early in life almost never feel pain. You see, pain is really just the fear of death. Pain is fear. Anger is fear. If you don't fear death, you're free. But instead, we're taught that death is bad, so our pain goes on and on. But you can't die until the pain stops, and the pain won't stop until you learn the lesson, not just in your brain, but throughout your whole self."

"What is it?" asks Buster, sweat in his eyes.

"Think," she says, taking his hand. "Or don't think. Open up to it. Let it come in."

Buster closes his eyes and takes a long deep breath. We sit in a lovely silence. His eyelids tremble. Now he gives me a startled glance, looks at Ruthie, and says, "I'm going. I'm going."

"Yes," she says, nodding.

He looks at me and cries, "Charlie! Be my witness!" He takes my hand and holds it with a strength beyond mine.

"Yes, Buster," I say. "I'm your witness. Tell me."

"Nobody's different," he gasps. "We aren't separate like we think. We're each a cell of this big giant thing, like a beehive." Now he looks at Ruthie. "Is that right?"

"We are one," she says, smiling sublimely. "Bees and people and everything."

He's going. I can feel him slipping away, the strength ebbing from his hand. I've never watched a person make the transition or whatever you want to call it. I've seen my share of dead bodies. I saw Lily kill a man. But I've never *watched* a person die.

Lily comes into the room. She hurries to the bed and adds her hands to mine. Ruthie has Buster's other hand in hers. She closes her eyes, and he dies. He leaves his body.

Ruthie cries out, but it isn't a cry of pain.

Lily's body shakes, and she clings to me.

I feel something, too. I don't know if I can describe it, but I'll try. I feel my body being lifted up by a powerful surging force. It's like having an elevator inside of you, a fast powerful one. But that's not really it. It's more of a pulling than a lifting. I have this image of Buster's spirit, or whatever you want to call it, shooting off into space with such incredible power that it easily gets past the gravitational pull of the earth, easily gets free. So maybe what I'm feeling is the force of his lift-off. Or maybe he's asking me to come with him if I want to, his spirit tugging at mine. Or maybe he's showing me what my death will be. Words are inadequate. I can only say for certain that as I stand up a few minutes later, I'm a different person. My perspective has completely changed. It's like Lily hearing the Brandenburg Concertos. Life will never be the same, and I will cherish it all the more.

16

"I can't stay any longer, Charlie," says Lily, giving my hand a squeeze. "Rain says the boy's gettin' outta hand. Needs my milk, I guess. So I'm gonna grab a cab, and you catch up later, okay?"

"Okay," I say, looking around anxiously. "I guess I better help Molly do whatever you're supposed to do at this point. But I sure don't like being apart from you."

"It's just for a few hours," she says, kissing me.

"I know that," I say, afraid to let her go, "but I just . . ."

"Charlie," she says, squeezing me, "everything's gonna be okay. Just finish up here as fast as you can and grab a cab. We'll be huggin' and kissin' and everything in no time."

"Okay," I say, letting her go, "but be careful, please."

I watch her move down the hallway, and I can't really believe she's my lover. There's something so lovely and buoyant about her, the way she moves, the way she talks, the way her eyes never stop taking everything in. I've never felt worthy of such a person before. And the feeling is so new, it needs constant proof of her existence to keep from disappearing in a puff of doubt.

All Molly has to do is sign four documents. But she won't. She knows all too well that once she leaves the hospital she's on her own, and that's no great consolation to her. So she decides to throw a tantrum. I try to calm her down. She spits at me, claws my face, and accuses me of causing Buster's death. She attacks a nurse, has to be subdued and tranquilized, and finally they wheel her into the psychiatric ward and strap her down for the night. Of course, that means I have to talk to the psychiatrist and spend three hours on the phone getting somebody from the track to say they'll be responsible for her. It's amazing how fast people who are supposed to be friends vanish in a crisis.

Fortunately, Buster made arrangements to donate his body to the scientists studying the effects of defoliants on humans, so by midnight all I have left to do is say good-bye to Molly and try to get a cab. But saying good-bye drags on for hours. She lies there in that bed, weeping and moaning, confessing infidelity, confessing that she prayed for his death, confessing all sorts of perversity and horror. I stay with her because Buster would have done the same for me. I know he would. But there's nothing else I can do, and so little I can say. Still, I think my staying helps a little.

An hour before dawn, a woman from the track arrives and I get ready to go. Suddenly, Molly blurts out that Buster's dream was always that one day he and I would have neighboring farms and that we'd go riding together and go to movies together. She says he used to talk about that all the time. I tell her the last thing he said to me was that he loved her. It may not be the literal truth, but it's true enough.

In the cab back to the Haight Ashbury, I keep wondering why death is dogging me. I wonder about Jerry, about the killings at Jerry's cottage, about Lily shooting that man that first night in Los Angeles, about Buster. I wonder if Juneau's okay. And I wonder about what I'd be doing if I hadn't stopped for Lily and the baby that night, if I'd gone back to my cousin's, parked the car, and fallen asleep on the couch. I'd probably still be making tacos for people in a hurry to get wherever they thought they were going. Or maybe not. Maybe I'd be dead, too. Maybe Lily is all that's keeping me alive.

I get to the city at dawn. I have the driver let me out a good distance from Rock and Roll Breakfast. I need to stretch my legs and clear my mind in the cold morning air. The alley cats are slinking off to bed. Delivery vehicles are drifting into the Haight.

I'm a couple blocks from the hotel. I hear gunfire, loud in

the quiet. Two shots! Two more! A fifth! My chest tightens. I can't breathe. I want to turn and run, to hide somewhere and then crawl away to anywhere. But I run toward the hotel. Sirens begin to wail in the distance.

When I get to the old house, the shooting is over. A sodden silence oozes from the walls. I push open the front door. The lobby is a morgue. Three men are dead, sprawled on the floor. Rain is standing behind the front desk, smoking a cigarette. She's wearing a blue bathrobe and pink netting over her hair. She seems oblivious to the bodies and the blood. She's working, tapping something into her computer. She looks up at me and says calmly, "Oh. You came back. Lily's gone."

"Where did she go?" I ask, stepping around a body I recognize as one of the goons from the racetrack.

"Oakland," she says, writing something on a scrap of paper and holding it out to me.

I'm stunned. It's a nightmare again. I try to wake up, but I'm already awake. "When did this . . ."

"I know nothing," says Rain, blowing smoke, then crushing out the cigarette. "I heard shots, called the police, came downstairs. These bodies were here." She blinks slowly a few times. "Vanish, Charlie. The heat is intense."

"My tools?" I say, coming close to her, taking the scrap of paper. "What about all our stuff?"

The sirens are deafening. I have no time.

"She took them," says Rain, her lips trembling. "She took a few clothes and your tools. That's all. Now get out of here. Go out the back door. Turn left down the alley, then right. Don't leave fingerprints. The back door is open."

"The front door! My prints!" I shout, glancing around in a panic.

"I'll get it!" she shouts. "Go!"

I can hear the armored cars arriving. I run across the lobby, dart down the back stairs, run through an alley, down another, and out into a crowd waiting for a crosstown bus. The air is thick with sirens. A police helicopter hovers above us in the sky.

A young black man turns to me and says, "Some heavy shit coming down. Bet somebody got killed."

"Yeah," I say, nodding. "Looks like it."

"Hope it doesn't hold up the bus any more than usual," he says, looking at his watch. "I got a new job. Don't want to be late. Trainee spot with a big corporation. Big chance for me, you know. Can't afford to be late."

Instinct tells me to flag a cab. I invite the trainee to join me and he does. As we're pulling away from the curb, two pursuit scooters come zipping through the alley and circle the crowd.

A few minutes later, I'm sitting down in the lobby of the Regency, shaking like a leaf. I order a beer, but it won't go down. I'm tired, wired, and scared. Dead bodies crowd my brain. I need sleep, but I'm afraid to close my eyes. I leave the beer and order some breakfast. No go. I keep thinking about those dead men. I give up on eating or drinking anything and look at the scrap of paper Rain gave me. There's an Oakland address written on it. Her handwriting is shaky. I go down the escalator, come out into the cold wind, and hail a cab.

Ghetto. Slums. Poor people. Broken glass. Garbage clogging the sidewalks. Sullen looks from bleary black men. The cab driver is a black man himself. He looks at me in the rearview mirror and says, "You sure you be going here, mister? You got that number right? Maybe it's not Oakland we want."

We come to a huge old warehouse built of bricks, with green glass windows, surrounded by a high voltage fence, topped with four lines of barbed wire. The gate is open, but the driver refuses to take his cab in. He pulls up outside. I pay. He lets me out.

I'm not afraid to be here. I've never had any trouble with black people. I owe them too much. Most of what I love I learned from them, and when they come close to me they can sense it.

I go to the door and knock. Nothing happens. I give the knob a turn and the door swings open. I walk in. The door closes behind me. No poverty here. I've stepped into a dazzling world of art and high technology. My heart begins to pound. I hear the baby cry! What a wonderful thing to hear the boy again! And now I know his name: Noah! Maybe it comes to me because I can feel the deadly waters rising, and this miraculous place seems like an ark. But I don't think so. I think it comes to me because it's his name. I follow the sound of his strong little voice and find him in his mother's arms.

She's sitting on a purple couch, about to give the boy a drink. Her fingers freeze on the button of her blouse. She gives me a pained look and very nearly cries. She hands the boy to someone and rises to embrace me.

I can die now. But I don't die. She holds me tighter and tighter, straining with all her strength, saying, "Oh, God, God, I am *so* glad to see you. *So* glad."

17

We're lying in bed, listening to the night rain drumming on the roof of the warehouse. It feels safe here, though I realize that's probably an illusion.

"Noah?" whispers Lily, snuggling close. "Are you sure?"

"Noah," I say, liking it more all the time.

"Kinda biblical," she says, doubt in her voice.

"All the good names are biblical," I say. "Joe, David, Peter, Moe, Larry, Curly, Paul, Danny, Felix."

"Yeah, but the thing about Noah," says Lily, worry in her voice, "is I kinda have this image of an *old* guy with a long white beard and a bunch of animals on a big boat without a rudder. But he's old, you know? A kid doesn't want to have an old man's name."

"He didn't start *out* old," I say. "I think it's a cute name."

"Well, it *is* pretty," says Lily, "but it doesn't rhyme with much, does it?"

"Sure it does," I say. "Rhymes with as much as any other name, certainly rhymes with as much as Charlie."

"What does Charlie rhyme with?" she asks, rubbing her hand on my tummy.

"Barley, gnarly, snarly. Not much."

"I was leaning toward Benjamin, actually," she says. "You like that at all?'

"That doesn't rhyme with *any*thing," I say, snapping at her. "I think Noah's a great name. I wish it were *my* name."

"No," she says, kissing me. "*You're* definitely a Charlie."

"Now what's that supposed to mean?"

"It means I want to make love," she says, crawling on top of me.

An hour or so later the boy wakes up, so Lily brings him to our bed and we try out names on him.

"Benjamin," says Lily, holding him up so he can run in place. "Benjamin? Do you like that name? Benjamin?"

"He hates it," I say. "Look at him frowning. He hates it."

"Charlie," she says, glowering at me, "this is serious. Don't prejudice him, please. Turn on that light."

I get out of bed to switch on a lamp. The boy watches me. He likes me. He's the first baby that ever liked me, and there's something so overwhelmingly sweet about that, I'm on the verge of crying half the time he looks at me. I'm not used to feeling so weepy, but I figure it's probably a good thing.

I get back in bed and Lily hands him to me. He dances his legs on my stomach and waves his arms, his little face tense with concentration. "Noah," I whisper. "Noah." He looks down at me, his eyes widen, and he blows a big spit bubble. "Noah?" I say. "You're Noah, aren't you?" He dances furiously, watching his feet, oblivious to me.

Lily says, "Noah."

The boy stops dancing, turns to his mother, and grins the most gigantic grin a baby ever grinned. He shrieks and giggles and shrieks again.

I hold my breath.

Lily stares solemnly at me for a moment, looks at the boy, and starts to laugh. What a beautiful sound! What beautiful confirmation! "Okay," she says, taking the boy from me. "Okay, kiddo, you chose it. Noah it is. Noah, Noah, Noah. Charlie and Lily and Noah. Here we are. Where's the goddamn ark?"

"I love you," I say to her, my eyes brimming with tears.

"You're crazy," she says, smiling at me. "And I mean that as a compliment."

The boy dances and gurgles for another twenty minutes, and to celebrate his new name, he poops a terrible poop. We change him together, and I think we each call him Noah at least a hundred times while we're doing it, but we never get tired of it, which is a good test of a name.

He falls asleep, and before we drift off ourselves, Lily says, "I like it, Charlie. It's not really an old man's name, is it?"

"No," I say. "No, it's not."

18

We're staying in the highest loft in the warehouse. Our host is a crazy artist named R.D. He captures moments of life with colored thread. He creates possible scenes from impossible movies.

He says we're safe here. That's all he'll tell us. It seems sort of hocus-pocusy, but the food's good, the art's fine, and there's space for Noah to crawl around in. R.D. says we can stay at least a week.

We ask about Rain. He says he believes she's safe.

I ask him if he knows why there's no mention of the Haight murders in the news. He says he doesn't follow the news.

We ask him if we're free to leave. He says yes, but he can't guarantee we'll be allowed back in.

We ask who owns the warehouse. He says he isn't sure.

We ask if he's sure of anything. He says he wouldn't bet on it.

R.D. is a character out of one of his tapestries. His hair is gray with a big blond spot in the front wave. His long ducktail is an iridescent blue. His eyes are friendly, but his face is a mask. He's a sturdy little man with an eager voice.

"I wonder sometimes if we can continue to hide," he says at lunch on our third day here. "It's beginning to feel wrong to me, though it's worked well for a long time now."

"You hide?" asks Lily, wrinkling her nose. "All the time?" She hands the boy to me and resettles herself in her chair.

"Our work goes out," he says wistfully, "But we remain anonymous. Personal fame is a detriment to creativity. We occasionally employ actors to impersonate us. Most of the famous artists in the world aren't artists at all, unless, of course, you believe that impersonation is an art."

"You like doing that?" I ask. "Having somebody else be you?"

"No," says R.D., raising an eyebrow. "But I believe in it."

"Why?" I wonder.

"It works," he says, nodding. "It works so well it's frightening."

"But how can you be free if you're always hiding?" asks Lily.

"Who said anything about freedom?" he asks, sighing. "I did a piece a year ago that was clearly sent to me from the future, and it was decided not to release it now. If my personal need to expose it, to show it off, had prevailed, the impact of the work would have been lost." He sighs again. "There are some things here that we've been waiting to release for nearly a hundred years."

"You mean the artist is dead?" asks Lily, giving me a worried look.

"Oh, yes," says R.D. "Of course. Most of our best artists are dead long before their creations come to light."

"Who decides?" I ask, my neck tingling. "I've always wondered. I knew it wasn't me."

"Uh . . . I can't tell you that yet," says R.D., suddenly uncomfortable.

"Who pays the bills?" asks Lily.

"All the money from the sale and dissemination of our creations is pooled," says R.D., reciting a favorite speech. "We each receive whatever we need to live comfortably, though not extravagantly. We can travel whenever we want, and we are given whatever supplies we need to make our art. If we desire to, we may move from one center to another, mixing with new artists, accelerating the fermentation."

"That part of it sounds real good," says Lily, winking at me. "But what's the catch?"

"You have to be invited in," says R.D. "And you have to agree to a lifetime of anonymity."

"I still don't get that," I say. "Where's the incentive if you can't . . . be somebody?"

"It is its own incentive," he says. "Freedom to make art."

"How do you mean?" asks Lily, deeply puzzled. "You sure this isn't some kinda religious thing? It's starting to sound like it."

"Okay," says R.D., putting up his hands. "We are an extremely large collective of anonymous artists. We get plenty of adulation and applause from each other. And we *do* share a common goal. The preservation of culture. That might be called religious, I suppose. The definition has become rather vague of late."

"And what does this organization call itself?" I ask, bracing myself for a mystical cliché. Noah looks up at me and makes an appropriate face.

"Nothing," says R.D. "A name would confine us. We're a bunch of crazy artists. We're a family of fools. We're a microcosm of what we'd like the whole world to be someday."

"Starting to sound kinda relidgy," says Lily, smiling, "but I like parts of it. I always thought we oughta spread the wealth around."

"How come you're telling us so much?" I ask, suspiciously. "What's to stop us from leaving here and telling the whole world?"

"No one would believe you," he says, shrugging. "What I've told you so far sounds like idealistic idiocy. The sixties reborn. They'd laugh in your face."

"That's true," says Lily, taking the boy from me and kissing him. "There's a kind of safety I guess about being ahead of your time."

19

We've spent five days in the warehouse. Lily played the piano all day long for two days, but she won't sing. She's afraid to let them hear her. I played guitar for her one day, and she liked what I was doing. Then she took it from me and played everything I played, only cleaner and faster. She can play anything she hears, and who knows what all she's listening to when she closes her eyes, leans back her head, and lets that stuff pour into her and out of her.

It's our fifth night here. We put Noah to bed and get deep into a game of Scrabble. We don't play for points. We just play. Lily likes to use all her letters each time, even if they don't spell a regular word. She lays them down, hooking them around other letters, making more words than there's ever been before. I didn't like her way of playing at first, but I've come to enjoy it, especially when I can get her making up definitions.

R.D. materializes, apologizing for the interruption. He asks us to come with him to a subterranean part of the complex. Lily gets Noah, though she hates to wake him, and we take an elevator down to an enormous room. The ceiling is high above us. Exquisite rugs float here and there on a sea of hardwood. The walls are white, the ceiling blue. The room is full of hundreds of paintings, sculptures, weavings. This is their private gallery. These are the creations they'll give to the world tomorrow, ten years from now, a hundred years in the future. And they will give them anonymously, for the pure thrill of giving. Lily doesn't trust it, and I trust her mistrust.

R.D. introduces us to a very black man named Andrew, then disappears. We sit on couches, facing each other. Noah falls asleep. We're in the middle of the vast room, just the four of us, a grand piano and a potted palm. Lily's wearing a loose cotton blouse and blue jeans. She's dolled herself up, put a little curl in her hair, and looks so good I can't believe she lets me love her. I've got on a baggy sweater and baggy slacks. Andrew's wearing a gray silk suit, a white silk shirt, a blue silk tie. His black, black shoes are outlined in tiny strands of pink neon.

He's a small, slender man, with wildly active hands. Big gestures. Enormous facial responses. A buttery voice and a jazzy vocabulary. "I heard a tape of yours," he says to Lily. "It changed my whole way of thinking. Changed, in fact, the course of my life. I am very, very excited to meet you."

"Where'd you get the tape?" asks Lily, looking away from him, frowning at her baby in my arms.

"Rain," he says. "She's a close, close friend."

"I made two tapes," says Lily, still avoiding his face.

"Four songs," he says, his hands fluttering up around his eyes.

"Yeah, they both had four songs," she says, turning to him, a sullen look on her face. "Same four songs. Different takes. I wonder which one you liked so much."

"How clever of you!" he says, smiling gigantically. "Hope I fell for the right one."

"Do you have it?" she asks gruffly.

"Yes," he says, taking a tape out of his pocket. He hands it to her. She looks at it, a blank expression on her face. She hands it back to him.

"You mistrust me," he says simply.

"Have to," she says, nodding slowly. "Too much we don't know. You could be working for anybody. These are pretty nice accommodations for starving artists."

"What would you like to know?" he asks, forcing a smile as his hands swoop through the air.

"Where's Rain?" she asks.

Andrew eyes me suspiciously. "Is he . . .? Do you . . .?"

"He's the only person in the world I trust," says Lily, pointing a finger at Andrew, shooting down his hands. "You got that? Him and that baby he's holding. You got that? The *only* person."

"I understand," says Andrew, nodding to me.

"So where's Rain?" I ask, smiling down at the sleeping boy.

"She's safe," he says, continuing to nod.

"I want to see her," says Lily, still pointing at him.

"She's in Oregon," he says, looking away.

Lily closes her eyes and laughs.

"We have a center there," says Andrew, his hands taking flight again.

"I want to go there," says Lily, breathlessly.

"You may," says Andrew, his eyes widening. "Possibly."

"What do we have to do?" I ask. "Say the magic word?"

He laughs and points at me. "You said it, Charlie! R.D. said you folks were quick, but I had no idea he meant lightning."

"And what word is that?" asks Lily.

"Words," says Andrew, waving his fingers in the air. "More than one."

"You want us to join," whispers Lily, taking my hand and squeezing it.

"No," I say, terrified at the thought. I'm ready to run, but I don't know where to go. Noah wakes up and yawns mightily.

"Yes," says Andrew, nodding.

Lily takes the baby from me, clears her throat and says, "We don't know enough."

"I'll tell you all I can at this juncture," he says, formally. "Ask me things."

"Why us?" asks Lily, shooting me a glance.

"I've told you," he says, looking dreamily at her. "Your tape."

"What's *your* art?" asks Lily, suspicion in her voice. "Or are you a front man?"

"No, no, no, no, no!" says Andrew, shivering, his hands clutching at his ears. "I'm an artist. I am. I really am. But my art is difficult, if not impossible, to classify."

"Try us," I say, not trusting his excuse.

He tips his head to one side, closes his eyes, and says, "Words, songs, sounds, clicks, pops, patterns, pauses." He opens his eyes. "Noise that means something. Or . . . meaningful noise. And I've written a few meaningless hits to keep the coffers full, though I haven't written anything in a long, long time."

"What hits?" asks Lily.

" 'Basic Concept' was my biggest," says Andrew, shrugging. "Sorry about that."

"I thought that was Random Death's tune," says Lily, impressed.

"I got no credit, of course," says Andrew, waving the memory away. "But we made tons of money for the . . . whatever we are. You'd be amazed at the earning power of anonymity."

"Do you run this show?" I ask, doubting very much that he does.

"No," he says, smiling at me. "Not a chance."

"Who let us in?" asks Lily.

He smiles enormously and his hands fly around his head. "When Rain called for help, I played the tape for . . . well, let's just say I used my influence in conjunction with your tape and . . ."

"Who killed the three men at Rock and Roll Breakfast?" I ask, hoping to catch him off guard.

Andrew gives me a sour look and says, "Why would anyone kill *any*body?"

"Why wasn't anything in the news about it?" I persist. "Ever. I know we live in violent times, but come on."

Before he can dodge that one, Lily asks, "Do you guys know who Pearl is?"

"Possibly," he says, folding his arms and ceasing to smile.

"You working for her?" I ask, getting a better grip on Noah.

"If I were," he says, leaning forward, "you'd be dead."

"Not necessarily," says Lily, frowning at him.

"You know her better than I," says Andrew, sighing in frustration. "I only know of her through others."

"Did Rain know Pearl was on our tail before we got to Rock and Roll Breakfast?" asks Lily, steel in her voice.

"Possibly," says Andrew. "I don't know all that Rain knows. She's highly telepathic, as you know."

"She didn't get it from me," says Lily, her voice dropping to a whisper.

"You'll just have to ask *her,*" he says, suddenly standing up. "Shall we go to a new level?"

"What?" I ask, squinting at him.

"We have another room below this one," he says, a challenge in his voice. "It's one I'm quite proud of. I think you'll find it highly intriguing."

I don't want to go. This thing is getting too big. They have too much stuff going for them. Art. Time. Money. Grand pianos. All I have is my desire to keep Lily and Noah as safe and happy as I can.

We take the elevator down to a state-of-the-art crystal laser recording facility. Lily almost faints. I've never seen anything so advanced. Andrew smiles sheepishly and says, "My little creation. My everything place."

"No!" Lily shouts, turning away from an electron synthesizer. "Let's go back up. I'll go insane if we stay down here."

We sit in the enormous room again. Lily puts the boy on the couch between us and he drowses off. R.D. brings us coffee and bran muffins. He's wearing polka dot pants and a torn gray tee shirt. His blond spot has moved slightly and now has a red line across the middle of it. His blue ducktail is braided. A tiny bell hangs from his ear.

Lily looks at the coffee and the bran muffins, turns to me and says, "They either want to keep us up all night, or they think we're constipated."

R.D. stays on. He's received some subtle sign from Andrew. The boy wakes up and Lily passes him to me. No one speaks for a few minutes. Lily reaches for a muffin and says, "Okay boys, what's the catch?"

"We simply ask you to remain anonymous," says Andrew, calmly. "For life."

"No thanks," says Lily, pursing her lips.

"Why not?" asks R.D. "What is it you would lack?"

"You know goddamn well," she says bitterly. "I'd lack *my* music in everybody's head, *now,* not when I'm dead. I want people to *know* it's mine. I want to be somebody in *this* lifetime. Instead of being nothing."

"You can't envision a creative life without fame?" asks Andrew, his voice quavering.

"I can envision it and it stinks," says Lily, standing up, ready to leave.

"Oops," says R.D., looking at Andrew.

"I wouldn't mind the anonymity," I say, taking Lily's hand and gently pulling her back down on the couch. "But I get the feeling once you join this club, there's no quitting."

"In a sense," says R.D., nodding at me. "It's exactly like life. Once you join, you're in until you die. But this isn't a prison. It's a hastening mechanism for cultural evolution."

"Look," says Lily, seething, "I've talked this bullshit all my life, see? You either tell me the catch or we're out of here. I'm not impressed by big words."

"A creation," says Andrew, putting his hands on his knees.

"A special song," Lily whispers, nodding in recognition.

"A special something," says Andrew. "It might be a song, it might be your soul."

"Do we sign in blood?" I ask, bouncing my eyebrows, trying to lighten things up.

"I did," says R.D., looking at his hands and wrinkling his nose. "Though it isn't required."

"What were you signing?" asks Lily, her eyes wide.

"You write your own deal," says Andrew, sharply.

"A contract," says Lily, smiling at me. "I always wanted a contract."

"I burned mine," says R.D., glancing impishly at Lily. "I signed it, waited a day, then burned it."

"You never told me that," says Andrew, glaring at R.D.

"I had to," says R.D., sadly. "I had to prove to myself that I could."

"So, how'd you feel afterwards?" I ask, remembering the day I signed the rights to my song over to a man who couldn't sing a note.

"I felt more committed than ever before," he says, nodding.

"To what?" asks Lily.

"I'm not sure," says R.D. He smiles at her, his eyes brimming with tears. "But whatever it is, it makes me work all day every day at my pictures, my tapestries."

"I know the feeling," says Lily, looking at him. "I'd do the same thing with my music, if I ever got the chance."

20

We lie in bed talking things over. We decide we have to get out of here, no matter how dangerous that might be. We have to make up our minds away from all this seductive stuff, all this potential music. We still have lots of money from our win at the track. I suggest we go on up to Lake Tahoe, rent a cabin in the woods, and think about things there. Lily says we should sleep on it, but I stay awake. After a few hours of bad ideas, I have a pounding headache, so I get up.

It's nearly dawn. Noah stirs. I pick him up, grab a bottle of juice and carry him downstairs to the enormous room, and down another flight of stairs to the recording studio. I gawk at the goodies again, and try another door. It's open. We go down a long flight of stairs into darkness. I feel for a light pad, touch it, the room materializes.

It's as vast and open a space as the room above, but the floor is exposed concrete, not wood. There are no rugs or pianos. There are only a few free-standing bookshelves, placed randomly on the flat gray expanse of cement.

That's all there is except for a few things sitting on these lonely shelves. I feel like an archaeologist finding all this, ten thousand years from now.

There are manuscripts of unpublished books, copies of unreleased movies, discs, tapes. And there really aren't very many of them, so I look at them all, reading their titles aloud to Noah. I figure his guess is as good as mine. He smiles at some of them, ignores the others, screeches at a few, but I'm never sure what his screeches mean.

I come to Lily's tape, and my heart begins to pound. I stick it in my pocket and turn away from the bookshelf. R.D. is waiting patiently for us at the bottom of the stairs, a sad smile on his tired face. "They've made copies," he says, nodding. "But that's the original."

"I've never heard it," I say, embarrassed that he caught me snooping around.

"It's an amazing thing," he says, leading us up the stairs. "An amazing gift."

"Can I ask you something?" I say, stopping. "Just between you and me, R.D.? No bullshit?"

"Certainly," he says, looking down at me from two steps above.

"What do they want to do with Lily?"

"Ah," says R.D., coming down a step and leaning close. He whispers, "They want to free her to make all the music she can. She's a fountain. She's a miracle. They want to give her creations to the world."

"Sounds pretty grandiose," I say, doubtfully.

R.D. winks at Noah. Noah attempts to wink back, but closes both eyes. "I once feared grandiosity, too," says R.D., shrugging. "But why deny the truth? Why deny what you really are, what Lily really is, what we all might be?"

"I don't know," I say, frowning at him. "I just don't trust it."

"And it doesn't trust you," says R.D., turning away, starting up the stairs.

"It's easy for *you* to talk," I say, calling after him, bitterness in my voice. "This is a pretty cushy setup you've got here!"

He doesn't answer me, and I'm left on the stairs with a whining baby and fifty tons of doubt.

21

They give us a car, an ancient turbo, hazard yellow, slow but durable. They don't ask us where we're going. Lily tells them we'll be gone a few days, but we don't really know what we're gonna do. R.D. says that no matter what happens, he'll be waiting for us to return. I ask him what he means by that. He says, "Don't ask."

We zoom past Berkeley, cross the Carquinez Straits, run through the flat plains around Sacramento, and climb up into the foothills, glorious with fall colors. We pass all the old gold mining towns, and I tell Lily that this is where Mark Twain got his start. She rolls down her window and lets the clean air fill the car.

We make it over Donner Summit, and drop down into the Tahoe crater. It feels good to be rolling along this bumpy old highway that curves around the shores of the great lake. But Lily says, "This was a bad idea, Charlie. We're near those damn casinos, aren't we? She'll have people there."

"Pearl?" I say, not wanting to believe it.

"Let's get off the main road," she says, giving me a worried look.

"We can go back to Oakland," I tell her, shaking my head. "It's a long way, but I'd rather do that than be paranoid for a week."

"I'm not being paranoid," she says, glaring at me.

We stop for fuel. I ask the attendant if he knows any out-of-the-way places to stay. He says he has a friend with a cabin in a place we might like. So I make a call, and the guy sounds friendly enough. He gives me directions and says he'll meet us there in an hour. He says we can have the place for half the usual price.

Lily doesn't like it that we're heading toward the casinos to get where we're going, but she stops complaining once we get off the highway and start up a narrow dirt road that runs through pine woods to the shores of a beautiful hidden lake called Fallen Leaf.

A bug-eyed fat man is standing with his springer spaniel in front of an old cabin near the water's edge. He wiggles his hands around in the pockets of his plaid shorts. His big tummy strains the fabric of his pink tee shirt with an alligator on it. He's got a gnarly old pipe stuck in his mouth. His tennis shoes and his spaniel are black and white.

We get out of the car. Noah shrieks with delight at the sight of the dog. The fat man says, "Name's Tillie, not me, the dog. I'm Willard. The dog is Tillie. Not me. I'm Willard. Willard Crenshaw. I hope you didn't think I was Tillie. I'm not."

He shows us around the cabin. It's old but clean. The floors dip and slant, but the bed is firm. Little waves are lapping against the shore, ten feet away. We've got electricity, a toilet, a kitchen, a fireplace and firewood. He says we can use the rowboat and fishing equipment if we want to. He shows us a trail that goes around the lake and runs off into the Desolation Wilderness.

"No way to make a call?" asks Lily.

"No," says Willard, taking the pipe out of his mouth. "Not in the house, but there's an old phone booth back the way you came not a hundred yards. Pretty sure it still works. It used to work. If you need anything, give it a try."

He leaves us his number. I give him five hundred dollars. He drives away in a car so old I've never even heard of it. Lily takes Noah down to the water and they play while I unpack the car, put the groceries away, and rig up a fishing pole.

I haven't fished since I was a kid. Feeding the line through the eyes of the pole gets me all excited. I feel that old hope rising in me that I'll catch something for dinner. For some reason that makes me think of my mother. By the time Lily comes in with the boy asleep in her arms, I'm sitting on the couch, staring at the floor, lost in a memory of before the divorce.

She puts Noah down for his nap. She takes me to bed and makes sweet love to me, soothing me with her strong warm hands, kissing me all over, moving slowly on me for a long time until she gets hot, runs hard, and comes a few seconds before I do. I drift off to sleep. I dream I'm in a war where the weapons are little angry people, a few inches tall. You give them to your enemies disguised as dolls. I wake up to the smell of trout cooking.

"You catch those things or did Noah?" I ask, coming into the kitchen. Lily's frying three rainbows. The boy is on a blanket in the little living room, drooling on a book.

"I was just standing by the water," she says, smiling radiantly at me, "looking at the mountains and the trees, the way they reflect in the water, you know, thinking how I've never been anywhere so beautiful, and this old guy in a canoe comes paddling along and asks if I want some trout, so I said sure. It was like something out of a movie. I almost didn't believe it."

"Can't beat that," I say, putting my arms around her and gently touching her breasts. "Thank you for making love to me."

"I sure wish I could have a baby with you," she says, softly. "Sure wish I'd waited."

"Thank you," I say, surprised to hear her say that.

"You're welcome," she says, turning to me. "I'll never join those people without you, Charlie. I don't care if they offer me the moon. I'll only do it if you do."

"We don't have to go back," I say. "We can go on up to Oregon now."

"I know," she says, leaning against me, "but let's think about it a while longer."

We go walking after supper. I carry Noah on my back in the baby pack Juneau gave us. We get to where we can't see anything made by humans. We stand on the trail above the lake and watch the granite mountains get in the way of the sun. That's how Lily likes to say it. There's one big cloud in the sky. It changes from white to gold to gray in about ten minutes. It's amazing.

We walk back to the cabin and sit by the fire until Noah conks out. I put him to bed, and Lily calls urgently to me. "Charlie! Charlie! Come here!"

I run to her. She's standing by the water looking up into the night sky. It's so dense with stars she thinks something must be wrong. "It can't be!" she says, shaking her head. "There can't be so many!"

"The dark Sierra sky," I say, quoting somebody.

"It's been here all along?" she asks, looking at me, taking my hand. "Are you sure this isn't the end of the world or something? It doesn't seem possible."

"They've been up there all this time," I explain. "City lights and bad air makes them dim."

"I feel cheated," she says bitterly. "I really do."

"We'll make up for it," I say. "They're not going anywhere."

"You don't think so?" she asks, looking up again. "Makes me feel kinda insignificant all of a sudden."

"You know what we'll do, Lily?" I say, kissing her cheek. "We'll drag the bed out on the deck and sleep under the stars. It's not likely to rain tonight."

"Can we?" she asks, sounding like a little girl. "Oh, can we, Charlie?"

"Yes," I say, holding her tight.

"And will you make love to me while I look up at the stars?"

"I will," I say, my heart pounding, my veins swelling.

"Then we can die," she says, leading me into the cabin.

But we don't die. We don't sleep much, what with the love-making, stargazing, giggling binges, and story telling, but we don't die. She tells me about a young blind woman she lived with.

"She was the only mystical sort of person I'd ever met," says

Lily, nodding to herself, "before Rain, and Rain doesn't talk much about it, she just is. But Cecily was an astrology freak. I was seventeen and I thought she was pretty weird in some ways, but she was nice to me, and every once in a while she'd get something about me from a reading that I hadn't told her."

"She do your chart?" I ask, remembering the time I had mine read.

"Yeah," says Lily, nodding. "Most of it came true, kind of."

"That's good to know," I say, sighing. "A guy read mine once and said if I made it to a certain age I was gonna do something important.

"How old are you, Charlie?"

"I told you," I say, muttering.

"You never did," she says, resting her leg on my belly. "I've asked you three times and you always dodge it."

"I'm pushing forty," I say, ashamed to be so old.

"You're a kid," she says, kissing me. "Men don't even *start* to get good until forty. It's me we gotta worry about. My voice is about as good as it's gonna get. I have to make my record soon or I'll never do it as well as I can. And I have to start singing in front of people, too, because I was born for that. That's why I can't be anonymous, Charlie. I can't be anonymous and still be what I'm meant to be."

"Did your chart tell you what you were meant to be?" I ask. "Mine was kinda vague on the subject."

"I don't know how I know, but I do," she says, trembling in my arms. "It's the one thing I know, Charlie. It's not really even something I want especially. I wouldn't mind that life they promised us. I think I'd probably love it if I could live somewhere like this. But it's not my destiny, Charlie. My destiny is to sing. And to give that boy as good a start as I can give him."

"I love you," I say, kissing her. "And that's what *I'm* here for. Because ever since I figured that out, I've been feeling pretty strong myself."

"You're too good to me," she says, resting her head on my chest. "Let's be together for a long time, okay?"

"That's what I had in mind," I say.

"Pretty soon I'm gonna have to tell you more about Pearl," she whispers. "Will that be all right?"

"Absolutely," I say. "Whenever you want to."

22

We're in the rowboat, soaking up the sun, watching the clouds, ree-laxing. I dip the oars and pull them through the still waters. We aren't going anywhere. We're just floating in the beauty.

"They don't *call* themselves anything," says Lily, smiling at me. "I like that. Do you?"

"Yeah," I say, "except maybe they don't *know* what they are."

Lily looks down at Noah in her arms. He lets go of her nipple and fidgets himself to sleep.

"Quick drink," I say. "He hasn't been nursing much, has he?"

"I'm weaning him," she says sadly. "Pretty soon he'll be on his own."

"What about me?" I ask, making a sad face. "You aren't gonna wean *me*, are you?"

"You can suck on me for a hundred years," she says softly. "I'll nurse you 'til we both die."

"Maybe I oughta row back to the cabin," I say, smiling at her.

"Maybe you oughta," she says, smiling back.

We barely get out of our clothes before I'm in her, going full tilt. She hangs on tight, her legs hooked around me, her lips at my ear saying, "Come on, Charlie! You beautiful thing! Just like that! Don't stop! Don't stop!"

After we've rested a while, she takes me in her mouth and makes me swollen again. She suckles on my tiny nipples. I'm the mama, she's the baby, we . . .

She lies down and I kiss her mouth, her breasts, her

thighs. She holds my head and I tongue her love and she shakes and rides the spasms of her miracle.

We lie under the quilt, holding each other, kissing and kissing, afraid to speak. But I have to say, "Lily, I love you so much, it hurts me."

The baby cries. I start to go to him, but Lily holds me down and says, "No, Charlie, he's just fussing."

We stay in bed, holding each other, listening to the tiny waves lap the shore. The afternoon sun pours through the window. The boy falls silent. Lily takes a deep breath and says, "I need to tell you about Pearl, Charlie."

"Yes," I say, though it's the last thing I want to hear about.

She hesitates, before she says, "She's so beautiful. You'd be amazed how beautiful and smart Pearl is." She closes her eyes and whispers. "I loved her, Charlie. She was everything I'd always wanted to be."

"What happened?" I ask, hoping I can listen without judging her.

"At first it was like being in heaven," says Lily. "She gave me anything I wanted. Clothes and money. The best food in the world. Parties. Music. Stuff I'd only dreamed about. I was almost dead when she found me, and then suddenly I was rich. And I thought it was because she loved me."

"Maybe it was," I say. "You'd be pretty hard not to love."

"I thought she did love me," says Lily, turning onto her side and facing away from me. "Until we went to Italy." She falls silent for a moment, remembering. "God, Charlie, that's the only time I've ever gone anywhere. It was like the best movie ever made. We went to Florence and Rome and Venice. I read so many books about the Renaissance, you wouldn't believe it. And we studied Italian every morning before we'd go out exploring. It was like the best dream I ever had. And then I ran off, but just for a few days. I didn't think she'd mind. I needed to be alone over there, to look at things without anybody telling me what I should be seeing. You know what I mean? I wanted to see it for myself. But she didn't understand that, or maybe she did, but when I came back everything had changed. She cut the trip short and we flew home."

"Sounds like love to me," I say. "Wounded love."

"She doesn't know how to love," says Lily, closing her eyes.

"Were you lovers?" I ask, assuming they were.

"We never made love, if that's what you mean," she says, stiffening. "But we did a lot of drugs together and shared a man now and then. We did all sorts of crazy things. And then she asked me to have a baby."

"Noah?" I whisper. "But . . ."

Lily groans and turns over, clutching at me, scraping me with her nails. She pulls her knees up to her chest and moans. I try to hold her, but she pushes me away.

"Tell me, Lily!" I say. "Get it out!"

I take her in my arms and hold her. She struggles to get away, but I won't let her. She arches her back and a spasm shakes her. Another goes through her, and another and another. She collapses. Her chest heaves and I pray to God she's not dying.

"God, God, God!" she cries. "What have I done?"

I hold her for a long time until her pain subsides. I lie her down on her back and pet her until she's calm. "You don't have to talk about it anymore," I say.

"Yes," she whispers, taking my hand. "I have to, Charlie. I have to tell you why I said I'd have a baby for her. It was because she couldn't have one herself, it was the one thing she couldn't do, and I wanted to pay her back. So I stopped taking drugs and did everything she told me to do. I exercised every day. I went to healers and they cleansed me. I learned to meditate and make my insides calm even if I was upset. I stopped eating junk food and things with sugar in them. I changed, Charlie. And then . . . I did it with the man she chose. I made my mind blank when he was in me. I never wanted to see him. I pretended he was God. And then I got pregnant, and it was a miracle, but . . ."

"What?"

"I couldn't . . . give her my baby. I couldn't do it. It was wrong. I couldn't sell him. Ever. No matter what she promised."

"What did she promise you?" I ask, knowing all too well.

"She was gonna pay for me to make a record," says Lily, sounding truly astonished. "She cut the deal. It was gonna be big, Charlie. So big. But I didn't care anymore. It was the wrong way, the wrong deal. So I ran. But they found me in the hospital right after I gave birth. Then they took me back to her house, and then before I was healed all the way, she let this dog-man . . ."

"Lily don't," I say, closing my eyes.

"No," she says sternly, "I can say it now. She wanted me to kill myself. She wanted me to give up the baby to her like I promised I would. She wanted me to say, 'Here! Take it! I don't want it!' "

"And when you wouldn't break?" I ask. "Why didn't she kill you then?"

"Because," says Lily, trembling. "Because she wanted me to breast-feed him for nine months. All her books said you had to do that. She used to say it every day. Every day. Every time I nursed him. 'The genetic mother must breast-feed the child for at least nine months to insure the proper development of the immune system.' She wanted him perfect. But I knew she'd kill me after nine months. That's why I told that poor fool — a stupid guard was all he was — I told him I'd marry him if he'd get me out of there. And he believed me."

"What happened to him?"

"They killed him," she says, getting out of bed. "Let's go, Charlie. Anywhere. But let's go. I don't feel safe here anymore."

"Tomorrow," I say. "Tomorrow's soon enough."

"Okay," she says, putting on her bathrobe. "I'll be out on the deck. Thanks for listening."

"That's what I'm here for," I say, watching her go.

I try to imagine her past, try to see it realistically in my mind, but it's too sad, too full of violence and mistrust. But I'm glad she told me. I want her to flush it all out, to exorcise it, to name it, and say good-bye to it, so we can get on with our new lives.

23

Lily nurses Noah for what she says will be the last time. We put him to bed and smoke the last joint of Jerry's weed. The first thing Lily does is go outside and look at the stars. Second thing she does is take off her clothes and swim out into the icy lake. Third thing she does is sit and stare at the fire while I make popcorn. Fourth thing she does is eat the popcorn.

We're sitting, laughing, getting greasy, when we hear tires crunching gravel. We jump to our feet. I'm dressed. I've got on jeans, tee shirt, sweatshirt, tennies, but Lily's barefoot and naked under her robe. She runs to get Noah. I peer out into the darkness. The thing is still coming, but its lights are off and that seems rotten to me.

Lily comes out of the bedroom with Noah in one arm, a few things in the other. She shakes her head in disbelief and goes out the side door onto the deck. I grab the knapsack, throw some bread and a couple cans of juice into it, and follow her. We get into the rowboat and shove off, hoping we're imagining things.

We're fifty feet from shore, moving down the lake, when we hear glass breaking, and somebody starts tearing our little cabin apart. Flashlight beams cut through the darkness, touch the water and find us. Lily ducks down, shielding the baby. I row with all my might away from the lights.

"That's it," says Lily, her voice trembling. "If we get out of this alive, I'm never smoking pot again."

"Mighta saved our lives," I say. "I wouldn't blame the dope."

"Just row this thing!" she shouts. "Row!"

The lights stay with us. I wonder why they don't shoot. My mind is full of nonsense and I can barely think. There's no road beyond our cabin. There's just a trail into the wilderness. We have to get to the trail! That's all I know.

"Did you get some shoes?" I ask, hoping she did.

"Yeah," she says, "and that little pack for carrying the boy."

An outboard motor rumbles into life. I pull hard for shore. We have to get there before they trap us out on the water. I tell Lily what I'm doing, but she already knows.

They're right behind us as we hit the shore and scramble out of the boat. The trail is somewhere above us. I carry Noah under my arm like a football. Lily's ahead of me, clawing through the deerbrush. I hear their boat ram the shore and big bodies crashing into the undergrowth below us.

Lily overruns the trail, but I catch her and show her the faint path. She starts to run. There's no time for her to put on her shoes. The granite stones are sharp and I wince thinking about her tender feet. I run after her, holding the boy out in front of me. I'm sure he's gonna start crying, but he doesn't. He seems to know. The boy seems to *know*.

We run by starlight. We run until our hearts nearly burst. We run out of the brush onto a slope of loose rocks. The trail forks and we take the steepest path. The thin air burns our lungs, but we run on, wanting so much to live. We come to a switchback, a hairpin turn, and take it fast, not daring to slow down. And now we can see their lights on the trail below us, three of them, bobbing in the darkness, one of them outdistancing the others, only a few minutes behind us.

But I have to stop to catch my breath and calm my racing heart. Lily puts on her shoes. The lights are much closer now. We take off running again. A few minutes later, we're off the open slope, moving through deep woods, the trail climbing steeply. Lily asks me if we should try to hide. I say no, the baby might cry out and give us away. But my real fear is that they'll hear my heavy breathing and my pounding heart.

Lily takes the boy from me while I put the little pack on my back. She lifts him into it. She grabs the knapsack with our food in it, slings it over her shoulder and runs ahead, faster than before. We run for a long time without stopping. We pass a small lake at timberline, and start up a steep granite slope. The stars illuminate the white rock, making it much easier to follow the trail.

Lily runs on and on. She seems to grow stronger as I grow more and more exhausted. She takes the boy from me, but still leaves me far behind. I can't run anymore and have to walk. My body aches. I know I'm holding her back, and I hate myself for being so out of shape. But finally we reach a high pass. From here the trail runs down into Desolation Valley. We can look back and see the casino lights on the south shore of Tahoe. We stop to rest. We can see the trail for a long way behind us, but there's no sign of our pursuers.

"Shit," says Lily, breathlessly. "If I'd only gotten the gun. I couldn't think."

"We'll be okay," I say, panting.

"Oh, really?" she says, her voice trembling. "What are we gonna do?"

"You go on with the boy," I say, knowing I can't run much further. "I'll catch up later."

"No," she whispers harshly. "If we have to die, let's die together. I'm not going on without you."

"Lily," I say, hanging my head, "I can't keep this pace up. This may be our only chance. Once we start down into that valley, they'll be above us, and they didn't forget their guns."

"So what do we do?" she asks, stamping her feet. "What do we *do?*"

"You remember that steep turn a few hundred feet back?" I say, hoping I didn't imagine it.

"Yeah," she says, nodding. "What about it?"

"I think we can stop them there," I say, starting down the trail.

"Are you crazy?" she says, following me. "They have guns, Charlie. Let's just outrun them. I know we can."

"Maybe *you* can, Lily," I say, "but not me. They're too close."

"Come on, Charlie," she says, stopping. "We can do it."

"Go ahead," I say, gritting my teeth. "I gotta do this."

"No," she says, taking my hand. "I'll stay with you."

"I'm not just tired," I tell her. "I *know* they'll catch us on the downhill into that valley. I know they'll kill us if we don't fight them now. They're hunters. They'll chase us until we drop."

The switchback is a good place for an ambush. I can stand on the trail above and look straight down on the trail below. If they don't see us in the darkness, I should be able to drop a boulder down on them. But that might not do it. Lily has to drop one, too. So we find the biggest stones we can move and push them to the edge. The boy, still strapped tightly to Lily's back, doesn't utter a sound, as if he's aware of what's coming. And maybe he is.

Now we hear footsteps on the trail. A heavy shadow rushes toward us, moving incredibly fast! I lift a huge rock above my head and throw it down with all my might, crushing the man as he reaches the turn! He grunts terribly and dies!

I stand, trembling in disbelief at what I've done. Lily rushes down to strip the body of weapons. "Charlie," she calls to me, "I can't move this thing. Help me get his guns."

I stagger around the hairpin, fighting dizziness and nausea. She's crouching by the body. She's a killer cat. It's pinned under a rock so big I can't believe I threw it. I can't possibly have lifted such a thing. "No, no, no, no, no," I say, turning away. "No, no, no." I sink into shock. I sit on the trail and bow my head. My life is draining out of me.

"Get up, Charlie!" Lily cries. "*Please* get up!"

I can't move. I can't feel anything. She slaps my face and tugs at my arm. The baby whimpers. I can't move.

"They're coming, Charlie! Please!"

They are. They come up over a little rise, two more shadows on the white trail! Their flashlights jump on and they open fire! Lily pulls me down behind the dead man! The bullets strike the body! The bullets strike the stone! Lily thrusts a gun into my hand! "Fire at the lights!" she screams. "Fire at the lights!"

I do it not thinking. I do it! I fire and fire! She fires and fires and fires! The lights fall! We fire and fire! The shadows fall! We fire and fire and fire! Our guns go dead. The men are dead. The blood of the man I crushed is on my face, on my lips, in my eyes, on my hands, on my clothes, on my skin. They're dead. They're dead. They're dead.

We're still alive.

I hear a hissing sound. Steam escaping from a pressure cooker. Wind blowing fine sand across sand. And I know it's the stars. I look up at them and see their faces and hear them hissing and hissing and hissing. Yes. I'm a murderer. Yes. I'm out of my mind.

24

We hike on a few minutes later. We know we can't go back to our cabin on the lake. Our only chance is to make it across Desolation Valley and hope we can come out unseen on the other side. We'll hitch a ride to Oregon, Canada, anywhere far away. If there were another planet handy, we'd go there, but there isn't.

The dawn light shows us where we are. We're on a trail in a granite wilderness. It's cold and I can smell rain coming. Our bread is gone. We have one can of juice left. Lily's bathrobe is ripped and her shoes are falling apart. She's wearing my sweatshirt, but she's still cold. I curse myself for not stripping the dead men. Lily says she'd rather freeze, but that's a real possibility now. I know if we get wet on top of being cold, we're in bad trouble, not that we aren't in bad enough trouble as is.

I keep my eyes open for shelter. We're tired and hungry, and we're afraid to drink the water because Willard Crenshaw warned us about a microscopic thing that makes you sick for life. He says even if the water is crystal clear, the thing might be in it. But when we come to our fourth little creek, we have to take our chances and drink.

I've got a pack of matches, and I'm planning to start a fire if we ever come to some wood. But most of Desolation seems to be above timberline, and what wood there might have been near the trail has long since been scavenged by the hikers that come here in the summer. I still have a ton of money on me. If we happen to run into a late-season backpacker, I'll buy him out. I'll give him whatever he wants.

It's hard and cold and rocky, and we're miserable, puny

animals, walking on the edge of death. If we don't eat something soon and get warm, we're gonna die. Plain and simple. Or someone or something is gonna jump out from behind a rock and kill us. That's life. And I'm a killer of humans now. A killer. I'm a murderer. It doesn't seem possible, but it's true. And now there's this terrible humming in my ears. It started when I threw that huge stone down on that living man and *wanted* him to die. But I didn't hear it until the stars stopped hissing. I know I'll have to do something about it or lose what little sanity I have left.

I keep my eye on what I think is probably a cave a few hundred yards up the side of the mountain just to the north of us. We're heading for a treeless basin of polished granite with six lakelets in it. They look like quicksilver under the gray clouds. It starts to rain. Before Lily can argue, I hustle her off the trail, up the stony slope and into what I hope is a cave. It turns out to be little more than an overhang.

Still, it keeps us dry and there's enough wood to build a small fire. Noah starts to shriek hysterically. Lily tries to nurse him, though she's worried about her milk being full of dope. She's afraid it'll make him strange or retarded. But he doesn't want to nurse. He pushes her breast away from his face and screams until he turns purple, and he keeps it up for a long time until it starts to snow. That shuts *him* up, but makes *me* want to start screaming. The temperature drops and Lily says, "How we gonna get out of *this*?"

I start a fire with that wood there is. I leave the cave to hunt for more. There's almost none to be found, until I spot what looks like a whole pile of dead wood way up the slope. So I scramble up there, slipping and sliding on the icy rocks. It's much further than I think. By the time I get to it, my arms and hands are nearly frozen. It's a gnarly old pine tree, five feet tall, surrounded by twisty dead parts of itself. I drag two big chunks down to the cave, warm myself, and go back for more. I make three trips and that gives us enough wood for the day. I get the fire blazing and we share the last can of juice. I dry my pants and shirt, standing as close to the flames as I can.

It starts to snow harder. Lily asks in a trembling voice if I think it's gonna keep up. "No," I say bravely. "It'll snow some in late September, early October, but it never sticks. The sun could come out any minute now, melt this away, and we won't even know it happened."

It starts snowing so hard we can't see ten feet in front of us. Lily holds Noah close to her and stares out into the swirling whiteness. "Charlie," she says, "it looks like it's sticking to me."

"Better snow than rain," I tell her, lacking anything better to say on the subject.

"Why is that?" she asks, frowning at me. "Seems like too much snow would cover the trail."

"We don't need a trail," I say. "We'll follow the contours."

"Listen," she says, glaring at me, "you can follow whatever you want, but *I* need a trail because my crappy seven dollar deck shoes are about gone and I'm not going cross-country on this shit barefoot. You got that?"

"There will be a trail," I say. "This snow will *not* be a problem."

"You promise?" she says, biting her lip. "'Cause I'd rather make a run for it right now than in two days when we're starving to death and the snow is five feet deep."

"We'll be fine," I say, wishing the damn snow would stop.

"Oh, you're probably right," she sighs, closing her eyes, brushing the wet hair off her forehead. "And it's nice to be warm. Thanks for getting the wood. I think maybe I'll try to sleep."

She lies down, puts her head on the knapsack, and goes out like a light. I hold Noah and sing quietly to him. We watch the snow together and I can see it in my mind falling on the bodies of those three men I killed, those three men I know nothing about, except that I killed them. I crushed and blasted their lives away. That's all I know. The humming grows louder. So I hum along with it and Noah falls asleep. He likes the world we're in. He likes the snow, what he knows of it, and now he's dreaming about it, resting up for more adventures, as all innocent little children do.

I wonder if the men I killed had souls. I wonder if our souls are innocent of what our bodies and minds do. They were killers, those men. Is there some sort of justice in the way they died? Will I die that way, now that I'm a killer? Is there something else, some reason for our existence beyond mere survival? Is this snow some sort of answer? It seems so pure. I'm not sure why, but I'm glad it's snowing. I hope it keeps snowing until I figure things out, until this awful humming goes away.

I decide to give the dead men personalities. I want to make their dying a good thing for them. So I turn them into horrible monsters, the kind that deserve death. But I don't really know if anybody *deserves* death. So I change them into normal people, with friends. They laugh and cry and want to figure things out as much as I do. I make them sick to death that they have ever killed anyone. I make them want to be born again, or to sleep forever. I make them into me.

I have the man I crushed reborn a sweet mulatto boy in San Jose. I have him grow up playing the piano and singing and teaching music and traveling to Africa with his Mexican wife.

I have the man we shot reborn a white girl in London. She's sassy and pretty and has a natural talent for selling things. I have her grow up owning a bookstore and helping her husband market solar-everything.

I have the other man we shot reborn a black man in Africa. He grows up to be an agricultural expert, a storyteller, a world traveler.

I have them all come back to Desolation Valley and meet on the trail above Lake Tahoe. The woman from England is traveling with her husband. They hike in from Fallen Leaf Lake, looking for a view. The pianist and a friend of his are hiking out after two days of roughing it in the back country. The African man is with his son. They've just climbed a peak. They're going out to their car at the trailhead.

They think they're meeting by accident, not knowing it's the spot where they died. The view is incredible. Lake Tahoe seems to hover above them, a huge disc of water suspended above the earth. It makes the world seem enormous and small at the same time.

The Englishwoman says, "What a glorious view! Is it an illusion? The lake? The way it hangs in the sky?"

The pianist says, "It's a musical spot. I wish I had my piano here."

The African says, "It's good that we are able to share this moment without being afraid of each other."

I keep adding to their new lives, their new bodies, until they're almost real to me. I'm not trying to excuse myself. I can never do that. But I have to try to believe in some sort of good coming from my murder of them or I will *never* stop wanting to die.

Lily wakes up a long time later and takes Noah from me. He starts to whine, but this time he accepts a nipple. It's still snowing lightly. Darkness is falling. We don't speak for a while. I stoke the fire. Lily says, "We have to spend the night, don't we?"

"I think it's our best bet," I say, poking at the coals with a little stick. "Get going at first light."

"You should sleep now," she whispers.

"Lily," I say, "we'll be fine. I promise."

"Don't make promises," she says, looking away. "Just go to sleep."

"I don't think I'll be able to," I say, the hum still loud in my head.

But I sleep hard for a long time and as I wake up I think it's daytime, the fire's so bright. But above the flames is darkness, and in the sky, those big beautiful hissing stars, silent now. Lily's sitting cross-legged, staring into the fire. Noah's curled up in front of her, my sweatshirt wrapped tightly around him.

Only his little nose and mouth are exposed to the air. It's icy a few feet away from the fire. My body is cold and sore.

"I've been thinking," Lily says, as I crawl over beside her and put my arms around her. She's warm in front, cold in back. "I've been thinking about things and I've decided I don't need anybody to know who I am. I just want us to get somewhere safe."

"I know who you are," I say, "and I'll always be with you."

"Yeah, that's true," she says, nodding, "but I've been trying to figure out how we can get there, you know, taking reality into account and everything."

"Know anybody with a helicopter?" I say.

"No," she says, settling back against me, "but I think we oughta go back to Oakland and see about getting in with Andrew and R.D., give 'em some of my songs. That's all starting to sound pretty good now, anonymous or not, you know? Let 'em deal with Pearl and then we can go up to Oregon. And whenever we need to, we give 'em more songs. We can do that, Charlie. And then we can just go on being safe and warm. That's all I want."

"We can try it," I say, holding her tightly.

"But we'll come back here someday," she says. "Only we'll have sleeping bags and a tent and good shoes. And where we had to kill those men, we'll stack up rocks in a big pile, a *big* one, and people will stop and wonder why it's there."

"I hope I never have to kill a living thing again," I whisper, "except maybe a tomato."

"We could be vegetarians," she says, nodding. "I hardly eat meat anymore, a little fish now and then."

"Did you . . . did you ever kill anyone before that man, that guy with the pipe, that first night?" I ask. It's something I've wanted to ask her for a long time.

"Yes," she says quietly.

"When?" I ask, my heart pounding.

"About an hour before you picked me up," she says, sighing deeply. "I've been wanting to tell you, Charlie. I don't want there to be anything unspoken between us. But it's so hard to talk about."

"Can you try?" I ask. "It might help me."

"Okay," she says, putting her hands on mine.

"You don't have to," I say. "I don't know if I could."

"No, I want to," she says. "I want you to know."

The fire's getting low. I put another log on and the flames jump up. Lily waits for me to get settled beside her. She says, "They were ransacking the city looking for me. I'd gone into a porno house to sleep, but one of them found me in there. He chased me up into the projection booth. This little old man running the film tried to help me, but this big animal comes busting in there and puts a knife in him before I can shoot, but then I did, and then I got the knife out of the old man, but he died in my arms. I didn't really feel much of anything about killing that dog-man of Pearl's. He wasn't alive anyway, not in his heart, but I felt so bad about the old man. I was numb. Just like you were back on the trail. I tried to get his name out of his wallet because I wanted to name the baby after him, but he didn't even *have* a wallet. I dream about him, Charlie. I get his face mixed up with my father's, and I feel so terrible because I think he was probably a pretty nice old guy, because in all my dreams he has cats, and they're waiting for him to come home, and they're hungry, but he never comes, and I search his apartment and I can hear them crying for milk, but I can't ever find them."

"Lily, Lily," I whisper, trying to soothe her.

"If you hadn't stopped for me, Charlie," she says, nodding, "I'd be dead now. No doubt about it. I was just thinking about that. I was thinking how it doesn't matter if we die now, because we got to love each other, and talk, and laugh a little, and make love better than any dream. So if we die, it'll be too bad, but I won't complain. I won't, Charlie."

"Then I won't either," I say, kissing her.

I taste salt and look at her face in the firelight. Tears are falling from her eyes. She hugs me and says, "You know I don't ever cry and I can't ever say I love you, except I *do* love you, Charlie! I love you! And when you die, I'll die. That's just the way it's gonna be."

"I love you, Lily," I say, and as I say the words I see there's something greater than the sum of the parts.

25

We get out of the cave and down the slippery slope at first light. It's stopped snowing, but the sky is full of heavy gray clouds. We're hungry and cranky and cold, but even so, I feel a new strength in me. I brag to Lily that I could carry her a hundred miles if I had to.

We make good time. We cross the basin of tiny lakes and find a waterfull tumbling down a mountainside. It looks too good to pass up, so we drink our fill, and set off again, pretending not to have heard the distant thunder.

Hours later, we reach a huge lake, the palest blue I've ever seen. I assume the boy wants to touch it, because he loves water, but as I carry him close to it, he grimaces and whines. A sign on a tree says Lake Aloha, but Lily calls it Moon Lake because it seems so lifeless here.

The trail forks. A marker tells us we're three miles from Lake of the Woods and six miles from Echo Lake. I seem to recall from my boyhood that Echo Lake is near a road, but Lily says that Lake of the Woods sounds more like a place people drive to.

We flip a coin and Lake of the Woods wins, though my gut tells me Echo Lake is the way to go. But we're so tired, Lily's feet so bloody, I don't have the heart to ask her to go six more miles if three is gonna do the trick. So we take the path that runs down into a forest of big pines. The dirt trail is much easier on her feet than granite. Our spirits rise on the soft downhill. A big boom of thunder rolls overhead and we quicken our pace, making it to Lake of the Woods just before the rain starts to fall. There's no road here. No road anywhere close.

We stand under a big tree, arguing about what to do next. The longer we stand here, the wetter and angrier we get. We're both frightened, and we don't try to hide it. Noah sneezes and Lily panics.

"What are we gonna do?" she moans.

"Let's go back to Echo Lake," I say. "I think there might be a road there."

"You *think?*" she shouts. "Nine miles? I'll never make it!"

So we hike around the deep lake. The rain pounds us as we climb a steep gap between two peaks. We stand on the high ridge, looking out over endless wilderness. We're drenched and shivering and tired. That awful humming is in my ears again. I have the boy on my stomach in his pack, zipped up in my sweatshirt, but it's not keeping him dry anymore. Lily's out of her mind with worry about him. We find a scraggly little pine and squat under it, not knowing what else to do. The hum is a roar now, and I start to blank out.

A lightning bolt strikes the nearby peak, jolting the earth, shaking me out of my stupor. We have to get the hell out of this place! But Lily won't move! She holds me and stares out into the rain. *Another* raggedy shaft cracks the sky, strikes the peak, and rocks the ridge! The thunder annihilates the hum! Noah and I moan with fear. Lily jumps to her feet and shouts, "A car! Charlie! I saw a car! There must be a road down there!"

I tell myself she's crazy with cold and wet and fear. I tell myself we're dying and this is Lily's last little dream. I stare out at the barren mountains and valleys shrouded in swirling mist. I see only granite and trees and a distant lake. There can't be a road out there. We're going to die. There can't be a road. We will freeze to death. The hum grows louder. The hum is thunderous. The hum says there can't be a road. The hum says death. Death.

But now I see it! No! I don't! I only think I do. I look at Lily. She's frowning at the rain, trying to see it again, trying to make the road be there. She kneels beside me, leans her head on my shoulder and says, "Do you believe me, Charlie? I saw a car. I did. I saw one. Just out there, but now . . ."

There it is! The tiniest piece of a road! A gray patch on the side of a granite dome! "I see it!" I shout. "I see it!"

"Where?" says Lily, grabbing my arm. "Show me!"

I point into the distance. It's impossible to say how far, but it *is* there. A colored dot moves across the gray patch. We *both* see it. A car! A car! We hug each other, kiss each other, and struggle to our feet.

There's no trail, so we pick our way down the steep slope, following the paths of least resistance, trying to keep the top of the dome in sight. The rain beats down. Lily slips and falls, scraping her knees. The boy begins to shiver terribly, but there's nothing I can do. We traverse a sandy hill and come to a lake where we find a trail. Suddenly, lightning shatters a huge tree not fifty feet ahead of us! The explosion knocks us down, and Noah goes out of his little mind.

We get up and run along a faint path that crosses a mile of open granite, following a swollen river to the edge of a cliff. Here the water drops hundreds of feet down a granite face, and its roar drowns out the thunder. Far in the distance, far below, the road snakes around the dome. We stare out into space and I wonder how we'll ever get down there. My legs are trembling, my arms are stiff. I sit down before I pass out. The rain falls harder.

"How we gonna do it?" shouts Lily, turning away from the edge, dizzy and shaking her head. "I'm scared of heights, Charlie. I'm sorry, but I am. I don't think I can do this."

"Don't worry," I say, trying not to show my fear anymore.

It would be a tricky climb if the rocks were dry and we were strong. But it's so wet, and we're so weak and frightened. It's madness to try. But we're doomed if we stay so we start down.

There isn't really a trail. It looks like lots of people have climbed up from the highway to the top of the falls, marking their routes with stacks of stones, placing them here and there along the way. But it's impossible to tell one route from another. We keep finding ourselves back at the falls, where there's no way to go on. So I ignore the markers and angle us away from the waterfall, improvising switchbacks through the manzanita. We hold onto the little bushes as we make our way down the steep slope, but Lily has nothing to protect her skin. The thorny branches tear her legs and arms.

And now we come to a place where we have no choice but to climb down a sheer wall of granite. We scout for another way, but there isn't one. It's the last drop before the terrain flattens out. We can see the trail below us, running through the woods to the highway. All we have to do is climb down a cliff in the pouring rain.

Lily says she can't do it. She says it's impossible. I tell her I'll go first. I tell her to watch where I put my hands and feet and to follow me, though the truth is I doubt I can make it myself. With good boots, maybe, but not in the rain with my worn out tennis shoes. But there's no easier way down. There's no other way at all. No other way. We have to climb down here or die. I beg her to try, but she refuses.

"I'm not a goddamn rock climber!" she screams, trembling with rage and cold. "I'll fall! Can't you do something? Can't you help me?"

I can't think of anything to say, so I sit down and inch my way to the edge. It's a long, long drop and I can't see how to start. "I'll climb down a few feet!" I shout to her. "Then you climb down to me! Then I'll climb down some more! We'll do that all the way to the bottom!"

"Let's go back!" she screams. "Let's go to Echo Lake! We should have gone there! You were right! You were right, Charlie! I'm sorry. Let's go back. It doesn't matter how far. We can't *do* this! It's impossible!"

"If we don't do this," I say, closing my eyes, "the boy will die, and so will we. We don't have a choice, Lily!"

She sits down beside me, saying nothing. She helps me switch Noah to my back. She kisses him and soothes him. I start down, my face to the wall. There are handholds, but the rock is so wet and the soles of my shoes so smooth, it's nearly impossible to get a purchase. It takes me forever to get seven or eight feet down the face. I wedge one foot in a crack, press the other against almost nothing, and call for Lily.

She lies down on her stomach and backs her legs out over the edge. She lets herself down until her feet are dangling a foot above my head. I reach up with my right hand and grab her ankle, while I hold onto the rock with my left. She lets go up above and comes sliding down beside me. I can feel a muscle about to tear in my leg. There's nothing to do but hang on and let it tear if it has to.

There's no way I can hold her for long, so I say as gently as I can, "Lily I gotta lower you down as far as I can and let you drop. It'll only be ten feet or so. Just make sure you land on your feet. You'll be okay. I promise."

She must hear endgame in my voice, or maybe it's Noah's howling, but she goes without a word, hanging onto my right hand as I wedge the fingers of my left into a tiny crack. I lean down as far as I can and let her go. She falls a long way. Much farther than ten feet. And she's almost down when she strikes her head on a little nob of granite protruding from the face. She lands on her feet, but collapses unconscious on the wet stones.

Noah's squirming on my back, tearing at my hair. I'm afraid he's gonna wriggle free of his pack and fall. I can't take the chance of jumping with him on my back, so I keep climbing down, though it seems to take forever. My leg is on fire, and all I can think about is Lily. She has to be alive! She has to be!

Finally I get down beside her. The blood is gushing from a gash in her forehead. I kneel beside her, take the belt off her bathrobe and tie it tight around her forehead, covering the wound. I switch Noah to my front, get him under my sweatshirt and zip him up. And now I make a deal with God. I say, "Listen you sonofabitch. You make my leg okay until I get her down to that road, or I will come up there and kill you."

I stand up. I try to ignore the searing pain in my left leg, just below the knee, but it's too much and I have to scream, which terrifies Noah and starts him howling again. I lean down and pick Lily up. She weighs a ton with the bathrobe on, so I strip her, get her over my shoulder and start down through the manzanita.

It's storming so hard I can barely see. Now a long thorn rips through my jeans and gashes my leg where it's already hurting. I fall hard on my butt, Noah claws at my chest, and I drop Lily twice before I can get going again.

My body is wearing down to nothing under the strain, but I can't let myself stop. I can feel how near I am to the end of my strength. I *know* I can't stop. To stop is to give up. To give up is to die. Noah's screaming, struggling, furious at being trapped against my chest. He's already been born and doesn't want to go through this nonsense again, but there's nothing I can do to calm him. Lily is dead weight, but I won't allow myself to think she's dead. She can't be. She can't be.

The rain pours down. The bushes claw at me. The hum fills my head, drowns the thunder, drowns the pain. There's nothing for a long time but the hum. I stumble down a sandy draw, wade across an icy creek, slip and nearly fall, but somehow I stay on my feet. The trail turns to mud. The hum is in the mud! The hum is nearly to my heart!

But now I hear a big truck downshifting on the grade! I hear tires hissing on the wet concrete, but I can't see the road. I stumble through a swampy meadow, get a better grip on Lily, and start up the last muddy slope to the highway. I give it the last of my strength, but I fall a few feet from the top, dropping Lily on the sharp stones, falling hard on the boy. He doesn't cry out, and I think I've killed him!

Lily lies beside me, the water running off her freezing body. I unzip my sweatshirt and the boy looks up at me with such sorrow in his eyes, I want to die for hurting him. But there's no time for sorrow. I crawl up the last few feet, dragging Lily with me.

Cars roll by in the dusk, their lights weak against the storm. I take Lily in my arms and press her gently against her boy. I bow my head and listen carefully, but the hum is gone.

26

Murray's Gifts 'N Things would be a good place to die, but we don't die, so it's a good place for not dying, too. We're miles from the highway, down an old dirt road used by fishermen and the local hill people. We sleep on a mattress in the storage room adjoining the little store. We can hear Murray and his wife Dolores talking to customers about the weather. It's like listening to angels, because they saved our lives and brought a doctor to stitch Lily's forehead and sew up the gash in my leg. Noah has a fever, but no broken bones.

"I saw you there," Murray says, pausing dramatically, arching a bushy gray eyebrow, "and I was sure you were dead."

"Don't be senile," says Dolores, frowning at her skinny old husband. "How many times you gonna say it?"

"There you were," he says, ignoring her, his eyes on fire with the story, "naked and bloody. I figured you'd been murdered, dumped by the side of the road. And then I heard the baby cry! That's the only reason I got out of my truck. Because I heard the boy."

"Don't be senile," says Dolores, shaking her head and sighing.

She's a rosy-cheeked old lady with long gray hair. She and Murray dress identically most of the time. They wear red and black plaid shirts, blue jeans, and big clompy hiking boots. They talk tough, but they're a couple of old sweethearts. They've been taking care of us for two days now, but it seems like I've known them for most of my life. I never really knew my father's parents, but I've always imagined they must have been something like Murray and Dolores. Cranky old farts with hearts of gold.

"It's okay," says Lily, smiling at Dolores. "He can tell it forever if he wants. It doesn't bother me."

"He will," says Dolores, nodding rapidly. "Don't worry, he will. And you won't be here to hear it. But *I* will, so don't encourage him."

We're sitting at the kitchen table, eating soup and crackers, saying our good-byes. A friend of theirs called this morning and says there's a bunch of strangers in the area looking for a woman with a baby. Dolores says we can stay, that they'll hide us for as long as we need to hide, but we don't want to endanger them, and we know damn well that when Murray gets to telling a story, he can't be trusted to keep a secret.

"But you weren't dead," he goes on, still amazed to be part of a life and death adventure. "No. You weren't. You were frozen stiff and *about* to die, but I got you home in time and Mother brought you back." His eyes fill with tears. They always do at this point in the story. He reaches out and Lily hands him the baby.

"Don't call me Mother," says Dolores, making a face. "I'm not your mother. I'm your wife. Your mother is dead and I'm tired of this story. You never change it. At least the ones you make up you change." She looks at me and shrugs. "What good is a story if it never changes?"

But there's no stopping Murray. He's getting to his favorite part. He holds Noah on his knees and stares intently into the boy's eyes. "Now remember this, little man," he says, his voice quivering with emotion, "remember this. Your mother *sang* before she spoke. She sang before she was even conscious. That must be what a true gift is. Don't you think? I never knew what my gift was, but I have an inkling now. She sang *before* she spoke. That's the key. I know it is."

"This is a new part," says Dolores, frowning curiously at her husband.

"I'm not senile," says Murray, looking at Dolores. "I'm old, that's all. And it's inspiring to think that these people needed me. I didn't think anybody ever would again. *You* don't seem to. It's been a profound experience, that's all. Why should I change that?"

"We can't thank you enough," Lily says, her eyes brimming with tears.

"No, no, no," says Murray, looking at the boy again, "that's the point, now get this right. She *sang* before she spoke."

A car pulls up outside, coughing and squeeking. Lily and I both freeze in our seats, ready to run for cover.

"That'll be Jerome," says Dolores, waving away our fear. "His universal's shot. Can't miss it."

"We want to give you some money," I say. "We know it's not enough but . . ."

"No," says Murray, handing Noah to Dolores, "we wouldn't think of it."

We get up from the table and go out the back door. An old Mercedes is spewing gray smoke, stinking up the pine-scented air.

"Get it fixed or get rid of it!" shouts Murray, charging toward the car. "Goddamn you, Jerome! I retired to get *away* from this shit!"

"About that money," says Dolores, handing the boy to Lily. "We could sure use some. Just don't let Murray see you giving it to me."

"Thank you," says Lily, kissing the old lady's hand.

I give her half our cash. She tries to give most of it back, but Lily makes her keep it. I give her a kiss, we hug old Murray, and off we go, groggy from too much easy living.

Three hours later, Jerome drops us at the bus depot in downtown Sacramento. We wade through a horde of panhandlers and get in line for the bus to Oakland. We're going back to join up with R.D. and Andrew. We want to live. We want the hounds called off. We want to worry about artistic compromise in relative comfort, not with the jaws of death closing around us.

We're moving slowly toward our bus. Lily leans over and whispers to me that somebody's watching us. She says he's making a phone call. I turn around, acting casual, and see an Asian guy standing at a pay phone, looking right at us, talking to somebody. I don't like the looks of it, so as we get to the head of the line and the driver holds out his hand for our tickets, I grab Lily's wrist and pull her around the front of the bus.

We run through the dark depot, dodge down an alley, and come out on the busy downtown mall. We stand still for a minute, not knowing what to do, and a sleek new electric train slides to a silent stop in front of us. The door opens, we get on and off we go, cruising on a cushion of ions, going in exactly the opposite direction we want to go.

We ride the train to the suburban end of the line, it reverses poles and slides back toward town. It's a new system and everybody on board is chattering about how smooth and fast it is.

"Now," says Lily, leaning against me, "if they'd just build one that ran down to Frisco and joined up with old BART, we'd be fine."

"All in good time," says a tall young man with a silly looking white goatee. He got on when we did, and he's been gawking at Lily the whole time, making faces at the baby. "Comes the revolution," he says, "the age of the rail will be with us again."

Sensing a lunatic, I smile at him and say, "Hey man, listen, we're new in town. You know a place where we can hang out for a little while and make some calls? We can make it worth your while if you'll point us in the right direction."

"Next stop," he says, smiling strangely. "Follow me."

He introduces himself as Tolliver. He gives us his card. It calls him a Rail Advocate. He tells us he's a lobbyist for the Alternative Transit Association. He strikes me as harmless enough. His clothes tell me he's a poor man with a slightly outdated sense of style. His hair is clean but unruly. Lily and I whisper to each other as we follow him to his place. We agree that unless the numbers change suddenly, he won't be any problem.

His home is in the basement of a crumbling Victorian, a couple blocks from the lightrail line. The walls of his dark little home are covered with pictures of old trains, maps of subway systems, blueprints for mass transit stations, posters of Albert Einstein and anybody who's ever written a song about a train. He serves us chamomile tea and brings me a phone he built himself using a split pea soup can and scavenged components.

I call the warehouse in Oakland. An extremely friendly operator tells me that the number I'm calling is no longer in service. I ask her to double check. R.D. gave me the number less than a week ago. She puts me on hold, I listen to synthesized Beatles for a minute or so, but when she comes back on the line she says she's very sorry but the number is definitely no longer in service and there's no new one available.

I hand the can back to Tolliver, close my eyes and try to think of what to do next. Lily puts a hand on my shoulder and says to Tolliver, "You wouldn't happen to have access to a vehicle that could get us to Oakland, would you?"

"I can rent something," he says, frowning, "but I *hate* that drive. The road is so bad now, it's an absurdity. They should build a laser train that gets you there in five minutes and *generates* energy as it falls along its ion frictionizer."

"Hmm," I say. "I'm not too familiar with frictionizers, but I've heard lots of good things about them. In the meantime, however, we have to get to Oakland, so . . . could you use a little cash?"

"Possibly," he says, smiling nervously. "But what I'd *really* like is for you to stay a couple days. I so rarely have company. People find me rather bizarre, but I'm actually quite nice."

"I'm sure you are, Toll," says Lily, nodding sympathetically. "You mind if I call you Toll?"

"No, not at all," he says, smiling sheepishly. "I've never had a nickname."

"Well, listen Toll," she says, glancing at me, "we're in kind of a hurry, see? My baby has a real bad fever and we *have* to get home. It's kind of a life and death thing."

"Consider *this* your home," he says, glancing around the room, a wistful expression on his face. "We could have fun. I could show you a Sacramento you probably never dreamed of."

"Of that I have no doubt," she says, sincerely, "but we *have* to get to Oakland."

She hands Noah to me, but he doesn't want to come. Ever since I fell on him, he's been wary of me. I take him, but he starts to fuss and whimper, so Lily takes him back. My little buddy doesn't trust me anymore.

"Tell you what," says Tolliver, faking a smile, "for next to nothing we can take a train. It's a special sort of ride I reserve for special friends of mine. You see, I know the guys who run the freights. I'm kind of well-connected that way. It's a slow train, but it's a good train and it's the last place your pursuers will look."

"Who said anything about pursuers?" Lily asks, frowning at me. She turns to Tolliver and says, "Where'd you get that?"

"You said life and death, didn't you?" he says, punching a number on the bottom of the soup can. "I consider death the great pursuer. Is it not?" He winks at Lily, and says into the can, "Dexter, 'tis I, Tolliver. Seating for three on the night train to Oakland." He looks at me and asks, "The midnight special? Just a few dollars more?"

"Why not?" I say, smiling at Lily.

"But of course," he says into the can. "We'll be there at ten. Adios." He fakes that smile again.

"This is pretty weird," says Lily, forcing a smile at Tolliver. Hers is somewhat more convincing than his.

"Not really," he says, the smile fading. "I think you'll enjoy it. Now, if you'll excuse me, I have to dye my beard."

"Very weird," says Lily, watching Tolliver disappear into his little bathroom.

"Beats falling down granite," I say.

"Yeah," she sighs. "If only I'd been wearing my frictionizer, I coulda made some money on the way down."

I laugh. It's the first time I've laughed since they came to kill us in the little cabin on Fallen Leaf Lake. "I wish he'd come to me," I say, looking at Noah.

"He will," says Lily, putting a hand on the baby's hot forehead. "When you get over your little fever, you'll make friends with Charlie. Won't you, Noah? You know he didn't fall on you on purpose. He loves you. He loves you more than anything, doesn't he?"

"Yes, I do," I say, fighting my tears.

The boy buries his face in his mother's breast, clinging to her with all his little might, afraid she's going to let him go, afraid she's going to give him back to the man who hurt him so badly.

27

"The potential of the rail system is virtually limitless," says Tolliver, ushering us into a dimly lit caboose. We're at the end of a long freight train in Sacramento. The earth is spinning us toward darkness again. The sun is painting pinks on the big puffy clouds.

"Hard to believe, looking at this," Tolliver sighs, glancing around the stark little room. There are two old tables in the center of the car, surrounded by a few worn-out armchairs. At the front end, there's a bunk bed and a little door marked Pisser.

"Hey, you gotta start somewhere," I say, trying to make him feel better.

Tolliver's friend, Dexter, jumps on board and the train jolts forward.

"How'd you do that?" asks Lily, smiling at him. She bounces Noah and whispers to him, "See how that man got this old train going? See that?"

Dexter is a tall man with a big droopy moustache and piercing blue eyes. He nods and bows to us, but he doesn't speak. I pull an armchair over by a window for Lily. She sits down and rocks Noah, hoping to get him to sleep. She looks out the window at the fleeting clouds and gets herself in synch with the slow rolling train. She closes her eyes and smiles. She looks about sixteen in the fading light. She's got on a bright red sweater, baggy blue jeans, and cowboy boots, gifts from Murray and Dolores.

I think to myself, 'We are on a slow train on a fast track to somewhere, and this is not a dream. This is all really happening.'

Tolliver and Dexter get busy setting one of the tables. They cover it with a clean white tablecloth, and set out dishes and glasses and silverware from what they say were the golden days of railroading, when something called the Del Monte Special was the *only* way to fly! The table set, the two of them disappear into the little bathroom, emerging a few minutes later wearing white shirts, bow ties, gray slacks, and blue running shoes.

Dexter sits down with his walkie-talkie and mumbles to whoever's driving the train. Tolliver stands out on the back deck, talking to himself as he watches Sacramento disappear. He's a floaty kinda guy, as Lily puts it, living in a future that may never come.

At Davis, the train slows to a crawl, and a young girl with long red hair jogs along beside the train, laughing as she hands up a cardboard box to Tolliver. It's our dinner, catered from a local joint. Turns out to be good Mexican food, my favorite. Tolliver serves up the tacos and enchiladas while Dexter pours the beer.

It's a great supper. We drink a little too much, but it seems to make Lily feel better, and that makes Noah feel better, too. He has a raspy cough and a runny nose, but by some miracle he doesn't have pneumonia.

We drink some strong coffee and talk about the future of the world, which seems like the perfect thing to do on a slow night train to who knows where.

"See," says Dexter, his voice little more than a whisper, "people don't realize that the computer is nothing more than an ephemeralization of a giant rail center. Hundreds of tracks, thousands of cars, billions of particles going thousands of places."

"What's ephemeralization?" asks Lily, winking at me. She's tipsy and having fun. She grins at Tolliver and says, "That anything like a frictionizer?"

"Ephemeralization," says Dexter, raising a finger skyward, "is when you do more and more work while expending less and less energy. That's what a good rail system does. It's the salvation of the world. And if we don't have a rail renaissance soon, if we don't make the transition, we'll experience shortages that will make the current ones look like surpluses. Too many *good* things come from petroleum to keep wasting it as a fuel. It's insanity! It's like cutting down redwoods, damming rivers. It's massive, world-killing ignorance. I'm telling you, I fear the end of the petroleum age more than I fear a nuclear war."

"But you'd think people would know better by now," says Lily. "I mean, we can all see that the roads are falling apart."

"It's nationalism," says Tolliver, pounding his fist on the table. "It's borders and patriotism and all that shit. We need a trans-global society, and trans-global trains!"

"You know a guy named R.D.?" asks Lily, giggling. She finishes her fourth beer, turns to me and says, "Tell 'em the stuff R.D. told us, Charlie. All that utopian stuff that sounded so good."

"No," I say, giving her a warning smile.

"Please do, Charlie," says Tolliver, staring intently at me. "I'm very curious about you two. I didn't invite you on this ride accidentally, you know. I . . . actually, I followed you from the bus station."

Lily takes my hand under the table and gives it an apologetic squeeze. She tells me with her eyes that she'll handle this particular matter. "R.D.'s our minister," she says, sincerely. "He's always talking about a better world in this lifetime. A world without war, that kinda thing. It just reminded me of what you were saying, that's all, and Charlie tells it better than I do, so . . ."

"Oh," says Tolliver, obviously disappointed. "I thought you might have been talking about that art collective in Berkeley or some place around there."

"No," says Lily, wrinkling her nose. "What's *that* all about? I just love hearing about this idealistic stuff, don't you, Charlie?"

"But that's the sorrow of it," says Dexter, frowning at me. "We should have been there already. We should have laser travel by now, and we would, if the early automakers hadn't abandoned their plans to build methane plants for a piece of the petroleum action."

"That's a good point, Dexter," I say, faking a yawn. "But I'm actually more interested in why Tolliver followed us. Is that something he does all the time, or what?"

"Not usually," says Tolliver, frowning at Dexter.

"What are we talking about here?" asks Lily, a hard edge to her voice.

"Well," says Tolliver, fighting with himself, "I was actually kind of notified to be on the lookout for you, if you're who I think you are. I figured with the baby . . ."

"Who notified you?" I ask.

"A friend of the rail," says Tolliver, grimly.

"So, now what are we doing, Toll?" asks Lily, tensing. Noah starts to whimper. He always seems to know when something's wrong.

"We're . . . I'm . . . taking you to him," says Tolliver, swallowing nervously. "It's worth a great deal of money to us. But I'm sure there's nothing to worry about. He said it was for your own good."

I look at Lily. Her eyes are steel. She has a gun in her pocket. She bought it from Murray. She hands me the boy, and he comes without complaint. She's tense and ready.

"Will they kill you?" asks Dexter, giving Lily a worried look.

"You bet," she says, sneering at Tolliver.

"Why?" asks Tolliver, grimacing. "I can't believe he'd be mixed up in something like that."

"Believe it," she says, bitterly. "They're paying him a hundred times what he's paying you."

"That would be a fortune," says Tolliver, challenging her. "Because he offered me a ton."

"You didn't tell me that," says Dexter, frowning at Tolliver. "You said this was for a good cause, man."

"No, I'll tell you what it's for," says Lily, her voice trembling. "It's for the woman who owned me. I don't know if you can possibly imagine that, but it's true. I was her slave, and she made me have this baby, same as a nigger waving at the cute little train chuggin' on by the cottonfield, just like in your happy little fantasies about what never was. But I took him and I ran. I'm a runaway slave, Toll, and now you're taking me back to her. You're not a visionary. You're a fuckin' bounty hunter."

Dexter looks away. Tolliver sits, stupefied, his eyes full of terror. But Lily isn't finished. "She would spit on your rails, man. A railroad track ain't nothin' but a bump in the road to her. She *rules* by the automobile. And the money this bastard gives you will smell like gasoline, and the smell won't ever come out."

"Not if you get off in Berkeley," says Tolliver, red with shame. "They're waiting at the station in Oakland."

"Then you better get off with us," says Lily, "because they will kill you if they think you let us get away."

"We'll get off in Richmond," says Dexter, jumping to his feet. "Nobody ever stops there anymore."

"I'm sorry," says Tolliver, bowing his head. "I just . . ."

"Needed the money," says Lily, putting a hand on his. "I know how you feel, Toll. I do. A guy offered me a fortune once for a song of mine, a special song, and I almost gave it to him, but he was such a scumbag, I couldn't do it. I needed the money, but I just couldn't do it."

"Sometimes I just get so tired of scraping by," says Tolliver. "I'm sorry."

"Your time will come," says Lily, nodding. "This rail stuff is nice. It's a great way to meet people. You don't have to worry about falling out of the sky. And you can make love while you travel. That's what the people are looking for, you know? New ways to make love. Don't you think?"

"Exactly!" says Dexter, sitting down again. "I know a

writer. He's strange, he mostly writes about sex, but we might be able to get him interested in trains. We could make a video! Take the idea directly to the people."

"Is that Richmond coming up?" says Lily, taking Noah from me.

"That's our stop," says Dexter, picking up his walkie-talkie. "I'll let 'em know up front."

28

Dexter and Tolliver head back to Sacramento on a utility train. We get a room in an old falling down motel called the Richmond Rendezvous. Lily loses herself in an old movie called *Stardust Memories,* while I play with Noah and try to get him to like me again. After a couple hours, just as I'm just about to call it quits, he laughs at a silly face I'm making and holds out his pudgy little arms to me. Big relief. I'm addicted to the kid. I need him to want me.

The movie ends and Lily says, "Now that's the kind of show I'd want them to make about my life. Deep, you know? Didn't you think that was complicated in a real good sort of way?"

"Shit, I don't know," I say, exasperated. "I was working on Noah."

"Good for you, Charlie," she says, squeezing my leg. "Let's watch it again, and I'll explain it to you."

So we run the tape again and Lily interprets it all for me and it's great. When it's over, I say to her, "Yeah, I sure would like to see what that guy could do with what's happening to us."

We shut off the tube and make love, first time since that day at the lake. She sleeps, but I can't. I lie awake, watching over my family. There's nothing in the world I want to do more.

29

I don't know what I'm expecting, but it isn't a bombed-out warehouse. We drive right by it. Our cab driver, a little Russian guy named Yuri something, says, "Must be right after this mess? No? Oakland?"

"Should be," I say.

"Charlie, I think that was it," whispers Lily, going deathly pale. "Oh, my God."

"No," I say, refusing to believe it. "It's gotta be right up here."

But right up here is an abandoned shopping center and beyond that a chemical plant and beyond that, barren ground. Yuri turns around and drives us back to what's left of the warehouse. Mounds of bricks. Twisted girders. Charred wood.

"Let's get outta here," says Lily, closing her eyes.

"No," I say. "Pull over."

"Are you crazy?" says Lily, grabbing my arm. "They're probably waiting for us."

"Just a minute, okay?" I say, glaring at her.

"One," she says, looking at Noah. "A little one."

Yuri looks at me in the rearview mirror, waiting for orders.

"Pull over," I say.

"You want if I should keep the engine going?" he asks, nodding.

"Yes," I say, getting out.

It's a gray, drizzly day. I climb over the bricks to where the front door used to be and knock in mid-air. I wave my arms and shout, "R.D.!" I walk slowly back to the cab.

"What are you doing?" asks Lily, leaning out the window. "Are you out of your mind? What if somebody sees you?"

"That's the idea," I say.

"We going now?" asks Yuri, revving the engine.

"In a minute," I say. "One more minute."

"They blew it all to hell, didn't they?" says Lily, holding Noah up so he can see the interesting jumble of colored blocks. He gurgles and holds out his hands to me.

"All to hell," mumbles Yuri, nodding.

"How much to take us to Sacramento?" I ask him, thinking Dexter might be able to get us on a caboose to Oregon.

"Good buncha cash," says Yuri. "Bus is cheaper."

"Come on, Charlie," says Lily, reaching out to me. "Enough is enough. Let's quit tempting fate, okay?"

"One more minute."

"What are you waiting for?"

"R.D.," I say, closing my eyes.

"If he's not dead," she sighs, "he wouldn't be hanging around this graveyard."

But that's exactly what he's doing. He sticks his head out of a shed across the street, and whistles and waves to us. I get in the front seat and Yuri drives us over there. R.D. comes out with two large suitcases, puts them in the trunk, and gets in back with Lily and Noah.

"Canyon," he says, bouncing his eyebrows at us in greeting, "just over the hills from here."

Yuri gives me a questioning look, glances awkwardly at R.D.'s colorful hair, and hits the gas.

"So," says R.D., as if nothing much has happened, "you made it."

"Barely," says Lily, her voice trembling. "It's good to see you again. Thanks for waiting for us. Was anybody . . ."

"We'll discuss it later," says R.D., nodding toward Yuri.

"I'm sorry," says Lily, taking his hand. "I'm so sorry."

"Turn right," says R.D., watching the road, "and take this boulevard all the way to the top of the hill." He turns to Lily and says, "It's not your fault. It's never one person's fault."

"How can you be so calm about it?" she says, shaking her head. "They just trashed your whole life."

"They blew up a building," says R.D., shrugging.

"I'm still sorry," she says, taking her hand away.

Noah smiles at R.D. R.D. smiles back at him and says, "Well, then as much as one person can, I forgive you." He puts his hand gently on top of Lily's head and mumbles, "In dominus, in whateverus, it's just what is, you know? It really is."

"Yes," says Yuri, starting to cry.

"Oh, gimme a break," says Lily, imploring me to do something.

"You okay to drive?" I ask.

"I'm fine," sobs Yuri. "I'm fine."

"I'd be happy to drive," I say, figuring it might be a good idea.

"Fine," says Yuri, pulling over.

"For that matter," says R.D., arching a turquoise eyebrow, "*I* should drive since I supposedly know where we're going."

"Supposedly?" asks Lily, looking at me and rolling her eyes.

"Nothing is ever certain," says R.D., trading places with Yuri.

R.D. drives for a few blocks, frowns at me and says, "I think we're being followed. Hold on everybody, I'm gonna make some sharp turns!"

We race around the hillside neighborhoods overlooking the bay, and turn onto a narrow winding road that carries us over the top of the hills and down the eastern slope into wild country. A few miles further along, we turn onto a dirt road. We drive slowly through the thickening gloom, coming to a stop at a big iron gate.

"We get out here," says R.D., putting the car in neutral and setting the brake. We climb out, R.D. gets his suitcases, and hands Yuri a gold coin.

"Thank you," says Yuri, giving each of us his business card. "If you ever want to drive me around again, just call that number."

When the cab is gone, R.D. leads us back down to the main road.

"You didn't trust him?" asks Lily.

"I don't even trust myself," says R.D., looking around anxiously.

It starts to rain lightly. A moment later, an ancient panel truck with a long snout pulls up beside us. We get in and off we go. The driver looks familiar to me. He's a black man with a heavy beard and thick glasses.

"It's Andrew," whispers Lily.

"Nice disguise," says R.D., laughing with delight. "I knew it was you, but I couldn't tell it was you. Is the you-know-what ready?"

"We hope," says Andrew, winking at me.

We turn off the paved road onto another dirt track and the rain intensifies. Andrew puts the truck in low gear and we climb a steep muddy stretch that runs through dense poison oak. We emerge onto a flat expanse of sodden ground.

"The foggy moor," says Andrew.

"Yes, Watson," says R.D.

We drive across the muddy ground to a grove of old oaks and sprawling eucalyptus. R.D. and Andrew get out of the truck and hurry away. We stay inside. The rain drums hard on the van. Visibility is non-existent.

"Here we are," says Lily, kissing me.

"Any guesses?" I ask.

"No," she says, leaning her head on my shoulder. "I'm too tired to guess."

"Been quite a day," I say, rubbing her neck, "and it's not even lunchtime."

"Oh, shit," says Lily, looking over my shoulder.

"What?" I say, afraid to move.

"It's an airplane," she says. "A funky little airplane."

"I don't hear anything," I say, closing my eyes.

"That's becasue they're towing it with a rope," she laughs. "If they think we're getting in that thing, they're crazy."

"They *are* crazy," I say, turning to watch them drag the little plane into position.

"I hate little airplanes, Charlie," she says, a slight whine in her voice.

"I've suddenly decided to like them," I tell her. "I've always believed that the better you treat a metal object, the better it treats you. You know what I mean?"

"Yeah," she says, holding me tight, "I once had a guitar like that. Had to kiss it just right before I tuned it."

"So, let's love this little airplane," I say, kissing her, then kissing Noah.

"I'm in love," she says, sighing. "What choice have I got?"

30

Andrew and R.D. ride up front, Andrew piloting, R.D. consulting a manual and making suggestions. Lily and I sit in old bucket seats, single-file behind them, Lily first, then me. Noah sits in a little car seat between Lily's legs. There's just barely enough room for R.D.'s suitcases.

They take an uncomfortably long time getting the engine to turn over, and it dies twice before staying on. At one point, R.D. frowns at Andrew and says, "Are you *sure?*" and a few minutes later Andrew replies, "Oh, *that's* right. I always forget that." Lily keeps her peace while I count backwards from a hundred and seven and hope I don't wet my pants.

We roll along the bumpy ground to the edge of the field. We turn around and roll back the other way at roughly the same speed, right around *no* miles an hour. The little engine whines and coughs. How it's going to lift all our weight, I can't imagine. Suddenly the windshield wipers stop working. Lily looks around the edge of her seat at me and says, "I love you, and I love this plane."

"I wish we were sitting together," I say.

"Muddy," says Andrew. "Might be hard to get up speed."

"Pack it down a couple more times," suggests R.D., tapping the meters to make sure they aren't stuck.

We bounce over the takeoff route two more times. Andrew announces, "Here goes nothing," and we start to move again, only this time he gives it gas and the bumps come faster and harder. The plane feels like it's about to shake apart, and *right* as we're about to hit a *tree* . . . he lifts the nose of the plane up and we're in the air.

"Nice job," I say, noticing I didn't wet my pants.

"Except it doesn't want to climb!" shouts Andrew.

The plane is skimming along the ridgetop about thirty feet off the ground, R.D. is frantically flipping through the manual, while Andrew is steering the plane around tall trees that jump out of the gloom at us. I'm about to suggest that we turn around and go back to the beginning, when Lily leans forward between R.D. and Andrew and tells Andrew to do something. I can't hear her over the whining engine, but he does *something* different, and the plane starts to climb. Lily sits back, R.D. looks at her with such love I can't believe it, and I look down and see I *have* wet my pants.

We fly slowly and steadily up to about five thousand feet, where we break through the clouds into brilliant sunlight. We're flying due north, fighting a steady head wind. Suddenly the plane swoops wildly up and down, and I'm sure we're going to die.

"What was that?" I ask, my stomach in my throat.

"That," says Andrew, "is what happens when the wind wants to kick us around a little. Any time wind wants to, it can have us. We are shit to this wind, Charlie. This is like the most primitive flying situation since the beginning of aeronautics. We could get seriously killed."

"How reassuring," says Lily. "Thank you so much for the information."

After about an hour, Andrew asks me if I want to trade places with him. He says he hasn't slept in three days and could use the snooze. R.D. takes over piloting. I crawl forward while Andrew crawls back. Lily falls asleep with a slight smile on her tired face. Up front with R.D., the clouds lie below us like the surface of some fairy-tale kingdom.

R.D. smiles at me and says, "Well, we have about a million more hours of flying. I forgot the Scrabble game. So how 'bout I tell you the story of my life?"

"Sure," I say, "if you can fly this thing and talk at the same time."

"Flying is easy," says R.D., giving me a doleful look. "It's getting off the earth and getting back onto the earth that are the crazy parts. That's why trains are such a good idea. Avoid insanity. Go fast on ground. Safe. Mmmm. Very safe."

"So please, tell me," I say. "What did Lily say to Andrew to make the plane go up?"

R.D. looks back to see if Andrew and Lily are asleep. They are. He arches one of his eyebrows and says, "She simply said, 'You know what to do Andrew. What do you do to make a plane go up?' Then she waited exactly four beats to the measure and said, 'Now *do* it!' Which he did. You see, he was trying to make the plane climb too steeply before we had sufficient speed. He's always been rather impatient. It's his biggest fault."

"She never ceases to amaze me," I say, breathing a sigh of relief all over again.

"You've been together a long time," he says, nodding. "I can tell."

"So what about your life?" I ask, settling back into my seat.

"The long or the short?" he replies, looking at me. "Version I mean."

"I love to listen," I say. "It's one of my favorite pastimes."

"How you spelling that?" he asks, shifting in his seat.

"I'm sorry?"

"Well, I'll skip the first thirty-three years and get right to the good stuff. My death."

"You died?"

He nods. "I had a prescription for sleeping pills written for me by my therapist. One pill made me cranky, two made me drowsy, three made me sleep a leaden, dreamless, worthless sleep, from which I would always wake up tired. The pharmacist, a little man with very white skin, might have been a robot, the way he filled the plastic jar with little pink pills. I looked at the impulse items by the cash register. Breath mints. A booklet called *One Thousand Easy Ways to Shrink Your Calves*. Little bottles of flavored douche. I bought one called Herbal Essence. My plan was to overdose, then douse myself with the douche and die smelling sweetly sexy. It would be an ambiguous final statement, but it appealed to me. The pharmacist tapped the little bottle and said, 'Hmmm, never saw this before. Thought we just had the root beer, chocolate, and creme de menthe flavors. Hmmm. Seems to be the only one, too. Hmmm. No price on it. I'll just . . . oh, you can have it. On the house.' "

"Weird," I say, lost in the story, seeing the scene as clear as day.

"Yes," says R.D., "and when I arrived at my enormous home in the fine neighborhood where no one had weeds, I didn't want to get out of my car. I wanted to drive to where my wife and children were, three thousand miles away, bring them home, put them back in their previous positions, and carry on as if nothing had happened. It was like my house had been robbed, all the good stuff taken. I loved my wife and children. I did. I was a wealthy, slightly liberal man. I gave money to several good causes. I had three foster children. One in Sri Lanka, one in El Salvador, one in Beirut. It just didn't seem fair. And, of course, the late afternoon sunlight was streaming through the windows and illuminating the portrait over the fireplace, the big color photo, practically a hologram of the four of us with huge shit-eating grins on our faces. My children had just been thoroughly tickled, and my wife and I had just made love."

"I'm sorry," I say, bowing my head.

"You should be," says R.D., nodding. "All your fault." He smiles sadly and says, "There was a message, Charlie. On the answering machine. God, I hate those things. It was my wife. She said, 'Rob, listen, I know I said I wasn't going to call, and I realize this is fairly tacky, but could you send me ten thousand dollars as soon as possible, like *tomorrow*.' Click. Beep. Next message. 'Rob, it's me again. Listen, never mind. I figured something else out. Thanks. Bye.' Click. Beep."

"What had she figured out?" I asked, frowning down at the clouds.

"I wondered the same thing," he says, sighing. "Prostitution? Robbery? Pornography? I decided I'd better leave a big note by my body, clearly written, saying, 'Despite our separation, my last will and testament is valid. My wife gets everything. All the money, all the credit, the cars, the house! Quick! Before she catches venereal disease or my children become perverted!' "

"And then?"

"Then, I went into my office and wrote the note. But instead of taking the pills first, I opened the Herbal Essence douche, and summer came flowing out of that little bottle! Bees buzzed. Insects sang. I knew the names of birds for the first time in my life. I smelled fresh cut grass and jasmine. I began to weep! I got up from my desk and hurried out into the backyard, carrying the little bottle with me."

R.D.'s eyes are shining as he says, "I stood staring at the blood red sunset, streaked with gold, and then I poured the sticky stuff on my head and my scalp began to tingle, then to burn. A crow flew by, then circled back and landed on the ground a few feet away from me. 'What's going on?' I cried. I was dizzy. There was this sudden terrible pressure in my chest. The crow stood staring at me, then he pecked at the lawn and came up with a worm. 'Am I going to die before I can kill myself?' I asked, my legs giving way.

" 'Yaw,' said the crow."

" 'Call an ambulance!' I cried. And then I had a heart attack."

R.D. looks at me and says with complete sincerity, "I'm fairly certain I died, Charlie."

"Completely?" I say, not wanting to believe it.

"Completely and totally. And I deeply regret that I cannot say I saw God, or my beloved grandmother, or even a soothing white light. I felt nothing because I was not there to feel. Whatever spirit I might have possessed fled as I fell, eager to be free of my ignorance. And then I came to life again. I don't know how or why this happened, perhaps so I could tell you this story. That's not such an absurd notion, you know.

Hearing these words *might* change your life, Charlie, which in turn might influence the entire course of human history. I'm not asking you to believe that. But I would ask you not to *dis*believe it."

"Okay," I say, nodding. "I'm still with you."

"No ambulance came for me," says R.D., sighing. "No friend rushed to my aid and breathed new life into me. Yet, I opened my eyes, stared in amazement at the stars above me, touched my chest and felt my heart pounding, and knew before I got to my feet that nothing on the outside had changed, but inside I was wholly new."

"A new spirit?" I ask.

"Yes," he says. "An artist. A gardener. Born into the body of a thirty-three year old man who couldn't find a good reason to go on living. He was *that* dense."

"So what did you do?" I ask, loving the climax.

"I sold everything, sent my wife a big check, moved to California, and started making art. I joined the collective eight years ago. I met Andrew five years ago and convinced him to join. My body is forty-three, but I've really only been here for ten years."

"Interesting planet, huh?" I say, winking at him.

"Beautiful," he says. "Thank you for listening."

"My pleasure," I say, smiling at him.

"Mine, too," says Lily, leaning forward and putting a hand on R.D.'s shoulder. "I'm glad to know you. You're an inspiration, and I thank you."

"Stop!" says R.D., reddening. "This feels too good!"

31

R.D. coaxes the little plane down onto a remote landing strip in the redwood mountains a couple hundred miles south of the Oregon border. No one's here to greet us, but Andrew says we'll have company within the hour. There's a little sunlight left. The sky is a deep dark blue, patrolled by a few big billowy intergalactic warship clouds.

I hold Noah's hands above his head and he practices walking, which gives me a backache from leaning over him, but does my heart good knowing how much he appreciates the lift. He's a good kid. The more you give him, the more he gives back. Only he doesn't want *things*. He just wants tons and tons of attention.

Andrew spends an hour removing his beard, while R.D. and Lily go over the engine of the plane. Lily reads things out loud from the manual, R.D. tries to match them with the actual parts. They tighten them up if they need tightening.

Moments before dark, two covered wagons come down the strip toward us. They're painted spumoni green and brown for camouflage purposes. One of the wagons has fuel for us, the other is full of people and food. Their engines are completely silent.

They stop just long enough for R.D. to affix a tow line from the plane to the bumper of the biggest wagon. Andrew gets in the plane to steer it. We jump in the back of the wagon with R.D. and roll along a dirt track into the darkness of the redwoods.

As soon as we're hidden from aerial view, the caravan stops and people swarm out of the wagons. "My God," says Lily, clutching my arm. "Hippies. Just like way back when.

Unchanged. We've gone back in time, Charlie. Saints preserve us, look at that big guy with the braids and the beads and the long black beard. I'll bet his name is Moonstone."

His name is Buck. He's six-foot-nine, three hundred pounds of pot farming muscle. He's the boss of the clan. According to Andrew, he's the most feared man in these parts where cannabis grows to heights of forty feet and the buds are the size of big roses. Buck likes to shoot down helicopters and spotter planes. He routinely blows up forest service vehicles and armored transport trucks.

We sit around a big fire, bongos and guitars playing softly in the background, and Buck says, "Yeah, it's the war. Same one, only this time we're the gooks, you know. They don't *really* want to get us, 'cause where else they gonna get the dope? I mean this is the same as that prohibition shit. A profit scheme. And the so-called government of this bogus democracy is just a big front for the people with the real power, the people who know what's *really* valuable. Now *this* shit will take you out of your body in two hits, and cut with rag weed it still makes most people hallucinate. So you can see why it's so valuable. Want some?"

We decline. Buck continues.

"Yeah," he says, packing a corncob pipe with chunks of resin-heavy bud, "I was in *three* jungle wars. Asia. Africa. Latin America. Stoned the whole time. I sure would appreciate it if you'd have a hit, and I'll tell you why. So I can know you know what I'm talking about. That's important to me."

I decide to fake one to ensure things go smoothly. Lily declines again, saying she's still nursing Noah, though as far as I know she isn't. R.D. takes a bud and eats it. Andrew smokes most of a joint. Buck is right about his product. The fake hit gets me as high as five hits of anything else I've ever smoked. Or maybe I'm just getting old. "Seems to me," I say, trying to remember who I am, "that this stuff . . . what was I saying?"

"It's fine," says Buck, simply.

"Fine," I echo. The individual blood cells in my arms grab my word and take it to my heart. I see them do it.

"Yeah," says Buck, "see, the thing is, we're trillionaire Buddhists. That's why Pearl can't get in up here."

Lily tenses. "You know Pearl?"

"Know *of* her," says Buck. "National power. Nasty business. Clout in New York, clout in L.A. She's even got some goons up this way, but this is pushing it for her. You'll be fine in Oregon, as long as your deal with Rasmusen stays good."

"Rasmusen?" asks Lily.

"King of Oregon," says Buck, smiling. "That ain't his real name. They call him The King, that's all he cares about. He changes the other one all the time. Some weeks he's this, and some days he's that. But he's always the King of Oregon."

"The deal is good," says R.D., tossing a little stick into the fire. "And he's Gustafson now, for your information."

"Doesn't matter," says Buck, grinning at me.

"He and the Dominic have a *very* good relationship," says R.D., glaring at Buck.

"They better, man," says Buck, "or she won't stop at the border."

"She'll stop," says R.D., looking at Lily. "Don't worry."

We eat a dinner of venison, potatoes, and the last fresh zucchinis of the season, while a few of Buck's people play acoustic versions of some old rock 'n roll hits. Great stuff. And these potheads really seem to *care* about their music. Buck asks Lily to please grace the premises with a tune. Those are his words.

"I'd rather not," she says, smiling sleepily. "Been a long day."

Buck shoots a threatening look across the fire at Andrew. He's happily wrapped up in the arms of a lovely amazon, high as a kite, but he comes down fast when he sees Buck is unhappy. "Come on, Lily," says Andrew, forcing a smile. "Please? I kind of promised."

"Kind of nothing," says Buck, his eyes narrowing, his big hands twitching. "The only reason we're here is to hear her sing. We made a deal."

"What's the deal?" says Lily, her voice cool.

"I'm a music freak," says Buck, his voice filling with emotion. "My people love music. It's what we value now, because it *has* no value. It's priceless. It's ultimate money. We grow plants, and people give us anything we dream about. We're Buddhists. We collect experience. Andrew says you sing from God. That's why you could land here, and that's how you're paying for your fuel. Your voice is how you get out of here."

"No problem," says Lily, smiling. "The specifics of the deal were not made clear, but I'd love to sing for you."

She takes a guitar from a skinny blond guy with a feather necklace and eyes like a cat's. She tunes it low and starts strumming. The congas come in on the beat. The tempo is steady, simmering. Lily keeps time with her feet, her shadow huge on the trunk of a giant redwood. She plays a simple rhythm run for a long, long time, before she growls out a tune that has everybody up and dancing. I hold Noah aloft and he gurgles with his mama, smiling up at the stars. The drums thump! A rasta black man screams into his bamboo flute! Two boys try their young hands at guitar leads. A woman howls along, making up her own melodies. Lily drops the strum to a slow easy roll, the bodies reform around the fire, the flute falls away, and the congas die. Lily takes it to country, singing to the little cowboys and cowgirls she knows are lurking beneath the feathers and the beads. She sings,

I made a terrible mistake when I left you
But what can I do about it today?
I ran at the first sign of trouble
Now you're tellin' me to stay far away.

I was so lucky when I met you
Now I just can't seem to forget you
Please take me back
Help me find that loving track
What was I thinking of
When I made so little of such a great love?

The lynx-eyed blond picks a lovely lead, and Lily howls,

> I ran and ran
> And ran and ran
> Now I want to run back to you
> I want to run back to you
>
> 'Cause I've learned my lesson
> Won't you help me out of this mess I'm in?
> Please take me back
> Help me find that loving track
> What was I thinking of
> When I made so little of such a great love?

"God!" says Buck, his eyes moist, his hands clasped together. "God what a voice! How did this happen to you? How long have you known what you know? I'd pay a million tons of the finest everything to have you stay here with us!"

Lily sings three more tunes and the people love them, but her genius has vanished. It left the minute Buck mentioned buying her.

We go to bed in a plush little tent with air mattresses and down sleeping bags. Lily says she wishes we'd had the tent and the bags in Desolation that night. It seems like a lifetime ago. We talk about all that's happened since we first met. We make long, slow love. We relive the takeoff and laugh so hard Noah wakes up.

He crawls around the tent for a while, talking his special language, and he ends up sprawled across me, his little lips touching the hair on my chest, his breath warm on my skin.

32

I have a dream that Buck and his people kidnap Lily. But they *don't* want me. I chase after them, trying to get them to listen to *me* sing, but nobody will. The whole dream long, Lily keeps telling me to get her out of there. I tell her the dream when we wake up and she laughs about it. But at breakfast, Buck says he wants us to stay.

Fortunately, Andrew and R.D. refueled during the night. Andrew starts talking incredibly fast to Buck, R.D. joins in, making weird noises, and Buck gets so confused, we're ready for takeoff by the time he figures out what's going on. Andrew and Lily are up front. R.D. is in the first bucket. I'm in the way back with Noah.

All I can see is the dark side of R.D.'s chair and a little sunlight creeping around the edges. I can hear Andrew jiving up a storm and Lily flipping switches and turning pages in the manual to check her flips. Buck's head is sticking through Andrew's window. His voice echoes through the fuselage.

"You don't under*stand,*" he growls. "You missed the *point* of the agreement. I get to *hear* her. I define that as hearing her over and over again."

"Oh, Buck," Andrew sings, "believe me, please, we *respect* that. But we're being pursued and our songbird needs a haven. Oregon and King whatever his name is, dig? You got a beautiful place here. You know I love your valleys and your women and your women's valleys, but this is not *safe,* in the same way over there is. *Any* other time, Lily would stay."

"You bet," says Lily. "I'm a veritable Bob whatsits when it comes to entertaining the troops."

"Yeah," says Buck, pausing. "But . . ."

Andrew begins to taxi. Buck runs along one side of the plane, talking about God. The lynx-eyed blond is running along the other side, talking to Lily. He's a strong young man, with a beautiful face and striking blue eyes. He has a husky voice and looks good as a hippy.

"Hey," he says, "name's Hoover. What if I come up to Oregon? Maybe we can jam?"

"Tell him to come," I shout, knowing it's never a good idea to turn down a musical genius just because you're afraid he'll steal your woman. You jam with him and take the chance, otherwise there's always doubt.

"Okay," says Lily, waving back at me so I can see her hand. "You know how to get there?"

"I was born there," he says, laughing. "My grandfather is Dominic Kachetti."

"Head groucho," Andrew explains.

"Oregon," says Lily, reverently.

We take off, lifting ourselves over the grand forests. It is, from all reports, a glorious ride, but I can only say that it's smooth. We land on a tiny airstrip on the slope of an extinct volcano, a few miles from the Oregon border. It appears we won't be flying to our final destination. Andrew opens the door of a rusty old shed at the end of the landing strip. Lily and I look inside, but all we see are bicycles.

With his two green suitcases stacked behind him, R.D.'s bike looks like something from a child's fantasy of running away from home. I have Noah behind me in a baby bikeseat. Lily and Andrew's bikes are loaded down with camping supplies and packages of freeze-dried food. We're wearing camouflage helmets, leather gloves, and goggles. We look like a badly rehearsed circus act lost in the woods.

The trail's pretty good, about two feet wide and only a little bit rocky. Once we get used to the feel of the bikes on the uneven ground, riding's almost fun, until my muscles, the ones involved in pedaling a bike, start to go out. When I was ten years old I could ride all day long. It's three decades later, and I'm the first to cry uncle after half an hour of easy riding.

"There's really only one bad stretch ahead," says Andrew, handing around a quart of orange juice. "It's a steep pass about five miles from here. You'll want to be in your lowest gear, and even then you may have to walk it up."

"Where's the border?" asks Lily.

"The pass *is* the border," says Andrew, frowning, "and that could be the most dangerous part of this trip."

"Why?" I ask. I see an East European border crossing in my mind. Barbed wire. Cold soldiers.

"Well," says Andrew, wiping his brow, "if they've got a spotter plane in the area, we may get spotted. We're completely exposed going up the switchbacks on this side, and if they call in a copter, we're sunk."

"So, we may have to go at night," says R.D., adjusting his goggles.

"And even *then* they may spot us," cautions Andrew. "They have awesome nightscopes now."

"So this is creative freedom?" asks Lily, giving me a kiss.

"I haven't done a stitch in weeks," says R.D., patting one of his suitcases.

"Is that what's in there?" I ask. "Your tapestries?"

"The complete works," he says, bowing.

We make it to the base of the pass in two hours. We stop in a grove of big pines and stare up at the steep, barren slope. The sky is empty, save for a high-ranging hawk. We can hear no engines. R.D. estimates it will take us an hour to hike the trail, half that if we have the strength to ride it. Lily and R.D. seem to find riding easy. Andrew and I do not. So, we put Noah behind Lily, stow our supplies under one of the pines, gobble a handful of nuts, and take off.

Lily is amazing. She leaves us all in the dust. R.D. pedals up the mountain slowly, but surely. Andrew and I are walking our bikes before we get twenty feet up the trail. When we hear the plane, we jump on our bikes, and careen back down to the cover of the trees.

We wait a half an hour. The plane, whoever it is, floats over the pass for a long time before it flies away. We wait another half hour, but R.D. and Lily don't come back down the trail. I start to feel a little sick. I tell Andrew I think we oughta make a run for it. He says we should wait until dark.

"You think they're okay?" I ask.

"Unless the wrong folks were waiting up top," he says, throwing a rock into a little stream.

"Damn," I say, "my legs just wouldn't go."

"We're old farts," says Andrew, shrugging. "I broad-jumped fifty thousand miles when I was a young man. Now I get winded going up a flight of stairs. I'm not fat. I watch my weight. I'm just bereft of muscle tone. I think I'm twenty-five, when in fact I'm pushing fifty."

"You seem so much younger," I say. "A quality of your race, I believe."

"How old are you?" he asks, bowing slightly to acknowledge the compliment.

"Thirty-something," I say, hefting my tummy and shaking my head.

"Shame on you," says Andrew, shaking a finger at me. "Lose it now, daddy. Later on . . . impossible."

"I know, I know," I say, shaking my head. "I gotta get in shape before I die."

"Speaking of shape," says Andrew, rummaging in our supplies, "let's have lunch."

"I haven't been apart from her for even a minute," I say, still wanting to run up the slope.

"She'll be okay," says Andrew, winking at me. "She's a wily thing. She was *born* to survive."

I sit down and stare at my useless hands. A few minutes pass, maybe more. Now two big copters hover into view and drift over the pass. One of them lands up on the ridge, while the other cruises our side of the mountain, chopping around directly above us. We're hidden, our bicycles are covered by brush, but we know if they have a good scope on board, they could spot us. Ten minutes go by, slowly, before the copter on the ridge lifts off, joins the other one above us, and they move off together toward the south.

"Somebody's up there now, if they weren't before," says Andrew, rummaging in his pack.

"I guess we'll have to go another way," I say. "I gotta tell you, Andrew, I'm dazed by the scale of this manhunt that we seem to be . . . whatever we are."

"There's no other way," he says, shrugging, "unless you brought ropes and pitons and know how to use them."

"You mean we have to go up there *knowing* somebody's waiting for us?" I say, shaking my head in disbelief.

"I mean show time," says Andrew, nodding. "Can you play a part?"

"Badly," I say. "I may be the worst actor alive."

"You be strong and silent," says Andrew, faking a smile. "I'll do the talking."

"We aren't waiting until dark?" I ask. "This seems crazy."

"Not crazy," says Andrew. "People who come in copters are always more apt to shoot at night. Besides, what kind of homosexuals would hike at night?"

"We're homosexuals?" I say, uneasily. "I'm not a professional actor, you know."

"Do the best you can, Charlie," he says, getting into his role.

So we rig up backpacks out of the bicycle sacks, and start up the trail. It's a warm day. The sky is blue. The air is fresh and scented with pine. We trudge along, exhausting ourselves. It helps me calm down some, though I'm still tense. I have Lily's gun in my pocket, but it's the last thing I want to use. R.D. offered Andrew a gun, but he refused it. He says *art* is his weapon. Andrew verges on the pompous at times, but I like him.

It takes us nearly an hour to make the pass. Up ahead of us is a sign marking the California-Oregon border. There doesn't appear to be anybody between us and there, so we push on, only to be brought up short by five soldiers who materialize out of fissures in the mountainside.

We march right up to them, acting bored and bothered. Andrew waves to them and says, "Hello? Don't tell me they've started a *war*. Is this the big one?"

"No," says one of the soldiers, a tall young man with steel gray eyes and a crooked mouth.

"Good," says Andrew, stopping extremely close to the young man. "Bitch of a pass."

I say nothing. I smile at the other soldiers, but they look away.

"Where you coming from?" asks the soldier that talks.

"Jesus," says Andrew, running his hand through his afro, "where are we *not* coming from?"

"Long ways?" asks the soldier.

"*Tell* me about it," says Andrew, glaring at me.

"I never said it would be easy," I say, giving him a prissy look. It's wrong. I'm too close to the stereotype. I lighten up and say, "Besides, we *need* to get into shape. We're turning into grotesque old farts."

"Speak for yourself," says Andrew, flaring his nostrils at me.

"Seen a woman on the trail?" asks the soldier that talks. The others are permanently silent.

"We have seen nada, nunca, no one," says Andrew, impersonating an aging intellectual fag just right.

"Don't be senile," I say, quoting Dolores.

Andrew sneers at me. "Just because *you* think it's good for the soul to be out in this shit, doesn't mean *I* have to. Give me some decent music and some *people* to look at. I'm sick of trees!"

That gets a laugh. The soldier that talks says, "Where you headed?"

"To a road," says Andrew, sticking out his tongue at me. "Preferably one with about a jillion lanes. However, Robinson Crusoe here keeps the map."

"That would make you Friday or something," I say, remembering that from somewhere.

"Darling," says Andrew, wagging a finger at me, "play to your audience, please. We gotta go."

"Uh," says the soldier, glancing at the silent ones, "you never did say where you were going."

"To the Rogue," I guess.

"That's a long way," he says, eyeing me suspiciously.

"You don't think we can do it?" I say, trembling with indignation. "Are you *implying* something?"

"It's just a long way," he says coolly.

"Since when is it your business where backpackers go?" I ask.

"Lily."

He says it so suddenly I nearly show my surprise.

"Lily?" echoes Andrew, stepping in. "Pardon our gross ignorance, but what is Lily? A hurricane? An heiress? I have *not* seen news in two weeks. Who's Lily?"

"The woman we're looking for," says the soldier.

I take a deep breath, look him in the eye and say, "Listen, sonny, I've been called a woman all my life, but never Lily."

He looks away embarrassed. We hike past them. In my mind, I see them kneeling down, taking aim, and blowing us away. Andrew grabs my arm and shouts, "God damnit, Jimmi! I don't care if you *are* pissed off, I *want* a picture!"

And he hikes *back* to the soldiers and asks if one of them would please shoot a picture of us standing at the border sign. One of the silent ones comes with Andrew and takes two shots of us with his instant print maker. I give him ten bucks for them. In the first picture, we have our arms around each other. In the second one, just to prove I can do it, I'm kissing Andrew on the cheek.

We wave goodbye to the soldiers and start down the trail into the wilds of Oregon. We hold it in for maybe a hundred yards, but then both of us burst out laughing. It takes us an hour to stop talking like queens.

33

We hike until dark, covering another five or six miles, but there's no sign of R.D. or Lily and Noah. We make camp by a small, nameless lake, eat some hideous freeze-dried Chinese food, and sit by our small fire until the cold drives us into the inflatable sleeping bags Andrew was wise enough to bring along. We lie in the darkness, watching the stars. I'm too anxious to sleep.

"I wonder if we could have driven up to Oregon?" I say, closing my eyes. "How could they check every car on the road?"

"Because they *really* want her," he says gravely. "And they got nothing better to do. They killed Juneau, you know."

"No!" I groan, thinking of how devastated Lily will be. "Oh, God no, Andrew."

"Burned her house down," he says, solemnly. "They thought Lily was inside with her, thought they could flush her out. Juneau said she wanted to stay, to give you a little more time to get away, to make them think Lily might have died in the fire, too."

"How do you know all this?" I ask, feeling sick to my stomach.

"I was on the phone with her," he says, his voice breaking. "I tried to convince her to leave, but . . ."

"She was part of *your* organization?" I ask.

"A founder," says Andrew, sighing. "She was very close friends with Rain. And me. She called us the day you got to her house, trying to arrange for you to join us, but there was such a deep, deep dread of Pearl, that they just didn't want to take the risk, until they heard Lily's tape. Rain and I had been waiting for just the right moment to present it to the council, when . . ."

"God damn," I say, "this Pearl must be awfully powerful. How does she get away with all this shit?"

"You still don't have a sense of it, do you?" he says. "She is a major power in the world. She owns the bodies and minds of hundreds of extremely powerful people. And she would trade them all for Lily."

"You mean the baby," I say. "She wants the baby."

"No," says Andrew, shaking his head. "Not the baby. Lily."

"It's insane," I say. "The whole thing is insane."

"Welcome to the big time," says Andrew. "It's a pain in the ass, to be sure."

"How'd you get involved?" I ask. "I was just driving down Sunset Boulevard, going absolutely nowhere, when I see this beautiful woman, with long legs, running with a baby in her arms. I pull over, open the door . . ."

"'Twas lust brought me around, too," says Andrew. "A lady left an echo in my mind that wasn't answered until I heard Lily's tape. Her voice gave me hope again."

"Tell me," I say. "I don't think I can sleep."

"A long story," he says wearily. He muses for a moment and says, "Not so long. I'll close my eyes and tell it as I see it."

"Please," I say, wanting to get my mind off Juneau. It doesn't seem right that she's dead. She was so full of life, so ready to go on for a long, long time more.

"I won't bore you with the childhood particulars," says Andrew, "except to say I was black, as you can see, and I had my first female lover when I was forty. And then I was standing on a San Franciso corner, wondering which way to go, when a quiet voice called to me. I turned and found myself staring at the most remarkable woman I've ever seen, because she was precisely the one I had always imagined, only never believed could be real."

"What did she want?" I ask.

"She wanted me to listen to her story and then to tell it. That was *her* dream, or so she said. I don't know why she chose me, but she did." Andrew says something in French that sounds like a sad proverb or something. "We went to her apartment, a big white space, a bed, and thousands of books, stacked in dozens of piles. She was sorting out literature. She said to me, 'I want my story told in a whole new way. It must transcend all previous categories. It must do to the reader what my life has done to me. I have died and been reborn three times in this lifetime. I know how the universe works. I can tell you.'

" 'Why are the beautiful so insane?' I asked her, seeing there was no point in being polite. She was the most direct person I've ever met.

" 'We choose our beauty,' she said. 'We know *exactly* what we're doing.' "

"Amazing," I say. "Was she nice looking?"

"Well," says Andrew, "I'm not a great Lothario, Charlie. Indeed, when I think of the decades my life has spanned, I'm practically still a virgin. Still, I've done my duty more times than I can count, and the sum total of all the pleasure I have ever known, cannot *approach* the experience I had with whomever this woman was. Her sexual nature dominates my memory, not her body. She was literally without inhibitions! She was a sexual dream, accomplice, monster! We made love for hours! Orgasms were what they're supposed to be. Climaxes to magnum opus love! There had been order in my life, now there was this woman! There had been a dream of fame, now there was this woman. There had been an abhorrence of city life, now there was this woman. There had been a fear of death, now there was the fear of *her* death."

"Wow," I say, looking at him in amazement, "and I thought *I* fell in love fast with Lily."

"Oh, Charlie," he says, clenching his fists, "when her fingers touched my face, a sweet shock jolted through my brain! Her eyes devoured my thoughts! Her lips burned into mine, softened me, spread me, opened me for her tongue! When I came out of my daze, I was naked and willing to die for her!

My cock was swollen and she swooped down and engulfed me! I exploded so quickly you woulda thought I was sixteen! And then she made me hard again, straddled me, guided me into her softness, and rode me until a cry came from her that must have been the same sound the universe made when it broke into being, and then I shot another batch of love up into her sweet insides and vanished into ecstasy!"

A silence falls. I don't know what to say. I can hear the sorrow in his voice, so I know not to hope for a happy ending.

"In the morning she was gone," he whispers. "Disappeared."

"You never found her?" I ask, knowing that he never did.

"I searched for three years," he says, sitting up and lighting a cigarette. "Gave up everything else and just hunted for her. Along the way I met R.D. and Juneau, they introduced me to Rain, the organization, or whatever you want to call us. They all liked me and helped bring me back to life. I was dead, you see. I died that night and was searching for my soul. I know that may sound ridiculous, but it's the truth, believe it or not. And one night, my new soul still an infant, I was lying in bed with Rain, we'd just made love, and she played Lily's tape."

"I haven't heard it," I say. "Don't know if I want to. Might scare me, huh?"

"Might," he says, blowing smoke at the stars. "I can't possibly describe the experience of hearing her. I can only say that no one has ever sung so beautifully to me."

34

The sun is almost directly above us as we walk down the narrow trail into a wide, steep-sided valley. A river snakes through the meadows and forests. The nearest town is a hundred miles away. I can see no road.

We cross a mile of open meadow and approach the main lodge, the center of the community. It's an impressive structure, a triple geodesic, built of massive rough-hewn logs. A wide veranda runs around the building. Stairways with ornately carved handrailings descend to the ground. There are hundreds of windows and dozens of chimneys. The massive roofs are covered with a variety of solar panels. On top of each dome sits a solar wind turbine made of fiber optic glass and copper. On top of each turbine stands a huge wooden weather vane that looks like a banana. Andrew says they're porpoises, but they look like bananas to me.

We're greeted by two snarling malamutes and three big men. They take us to a cement bunker several hundred yards from the lodge. I'm strip searched and put naked into a small padded room without windows. I think of Lily saying, "So this is creative freedom?" I lie down and flatten my aching back.

Several hours go by. My emotions run from anger to frustration to indignation to amusement to boredom to fear to terror to boredom to indignation and back to being pissed off. Finally, the door opens. A man, a white giant wearing combat fatigues, walks into my room and hands me a gray sweatshirt and a pair of baggy white trousers.

"Elegant," I say, putting them on. "So this is creative freedom?"

"No," he says, slowly shaking his enormous head, "this is the beginning of an examination. My name is Ken and I'm here to protect everybody and answer any questions you have, if I can."

"Where's Lily?" I ask.

"I don't know," he says, shrugging his massive shoulders.

"Do you know *who* Lily is?" I ask.

"Yes," he says. "Follow me, please."

I follow him. We walk down a long hallway to a brilliant blue door. As I stand beside him, I get a sense of what Noah must feel being next to me. Overwhelmed. Ken unlocks the door and ushers me into a white room with a blue tile floor.

A mousy little man with a mousy little moustache introduces himself as Dr. Klemmer. He has a chirping voice that makes me want to scream. He asks me to sit in a chair. He examines my eyes, using various colored lights. He has me lie down on my stomach and seems to do little more than tickle my feet.

"Fine," he chirps. "Fine." He writes something on a piece of paper, hands it to Ken and says, "That's it. Bon voyage."

"Now where?" I ask, following Ken out the door.

"Eagle's Nest," he says, his voice unbelievably deep.

We stop at the exit, and he hunts in a cardboard box for a pair of shoes for me. He comes up with a tennis shoe for my right foot, a running shoe for my left. I put them on. They fit. We go out into the world. The sun is just setting. I miss Lily so much I want to shout for her, but I hold it in and trot after Ken.

"Kinda cold," I say. "Any chance of food?"

"I don't know," he says.

We hike past the lodge. In the fading light, the place appears to be abandoned. We cross a sturdy wooden bridge spanning the river of the valley. "Good fishing?" I ask, trying to be friendly.

"They say so," says Ken. "Personally, I don't fish. I'm a vegetarian."

"What do you do?" I ask. "I mean, do you have like a title?"

"I guess you could say I'm a bodyguard for Mr. Kachetti," he says, "and I sing bass parts, and I go to Australia in

Junior's . . . uh . . . I work as a sound man on movie shoots. I hold the microphone boom. I can hold a twenty-foot boom above my head, fully extended, carrying three broadcast-quality mikes for a half hour at a stretch. In Australia, that's worth something."

"Who *is* Dominic Kachetti?" I ask.

"If you don't know, I can't tell you," he says, grinning for the first time. "And I mean that."

We hike across an enormous meadow and into the woods. We climb a steep trail to the top of a granite crag that overlooks the valley. "Nice," I say, gasping for breath. "Beautiful."

"Yeah," he says, barely winded, "but vulnerable as hell from the air."

The first stars are twinkling on. I start to shiver. The trees around us turn from real to shadow. A slight breeze chills my neck. I wait for Ken to say something more, but he remains silent. So I say, "Hey, I'm freezing, man. Can we go someplace warm?"

"I don't know," he says, his voice monotone.

"What *do* you know?" I ask, trying to keep my anger in.

"I was told to bring you here," he says. "I was told to see what happens."

"So this is creative freedom?" I ask, tired of games.

"Would you quit saying that?" he growls. "It's irritating."

"This *isn't* irritating?" I snarl back. "I'm cold. I'm hungry. I miss my wife and baby. I have worked *very* hard to get us here safely, and now you're bullying me. I'll say whatever I want to until you or somebody else tells me what the hell is going on!"

"I brought another guy up here last night," says Ken, his tone changing. "He was supposedly a friend of ours, but he wasn't. That's a four hundred foot drop there. Right behind you. Sometimes people have to be right on the edge before they'll tell the truth."

"I don't like edges and I don't like drops," I say, a warning in my voice. "I been there and it sucks."

"Go to the edge," he says, moving toward me.

I stand my ground. He comes so close, my nose touches his shirt just above his waist. He is easily the biggest man I've ever seen. "Just one more question," I whisper.

"What?" he says, looming above me.

"Do you like women? Sexually?"

He steps back slightly. "Why?"

"Oh, I don't know," I say. "I just . . . oh, never mind. I just . . ."

"What do you mean?" he asks, bothered by whatever he imagines I'm implying.

"I mean, Ken, that I'm going down to find my woman," I tell him. "I just wanted to see if you could identify with that."

"I can't let you," he says, moving toward me again.

I back up two steps, almost to the edge. Suddenly I step forward and kick him in the balls as hard as I can, dodging around him and running back down the trail. I don't care that he'll kill me when he catches me. I'm fed up.

I get down to the meadow. It's fully dark. I run across the bridge, look back, and see Ken lumbering toward me. In the darkness he seems twenty feet tall.

"Lily!" I shout. "R.D.! Lily! Help! Lily!"

Lights go on in the lodge! People open the doors and stand silently on the veranda. Ken's close now. I run up the stairs and fall on my knees in front of a man and a woman. "Help me!" I cry. "He'll kill me!" They say nothing. I jump to my feet and run along the veranda. Ken is only a few steps behind me, his huge body shaking the floor as he runs. "Lily!" I scream. "Lily!"

Dogs begin to bark. More lights come on. People converge on the lodge, coming from the woods, coming across the meadows. I run down the stairs and sprint into the open. "Lily! Lily! Lily!"

And now I hear her calling to me, her voice faint in the distance. I run toward the sound. It seems to come from upstream. I run and run along a path that follows the twists and turns of the river. I glance back and see dozens of people following me. Some have flashlights. The terror of the chase into Desolation comes back to me. "Lily!" I cry. "Lily! Lily!"

She calls again. She's closer now. I run on, caring only that I might see her one more time before they kill me. The trail dips down off the embankment and runs to the water's edge. Two massive planks span the rushing stream. I run across them and find the trail on the other side. A cabin sits all alone near a wide bend in the river. A dim light is shining inside.

"Lily! Lily!" I scream.

"Charlie," she says, almost in a whisper.

She's standing by the door, waiting for me. I run to her, embrace her, hold her to me, smell her, tell her I love her, and wait for the deadly blow. I can hear the people behind us. Their lights play at our feet. I feel a huge presence behind me and know that it's Ken.

A small, thickset man with a wild mane of hair opens the door and looks out at us. He leans on a crooked cane. A fire flickers behind him. "It's all right," he says calmly. "Go back to the lodge. Go to your homes. It's all right. There's nothing wrong. Nothing wrong."

"What about me?" asks Ken.

I can hear the hurt in his voice, but I'm not brave enough to turn around and look at him.

"You come in with us, Ken," says the old man, turning away from the door.

Ken moves past us, mumbling something that sounds apologetic as he ducks through the doorway.

"Who was that old man?" I ask Lily.

"I'll introduce you," she says softly.

"I missed you so," I say, holding her tight, kissing her cheeks and throat.

"We'll be together from now on," she says. "I promise."

"I thought you didn't believe in promises?" I say.

"I don't," she says wistfully. "But you do, and I want to give you everything, Charlie."

35

The little man with the wild mane of hair sits beside the giant on the sofa. He stares into the blazing fire, sighs deeply, and folds his arms. An older woman sits in a rocking chair to one side of the fire, holding Noah on her lap. Her long gray hair is done in braids and her dress is blue calico. R.D. sits opposite her in another rocker. He's wearing magnifying goggles and pale blue pajamas. He's working on a new tapestry. He smiles at me as we come into the room and says, "Welcome, Charlie. Heard you put on quite a show getting here."

"So this is creative freedom?" I ask, aiming my remark at Ken. He looks away.

"Be nice," says Lily, taking my hand.

"Why should I?" I say, the anger rising in me. "These jokers were gonna kill me."

"Not so," says the old man, looking up and frowning at me. "We don't kill people here. It's forbidden."

"But torture is okay?" I ask. "Being threatened with a cliff? Listen, I don't like cliffs. I've never had a good experience with one. You know what I'm talking about? Ken? Fuckin' bully!"

"I didn't mean to torture you," says Ken, clenching his giant fists. "I was just doing what they told me to do, and I'm sorry I did. Okay?"

"I apologize," says the old man. "We haven't had a crisis like this in . . . well, ever. We have traitors now. We never did before. It's completely upset the balance, the ether, everything."

"I'm not a traitor," I reply. "I barely know what the cause is."

"We were just talking about that," says Lily, putting her

arms around me, sending a thrill through me. Drama's okay. An adventure now and then is fine. But the main show, the center of my universe, is Lily.

"I'm Charlie," I say to the room, feeling Lily's strength pouring into me. "In case you didn't know it, I'm Lily's man. Now, she mighta made it here without me, but she didn't, so if you're dealing with her, you're dealing with me. I can handle just about anything, but I don't like being roughed up, especially when I haven't done anything wrong."

"He's fairly ferocious," says Ken, glancing at the older woman in the rocking chair.

"Impressive," she says, her voice lazy and sweet. "And loyal. I like that."

"He certainly *loves* her," says the old man. "Even *I* can hear that. The room is fairly vibrating with the message."

"Guy talks like a crazy. Is he?" I whisper to Lily.

"Hah!" says Ken, glancing at me from across the room.

"What?" asks the old man, glaring at Ken.

"He was asking if you were crazy," says the giant. "Struck me funny, that's all."

"You heard me?" I ask, amazed.

"One way or the other," says Ken, shrugging.

"Ken is of this place," says the older woman, her voice pulling me toward her. I bring Lily with me and we sit at her feet, our backs to the fire. "We found him here," she goes on. "He was a wild child, left by someone. He came to me, whining like a lost pup. We took him into our family and raised him. He's always had an extraordinary ability to hear. It's one of the things he tries to teach us."

"I'm sorry I kicked you," I say to Ken. "You scared the shit outta me."

"I deserved it," he says, nodding slowly. "I heard it coming. I musta wanted it. I don't like violence. It makes me sick."

"Who are you?" I ask the woman.

"I am Hilda," she says, smiling wryly. "They call me Queenie, because my father was the first Dominic."

"I'm sorry," I say to her, "I probably oughta know by now, but what's the Dominic?"

"He is the leader of our movement," says Hilda. "My father was the first, and by no coincidence my husband became the second. The third and current Dominic sits before you, also my husband."

"You're the power behind the throne?" I ask.

"Quick," says R.D., lifting his goggles and winking at me. "Very shrewd, Charlie."

"Food," I say suddenly. "I am so hungry I could die."

"Don't," says Hilda, handing Noah to me and floating out of her chair. She drifts toward the kitchen. Ken lumbers after her.

"So you're Dominic Kachetti," I say, giving my boy a kiss. "We met your grandson, I believe."

Noah's drowsy, but he comes to life to talk a little to me. He burbles and gibbers and drools, gives me some big four-toothed grins, waves his pudgy little arms, yawns, and goes to sleep, an impish smile on his face.

"Yes," says Dominic Kachetti, sighing, "I am the supposed boss of this supposed whatever we are, that has suddenly become wholly redefined. We are, after nearly a hundred years of blissful invisibility, *completely* exposed." He takes a deep breath and smiles. "Of course, we knew it was coming. Predicted by the first Dominic almost seventy years ago. But even so, it's a grievious shock. Premonition is one thing, belief is another."

"What did he predict?" asks Lily.

"Ah," says Kachetti, placing both index fingers on the tip of his nose. "There will come a time near the end of this millenium, when the critical mass of our movement will centrifuge us to the surface, anonymity will die, and we will come into contact with an unconscious genius. And *she* will lead us into notoriety, conflict, and either destruction or an unimaginable acceleration of global influence."

"What do you mean by unconscious genius?" I ask. "Those are two extremely loaded words."

"She doesn't distinguish between art and life," says Kachetti, nodding. "Lily's not eccentric, academic, gaudy, forced, or even a little bit obscure. She's pure. She's connected to the essential . . . uh . . . thing . . . of all humans. She is, to quote my predecessor, 'omni-presently interactive.' Or something like that."

"I know that," I say, putting my arms around Lily and kissing her.

"Watch out you don't squish the baby," she says, reddening as we smooch.

"Lucky man," says Kachetti, watching us with a glint in his eye. "The evolution of culture depends on such pairings. You're a brave man, Charlie. I hope you can handle it."

"He can handle it," says Lily, smiling. "He's been road-tested."

"Good," says Kachetti, nodding. "Good."

Hilda brings me food. She sits in her rocking chair, takes Noah from me and says, "The war has finally reached us, and we don't know how to fight. How would you combat Pearl, Lily?"

"I'd have to know the particulars," says Lily, answering calmly.

"Ah," says Kachetti, fingers to his nose again. "As we know them to be, the particulars are, that she wants to possess you and this child. She hasn't influenced our benefactor, Gustafson, to allow her access to us, *you* being part of us now, but she may be close to that. He's a rather flexible soul, shall we say, and in the meantime she's attacking what centers of ours she's been able to find, and simultaneously exposing us to the media as a group of lunatics who are very, *very* bad for the status quo. We represent change. And you, Lily, represent *our* change."

"Are you *blaming* Lily?" I ask. "Because if you are, we'll just get . . ."

"Charlie," says Lily, putting a hand on my arm, "calm down."

"At this point," says R.D., "Gustafson can hold Pearl off for as long as he wants. But she's putting tremendous pressure on *all* her connections, trans-globally, so . . . there's no telling what might happen."

"God," says Lily, shaking her head. "I had no idea."

"It's perfectly appropriate that she should covet you," says Kachetti, nodding. "You're possessed of the one currency more precious than all the metals and narcotics combined."

"I got rhythm, right?" says Lily, waving a finger skyward.

"You have the three elements of great art at your command," says R.D., impressively. "You have wind, style, and flower."

"I call it magic," says Hilda, "but then, I'm considered very old-fashioned."

"If you need any low vocal parts," says Ken, "I might be just the guy you're looking for."

"I might be shit," says Lily, her voice hardening. "You guys are calling me a genius, but what if I'm nothing. Happens all the time."

"Ah!" says Kachetti, clapping his hands together, "but it's a *group* delusion, so it doesn't matter."

"I don't know about that," says Lily, looking to me for help, "but it seems to me we've got to move fast or Pearl is just gonna come up here and take whatever she wants."

"It's highly unlikely that she would venture such an attack," says Kachetti. "You see, we're guarded by Rasmusen's, I mean Gustafson's, soldiers. Crack troops. Lots of them. Guarding all the passes. How you were able to get by them . . ."

"Where's Andrew?" I ask, smiling as I remember our charade at the pass.

"He's with some chick," says Ken, dolefully. "Partying."

"Don't say 'chick,' " says Hilda. "It's regresssive."

"We need to meet with this Ramusen or Gustafson or whoever he is," says Lily, frowning at Hilda. "And we need to start a public relations campaign or something before they get us looking too weird to the people. Can't lose the people or we're sunk."

"How we gonna do that?" asks Ken, giving Hilda a perplexed look. "I don't even know what that *is*."

"He's right," says Kachetti, his shoulders sagging. "We've *survived* on anonymity. We practically *worship* being unknown. We don't know the first thing about notoriety."

"Sorry," says Lily, her voice taking on a hard edge, "but if *they* tell people what we are, that's what people will think. So we gotta beat 'em to it."

Hilda leans forward in her chair and says, "We are perilously at the mercy of Ras . . . Gustafson, and . . ."

"I'll take care of him," says Lily, turning to me. "You got any bright ideas, Charlie?"

"I'm with you," I say. "We gotta let the people know the truth before Pearl can twist it to her advantage."

"But how?" asks Kachetti, his weary voice cracking.

"Well," I say, "I think we create our way out of the situation."

"Rather vague," says R.D., disappointed. "I was hoping for specifics."

"I'll give you specifics," I say, wishing they'd all just disappear. "But right now I need to go to bed with my wife and my baby. Where are we sleeping?"

"This is our house," says Lily, leaning aginst me. "They gave it to us. It's ours."

"You're kidding," I say, looking around and wrinkling my nose. "I was hoping for something a little more futuristic."

"Cut it out, Charlie," she says, embarrassed.

Kachetti, Hilda, and Ken rise. R.D. stays where he is, rocking slowly, watching everyone with great amusement.

"Coming?" says Kachetti to R.D.

"Not just yet," he says.

We walk them out into the cool night air and watch them move along the river path under a sky impossibly full of stars. We go back inside. R.D. looks up at us and says, "You guys were wonderful. They liked you. I could tell."

"They're desperate," Lily says, taking Noah from me.

"No," says R.D., shaking his head. "They're just artists."

"Where are you sleeping?" I ask him.

"I'm not," he says cheerfully. "I'm working. All right if I use the couch?"

"Sure," I say. "But why . . ."

"I'm sorry about the rough stuff," he says, concentrating on a stitch. "Ken wouldn't have hurt you, though he *is* rather scary to the uninitiated. I told them it was unnecessary, but there were several people on the council who . . ."

"The council? This wasn't the council?" I ask.

"No, no," says R.D., slowly shaking his head. "You see . . ."

"Tell us in the morning," says Lily. "We don't want to get depressed."

"Hell, no," I tell him. "We just got here."

36

"Did they tell you?" Lily asks, as we lie in each other's arms. "About Juneau?"

"Yes," I say. "Andrew told me last night."

"She was so stubborn," says Lily sadly. "I can just see her doing it, too. Standing there, daring the flames to burn her."

"Talk about brave," I say, admiringly.

"I don't know about brave, Charlie," says Lily, sighing. "She must have wanted to die. She talked about it a little when we were there, about not seeing the point anymore without love."

"Lotsa lonely people," I say, holding her tight. "We're incredibly lucky to have each other."

"Yeah," says Lily, "but I always thought Juneau would go on forever. She was the strongest person, man or woman, I've ever known, besides you. She was such an inspiration to me. She's the one who liberated me, you know? She was the first person who really made me realize that women are superior to men in a lot of ways. And she didn't take shit from anybody."

"I'm sorry she's gone," I say. "I'm sorry I didn't get to know her better."

"She's not gone," says Lily. "She's *in* me. Most of what I am comes from her. I just never wanted to be her lover. I loved her, you know, and I liked to *hold* her, like an old baby doll, and I liked to kiss her on the cheeks, and every once in a while on the lips, because I really did love her, I just didn't want to have sex with her."

"Nothing wrong with kissing anybody," I say, kissing her.

"She used to say, 'Lily, I don't worry about death. Death is just death. Life is the complicated part. Life is the real magic trick. Seeds a hundred years old can still be made to sprout.' "

"Is that true?" I ask.

"You know it is," says Lily, holding me tight. "Look at us."

"I know you're the best thing there's ever been," I say, kissing her again.

"I'm just a good singer, Charlie," she says, wearily. "You know that. All I want is a decent place to sleep and a little recording time."

"You can't say that anymore, Lily," I say, rubbing her head. "You're too important now. They're counting on you."

"*Us!*" she says, urgently. "You and me! I'm not doing this alone, I can tell you that right now."

"Don't worry," I say. "I guess maybe I was thinking about how nice it would be to just hang out here for a while before we actually had to *do* something. But I'm ready to go to work. Don't you worry about that."

"Be nice if there was a Santa Claus, too," she says, drumming her fingers on my chest. "But there isn't. There's just you and me, and this bunch of whatever they are."

"Big bunch," I say. "Andrew was telling me there's thousands of them, with centers all over the world, and Pearl's been bombing and burning every one she can find. I don't know how we did it, Lily, but we landed right in the middle of a major thing. I guess it's a war, except we don't have an army and she does."

"You were talking pretty brave out there a little while ago," says Lily, pulling away from me and sitting up. "They're expecting a game plan from us tomorrow. Did you really have an idea, or were you just tired?"

"I got a plan," I say, my heart pounding. "I know you're gonna say I'm crazy at first, but I think it'll work."

"What?" she says, holding her breath.

"For you to make a recording," I say, breathing hard. "Something that goes out and stuns the whole world, so Pearl won't have any choice but to leave you alone. You'll be too famous."

"Charlie," says Lily, sighing and relaxing against me, "this ain't no Mickey Rooney musical. We can't just put on a backyard extravaganza and save the world. That's not gonna stop her. If I make a record and it turns out any good, it'll only make her hate me more. Besides, I might cut a pile of crap. That's a real possibilty."

"No, you won't," I say, urgently. "No, you won't. You'll make a record so great, that . . ."

"Charlie," she says, putting a hand over my mouth, "don't make me crazy, and don't go having expectations like that. I'm a person, remember. You know that better than anyone. I shit same as you. I fart and get cranky and feel bad most of the time, and hate myself and worry too much and think I'm something special and think I'm nothing. Same as you, and same as them. So don't go making me into whatever *they* think I am. They don't *know* me. They heard my tape and I sang a little yesterday in their studio, just to prove it was really me. You aren't the only one they put through some tests."

"That little doctor look at you?" I ask, frowning. "He was *weird.*"

"Yeah," she says, nodding grimly. "He just made things worse. He said I was a power source or something. Pissed me off."

"A power source?" I ask. "Did he say how many kilowatts?"

"Something," she says, waving it away. "Said I had this concentration of negative or positive ions or some such bullshit. Made everybody start treating me like I had cooties."

"You don't want to be something special, do you?" I say, teasing her.

"'Course I do," she says, sitting up again. "But *I* want to say what that is. *I* know what I am, Charlie. I'm a singer. And sometimes when I get opened up just right, songs come through me from somewhere that are just too good not to give to the world. Other than that, I'm just a woman. I have a man I love, and a baby I love, and I didn't tell you that this is the place I was talking about. This valley."

"What?" I say, stunned. "What place?"

"This is the place I couldn't tell you about," she says. "The secret place."

"You *knew* about this valley?" I ask, not believing it.

"Yeah," she says, lying back down beside me. "But I didn't remember it completely until R.D. and I came riding down the trail, and I saw the river running through the meadows, and I heard the sound of the water and the wind in the pines. Then I remembered all this stuff I'd been trying to forget all my life."

I hold my breath. I can feel something big coming.

She cries as she says, "We lived like rats, Charlie! We scavenged through garbage and slept under piles of rags. We were hungry all the time. I used to chew on sawdust just to have something to chew on. We'd go into towns and beg on the streets. My father was crazy. Violent. He thought the world was one big torture chamber, and maybe it is. But one time, we came to this valley, this very place, Charlie, and I remember playing by this same river with a gang of kids. And one of the kids was as big as a man and never said a word. And I remember eating the first good food I ever had, and I remember watching a girl making pots on a wheel. She let me try. And I remember my father trying to get well. They were helping him learn not to be insane, not to have to shout all the time. And I remember my mother sitting at a table with other women, and how they got her to talk and laugh. I loved it so much, Charlie. I loved it more than anything I'd ever dreamed about. But then my father was shaking me awake in the middle of the night, his hands so rough, and then we were back to the cold and the hunger and the shouting and the always hurting for another thousand years until he mercifully died."

She cries for a long time, and I cry with her. I think for a little while about my own sorrow, but mostly I think about hers.

"How'd you turn out so sweet?" I ask, after a long time.

"So I could meet you," she says, kissing me. "I knew you'd want a sweet woman."

"How'd you know?" I ask, squeezing her.

"I've been looking for you all my life, Charlie," she says, kissing me. "I just didn't know it was you at first."

"What finally gave me away?" I ask.

"Everything," she says, holding me tight. "Everything did the trick. Your face, your eyes, the way you talk, the way you keep saying you love me, the way you never run away no matter what. The way you only want me. You still do, don't you? 'Cause I don't think I could stand it if you . . ."

"Lily," I say, kissing her, "will you marry me?"

"Yes!" she says, bursting into tears again.

"And then we'll save the world," I say, crying along with her. "I guess that's why we get each other, so we don't have to worry about being alone, so we can concentrate on the other stuff."

"Maybe so," she says, kissing me and kissing me. "That sounds good."

"I missed you so much," I say, kissing her sweet breasts.

"Show me," she says, whispering her hot breath in my ear.

So I try to show her. I try to love her with more of me than has ever loved.

And afterwards she says, "If that's what missing me does for love, I'm all for it now and then."

37

We walk along the river in the cool morning air, holding hands, strolling the valley. It's the best dream I've ever had, only I'm awake. R.D. walks along behind us, carrying Noah, making silly whistling sounds at the boy. Noah likes R.D. He thinks he's hilarious.

We eat a gorgeous breakfast in a sunny corner of the lodge. We sit with Hilda, R.D., and Dominic Kachetti. We're served by the woman and the man I threw myself down in front of last night. I try to explain why I was so freaked out, and she laughs and says, "We thought you were crazy, on a bad trip or something, because Ken wouldn't hurt a flea."

"It was my fault," says Ken, calling to us from a distant table. "I can be kind of scary at first."

"I don't know why," Lily whispers. "He's only about nine feet tall."

Ken laughs at that. Lily blushes. She forgot he can hear us from a long way off.

'How do you do that?' I think to myself, wanting to see if he's a mind reader. I look down the room at him. He shrugs his big shoulders and goes back to eating his pile of veggies and rice. Hard to know if he heard me or not.

Andrew comes in as we're finishing our meal. I get up and give him a bear hug. I don't usually hug other men, but when you go through something together, as frightening as what we went through on the pass, you can't help but feel a bond. We laugh for about five minutes, and he introduces me to the woman he's with, a dancer from Greece. Everybody gets up from their tables and we troop out of the lodge. We go down the stairs, cross a clearing, jog past the bunker, and hike through the woods to an abandoned quarry. They've carved a beautiful amphitheatre out of the rock.

Dominic Kachetti opens the meeting with a brief speech. He says, "This is Lily, her child Noah, her husband Charles. They have joined us here as we expected they would. We've given them the cabin at the wide curve in the river for as long as they choose to stay here."

"I think it's insane," says a tall, skinny man with extremely short blond hair. He stands up and points a finger at Lily. "She's a threat to the continued existence of the community. I'm very sorry to burst everyone's bubble, and that's *all* it is, but she should *not* be here. It's asking to be attacked."

"How do you know she's a threat, Kyle?" asks Andrew, scratching his head. "Maybe she's our only hope of survival."

"We were doing just fine until she came along," he says, sneering at me for some reason. "Or should I say *they?*"

"Were we?" asks Kachetti, looking questioningly at the sky. "Because it hadn't been diagnosed? The cancer? There *were* people working to destroy us from within. There still are. Her arrival has merely hastened that revelation. I think we should be thankful for that, not fearful."

"This is old business," says a black woman with a powerful voice. "We all crawled in here one way or another, and we all brought shit with us. We voted her in. So she's in. That's the rules. Once you're in, you're in. No matter what. The question now is, what's the plan? How do we get out of this mess?"

A guy with a French accent says, "We aren't warriors." His accent is thick, his voice is deep and resonant. "We're thinkers and creators, but we die much more easily than we kill. My main concern is our vulnerability."

"What about Rasmusen?" a Japanese woman asks.

"Gustafson," says Kachetti, nodding. "He's agreed to continue his defense of us here, but the outside centers are having a hell of a time. We'll have to close some, but we can open new ones. This isn't the end. It's a shifting to a new course. We're more visible now, but ultimately we'll be more secure. That's the great challenge."

"The end of elitism," grumbles an old, old man wearing a suit and a floppy bow tie. His eyes are shining under craggy brows. The hair on his head is a curly white mountain. He talks tough, and the people hang on his words. "Don't know what it will bring," he says, frowning, "but there it is, and here we are."

R.D. gives me a look. "Charlie has a proposal," he says, smiling. "A possible solution to some of the immediate pressure that's being put on us. Charlie?"

"It better involve Rasmusen," snaps Kyle, our main opponent. He continues to glare at me.

"I want to meet him as soon as possible," says Lily. "Whatever his name is."

"Why do *you* want to meet him?" snarls Kyle, his hands trembling. "You couldn't *do* anything to influence him. He'll squish you like a bug!"

"Would you cool down, mister?" says a big guy with a German accent. He glowers at Kyle, then looks away and shrugs.

"Don't talk to me like that!" screams Kyle, scaring Noah. "I won't stand for it! Kachetti, tell him to apologize! I won't tolerate it!"

"He's sorry," says Kachetti, bowing slightly. "But please, Kyle, we need to discuss this rationally."

"When *they* leave, I'll become rational!" he shouts, striding away into the forest.

"If there are no further comments," says Hilda, smiling sweetly at Lily, "we would like to hear your proposal, Charles."

"Charlie," I say, standing up. I'm nervous, but I feel good. It's so quiet here, and everybody's listening to me. Nothing like this has ever happened to me before.

"I love you," says Lily, smiling at me.

"Well," I say, looking at everybody looking at me, "we're gonna make a record. And then we're gonna launch a massive publicity campaign. And we're gonna make a definite political statement to go with the music. We're gonna announce our complete and total dedication to worldwide artistic liberation. Anybody here who wants to stay anonymous, go ahead, but here's the thing, what*ever* you do, you have to spend at least *half* your time working *directly* for liberation. I'm talking about if there's a war going on, we have to tell everybody we can, in any *way* we can, that it's bad for art, and we're not gonna support it. I'm talking about if there's a heavy-duty government somewhere oppressing people, we have to blitz the airwaves and tell that government to lighten up! We have to scream about anything rotten that gets in the way of people making their art. That's the way we're gonna fight Pearl. By getting the people on our side before *she* gets them thinking we're just a bunch of wackos."

Kachetti frowns at me and says, "Don't you think it might be less offensive to people if we said that we were, oh . . . I don't know, dedicated to the preservation of culture? Artistic liberation sounds a bit combative, don't you think?"

"No," I say anxiously. "It *is* endgame for elitism. If we come out saying *we* know what culture is, like God appointed us and nobody else, people are gonna think we're a bunch of pompous assholes. I don't think artistic liberation offends anybody, and if it does, then we just have to work that much harder until it doesn't."

"We had no idea you were such an orator," says R.D., squinting curiously at me.

"He can talk, can't he?" says Lily, beaming at me.

"I like it," says Andrew. "It's not nonsense. It's *real* work."

"As for your music," says a thickset man with what I think is a Polish accent, "you need no permission to *make* it. We ask only to approve of it before dissemination. Can you agree to that?"

Lily gives me a worried look, and says, "I don't know. This system has got to *move* or you'll be preserving things for a future that already happened."

"Impatient," says the old man, grinning at Lily. "My name

is Junior. I'm the transportation person around here. I'm glad you could make it. I love the way you talk. But I must remind you that you can't push time. You may think you can, but that's an illusion. When the time is right, the egg hatches. Before that, no chick, just goo."

"We have a certain wisdom," says the Japanese woman. "We are . . ." She frowns at Andrew. "Say it for me, please."

Andrew smiles, tips his head slightly to one side and says, "Blackjap francewhite rusafro. Asia Minor, Asia most. Old man, young man, womanboy, ghost. Lyrics, Lily, that's *all* we are, and you gotta try to put it to song. It may *seem* an impenetrable confusion, but believe me, if you make a truly great tape, we will *all* know it. And if you don't, we will know that, too. It's not enough that you have whatever you have, if you don't know how to play it. But we're here to help you, that much we know. That is the beauty of whatever it is we are. We help."

"But we demand excellence," says a man with no accent at all. "We're not easily bluffed."

"How do you define excellence?" asks Lily, taking a deep breath and giving me a terrified look.

"Ah," says a man with what I think is a Russian accent. He looks over at Kachetti and says, "Our favorite point of debate. I always define it as unadulterated honesty. Simple and clear. But . . ."

"I can't define it," says the Japanese woman. "I concentrate on the purity of the form."

"If it makes my heart pound and I hear God in it," says the black woman, "then I say yes."

Junior grimaces, frowns at the sky, and says in a strong, gruff voice, "If ya got it, ya got it."

Kachetti laughs, shakes his head and says nothing.

Hilda stands up and says, "The meeting is over."

"But what about this Kyle person?" asks Lily. "How does he define it?"

"Not to worry," says Hilda, putting her hands on Lily's shoulders. "He will become your greatest advocate."

"And what about Rasmusen?" asks Lily, her voice trembling.

"Gustafson?" says Hilda. "He's flying in today. Later this afternoon."

"So I can get started on the tape?" asks Lily, taking my hand.

"Yes, yes," says Kachetti, his eyes twinkling. "The sooner the better!"

"I'll need an engineer," says Lily, her eyes shining.

"Which I am," says Andrew, bowing deeply. "I am, in fact, *the* engineer."

"Maybe so," says Lily, nodding to him, "but I want everybody here to know that Charlie is gonna be overseeing the whole thing. He's the producer, okay? Anybody has any questions, he's the boss in the studio."

I nod and smile and try to act fairly cool in front of everybody, like it's no big surprise to me, but when we're alone I tell Lily that nobody has ever honored me as she does.

38

Lily's worried about what to do with Noah while we're recording. I guess Ken hears us talking about it, because he comes over to the house a while later and asks if he can get to know the boy and learn to take care of him.

We're standing by the river. Noah's sitting on the sand, playing at our feet. Lily leans down, picks the boy up, kisses him lightly on the cheek and hands him to Ken. And though the giant's *hand* is nearly as big as the baby, though Noah seems like a tiny toy cradled against that mountainous chest, it feels like a good match. Their eyes meet. Ken wrinkles his nose at the boy. Noah wrinkles his nose at Ken, and starts gurgling and gibbering and waving his arms and smiling.

Lily decides to give Ken a try as a babysitter, but not before she talks him through two diaper changes and a mock lunch. Noah is ecstatic about Ken, and Ken seems to really like the boy, so we leave them playing by the river. Ken gets down on his hands and knees in the sand, making a bridge with his body. Noah crawls back and forth underneath, stopping each time to look up in amazement at the human arch above him.

The studio is located in the same building where they kept me in the padded cell. It's not as high-tech as the Oakland facility, but it's better than anything else I've ever seen. Andrew is readying the engineer's booth. He introduces us to a painfully thin young man named John, who immediately tells us he's a philosopher. He gives us a tour of the studio. He knows everything about every knob and dial, every channel and every switch.

"Now," he says, leading us into the performance room, "I

am fully cognizant of this being your gig, and I'm totally supportive of that proposition, and by proposition I lean heavily on Wittgenstein, though he's mostly wrong."

"How old are you?" asks Lily, eyeing him curiously. "Are you making any sense, or is this just bullshit?"

"Probably not," he answers, pushing his glasses up his slightly crooked nose. "I use the Picture Theories as inspiration, especially on any blues." He demonstrates his talent on a pulse tone synthesizer. He plays a blindingly fast run of notes full of sorrow.

"I don't care if he gets his inspiration from chocolate chip cookies," whispers Lily, reverently. "If he can play like that, he can play with me."

"Andrew revealed your tape to me," says John, shaking his head. "Opened up infinite interconnections." He glances at me and raises his eyebrows. "I saw it save the world."

"That's nice," says Lily, looking at me and rolling her eyes, "but right now we gotta get cooking."

"I'm here," he says, winking at her, "and I think I'm correct."

"Okay," says Lily, frowning up at Andrew. "We got some guitars around here?"

"Ah," says John, his hand shooting skyward and swooping down across invisible strings. "The Arab's answer! I salute your mastery of its rhythmic potential. And by the way, I might be able to show you some pretty nifty tricks."

Lily and I crack up. Andrew howls silently from behind the soundproof glass of his booth. John brings forth a dazzling array of guitars. Lily grabs an old one, plugs it in, tunes it up, gives Andrew a nod, and starts to rock. John touches a few panels on a synthesizer and sits down to play a catchy bass line. Lily smiles at him and kicks up the tempo. I stroll over to the percussion zone, pick up some brushes, and get into it, too. We bump into a nice, danceable bottom, and toy with it until we find the groove. We make it happen for fifteen minutes.

"There," says Lily, finishing with a rush of notes, "that

should do for this Gustafson guy. I hope he likes to dance. We know he likes to change his name. You know why he does that?"

"He's insecure," says Andrew, his voice booming over a speaker. "You'll understand when you meet him. He's an old fart. Might want a ballad, Lily."

"Won't need any backup tracks for that," she says. "But my philosophy—you listening, John? My philosophy is, if you start with something you can dance to, nobody's gonna doubt what you're doing."

We fool around a while more before we break we for lunch. Andrew and Lily walk ahead, talking about sounds, while John and I trail behind.

"See," he says, his hands as wild as Andrew's, "I was reading Buckminster Fuller yesterday *and* listening to Lily's tape, when suddenly her *voice* destroyed all my preconceptions, and I *heard* the new theory."

"The one that's gonna save the world?" I ask, doubtfully.

"Yes," he says, smiling at the sky. "It's the missing link between mathematical principles and human emotions. See, what we do is, we *use* music to provide the *equations* for feelings. Would that be a trip, or what?"

"To be continued," I say, putting a hand on his bony shoulder. "You're making me dizzy."

We get to the lodge and find Ken in the middle of a major lunchtime experience with Noah. Ken's shirt looks like abstract art. Noah is seated in his highchair, smearing the enormous canvas of Ken's chest with yogurt, applesauce, strawberries, blueberries, muffins, and milk.

"Nice job," says Lily, stopping to admire the mess. "Looks kinda scary."

"I'll have him cleaned up in no time," says Ken, holding a spoonful of applesauce an inch from the boy's mouth, waiting for it to open.

"Doesn't bother me," says Lily, smiling at the giant feeding her boy. "Maybe he'll end up a painter."

"We went on a hike," says Ken, wiping the boy's face with one huge finger. "Showed him a hoot owl and a deer. He liked it."

"I'm jealous," I say.

"I'll take you, too, sometime," says Ken. "I can show you raccoon babies, golden trout, trees in a circle that make a power space, and a waterfall that carries all the answers, if you listen long enough."

"How about tonight?" I ask.

"To the waterfall?" asks Ken, his eyes widening. "Sure."

I feel a strong need to get closer to this big guy if he's gonna be the protector of my son. My son. I never dreamed I'd ever get to say that. It doesn't matter that some other guy gave Lily the other half. It's all good at birth. Noah is my son.

So who should be waiting for us down at the sunny end of the lodge, but Dominic Kachetti, Hilda, R.D., and Rasmusen Gustafson whatever, the King of Oregon. Andrew and John sit down with Ken, so it's just me and Lily going to meet him.

The man is almost a cartoon character. He's skinny and has a perfectly kept white beard. He might even be handsome, except he sneers so much it makes him seem permanently pissed off. He's wearing a gray jumpsuit and fine Italian boots. He has a tiny computer on his wrist and a pearl-handled six-gun on his right hip. He nods for us to sit.

Kachetti smiles and says, "Please. Sit anywhere."

We sit across from Gustafson and smile at him. He looks us over for a minute, frowns at Kachetti, scratches his cheek, squints at Lily and says, with unmistakable suspicion, "So are you a duo, or what?"

The air around him vibrates with the word "what." He pronounces it "wut." He can call himself anything he wants to. We know who he is. He's a country music freak. Country. Nothing else will do.

"Yeah," says Lily, winking at me, a slight drawl creeping into her voice, "Charlie here likes to sneak around on the guit box a little, while I'm playing rhythm and singing up front."

"Great God!" he cries, his eyes going wild. "Country-style lead guitar? Shit man, that's my favorite kind of music!"

Lily turns to me and gives me a very clear message with her eyes that says, "Charlie, you better say that's *exactly* what you play, even if you've never gone *near* it."

"Yeah," I mumble, "I like to run that way some."

"Hallelujah!" he shouts, jumping to his feet. "To hell with lunch! Let's go to the studio!"

He *storms* out of the lodge! Nearly everybody in the place jumps up and chases after him. I can't blame them. He's got the power. I turn to Lily and say, "I ain't never played none a that shit."

"You will today," she says, her eyes narrowing. "You will play that shit like you were born in Nashville to a picker's son of a picker's son back to Morocco or wherever."

"And if I can't?" I say, my palms getting sweaty.

"Then I doubt very much we'll be staying here," she says, shrugging.

We stop by Ken. Lily tells him to get the boy cleaned up. "Put him in some little blue jeans and a cowboy shirt if you know somebody around here with a kid his size," she says, licking her lips. "Then bring him down to the studio and let him crawl around." She turns to me and says, "Charlie, you make damn sure that place is babyproof."

"What are we doing?" I ask.

"Are you kidding?" says Lily, flabbergasted that I don't know. "We're putting on a *show,* Charlie! You knew that!"

"I know, but . . ."

"You're the slightly delicate good-old-boy," she says, taking my hand. "Otherwise, you'd be killing somebody or playing football, and I'm the tough chick with a great ass who fought every inch of the way to get where she is, and Noah is the holy child, the little country gentleman of the future. And if we can get him sitting by that guitar, touching the strings, then you can play Beethoven, and this old fart'll think you're the reincarnation of Chet Atkins."

"But what if he really has an ear?" I ask, trembling. "What if he can tell one note from another? Then what?"

"Then you dig down," says Lily, squeezing my hand. "You dig down and get it. You've heard it in your head, you can play it. You just have to trust yourself, Charlie. Open up and let it fly. That's what I'm gonna do. I don't see that we have any choice if he's who they say he is."

"Rasmusen?" says Ken.

"Gustafson," I say.

"The King of Oregon," says Lily, nodding slowly. "The guy with the army. The guy paying the bills."

39

Ten minutes later, we're in the studio, guitars in our hands, microphones all around us. Lily says she wishes she'd worn a skirt, but I think she looks great in her tight blue jeans and tighter little tee shirt that shows a little bit of tummy and goes tight around her breasts. She squeezes my hands again and whispers, "Take your time, Charlie. A few good notes are worth a million bad ones. And remember I love you." Andrew fades in the rhythm bottom we recorded earlier, and we go live.

I stroke a tentative run of notes, nothing bad but nothing great, and Lily starts to sing. What a voice! What am *I* doing here? I'm a hack, a pretender, a nothing trying to play along with a genius! I close my eyes and I can't *believe* her voice! How can such purity, such emotion, such power, be human? I open my eyes. Her whole body is trembling with song. The room is too small to contain her. There's nothing that can ever capture her. She isn't merely human. She's divine as she sings.

I been working real hard
At making myself invisible
I want to get into your life
Without your knowing
I wanta learn a few of your secrets
'Fore I make my move
And when I do
I want to get you alone.

I look down at my hands, fumbling to keep up, and I wish they were *her* hands. I wish she could play it for me, but I know I'll have to give it a try. Whatever his name is wants a duo, a sexy gal up front and her wizard guitar man playing hot licks behind, so I'll give it my best shot and hope he's a fool, but I'll never stop wishing she'd do it for me.

I'm gonna find out all I can
About your fantasies
That's the way I'm gonna learn
How to play my part
I want so much to love you,
You know it's hard to wait
But I will if it will help me
Get into your heart.

Now she hits a swooping change of chords and I'm alone with the rhythm track, alone with my ignorance, alone with the knowledge that what*ever* I play it will sound like shit next to Lily's voice. But I have to play *some*thing, so I close my eyes and give it a try.

But what comes over the speakers is *not* what I'm playing. My guitar's been turned off. Lily has her back to the audience, playing the lead for me. I'm truly the dummy up front. The fraud. The thing The King wants to see. And for a split second I'm furious that she's pulling this stunt without warning me. I toy with the idea of stopping completely, blowing the charade, except for one thing. I got my wish! All I have to do now is *pretend* to play, and the lead is as great as her singing. It's pretty and joyous and endearing, and long before she finishes, the audience is applauding, laughing, crying, shouting. It's the loveliest music I've ever heard.

And now they're chanting my name. "Charlie! Charlie! Charlie!" I feel kinda foolish, but I keep on faking it, chasing after the notes I'm hearing. They run ahead of me, teasing me, making it almost too hard to fake. I look up at Lily to warn her to slow down, and she's not playing! *I* am! She's standing there watching me, her hands at her sides, the tears rolling down her face. She's tricked me into freedom! She's tricked me into playing from my heart!

And when I lose it, Lily's hands fly to the strings and she picks out a melody that makes what I do seem like a baby crawling next to his sexy swinging mama. God, can she play! Now it's my turn to cry. Let the old fart think what he wants about me, my Lily's on fire and I can't pretend not to care.

Andrew fades us out perfectly. Gustafson rushes forward, shakes my hand, kisses Lily's hand, and actually bows to her. "Yes, yes," he says, his eyes all jittery and wild. "Now, now, now do one where you *both* sing! God, if you can pull *that* off, there's nothing can stop you, nothing!"

"You think so?" says Lily, batting her eyelashes at him.

"*Know* so!" he shouts. He turns to Kachetti and says, "She's obviously far more experienced than her husband, but he's got the chops. He'll come around. She oughta play most of the longer leads. Can we agree to that?"

"We'll consider it," says Lily, smiling at him.

"I *like* her," he says, still looking at Kachetti. "I do. I really like her. She's strong. You know? She's like a sturdy . . . thing. I like her. I'm not just *saying* that."

"How old are you, Mr. Gustafson?" Lily asks. "Or is it Rasmusen?"

"Gustafson," he says, frowning at Hilda. "Sixty-three. Why?"

"Married?" asks Lily, her voice verging on the flirtatious.

"Several times. Why?" he asks, still refusing to look directly at her.

"Texas?" I ask, hoping I'm right.

"For starters," he says gruffly, "but I'm all Oregon now. It's a great place once you know the dry spots. Why do you ask?"

"I had you single and pushing forty-eight," says Lily, winking at me.

"You flatter me," he says breathlessly, looking at the ceiling.

"Truth is," says Lily, "we don't have a harmony tune rehearsed yet that I think would be good enough for a man of your taste, Raz. You mind if I call you Raz?"

"No," he says, nodding and blushing. "You call me anything you want, honey."

"We have a ballad," says Lily, taking my hand. "Charlie kind of hums it with me in parts, and it's real pretty." She says "pretty" "purty."

"Well, that'll certainly do," says Raz, grinning gigantically at the floor.

Lily calls John over to her and whispers something to him. He goes to the synthesizer, touches a few panels, puts on headphones, and sits down to play. Lily sweeps into a sweet long version of the ballad she sang for the marijuana chieftain and his people. I poke in a lick or two and hum a pretty good harmony on the chorus. Lily nods to John, and he runs a pedal-steel guitar lead behind us that's so nice you can practically *see* the plains of Texas rolling by. Lily finishes with a lullaby falsetto, and Andrew fades us into a recording of rain falling on a highway, a train howling in the distance.

Gustafson is delirious. He paces around excitedly and shouts, "I know a guy in Portland! The audio jock of the Northwest! He'll *spear*head the drive! We're gonna make Nashville *green* with envy! We'll annihilate them!"

"Well, Raz," says Lily, taking her guitar off, "I hate to disappoint you, but we do other stuff, too, you know? It's only fair to tell you that we do *what* we want or we don't do anything. We *love* country, but we like to rock 'n roll. You know what I'm saying?" She takes his hand and frowns at him, but he still won't look at her. "Raz, what I'm trying to tell you is that I tend to get jazzy sometimes, and we get radical now and then, *very* radical. So we need to know if that's a problem, 'cause if it is, we may not be able to accommodate you. You know what I'm saying? We play free, or we don't play."

"God, I like her," says Raz to Kachetti and Hilda. "I like direct people, I really do. I like her. I like her voice, I like her style, I like the way she just . . ."

"So tell *me*," says Lily, tapping him on the shoulder. "Tell me. I'm right here."

Well, he turns to her, and I'm pretty sure the old guy is gonna take her in his arms and kiss her. But he doesn't. Instead, he rocks up on his toes, digs his hands into his pockets and says, "I like you, Lily, I do. And I like your husband."

"He's here, too," says Lily, encouraging him like a mom helping her son get over being shy.

"I like you, too, Charlie," he says, shaking my hand, matching my grip.

And now, as if by heavenly decree, Noah, dressed as the infant Hank Williams, crawls over to his mother's guitar and plucks three clean notes in a row, perfectly in time with the song we just finished. Raz sees it. He walks slowly over to the boy, and looks down at him, waiting for him to play again. Or maybe he's seeing himself, the way he's always wanted to be. Innocent, gifted, and just starting.

40

"What a thing it is!" says Hilda, presiding over the celebration feast in the lodge that night. "Our benefactor," she proclaims majestically, "Raz Gustafson, has promised us renewed funding, a strengthening of our defenses, and much more. Thanks to Lily and Charlie, a great victory has been snatched from the jaws of defeat!"

Thunderous applause fills the vast hall. It's awesome to feel all this gratitude!

"I wish she wouldn't talk like that," says Lily, whispering to me. "She's blowing this way out of proportion."

"Let her ramble," I say, liking it. "She's just letting off steam."

"I don't like it," says Lily, sneering at my forehead. "I don't trust Raz, and I don't like getting credit for something that could still fall through. 'Cause then we'll get the blame, too."

Hilda beams at Lily. There are calls for Dominic Kachetti to speak. The old man struggles to his feet. He's exhausted from the weeks of tension and despair. He muses for a moment. His voice trembles with emotion. "I do not wish to detract from this afternoon's performance. I am relieved and happy, as many of you are, but I must remind you that we will never be safe, until everyone is safe. We will never be free, until everyone is free. Charlie spoke the truth this morning when he said it is endgame for elitism. We have the technology to give every human being on this planet a safe and meaningful life, yet we squander our wealth and energy on petty wars to protect a petty few. Today, Lily sang us a victory. Perhaps. But what did we gain? More for ourselves, and little for the world. Our purpose is clear! To share our wealth by giving our creations and our energy to those less fortunate than we. *That* is victory!"

There's applause, but it's not as strong. The people like Hilda's fairy-tale stuff better.

"That's more like it," says Lily, leaning her head on my shoulder. "Now let's go home and go to bed. I'm pooped."

Ken carries Noah home for us. He hands the boy to Lily at the door, turns eagerly to me, and says, "Ready to go?"

"Where?" I say, worn-out and longing for bed.

"The waterfall," he says, disappointed. "You didn't remember?"

"He's been talking about it all day," says Lily, lying sweetly to him.

"I didn't hear him," says Ken, bowing his head and looking away. "I would have heard him."

"I'm sorry," says Lily, embarrassed. "I forgot that . . ."

"Maybe some other time," says Ken, shrugging his giant shoulders."

"No," I say, rousing myself. "I want to go. I'm tired, but I want to go."

"Don't stay up too late," says Lily, kissing me. "I want to get started early tomorrow."

We hike up through the meadows, and turn northward as we make our way into the forest. The trees block the starlight and we're in total darkness. I can't see where I'm going. I have to stop. Ken comes back to get me. "Hold my hand, Charlie," he whispers. "I can see just fine."

"Should have brought a flashlight," I say. "This is spooky."

"No," he says, his voice suddenly harsh. "Don't ever bring a factory thing here. You promise?"

"Why not?" I ask, a tremor of fear running through me.

"Spirits don't trust things made by machines," he says, engulfing my hand in his. "Don't know why, they just don't."

We climb a soft slope. We traverse the shoulder of a rocky hill. We pass between two massive granite domes. The forest thins. Starlight again. The waterfall. It's a paper-thin sheet of water, several feet wide, falling unbroken from the top of a sheer cliff, dropping into a massive crack in the earth. It falls *so* far before hitting bottom, that even though we can reach out and touch it, the sound it makes is a distant one.

"Jesus," I say, my voice echoing off the quiet water.

"You can play it like an instrument," says Ken, reverently. "Bring Lily here and she'll make sounds you won't believe."

He tips his mighty head back and sings a deep bass note. It runs up the strand of water, grows faint as it approaches the top, and gets louder again as it rides the water back down to us, turning into a whisper as it vanishes into the earth.

"God," I say, "that's an amazing thing. Unbelievable. *Look* at this thing!"

"Yeah," says Ken, nodding, "and that's only one of the things I've figured out. I got four voices going one time."

"What do you call it?" I ask, overwhelmed by the power of the thing.

"Call it Nanza," he says, "but you can call it anything you want. Andrew comes up here all the time. He says he can talk directly to the mind of the earth here. It's a kick, Charlie. We'll have to come up here and listen to him sometime. You and me and Noah. Yeah. Noah would like this."

"You love that *kid!*" I shout. My voice rings off the water like a metal spoon striking a tile floor.

"Maybe he's my brother," says Ken, nodding, his huge head a mass of darkness against the silver band of water. "Hilda said I'd get a brother someday. Maybe it's Noah."

"Ken," I say softly, "I'm really sorry about kicking . . ."

"That was years ago," he says. "Forget it."

"It was last night," I say, shaking my head. "But it sure does seem like a long time ago."

"I like to sit on the rock over here and listen for a while," he says, leading me to a flat boulder. "You ask the falls anything you want to know the answer to. You don't have to ask out loud, unless you want to."

We sit. I think for a moment, asking, "Are we home free?"

The falls continue to fall. Their distant sound is like steady waves washing a beach of pebbles. Abruptly, the water breaks into separate sheets, some long, some short, some solid, some fragmented. Moments later, this pattern of water hits bottom far within the earth, and I distinctly hear a voice say, "From the air."

I ask Ken what he heard. He says, "Guns of air."

We walk home. Ken tells me about Noah and all the things the little guy did today. "I'll take him any time, all the time," says Ken, putting his huge arm around my shoulder. "You just let me know."

"He makes you happy, huh?" I say. "Me, too."

"Happier than I've been in a long, long time," he says, nodding. "I had a lover once, but she went off. I know it's hard to believe that I had one, but I did. She said it was to be free as an artist, but I know it was to get away from me. It's lonely being what I am, so it was lonely for her being with me, but I guess that's just the way it is."

"You're a good man, Ken," I say, patting his massive arm.

"I been seeing a girl over at Medford," he says, sighing. "Not too often. She's only seventeen, but she's six-foot-nine and she's petite next to me. She likes that. Gets her pretty excited. I might see her again soon, I hope."

"Well," I say, my heart breaking for him, "Noah sure likes you."

"I sure love him," he says emotionally. "He's got a head full of stories already. Man oh man, shoulda heard what he said about his mama and you. You might wanta get that boy in another room if you're gonna be *that* wild in bed."

"He exaggerates," I say, trying not to show too much surprise. "All babies do. He hasn't seen enough to know what he's seeing."

"If you say so," says Ken, embarrassed he brought it up.

"Well," I say, stopping at the door to our little house. "I'm not sure what the waterfall meant, but it was a wonderful experience. I guess we'll see you tomorrow."

"I'll be here," he says eagerly. "First thing."

"We'll meet you over at the lodge," I say. "No need for you to come all the way over here."

"No problem," he says, turning to go. "See you in the morning."

Lily's awake, reading a book about horoscopes. I tell her everything I just saw and heard, and we end up moving the boy's crib out of our bedroom into the other little room.

"You don't believe he can really communicate like that with Noah, do you?" I ask her, as we get into bed.

"I don't want to discuss it," she snaps, turning away from me.

"Beauty," I say, taking her in my arms. "What is it?"

"No," she says, closing her eyes. "I don't want to remember."

"Tell me," I whisper. "I want to help you with it."

"Pearl," says Lily, her voice quivering with rage, "used to hold Noah while she watched me getting it from the boys."

"Oh, Lily, I'm sorry," I say, my skin tingling with rage.

"I just pray that Noah was too young and too pure to know what he was seeing," she says, clutching at me. "I just hope he saw it like some big blurry Picasso thing."

"I am so sorry," I say, kissing her.

"You're a saint, Charlie," she whispers, kissing my forehead.

"You're pure and good and the best thing there's ever been," I say, holding her tightly.

"No, you," she says, kissing me.

"No, you."

41

We hand Noah off to Ken after breakfast and hurry down to the studio. Lily's bursting with tunes and we tape a jazzy rhythm track in no time. My hands are still goofy from yesterday's miracle performance, and I can't do anything coherent except play the drums. Lily knocks out a beautiful salsa lead on an old wooden electric guitar, John synthesizes a Brazilian big band, and we take a break before Lily gives the vocal a try.

John goes into a blab about his search for emotional equations. He says he's feeding Lily's song into a digitizer, then using a computer to scan the digits for what he calls reduceable patterns.

"Why?" asks Lily, shrugging. "Why not just enjoy it?"

"Because we have to use all our resources to help the world. That's what the Dominic says. And what if I *could* find the equation of love," he says simply. "The equation of hope? Of joy? Think of the applications! Think of the equation of joy applied to aero-dynamics, architecture, computers!"

"I can't," says Lily, glaring at him. "I *don't* think about it. That's the way I do it."

Suddenly Andrew shouts into us, "We're being attacked! We're being attacked!"

We freeze, not believing it. It can't be. Lily looks at me, stunned. "Noah!" she cries, and runs out of the studio.

The hallway is already crowded with people. Hundreds more are rushing into the building. It's the closest thing to a bomb shelter we have. Lily pushes through the terrified crowd. She's about to go outside, when Andrew grabs her arm. "Don't go out there, Lily!" he shouts. "It's death!"

"My baby's out there,!" she screams, breaking away from him, pushing open the massive door.

I follow her. It isn't only sunlight that startles us, but chaos. Dozens of people are rushing toward us, terror in their eyes. They're desperate to reach the thick cement building. Some carry children. Some carry manuscripts. Paintings. Tools. Instruments. Some carry food and blankets. Others are running with us away from the fortress, searching for loved ones or going for more supplies.

Over the meadow, beyond the lodge, approaching slowly, are three enormous helicopters. Troop transport gunships. Their chopping blades fill the air with an ugly unnatural mechanical coughing. Ahead of them, running like a herd of frightened deer, come more artists, more children. People we have never seen. People who have never known such terror. There has never been anything more terrifying than this.

Lily and I crouch on the lodge veranda. We search the passing crowd for the giant Ken, but he isn't among them. Lily closes her eyes and keens, "No! No!" She runs toward the stairs. I catch her and pull her down behind a heavy oak table. A burst of machine gun bullets rip apart the windows behind us! We're strays and they're trying to round us up. They want us all in that bunker. Then they'll starve us out or worse. They know exactly what they're doing.

We look upriver to where our cabin sits small and pretty, where the waters make a slow graceful curve. We see a gunship hovering over our house, about to land. But it doesn't come down. A missile flies from its belly, crashing through the shingled roof! The cabin erupts in a cloud of flames!

Lily goes berserk. She rises with a strength I can't overpower, breaks away from me, and runs down the stairs. She crosses the bridge and runs directly under the two nearest choppers. I'm right behind her.

The copters above us continue herding the panicked mob toward the bunker. But the copter that blew up our house turns smoothly in the air and spews bullets in front of us, rototilling the ground, trying to turn us back. But Lily runs on. She's about to hurl herself into the flaming pyre, when I catch up to her, grab her and turn her with all my strength to the east, so she can see that Noah is still alive.

Ken is carrying the boy, lumbering toward the shelter of the woods. Running with him is a woman dressed all in gray. Lily hesitates in my arms, breaks away and runs after them. I stay where I am, hoping to draw the helicopter away from them, but it's no good. Whoever's directing that ship knows what they want, and it isn't me. A last burst of bullets falls close by. The ship turns and drifts after Lily.

I glance toward the lodge. The other copters are about to land and discharge Pearl's warriors. I run after Lily. The gunship begins to fire at Ken and Noah and the woman! I hear Lily scream as the woman falls! I see Ken stagger. He stumbles into the dense forest. Lily runs on. I run after her, feeling a terrible coldness in my bones.

And now there comes a sound beyond all sound! I'm about to cover my ears, when I'm picked up like a rag doll and thrown across the meadow. I land well, somersaulting, and press my face down into the mossy earth, wishing I could burrow like a gopher! There's a terrible crash! A moment later, I'm engulfed in waves of unbearable heat.

I look up. Not fifty yards away is the flaming wreckage of the gunship! I can't see Lily, and I can't move forward to find her. The heat is too intense. I stagger to my feet and run back toward the river. The air becomes cooler. I fall on my face again as a supersonic jet materializes fifty feet above me. A deafening sound wave follows a second later.

One of the other choppers turns away from the bunker and moves out over the river, coming toward me. I get to my feet and start to run. Suddenly, a blur of silver streaks the stinking sky, hits the copter, and blows it to pieces! Hot shards of metal whizz over my head, though I'm a quarter mile away.

The surviving gunship is just touching down, but it takes to the air again and makes a run for it. Three little jets flash out of the blue, swarm the thing, and tear it to pieces with their missiles and bullets. They roar away and a silence descends, broken only by the crackling flames and the beating of my heart. The air is so thick with death I know I can die if I want to, but I have to get to Lily if I can.

I run to where I saw her last. For a long time black smoke obscures everything. But now I see her, crawling toward the woods, calling out to her child! I run to her and help her to her feet. She grimaces and says, "Oh, shit! I stepped in a fuckin' gopher hole! Twisted my ankle!"

"I'll carry you," I say, putting my arms around her.

"No," she says, pushing me away. "Go see about the boy and Ken. I'll see if I can help this one."

I run toward the trees, glancing at the shattered person in the grass. I know without knowing that it's Rain. Lily hobbles toward her body. As I reach the forest, I hear Lily's sorrowful cry.

I rush into the woods, stumble over a log, fall to my right, and nearly land on top of Ken. He's sitting against the backside of a big redwood tree, weak from loss of blood. Noah is wide-eyed and pale, trembling in the giant's hands, shocked out of his little mind. Ken hands the boy to me, gives me a quivering smile and says, "It's in my calf, my left leg, down low. I'm bleeding buckets, Charlie. Lily okay? I can feel the stuff running out of me fast. Lily okay? The boy's okay. Just scared."

I set Noah down and take off my shirt. I tie it around Ken's enormous leg, above the knee, making the knot a tight one. I pick up Noah and hold him to me. He's shivering. His breathing is erratic. I check him for a wound, but his little body is unscathed.

"They hit Rain, huh?" says Ken, closing his eyes. "She must be dead."

"Yeah," I say, breathing hard, feeling dizzy. "I don't know."

We hear more choppers coming.

"Shit!" cries Ken, struggling to his feet. "I know a cave near here."

"I'll get Lily," I say, handing him the shivering boy.

Ken sits back down against the tree to wait for us. I run out of the woods onto the meadow. The sky is full of choppers. Some have already landed. But they're Gustafson's boys. The people are rushing out of the bunker, coming out of the lodge, dazed and happy, greeting the young soldiers, the troops of liberation.

Lily lies beside Rain, sobbing, clutching at the body of her friend, trying to love her back to life. I run past them, knowing I have to get help for Ken before he bleeds to death.

Two young medics run toward me. I wave frantically to them. I don't want this to be happening. I don't want to be in a war. But as I wave, I realize for the first time in my life, that I've *always* been in a war. I've just been lucky enough to avoid the front, where the actual bleeding and dying goes on.

42

Cold winds. Steady rain. We bury the body two days after the invasion. Andrew, R.D., and I dig the grave in a beautiful spot overlooking the river, not far from the charred remains of our house.

Lily rouses herself for the burial, but otherwise she stays in the studio, keeping the lights low, sitting in the corner, holding Noah, humming to him, trying to get him to nurse, but he won't. I try to play with the boy, but he's listless. Lily eats almost nothing. Noah takes a bottle now and then, but he doesn't drink much. Mostly they sit and hold each other and wait for the overwhelming sorrow to go away a little.

We lie on a futon at night. Sometimes I sleep. Lily rarely does. She lets me hold her. Sometimes she comes to me and presses herself against me for comfort, but she can't give any comfort to me. I accept that. I hold the boy and tell him I love him. I tell him all the things we're gonna do when he's feeling better.

And now it's the afternoon of the fourth day. Lily looks up at me from the corner. "It's time, Charlie," she says, nodding slowly. "I want to get in the river. I want to wash away this fear, okay?"

So we go out. She leaves Noah at the lodge with Hilda. The clouds lift a little. We walk over to the ruins of our house. We leave our clothes on a big stone beside a blackened tree. We immerse ourselves in an icy pool in the middle of the stream. I can stand it for only a few seconds. Lily stays in for several minutes. We dry ourselves, hold each other, dress and go back to the lodge to see what we can do, to see if there's any reason to keep making our music.

A meeting is in progress. A hundred people are present. Kyle Dobbs is speaking. He's gaunt and tired, his eyes bloodshot. "More than half our people have fled and more will follow," he says, indignantly. "And I say that it's the fault of Lily and her child. A good friend is dead, three people are wounded, our children are traumatized forever, and everything we've worked for, everything we've ever believed in, *all* the years of struggle are to be wasted so *one* egotistical artist can be famous? That's insanity!"

"He's right," says Lily, going up in front of the group, standing beside Kyle. "We're leaving."

"You are?" says Kyle, squinting suspiciously at her.

"But I need to say one thing," she says, her voice trembling. She brushes the hair out of her eyes and takes a deep breath. "I'm sorry. I am. I'm sorry I ever knew Pearl. But I'm sure you all know about jealousy. The way a person acts when a relationship ends and they don't want it to. How sometimes they hit somebody, break things, chase you. There's not a doubt in my mind that everybody here has *been* that crazy or had somebody *be* that crazy to them. The difference is, my crazy friend has her own army."

"Well," Kyle simpers, "thanks for the disclaimer but . . ."

"I'm not done yet," says Lily, burning him with a look. "Rain was my best friend after my husband and my boy. She saved my life a thousand times, and I saved hers a few times too. We traveled together, you know? There was nothing we didn't share. I miss her so much it's like my soul has been torn in half." Lily scans the faces of the frightened people. "I came here ignorant of you, you of me," she says, her voice full of passion. "I haven't had a chance to get to know many of you, but I want to thank you for what you've given me. I can't seem to ever stay here for long, but I would dearly like to come back here someday when I won't be a danger to you."

"Wait," says Dominic Kachetti, striding to the front. He faces the people, his voice strong and clear. "Kyle is absolutely wrong! Totally, shamefully wrong! The loss we suffered was the consequence of *our* action, *our* commitment to truth, *our* choice. To scapegoat Lily would be the death blow to our movement. To blame even our enemies is primitive and stupid. The government of this nation has done this kind of killing all over the world. And now it's finally happening here." He scowls at Kyle, and scowls at the people. "Well . . . tough shit for us. This is reality, Kyle, as much as we hate to admit it, and if you don't like it, *you* leave, because I'm gonna beg Lily to stay. I want to work this out. I want to get through this violent time and emerge into a new age, strengthened by adversity, emboldened by what I know will either be the victory of goodness, or the decline and fall of the human race!"

"And that," Hilda whispers to me, "is why he is the Dominic."

"No," says Lily, moved by what the old man said, "I can't ask to . . ."

"A vote!" shouts R.D., jumping to his feet. "Of the council and everyone here. How many want Lily and Charlie to stay?"

Everyone, save for Kyle and four women, raise their hands.

"To leave?" asks R.D., batting his eyelashes at Lily.

Kyle and the four women lift their hands.

"Then if you wish, you may stay," says Kachetti, embracing Lily.

"No," she says, gently pulling away from him. "We won't stay unless Kyle and these women ask us to. I never liked a person who displaced somebody else, so we'll be getting out of here as soon as we can."

Kachetti and R.D. rush over to Kyle. Hilda gives Noah to me and runs to Lily. Andrew comes and stands silently beside me. A dozen people ask me to tell Lily that they want us to stay, that they don't blame us. But there are many, many more people who say nothing, who stand waiting, wondering, dazed by the sudden and frightening change in their reality. Lily moves away from Hilda, comes to me, takes my hand, and we go upstairs to see Ken.

He's lying on his side, reading the screenplay to *Stage Coach.*

His enormous bed nearly fills the tiny room. The walls are covered with masks he's carved out of redwood, decorated with feathers, and painted with the colored juices of berries and seeds. They are perfectly symmetrical pieces. Most of them are surprisingly fine. He has a big bookcase crammed with books. He has a huge rocking chair. He has a Navajo rug. He has a view out over the river. Hanging on the wall between two windows is a painting of a minotaur. On the night table beside his bed there's a lamp with a base of manzanita, and beside the lamp sits a pipe, a round bowl of clay sculpted in the shape of an eagle's claw.

Ken puts his book down, rolls onto his back, and holds out his big hands for the boy. Lily gives Noah to him. A light comes into the baby's eyes. He gives the giant a tiny smile, and speaks for the first time since the terror came into him. He says, "Glrrrbshl frezgurfburdle."

"How's your leg?" I ask.

"My butt hurts more than my leg," says Ken, smiling. "If doc doesn't let me get up soon, I'm just gonna get up. I'm mostly okay. Boy looks thin."

"He won't eat," Lily says, bowing her head.

"Yeah, he will," says Ken, looking at the boy. "Now he will. He's just been resting up."

The giant offers the boy a cracker. He takes it, gives Lily a sly little look, and devours it.

"That's a relief," says Lily, smiling at her boy.

"He'll be okay," says Ken, puffing his cheeks out at Noah.

"Tell me about Rain," says Lily, handing her boy another cracker. He snatches it from her.

"She wanted to surprise you," says Ken. "That's why she waited at the house. She was taking a nap with Noah when the choppers came."

"Why didn't she come to the valley before now?" asks Lily, sitting down on the bed.

"I'm not sure," he says. "She told me it wasn't safe until you got Ras . . . Gustafson to say he was gonna . . ." He stops talking and looks out the window. A squadron marches by, returning from perimeter patrol.

"Sorry about that," says Lily, seeing Ken frowning at the soldiers.

"Not your fault," he says, handing Noah to me. "Like Kachetti just said, it's a consequence of our commitment to truth. Honesty doesn't pay all that much, but it's the only way to be. The rest is just *greedy.*"

"I don't know how you guys can be so forgiving," says Lily, looking at the floor.

"What do you mean?" says Ken, frowning at her. "I want you to make that record. There's no time to waste. If you're to blame, everybody's to blame. This is a group, remember."

"We'll probably be leaving," says Lily, staring grimly at me.

"No," says Ken, wrinkling his nose. "Kyle'll come around. You'll see."

"I don't know," says Lily, her eyes filling with tears. "That's maybe not the problem, Ken. Maybe I don't believe in this anymore."

I want to say something, but I hold it in.

Ken reaches out a huge hand, grabs Lily's arm, and whispers, "I'm gonna tell you something I've never told anybody. You promise not to tell anybody else?"

"Okay," says Lily, looking at him.

I bring Noah over and we sit beside Lily. The giant frowns, looks up at the ceiling, and says, "I remember when they killed my mother. She was big like me, only different. My father was more like you. She caught him to make a baby, 'cause all the males of my people were gone. She was wild, see, and big. You probably couldn't believe how big. One day, I was maybe five years old, we were coming down a steep hill. I remember it because I kept falling and rolling and tumbling. And then from way off, somebody shot her. She dragged herself and me far away to a cave I'll show you someday. Then she died. I sat there, thinking she was asleep. I didn't know what death was. We never killed anything. I'm a vegetarian. I once ate a burger in Medford. I almost died. They said it was food poisoning, but I know I was choking on the spirit of the cow."

"God," says Lily, looking at me, "I never thought of it like that."

"Well, anyway," says Ken, eager to continue, "I remember I finally stopped waiting for her to wake up. She was starting to stink. I came wandering down here and sat on this spot where the lodge is. I sat until death was taking me. That's when I realized what had happened to my mother. But I wasn't afraid. I was irritated, because somehow I could tell it was unnecessary, but I wasn't afraid. And then this old guy, the first Dominic, and a bunch of other people came hiking in here. I was too weak to run. He came up to me, put his hand on my head, looked in my eyes, and tamed me. The way Hilda does to people. He died a few days later. But Hilda smelled like him, so I trusted her. Nobody else could get close for years and years."

"Could you talk?" I ask. "Did you have a language?"

"No," he says. "Not an out loud one anyway. But we could hear each other, my mother and I."

"And then?" Lily asks, her mouth open in astonishment.

"Well," he says, blinking at her, "that's it. I was telling Charlie that the loneliness was killing me. And then I met Noah. And now you want to take him away."

"Now wait a minute," says Lily, pointing at Ken.

"No, you wait a minute," he says, snarling at her finger. "People been running out on me all my life. And if I have to make you feel guilty to get you to stay, I will. Because I don't have a good reason to live if you guys leave."

"I never thought I'd see the day again," says Lily, shaking her head as she takes Noah from me and hands him to Ken, "when somebody could pull this shit on me and get away with it. But you did. So I'll go talk to this Kyle Dobbs character and see what I can do."

"And his four wives," says Ken, smiling.

Lily freezes. "Those women are his wives?"

"You don't know about Kyle?" asks Ken, surprised.

Suddenly, the irritating Dr. Klemmer strides into the room, gives each of us a prissy little bow and goes to Ken's enormous feet. They're sticking out from under the covers at the bottom of the bed. "How are you feeling?" he chirps, talking to Ken's soles.

"Better," says Ken, ominously. "My little brother here wants to play. Tell me I can get up."

The doctor takes a thick needle out of his vest pocket and runs it down the center of Ken's left foot. He repeats the procedure on Ken's right foot. He comes around the side of the bed opposite us, looks into Ken's eyes, frowns and says, "You can get up, but take it easy or you'll start bleeding again. They did some deep damage to you. It needs time to heal. Amp up on your vitamins E and C, and keep on with the comfrey and the black kohosh. If you insist on remaining a vegetarian, take extra B, all of them, tons of them."

"I don't like pills," says Ken, grimacing.

The doctor ignores him, turns to me and says, "Ah, I see you've cut down on the pot. Good for you."

"Anything for my boy?" asks Lily, smiling hopefully at the doctor.

He peers into Noah's eyes for a moment, then starts backing out of the room. "No," he says in a hushed tone. "He's fine."

"That's a weird guy," I say, watching Klemmer scamper down the hallway.

"You should see him work his crystals," says Ken, lifting Noah high in the air, making him squeal. "I've seen him get light to actually *do* things. I once saw a blue light dissolve a big sore."

"He seemed afraid of Noah," I say, baffled.

"Oh, he is," says Ken, smiling. "I heard him say he's just like his mother. A power source."

"Now where does he get off saying that?" asks Lily, giving Ken a frustrated look.

"He says the feet are seismographs of the body," says Ken, nodding. "They give kind of a summary of where the body is now. But the eyes hold a history of us, and show our power. He tried to teach me, but I couldn't ever see what he was seeing. I could *hear* it sometimes, but I almost never saw it. I don't know, maybe it *is* all bullshit, Lily, but he's been healing people around here pretty well for as long as I can remember."

"You want the boy for a while?" she asks.

"Sure," says Ken, smiling.

"Where does Kyle live?" she asks.

"Up above Eagle's Nest. Charlie's been that far. Just keep following the trail on up for another hundred yards or so."

"Stuff his little face, would you?" says Lily, kissing Noah.

"My pleasure," says Ken, swinging his giant legs out of bed. "We'll just go down and decimate the kitchen."

43

Kyle Dobbs lives high above the valley in a white stone mansion. His wives move quietly through the ivy-covered corridors. We're ushered into a cool dark room. I can feel that we're inside the mountain. The lighting is subdued. The space is elegantly designed.

Kyle enters in a white silk robe. He's a frighteningly thin man, with hungry eyes. A long thin ebony pipe hangs from one corner of his mouth. A little line of blue smoke drifts skyward. I guess hash. Lily nudges me and whispers, "Hash."

We sit on an onyx couch with blue silk cushions. Kyle sits across from us on a black marble swing suspended from the ceiling by gold chains. He takes a deep toke, turns profile, and blows the shit out at a perfect forty-five degree angle. "This is a power struggle, no?" he says, looking at Lily.

"Yeah," she says, looking away. "I guess it is, and I hate this stuff. I'm lousy at it."

"Disarming," says Kyle, playing an imaginary violin, "but I don't buy it. You're doing this, Lily. It's not just happening. You're making an incredible move on this place, so don't plead innocent."

"How would you know what I'm doing?" she asks.

"*I* was a musician," says Kyle, a terrified smile on his face. "I was starving, too. Really. I was."

"What happened?" asks Lily, genuinely curious.

"I grew up," he says simply. "I got tired of playing in the mud. It was beginning to smell like shit. I was tired of being powerless. Impotent. Do you see what I'm saying? I wanted better toys. Now! Not when all men are free, as the Dominic would say. I want them now. I can't wait. There's not enough time. Is that wrong? After all, Lily, here you are. It's nice to be free to sing, isn't it?"

"Now wait a minute," I say, stiffening. "I don't think . . ."

"Ah, the caveman speaks," says Kyle, yawning at me. "I wondered if you could."

"Hey, I'm not the one with four wives," I say, bristling.

"Precisely," says Kyle, his eyes widening. "You couldn't *possibly* handle more than one. If that."

"Okay," says Lily, shaking her head. "Let's cool the macho stuff right now."

"I'm not being macho," I say, glaring at her and feeling very macho.

"A conflict," says Kyle, putting his hand on his cheeks in mock surprise. "How sweet. You two are really *very* good. It's almost believable. Except I know it's not."

"Why do you doubt it?" I ask, wanting to scream at him. "What makes you think . . ."

"You're here, aren't you?" he snaps. "I can *hear,* Charlie. Ken isn't the only one with that gift."

"Are you saying you read minds?" I ask, wishing we could leave. "Just come out and say it, okay?'

"But he's not saying that," says Lily, annoyed with me.

"I *hear* you," says Kyle, scornfully. "I hear what you *mean.* I don't *want* to read your mind. Your words tell me too much as it is."

"So what's the deal?" asks Lily, glaring at him.

"I want to produce your record," he says. "I want to be known as the man who made you. I get the credit. I get my name right under your name."

"That's Charlie's," says Lily, taking my hand. "We cut our deal a long, long time ago."

"Don't be so sure," says Kyle, snapping his fingers.

One of his wives comes running in. Lily nudges me and whispers, "Speed freak."

"I can *hear* you," says Kyle, singing it. "And yes, she is."

The woman is slender, her eyes fiery. She's wearing a pale blue jumpsuit. Her head is shaved. Her hands tremble and she can't stop moving. She blasts Lily with a look. It bounces off. She tongues the air at me. I turn away. She's a cat in heat. Scary.

"This is Hava," says Kyle, squinting at me. "Interested, Charles? She runs hot and fast. I'd be happy to loan her."

"No thanks," I say.

"Darling," says Kyle to Hava, "my disc, the latest one."

She darts away. A moment later the air fills with techno-pop dribble. It's so bad, it's almost good, but not quite because it goes on and on for a long time, and never changes, never sings, and never once makes me feel anything, except relieved when it finally stops.

"*That,*" says Kyle, pausing dramatically, "is the kind of thing I can do for you, Lily."

"No thanks," I say. "We like a melody."

"But the people *expect* wall of sound now," says Kyle, standing up. "Where have you been? I *know* about marketing. The people are terrified of silence. God forbid that it should ever be quiet again. They'd have to *think.*"

"I happen to respect the taste of the people," says Lily, "because that's all I am."

"So you can't have that," I say. "What else do you want?"

"The boy," says Kyle, nodding. "He's probably a genius. With the proper training, he might become someone very, very important."

"You sound like Pearl," says Lily, flinching.

"Pearl is an acquaintance," says Kyle, checking his fingernails.

Lily freezes. She gives me an anguished look. I take her hand, turn to Kyle, and say, "Listen, man, get this straight. We have the votes here. We don't *need* to talk to you. If you don't want to play with us, okay. But forget about the boy and the recording. Is there anything we can do to make you more comfortable about our being here in the valley?"

Kyle snaps his fingers three times. Three of his wives appear.

They're very different from each other, and yet they might be sisters. "Witnesses," says Kyle.

"To what?" asks Lily, glancing around the room.

"Any possible verbal agreements," he says, yawning again. "I'm very eager to make arrangements with you. I feel that we're very close, don't you?"

"Be careful," I say to Lily. "Maybe we oughta just go."

"No," she says, taking her hand away from me. "I can do this."

"Good," says Kyle, sitting down on his swing. "I want fifty percent of the residuals from everything you ever do."

"No. You get nothing," says Lily, "except what I give you as a gift."

"Brilliant," says Kyle, his eyes sparkling. "I want all the residuals from your first recording."

"You get nothing," says Lily, "but I'll give you a gift."

"Nice," says Kyle. "Ambiguous, but a concession."

"Not necessarily," I growl. "The gift might *be* nothing."

"I want something from your third recording," says Kyle, shrugging. "Anything you'd like."

"Okay," says Lily, "I'll give you . . ."

"No," I say, intervening.

"Charlie," says Lily, glaring at me, "let me handle this."

"No," I say, standing up. "We're going. You get nothing, Kyle. You got that? Nothing. She could give you the tiniest piece of the suggestion of a possibility of an idea of a fantasy, and you'd use it to haunt us forever. I know what I'm talking about. I sold out before. I remember how it feels, and this is it." I turn to Lily. "Let's go."

"Okay," she says, reluctantly getting up.

"God damnit!" says Kyle, standing up and pointing a trembling finger at me. "You are a colossal pile of shit! She *wanted* to deal with me."

"That's because she wants to make this record more than anything," I say, taking Lily's hand again. "But we'll do it clean or we won't do it."

"I will not forget this," says Kyle, clenching his teeth. "She was dealing with me, and *you* wrecked it. *I* might have produced her album! But no, idiot here is going to do it. This human turd is going to handle the greatest vocal talent of our time. Instead of me. How dare you! How dare you!"

"Now wait a minute," says Lily, confused. "Charlie was always gonna produce it. That was never in doubt. What are you trying to do, Kyle?"

"That's the way they do it," I say to her. "Twist every word."

"*You* did it," he says, sneering at me. "You will pay for this, mister." He barks at his wives. "Show our guests to the *back* door. They can *walk* down."

"How else?" I ask.

"We have a glider tram," says Kyle, lighting up another pipe. "But *you'll* never ride it. And if you think Raz is committed to you, I got news, you aren't shit to him. He's very much into contracts, and he hasn't signed one yet. So. . ."

"We like to walk," I say. "It's good for the heart."

"You better like to walk, Charlie," he says, moving to the window. "Because that's all you'll ever do. Until you die."

On the way down the trail, I look back up at Kyle's mansion. He's standing on a balcony, watching us with binoculars. And I realize he must have watched the invasion from there, too.

44

Our spirits are muddy. We play and play and play Lily's tunes, but the magic, the joy, whatever it is that makes her great, isn't here. Andrew can't do anything with his machines to restore her power. He blames himself.

"It's me, not you," says Lily, putting down her guitar. "We been at this almost a week and we're gettin' worse, not better."

John turns away from his synthesizer and says, "Maybe old Aristotle was right. Maybe mathematics *can't* prove emotions."

"Did *he* say that?" asks Lily. "I always wondered what his trip was. You got any hot Aristotle for us?"

"Well," says John, "he said, among other things, and I paraphrase, that when it's not flowing, it's because there's no germ motif to flow *from.*"

"How did he know that?" I ask.

"He didn't," says John. "He was just a philosopher."

"Why do they always use such big words?" asks Lily, her voice full of bitterness.

"Part of the job," says John, frowning at the ceiling. "Philosophers have to look for a universal application."

"Look," says Lily, closing her eyes, "I'm probably just in a bad mood, John, but I really am kinda tired of your always trying to put words to things that don't take words. A song doesn't work because it doesn't have charm. If you try to define that, I'll kick your ass. A song has got to uplift. What's that mean? Don't mess with it. Now you could say A squared plus B squared equals C squared, but that's only true if you *believe* in whatever those letters stand for." She unplugs her guitar and puts it in its case. "It's something my mother used to say. And I just remembered it. The truer to myself I am, the less a sinner."

John is stunned. "You just posited some tremendously heavy stuff," he says, swallowing. "You just referenced a whole new plausible universe. You're not unconscious at all. You know exactly what you're doing, don't you?"

"In a way I do," she says, nodding, "but I don't want to try to explain it. The knowing is inside me, it's not a theory, because it doesn't come from words. I *know* how to sing."

"I'm blown away," says John, running out of the room.

"Me, too," says Lily, looking up at Andrew. "Shut us down, friend. We need a break from this."

"You got it," he says sadly. "I'm sorry about that problem with . . ."

"My fault," says Lily, taking my guitar off of me.

"So what are you gonna do?" asks Andrew, putting a little reverb into his voice.

"Get out of here for a couple days," says Lily. "How about you?"

"Might go down to the redwoods," he says, turning on the echo so it goes redwoodsredwoodsredwooredwooredwoodsss. "Visit Buck and his people."

"His women, you mean?" asks Lily, smiling sadly up at him.

"I might give that a try," says Andrew, sounding doubtful. "I'm not much in the mood anymore. Maybe. Don't know."

"We'll get over this," says Lily, putting my guitar in its case. "We have to."

"I don't know," says Andrew, turning off the special effect. "I've lost so many good friends."

"No matter how far down you get, you gotta get up," says Lily, nodding to herself.

"If you say so," he says, getting up out of his chair. "I'm gonna have to go on your say-so, Lily, because I haven't been able to find mine."

"You will," says Lily, taking my hand. "You will."

We go to see Dominic Kachetti and Hilda. R.D. leads us on a steep climb. We come to a vantage point even higher than Kyle's, almost too high for my taste. The view is grandiose. The people down at the lodge look like ants from up here.

The house is small. It's a dome lying on its side, the bottom pressed against the face of the mountain. A wide deck curves around the round-curved house. There's nothing above us but a granite wall, rising to a jagged peak.

R.D. opens the front door without knocking. He ushers us down a hallway, into an intimate living room. Lily stops suddenly. I bump into her from behind. Kachetti and Hilda are making love on the rug. The old man is behind Hilda, on his knees, thumping steadily into her. She's sprawled forward, her head on a stack of pillows. Kachetti smiles at us. "We'll be done in a minute," he says, breathlessly. "I'm just about to come." He closes his eyes and rides along furiously. Hilda begins to groan with delight. Now he comes. His skinny little body spasms, he throws his hands above his head, sighs, and collapses onto Hilda's butt and kisses it about twenty times.

Lily is outraged that we just stood here watching them. She wants to leave. R.D. assures her that it's perfectly all right that we watched. "It's no big deal," he says, smiling nervously at us. "It's not. Really. They don't mind. I promise. They don't."

"Yes," says Kachetti, dismounting. He wraps a towel around himself. "We actually like being caught in the act now and then. Adds a little drama, which helps us feel more romantic."

He sits down on a sofa and gestures for us to sit. We choose colorful matching armchairs. Lily squirms. Kachetti fidgets. R.D. is embarrassed about not being embarrassed. I feel silly. No one speaks. Lily tries to smile, but can't. Kachetti clears his throat and readjusts his towel. R.D. coughs. I start to say something, but Lily shakes her head.

Hilda gets up. She's a lovely woman, soft and white and ample. She's not embarrassed at all. "This," she says, "was our first time since the attack. We normally make love every day."

"Wow," says Lily, frowning in disbelief. "How old are you guys?'

"I am seventy-eight," says Kachetti, yawning. "Can you believe it?"

"I am at least that," says Hilda, putting on a red silk robe and gliding across the room. "I was a young woman with a baby in Sweden before a number was given to me. I might be as old as Junior."

"I'm sorry," says Lily, forcing a polite smile. "Did you just say you don't know how old you are?"

Hilda sits on the sofa beside her husband. She kisses him and looks into his eyes. She looks at Lily and says, "I don't come from around here originally."

"You mean Oregon?" I say, frowning. "Didn't you just tell us you were from Sweden?'

"Yes," says Hilda, nodding mysteriously. "I come from . . . somewhere else."

"Sweden," says Lily, nodding to show that we understand.

"Before that," says Hilda, arching an eyebrow.

"Your mama's womb!" sings R.D., falling on the floor at Kachetti's feet. "They want to get out of here for a couple days."

Kachetti looks at Hilda. She's thinking. They're letting us know who's boss. "Why not go to Raz's?" she says, smiling at Lily. "He has a lovely estate. Junior will take you. You really should experience a ride with Junior."

"Will we have to go back to our drawls?" asks Lily. "Took me three days to get rid of mine."

"Little hangin' on still," I twang.

"Don't get me started," says Lily, shaking her head wearily.

"He *does* love it," says Hilda, looking Lily in the eye. "And my brother *is* the power at the moment."

"He's your brother?" I ask dumbly.

"You don't like the nepotism you smell?" asks R.D., nodding. "I had the same reaction initially, and I'm related to no one. I'm barely related to myself. But you'll transcend it. You will. There's a very good reason for it at this stage."

"Raz didn't come over to our side until a very short while ago," explains Kachetti, his index fingers floating up to the tip of his nose. "We had other arrangements, but they weren't sufficient. You see, we used to just need money. But our ideas, our movement, has evolved so quickly, has gained such momentum, we're now interfacing with the power elite of the world. And when you enter that realm, all the rules change, reality alters, and experience becomes both ethereal and dangerous. Raz is our first ally in the new world."

"And what does he get out of it?" asks Lily, tensing.

"You," says Hilda, pausing dramatically. "You."

"So we're going up to Raz's for a reason, right?" I say. "You came up with that vacation plan just a little too fast."

"He's requested that you come," says Kachetti, looking away, ashamed.

"You mean he's commanded it," says Lily, giving me a look.

"Yes," whispers Hilda, loving the regal word.

"Okay," says Lily, crossing her legs, "if I'm gonna swim here, tell me about the sharks. Is Kyle anybody I have to worry about?"

"We owe him a great deal," says Kachetti, shutting his eyes. "We were about to lose this land and close most of our centers. The money just wasn't coming. And then Kyle appeared, and . . ."

"Okay," says Lily, her voice softening. "I been there." She takes a deep breath and says, "We'll be happy to go visit Raz. I've been wanting to talk to him alone anyway."

"Leave the boy with Ken," says Hilda.

"I will if I want to," says Lily, eyeing her suspiciously. "Nobody tells me what to do with my baby. Nobody. You got that? I don't mean to be crude. I like you. I like all of you. But my child is *my* business. Mine and Charlie's. Okay?"

"Sorry," says Hilda, bowing her head slightly.

"What the hell, Charlie?" says Lily, looking sadly at me. "Wanta go?"

"Yes," I say, though I don't.

"Okay then," says Lily, standing up slowly. "Let's go see if Ken wants to come with us."

Kachetti and Hilda both jump about a foot in the air, terror in their eyes. R.D. rises with us, but Lily says, "No! I need to be alone with Charlie."

R.D. looks hurt, but puts on a smile and says, "Okay."

We hike fast down the mountain, not talking at all. When we reach the bottom and are out on the meadow, Lily slows down and says, "I don't like this shit, Charlie. It's not right. Rain's dead. That's what *I* know." The tears fill her eyes. "That's what I know, Charlie. She's dead. Dead! She was a beautiful, wonderful person, Charlie! God talked through her all the time. And now she's gone, and they're fuckin' around with our lives!"

She falls to her knees, sobbing. I sit down beside her and hold her until she stops crying. We get to our feet. I keep my arm around her as we walk toward the lodge. I tell her we don't have to go go Raz's.

"I want to," she says, urgently. "This is bigger than we thought, Charlie. We need some power. Now! And I know who's got it around here. So let's get up to Raz's place and talk money."

"You'd cut a separate deal?" I ask, shocked.

"I will cover my ass," says Lily, seething. "And yours and Noah's. I'm ready to expand my consciousness, Charlie, but I'm not sacrificing you and Noah to do it. You're the only part of my life I *know* is real."

Ken is sitting on the veranda, holding Noah, humming to him. Lily sits beside them. She sighs deeply as she looks around at the lovely day. The clouds are little cotton balls in the blue. She looks at Ken and says, "You'd die for that boy, wouldn't you?'

"Yes, I would," says Ken, without hesitating. "He's my best friend, even more than Hilda now."

"If we go away for a couple days, can you watch him for me?" she asks, shielding her eyes from the sun.

"Of course," he says, smiling. "We could go on an overnight to the Valley of the Loons. I know a sacred rock where . . ."

"No overnights," says Lily, cutting him off, "and don't take him up to Kyle's, you hear me?"

"Yes," says Ken, humbled as only a giant can be.

"And one other thing, Mr. Audio," says Lily, tapping Ken's chest, "I'd appreciate it if you wouldn't tell Hilda or Kachetti or anybody what we're saying when you hear us. You know what I'm saying? Keep it to yourself if you have to listen."

"I can stop hearing you," says Ken, "but . . ."

"I wish you would," says Lily, glaring at him. "We need our privacy now and then."

"But what if you're in trouble?" he asks, his brow wrinkling. "What if you're calling me and I'm not hearing you?"

"Ken," she says, taking Noah from him, "I like you. I like the way you love Noah. And *he* loves you, and I trust his judgment more than anybody's, but I gotta tell you something. *I* don't need your help. Charlie helps me. I'm not saying I won't take your help when I need it, but my baby needs it from you right now, not me. You understand?"

"Yes," says Ken, smiling at her. "You're getting in touch with your power."

"Don't get cosmic," says Lily, pointing at him, a warning in her voice. "I'm sick of this cosmic stuff."

"I'm sorry," says Ken, "but I'm not being cosmic. You *are* powerful. You can sing and make music much better than I can do anything, so no wonder you don't need me."

"What I'm saying is," says Lily, waving the compliment aside, "the kid comes first. If he's snug and you don't have anything better to do, then you can worry about us."

"Okay," says Ken, nodding.

"One last question," Lily says, handing Noah to me. "In your honest opinion, Ken, can I trust Hilda?"

"Yes," he says, nodding slowly. "I know she comes across kinda strange. She has some pretty weird ideas. But she's generous. She's really why you're here. She was the swing vote."

We go back to the studio to be alone with Noah for the rest of the day and that night. Lily's never really been apart from the boy. She's frightened about it. She keeps Noah up *way* past his bedtime. She's afraid he'll take his first steps while we're gone.

She can't sleep. We try and fail to make love. She weeps off and on for about an hour. I have a nightmare about being in a crash. In the morning we're both nervous wrecks.

After a cold dip in the river, we choose a few good instruments, including John, and go out on the meadow to wait for Junior.

Lily hands Noah to Ken and says, "Four times a day, food. I showed you the bath routine. You *know* everything, but this is hard for me, so . . . go over everything one more time."

"I feed him good food," says Ken, nodding. "I keep him clean and warm and happy. I can give him to Hilda, but I can't leave him alone with her. I make sure he gets good exercise. Sing him to sleep."

"And kiss him," says Lily.

"May I?" asks Ken, smiling sheepishly.

Lily's shocked. "You haven't yet?"

"No," says Ken, looking at the boy, "I wanted to, but . . ."

"How could you resist?" asks Lily, staring in disbelief at the giant. "My god, Ken, that's what babies are *for!* Now for godsake you kiss that boy at least ten times a day, or shame on you!"

"Okay," he says, shrugging his shoulders and making a face at Noah.

And now it comes. A dazzling turquoise dirigible! Two hundred feet long! It lands silently. The lift-off paddles slow. A door opens. Junior hops down from the ship. He's wearing cowboy everything and looks fairly authentic. He comes to us and shakes our hands. We load our instruments, kiss Noah good-bye, and jump on board. A few seconds later, we drift off the earth and float away.

45

We settle into our seats. They're padded body pods. Junior says they're engineered to close protectively around us should the aircraft experience any unforeseen difficulty. We're sitting in a cylindrical cabin made of crystal-clear resin, hanging beneath the dirigible on ten million strands of titanium.

"This thing can go forever," says Junior, his voice deep and raspy. "Fuels off the sun, makes no noise, and gets you there when you're *ready* to get there, unless you're in a hurry, then you take a jet, but then you miss the party, and you get there long before you should, and you have to wait around for your body-mind to catch up to your mind-mind at its natural pace. This is better. This is how you do it on earth, if you know what's good for you."

"You a poet?" asks Lily, smiling at the old man.

"I will take that as flattery," he says, beaming at her. "My words of late are babble, God-talk mostly. I'm a hundred and seven after all. I'm almost past the human. See? I watched astounded as my sexuality evolved from the purely physical to the mostly emotional to the virtually spiritual. It happens to everybody, if they allow themselves to grow old naturally and healthfully. It's a profoundly richer experience than dying of an illness or through self-destruction. Or so I'm told."

He gives us each a bottle of dark brew. It's a rich and earthy beer. We stare out at the world moving by. Green. Brown. Green. Gray. White. Clouds. Green. Green. Brown. Green. Oregon.

"This is home brew," says Junior, hoisting his bottle. "I made it myself. Some secret ingredients. A few Indian addendums and . . ."

"Is there mescaline in this punch?" Lily asks, looking at her empty bottle.

"Not enough to *do* anything," says Junior, bouncing his eyebrows. "Just enough to taste."

"We've been spiked, Charlie," she says, half-smiling and half-frowning at me. "No wonder people like to travel with this old fart. He's the candy man."

"Keep talkin' " says Junior, settling back in his seat. "I love the *way* you talk. Total spiritual mind. Good, honest poetry. You're no bullshit, Lily. And believe me, I've heard it all. I've seen it come and go, and it almost all goes, save the truth. I cannot tell you how much I admire you. I see you as the sign the big change is near. I'm glad I hung around to meet you. It was worth it. Definitely worth it."

"The change?" I ask, feeling euphoric.

"The acceleration of enlightenment," says Junior, clearing his throat. "We're *in* it right now, but we ain't seen nothing yet. That's a hundred and seven years talking."

We drift up the Willamette Valley. We grow dizzy looking at the soggy richness of the planet.

"Humans love beer," says John, speaking for the first time on the voyage.

Lily and I brace ourselves for an extended blab.

"Do tell, Johnny," says Junior, smiling proudly. He says to me, "I taught the lad some tricks. Gave him my reading list, but he went berserk on the philosophers. Mighty lonely sometimes, huh, Johnny?"

John points at Lily and says, "She knows what she's doing, Junior. This is no accident her being here. Everybody thinks we invited her because of her songs and Rain and Juneau, but the fact is, *she* planned this whole thing."

"Of course," says Junior, conducting an imaginary orchestra, "that's the way you do it. You can blame your father and mother and this and that. That works for getting started, but then what? Blame is irrelevant once you know who you are. And then it's a stumbling block. And then it's a brick wall!

Awake! Wake up, Johnny! Enlightenment isn't some royal flush of magical rainbow horseshit! Enlightenment is *knowing* you're God, along with everybody else! Indivisible, with liberty and justice for all! Got that?"

"You knew," says John, scowling. "You knew and didn't tell me."

"Of course I told you," says Junior. "But your ear was the wrong shape. The first Dominic predicted it. I was there when he said she would come."

"Hey," says Lily, putting her foot down forcefully, "you just said *everybody* was it. So don't go putting it all on me, or I'm gonna start kickin' some butts. You got that?"

"Got it," says Junior, his eyes sparkling. "Tell me how it is, Lily. Tell me how it will be."

"I'm a musician and a singer," she says carefully. "Charlie is my man and we love each other more than anything. And we love Noah more than we love ourselves. Johnny likes my music and he thinks I know what I'm doing, or something. And you're a rich old fart with tons and tons of knowledge. And we're going up to see Raz. Okay?"

"Okay," says Junior, pushing a button on the wall. "I was planning a side trip, but that's not for now. Let's just get you there."

46

We see the geodesic dome from many miles away. It's bigger than anything man-made I've ever seen or heard of. A flock of aircraft come out to meet us. Military jets, private planes, helicopters, gunships, hovercraft. Junior opens a communication channel. We're asked to identify ourselves verbally. We each recite the line, "Around the rugged rock, the ragged rascal ran." A moment later, we're cleared for landing.

"What exactly does he have *under* there?" I ask, awestruck at the grandeur of the dome.

"A palace," says John, nodding slowly. "And a stage."

"And a big lake, and five thousand acres of organic gardens," says Junior. "Not to mention the facilities for his countless lackeys and servants."

"It sure is *big,*" says Lily, as the dome looms closer. "Looks like a whole planet, craters and everything."

"For what it's worth," says Junior, sighing. "I prefer the free floating life myself."

"Still, it's nice to have places to land," says Lily, nodding. "If you know what I mean."

"Must be priceless," I say, shaking my head in disbelief at the *scale* of the thing. Our big dirigible is a dot next to it.

"It pays for itself," says Junior. "Produces all the energy it uses, exports the surplus, controls its own internal environment. It makes sense, but it may not be here for long."

"Are you trying to tell us something?" asks Lily, frowning at Junior. "Because if you are, I'd prefer the direct method. I never have been much good at deeper meanings and stuff like that."

"Don't underrate yourself," says Junior, shaking his finger at Lily. "Don't ever do that. It's the worst thing you can do, believe me. What I'm trying to say is . . . that domed city is a good idea. But a good idea isn't worth shit without the power to make it happen."

"There *is* something he's trying to tell us, Charlie," says Lily, sighing and shaking her head. "But I still don't get it. I *see* the dome. There it is. So what are you trying to say, Junie? You mind if I call you Junie?"

"No," he says, nodding. "I like that. How 'bout I call you Lil?"

"It's a deal," says Lily, winking at me. "Is that okay, Charlie?"

"She knows what she's doing," says John, shaking his head, "but . . ."

"If you don't know, I can't tell you," says Junior, smiling sadly at Lily. "I'd like to, but I can't."

"Wait a minute," I say, "this is getting a little thick. Can you give us any hints?'

"Only this," says Junior, staring grimly at me. "Try to imagine the world before money."

"That was before my time," says Lily. "Sorry."

"True," says Junior, coughing. "But . . . true."

We're given a large suite of rooms. They open onto a stylized garden of white pebbles and bonzai pines. Stepping stones traverse the expanse of white, leading to an azure pool full of red koi. The sky above us is an amplified blue. There are billowy white clouds inside the dome with us. It will rain, Junior tells us, during the night. Condensation. They open the dome on delightful spring days and for several hours each morning during summer. They keep it closed throughout the cold winter months. The massive shell catches sun and wind and sound, transforming them into power for Raz, making it southern California inside.

John goes off to find the stage. No one has said we're performing, but we can feel it in the air. Thick and tangible. It's the last thing I want to do. I want to go back to the valley, break out my tools, and build a simple place by the river. We're worn out. The sun is setting. Our clouds are turning gray. We lie down on the bed and hold each other.

"Wonder what Noah's doing right now," Lily muses, resting her head on my chest.

"Eating," I say. "Or screaming. Or pooping. Or laughing."

"He's got a great laugh," she says, trying not to cry.

"He's the greatest thing," I say. "Right after you."

"*You're* the greatest thing," she says, kissing me.

"No you . . ." I start to say, but someone knocks on the door.

We sit up. Junior enters. He's carrying a stack of boxes. He bows slightly and says, "Raz would like to see you two as soon as possible. He would very much appreciate it if you'd wear these clothes. The ones in these boxes."

"What if we don't like them?" asks Lily, yawning.

"Please like them," he says, closing his eyes. "Please?"

An hour later, we're following Junior through the deserted halls of the palace. Lily's wearing a body-hugging black dress with a neckline that swoops down to the sweet round tops of her breasts. She's wearing lacy black stockings and bitchy black heels. She's got a diamond necklace, she's got diamond earrings, she's got diamond bracelets. *Big* diamonds. Her face is radiant. She looks like the most beautiful twenty-something-year-old God ever made. I'm wearing shiny black cowboy boots, tight black jeans, and a long-sleeved shirt. Lily likes it unbuttoned to half-way down my chest. She says she wouldn't have it any other way.

"Where are we going, Junior?" I ask. We're on a moving walkway, sliding down a long hall of mirrors.

"If you don't know . . ." he says, his voice trailing off.

"Charlie," says Lily, pressing close to me, "I think we're gonna make a deal. I can feel it coming."

"Maybe," I say, my heart pounding, "but remember, *we've* got the ultimate leverage."

"What's that?" asks Lily, giving me a frowning smile. "I forgot."

"We can die," I whisper.

"Oh, yeah," she says, looking away. "That."

We're nearly to the end of the hall when the walkway slows, then stops. "I must leave you here," says Junior, his voice trembling. "Go through that door there. The big red one. And remember, don't underrate yourselves, whatever you do."

Lily kisses him. I shake his hand. We step off the walk. It reverses itself. Junior slides away from us, waving slowly. I take Lily's hand and give it a squeeze. Something big is about to happen. I'm sure of it.

"Charlie," she says, stopping a few feet from the door. "Are you gonna let me handle this?"

"What do you mean?" I ask, tensing.

"Well," she says, looking down. "I mean . . ."

"You mean you want me to keep my mouth shut?" I say, flushing with anger.

"I want you to trust me," she says, resting her head against my chest. "I know what we want. I do. Believe me."

"Okay," I say, my eyes burning. "I will, but if you . . ."

She kisses me. We stay in the kiss, giving ourselves to each other. We open the door. We're backstage. People are running all over the place, getting ready for a show. We can hear John shouting at somebody. We can hear a big, restless crowd out front. Raz comes around the corner, talking a mile a minute into a walkie-talkie.

He's startled to see us, but relieved. "Well!" he barks. "It's about time! You look great! Just great. Why no lipstick, Lily? And what about the hats? Didn't Junior tell you, that . . . oh, never mind. You look just great. How about I have a makeup man touch you up a bit? As you can see, you're going to be performing." He glances at the little computer on his wrist. "Any minute here."

"What's going on, Raz?" says Lily, her eyes narrowing.

"*You* are," he says, laughing nervously. "The crowd is *very* ready. Your man has everything set up. You just walk on and . . ."

"No," says Lily, lowering her voice. "What I mean is,

what's going on that you didn't tell us about this? This feels like some sort of setup and I don't like it."

"It's no big deal," says Raz, trying to seem unconcerned. "I invited a few friends, a few very influential people. They can help us. Your man has everything ready. It'll be a breeze."

"*Is* he my man?" asks Lily, suspiciously. "Or is he one of yours?"

"John?" he snorts. "Mine? He'd never work for me *directly*. He's a philosopher. And I got that other one here for you, the hippy kid. From the redwoods. I figure let him do the leads, put Charlie on drums."

"I'm not great," I say, wanting very much to hit the guy.

"You're fine," says Lily, looking around. "Hoover's here? Hey, this could be fun. Who's our opening act?"

"Nobody," snaps Raz, his jaw shaking with anger. "You're it. This isn't some sort of fun show. This is a big thing, Lily. They'll be expecting you to . . ."

"We'll do whatever we want," she says, cutting him off. "Remember, Raz? If we want to go out there and tell jokes, we will. And if we decide to let Charlie do all the singing, then that's what we'll do."

A disbelieving smile creeps over Raz's face. She has him by the balls. He set some sort of trap for us, but he caught himself, too. He laughs awkwardly. He coughs. He looks at his computer. He chews on his bottom lip. He coughs again.

"You want to level with us, Raz?" asks Lily, looking away, tired of watching his discomfort.

"Look," he says, bowing his head, "just be good. If Charlie sings, it better be the best singing God ever heard. And if you tell jokes, I sincerely hope that they're the funniest jokes that have ever been told. Because if they're not . . ."

"This keeps getting more important-sounding all the time," says Lily, wrinkling her brow. "I can't remember how much we're getting for this. Can you, Charlie?"

"It's more than important," says Raz, his hands beginning to shake. "It's absolutely crucial."

"How crucial is it, Raz?" says Lily, almost sneering at him.

"We'll discuss it later," he says, breathing hard, giving her a pained look.

The crowd starts making angry noises.

Raz looks around, terrified. "You'd better get out there, Lily," he says, reaching out to her. "These are not people who like to wait."

"We're in no hurry," says Lily, smiling a big phony smile. "Are we, Charlie?"

"Not really," I say, though I can tell that the old man is about to explode.

"God damnit, Lily!" he cries, panicking. "Don't you realize what's happening? You do. Don't you? Junior told you, didn't he? You know what this is. Don't you?"

"Junior told me nothing," says Lily, almost whispering. "Why don't you explain it to me? And use little words, please."

"They warned me about you," says Raz, taking a step back. "They said you were . . ."

"Who?" says Lily.

"Okay, okay," he says, shoving his hands in his pockets, glancing around nervously. "The rules have suddenly changed. I'm not used to being in this position. I'm used to being in control. But . . ."

"Make it *very* easy to understand," says Lily. "I'm not stupid. But I figured out a long time ago that if you make people use little words, they have a much harder time lying."

"I've never lied to you," says Raz, lying. He realizes the absurdity of what he's just said, puts a hand over his mouth and looks away. He takes a deep breath, looks Lily in the eye and says, "Okay, I'll make it simple. It's two out in the bottom of the ninth. We're down by three runs. Bases loaded. You're up."

"What game is this?" I ask, the hair on the back of my neck standing up.

"It's the last game of the World Series," he says, closing his eyes. "The *last* game. World Series."

"I don't talk baseball," says Lily, shaking her head slowly.

He looks at her, his eyes bleary, his hands trembling. He seems so old and helpless. He can call himself anything he wants, but nobody seeing him now would call him the King of anything. His jaw begins to tremble. Tiny tears drip from his eyes. "I'm out of power," he whimpers. "Pearl . . . I'm not sure how, but . . . she cut my lines. She . . . she . . . she made some deals with people I thought . . . the people I thought . . . I *knew,* god damnit! She . . . ripped my organization apart to get at you! And now . . ."

"Who's in the audience?" I whisper.

"The way to get *around* her!" he says, reaching out to Lily again, touching her hand. "The way to beat her. The way to get back the power, and then some!" He swallows his tears. "There's more power out there than I've ever had. The most powerful people in Japan are out there. And China! Three from Africa. Two from Brazil. Europe. Australia. If I can cut big enough deals, *global* deals, with these people, we're home free! Pearl won't be able to touch us!" His eyes glaze over and he starts to shout. "Do you realize what I'm saying? They *all* want to deal with me! They heard your tape. They *all* want a piece of the action! The whole *world* wants you! We can do it, Lily. We can get it all back and then some! If you'll just help me. If you'll play this concert and *win!* But if you don't, then Pearl . . . oh, God." He puts a hand over his mouth and turns away.

The color drains out of Lily's face. Her cheek twitches. Her hands start to shake. "But I'm just a singer," she says, weakly. "I don't quite see what I can do for you, Raz. I mean . . ."

"You *don't?*" says Raz, looking at her, terror struck, grimacing horribly and clutching at his chest. "But I thought . . ."

"What?" asks Lily, terrified.

"You *planned* this, didn't you?" he says, the blood draining from his face. He staggers.

"No," says Lily, shaking her head. "I'm just a singer, I . . ."

"Oh, my God!" groans Raz, doubling over. "Oh, my God, what have I done?"

"She's *fucking* with you, Raz," I say, grabbing him and shaking him. "She's playing innocent. Can't you see it? Are you too freaked out to see it?" I turn to Lily and say, "Lighten up, honey. Can't you see he's beat." I push Raz up against the wall and hold him there, saying, "Get it together man. She was just toying with you. She gets like that. We know what we're doing. We thought you were stronger, you know? We were bowled over by your palace. The dome. All your stuff."

"But, Charlie . . ." says Lily, her whole body shaking.

"Enough!" I shout, slapping her hand so it stings.

"Ow! You fucker!" she says, taking a swing at me.

"Okay, okay," says Raz, collecting himself, moving away from the wall. "You don't have to put on a show. Kyle already told me. . ."

"Oh, I get it," says Lily, snarling at him. "Kyle's your front man, huh?"

"Who gives a shit?" screams Raz, his eyes wild. "It's *all* on the line here. And *you* have the power. I don't know how you got it, but you did. Pearl says you got it from her, but she doesn't say how. She just wants it back. Hilda says you have it. Kachetti swears you do. I *heard* it in your music! You *have* it! So let's deal! What do you want for it?"

"We want half of everything," I say, smiling slightly. "That was Kyle's opening bid."

"No," he says, shaking his head. "Definitely no. And if you don't make a deal with me, power or no power, Pearl walks in here and takes everything, including you and your baby and everything. Am I right, Lily? You know what's going on."

"We can die," says Lily, taking my hand and staring steadily at Raz.

"That's right," he says, calming down. "That's right. And it would be such a shame to lose such a voice, a gift from . . ."

"Don't say it," says Lily, steel in her voice. "Don't get sentimental on me, Raz. It doesn't suit you."

The crowd starts to boo. We can feel their anger. Fear. Frustration. They've been waiting far too long.

"Okay," says Lily, nodding to me. "Here's what we want. To live in peace and comfort in the Dominic's valley, me and Charlie and Noah and our friends, until the end of our natural lives. We want Pearl . . . gone. And we want to give at *least* as much to the rest of the world as we give to you."

"It's a deal," says Raz, pounding his fist into the palm of his hand. "If, and only if, you blow this audience out of their seats. There are a thousand people out there, but only a dozen of them have the power we need. Do you understand? If you don't convince them, we have nothing to trade. Nothing. And then we'll die. And it won't be our choice anymore. It will just happen."

"Then you better wish us luck," says Lily, somehow managing to wink at him.

"No," he says, taking a deep breath, standing as tall as he can. "Not luck. We know it isn't that. It's power. So be better than great. Be better than you've ever dreamed you could be. Be everything. Please."

47

A big concert stage, the lights burning down on us, a very ready crowd, the best show in town. We walk out and the power washes over us, the power of expectation, the power of what might be, of what *we* might be. All we have to do is make it happen. They've got the light just right, the sound just so, all we gotta do now is blow, baby, blow!

I go to the drums and pick up my sticks. I know what to do. I'm just waiting on my cue. Lily looks at me, smiles and shouts, "One! Two! Three! Four!" I hit the skins and the crowd starts to roar!

Hoover plays a lead that just can't be! It's too fast, too clear, too strong! John floods the background with lush undertones, and Lily strokes a rhythm and starts her song. As her voice rolls over those people, they fall silent in their seats, I switch to brushes and I swear you can hear their hearts beating, a thousand of them, thumping in their chests. They can't believe their ears, so they listen to their hearts, and when she finishes the first *verse* they are on their feet cheering! This woman can *sing*!

Now she crushes them with her sorrow. She cries out a blues that is too full of sadness for anyone to stand, so they all sit down and wallow in their lost loves, their missed chances, their shattered dreams. But she doesn't leave them there, not Lily. No, she winks at me and I kick up the pace, and we rock into a dance tune and shake up the place. Hoover knocks out a sweet happy lead on top of Lily's voice, and Johnny stings the keyboard with a choice bunch of sounds that resound and boom and echo in the dome, so nobody in that amazing place ever, *ever* wants to go home!

And now there comes a silence louder than any explosion! Lily walks to the grand piano, her heels clicking on the stage. The people sit down and settle themselves. They can feel it coming, they can feel something more than they expected, more than they dreamed, but they don't know what she's going to do, and she knows they don't, so she milks it. She takes her time sitting down. She can be *so* sexy making me wait.

She plays alone. She doesn't sing. This is not a song with words. This is not a song I know. It sounds like Bach, and it sounds like Basie, it sounds like nothing, and it sounds like everything. It sounds so deep and rich and complex and simple, there is nothing really to call it, except music, beautiful music. She saturates the air with harmonies, playing a slender line of notes that dodges around among the keys, resolving itself in E or G.

Now she shifts it to a song, leans back her head, closes her eyes, and gives her man, that's me, a big surprise. But that's not really the word for it, no. It's not a surprise, it's the loveliest of gifts. She's put music to that song I wrote for her, that song I kinda spoke and sang for her that day on the Big Sur coast, when we were resting our ears from the howling Volkswagon, when I wanted to tell her I loved her. But she's made it so pretty and so full, I don't recognize it at first. It's so tender and sweet and strong, I don't realize it's my song until she's halfway through the second verse. Her voice soars as she sings, "I'm jealous of the time that we were not together, I'm jealous of the time we did not have. I'm jealous of every minute, of every hour, of every day, that we were apart. I'm jealous of the time, baby. So jealous. Of the time."

Well, we do a lot more playing, and we bring the house down more times than I can remember. We rock, we roll, we samba, we blues. We reggae, we ramble, we do whatever we want to do, because after that jealous song, they don't give a shit *what* we do. Lily *owns* them now. She *does* tell a joke, I *do* sing a song. John makes his synthesizer sound like a gang of old ladies singing gospel, and Hoover jams along. There's nothing we can't do! And at the end of the show, the people start screaming for Lily alone.

"So she walks to the edge of the stage, a microphone in her hand, and she says, "HEY!"

And the crowd says, "HEY!"

And she says, "How about I sing a song without music? How about I tell you a little bedtime story and then you all can get the hell outta here?"

"YEAH!" says the crowd.

"Well," says Lily, sitting down, dangling her legs over the edge, "here's the thing. We almost didn't make it here, Charlie and me. We almost got killed about two dozen times. But we love each other, so we made it, and that's what *you* gotta do. You gotta find somebody to love, and I don't just mean screw. I mean love. And if you don't have somebody handy, lemme tell you about the hospitals, and the old folks' homes and the day-care centers full of people and children that need your love. And the thing is, if you put it out, it's gonna come back. Just like we're putting out this music, and your love is washing over us in big, beautiful waves. That's what it's all about! It's the only job worth doing! It's the only show in town! So right now," she says, standing up, "let's . . . get . . . DOWN!"

And now we rock! And now we roll! And now we run off, fearing for our lives as those crazy love-hungry people charge the stage!

And twenty minutes later, hiding in our room, we can still hear the chanting booming through the dome. "LIL! EEE! LIL! EEE! LIL! EEE! CHAR! LEE! LILY! LILY! LILY!"

An hour or so later, we follow Junior to a big ballroom where he leaves us alone with Raz. The King is an emperor now, trembling with power, our power, but half of it is his, and half of what Lily did out on that stage would light most major cities for a long, long time. Weird little Dr. Klemmer knows what he's talking about. My Lily is a power source, indeed.

A door opens. Men and women come in. They are all dressed to the nines, or maybe to the tens, one never knows about fashion these days. There are roughly a hundred of them, and they all have their eyes on Lily. They all want to get close to the god. Servants appear with drink and food. Junior waltzes in wearing top hat and tails. We sample shrimp and caviar. We sip champagne. Each person comes and speaks to us. They nod and bow. Whatever we say, they adore. Whatever we do, they admire. Junior guides us, helps us, keeps things moving. This is his art, and we're glad he's here. Raz stands apart from us, chatting, nodding, shaking hands, winking. Power is happening. Power is flowing.

Now suddenly we're alone again, the four of us. Raz, Junior, Lily, and I. Lily writes something on a piece of paper. I read it and nod. Junior reads it. Raz reads it, puts it down on his desk, and is about to sign, when Lily puts her hand on his and says, "In blood, Raz. We sign in blood."

"By God," says Raz, his eyes widening, "you are really something, Lily. I never should have doubted you."

Junior gives Raz a knife. He boldly slashes his hand, cutting the plump flesh below his little finger. He hands the blade to Lily and she does the same. She hands the knife to me. I position the blade, close my eyes, and draw it down. We put our bleeding hands together over the desk. Mine's on the bottom, Lily's is next, then Raz's. Our blood drips down onto the dark wood. We dip a quill into it, and each of us signs. Junior is our witness.

Lily presses her wound against mine and we close our eyes. Raz leaves the room. Junior says he's crying.

The paper says,

> Lily, Charlie, and Noah will live in the valley where the Nanza Falls are, where the Dominic lives, forever or until they die, whichever comes first. And so will any children they might adopt or by some miracle have. They will be free, as free as anybody can ever be, but they will sing their best for Raz. In return, he'll protect them and will never sell them out, never, even after he's dead. We sign with our blood, making this pact eternal.

48

Junior brings his dirigible out of the sky into the Nanza Valley. Hundreds of people are waiting on the meadow to greet us. "Your adoring friends," says Junior, holding us aloft a moment longer.

"Is this absolutely necessary?" asks Lily, wrinkling her nose.

"Good question," he says, nodding. "Often wondered the same thing myself. Might be. Might not be."

We step out of the dirigible into sunlight and polite applause. Dominic Kachetti shouts an embarrassing speech about Joan of Arc. Hilda makes a major ceremony out of handing Noah to Lily. They've dressed him up in a blue kimono. They've curled his hair. They've put little silver slippers on his feet. He looks incredibly cute, but I still resent the costume. They've tried to clean Ken up, too. His shaggy hair has been cut and his baggy clothes have given way to a three-piece suit, which makes him look like the biggest salesman in history. He's red with shame.

"Did you enjoy your brief vacation?" asks R.D., leading us to the lodge.

"Wouldn't call it much of a vacation," says Lily, looking around uneasily at the people following us. "Hey R.D., are they all planning to come to bed with us, or what?"

"They'd like to," says R.D., giving her a sad smile. "But right now they just want to thank you for giving them tons and tons of money."

"Raz is being remarkably generous," says Kachetti, his voice quivering. "Remarkably."

"He can't make us do anything we don't want to," says Lily,

looking at me. "He signed the contract. We're gonna make our recording and get it out to the people. He can't . . ."

"He's not violating the contract," Junior warns her. "He's being generous. That's all. If you could see the *other* contracts he signed last night, you'd understand that this is a pittance."

"You'll be staying in the *pent*house suite," says Hilda, bowing slightly. She is radiant with new wealth.

"Raz had it installed a year ago," says R.D., impressively. "It was built by artisans from China and Italy and Japan. It's all redwood, ebony, alabaster, and jade. I think you'll find it *very* comfortable."

"I don't want to stay there," says Lily, stopping on the veranda.

An uncomfortable silence falls. Dominic Kachetti glances nervously at Hilda. R.D. looks at Junior. Hilda looks at me. Junior sticks out his tongue at Kachetti. R.D. puts his thumbs in his ears, waves his fingers around, and says, "Yada yada." I shrug about thirty times and Noah farts.

"It's *very* nice," says Hilda, forcing a smile. "It's an art *treasure.*"

"I want to stay in a regular room," says Lily, almost whispering.

A hundred people strain to hear her.

"There's an empty one next to mine," says Ken, pawing at the tie around his neck.

"Fine," says Lily, glaring at Hilda. "We'll take it. That way we'll only have to walk ten feet to get to the babysitter's.

"But we thought . . ." says Hilda, genuinely perplexed.

"Listen," says Lily, handing Noah to me. She turns and faces the people following us. "Listen, I appreciate your coming out to meet us, I do. And I'm glad you got that money, I am. Never hurts to pay those bills. But listen, here's the way it is. I'm very, very happy to be here, okay? I love it here. But the thing you've *got* to remember, and I mean this, is that I'm the same as you. The same. Got that? I'm not a genius. I'm not from another planet. I'm a regular person, same as anybody. I've spent twenty years learning how to use my voice. That's all. You can do the same and better. So . . . let's keep this thing going. What I'm gonna do is basically work as hard as I can for as long as I can, making the best music we can. And then I'm gonna give it to the world. But we're still gonna take our turns doing the dishes and I'm gonna teach Charlie how to cook."

"Good for you," says Junior, his eyes shining.

"How do you give things to the world?" someone asks. "I've never known how to do that."

"I don't know," says Lily, her voice quivering, her eyes filling with tears. "I guess you have to figure that out for yourself. I only know that me and Charlie and Noah want to live in a regular room, here at the lodge, because I like a big house full of people."

"Ahhhrgh!" roars Ken, ripping the tie off his neck and flinging it away. Noah laughs and holds out his hands. The giant takes him from me and gives him a kiss.

We go to our room. We get Noah out of his costume and into his clothes. Lily goes down to help make supper. I change into my boots, put Noah on my back, and hike with Ken to the Nanza Falls.

I ask them if we're home free, but the waters don't speak, or I can't hear.

49

Dear Charlie,
Here's a poem for last night.

me
first time rain gone you in me
first time you in me
time you in me
you in me
you n me
you me
youme
youm
you
yu

Lily

50

We make a recording forty-seven minutes long. Twelve tunes. It takes us eleven weeks to make. We ship it to Raz and he rockets it to Japan, and we take a break while they get it ready for release.

Lily gets heavily into cooking and spends a lot of time with Noah. I knock out a wall, so we can have *two* regular rooms, one for her and one for me. Feels good to be a carpenter again. Feels good to hit some nails.

It's almost Christmas. We've had some snow. Noah is standing at the window, staring down at his feet, a frown of concentration on his little face. I think he's finally made the connection between his legs and what he's been trying to do for the past three months. Walking has only been an *idea* for him up until now. But here he is about to take that fateful step that will end his infancy forever. He's balancing himself with one hand on the window sill, preparing for a launch.

Lily is sitting across the room from him, her feet up on the coffee table, her nose buried in a fashion magazine. She's mad at me because I left my dirty clothes around for too long. I'm lying in my underwear, flattening my back, hoping for one of those miraculous pops that makes everything okay again. Somebody knocks on the door. The sound startles Noah. He breaks away from the window and rambles across the room like a groggy halfback. He topples forward off the rug, goes down on his knees, and falls hard on his face. He howls!

Lily scoops him up and tries to soothe him and praise him at the same time, while I put on my bathrobe and open the door. It's R.D. He's extremely agitated. "You've gotta come with me *right* now," he says, breathlessly. "Junior is about to die."

"What?" says Lily, bouncing Noah. The boy falls silent.

"He's going to leave his body," says R.D., turning away. "Hurry!"

We follow him downstairs. Lily carries Noah. At one end of the lodge there's a huge stone fireplace. In front of it, seated naked and cross-legged on a small oriental carpet, is Junior. He's almost a skeleton. His huge mop of curly white hair seems completely out of proportion to his body. Gathered around him are about fifty people. Junior's taking questions from the audience, but seems eager to be going.

"How do you know?" a young woman asked. "How do you know it's death?"

"Very distinct feeling," says Junior, winking at her. "Very. Very much a sure thing. You couldn't *not* know it. Profound tingling sensation, spirit disengaging from flesh. Fabulous! Once you get used to it."

"You're really a hundred and *seven?*" asks a little boy.

"One hundred and seven trips around that star," he says, shaking a finger at the ceiling. "I was a psychoanalyst for seventy years. I think I helped three or four people."

"How did you get over your fear of death?" Kachetti asks. "I don't mean the first seven times. I mean the last time."

"Aw, shit, Jack," says Junior, rubbing his nose. "I just did. It just went away completely. It was *such* a relief. It was like becoming weightless. Made the last thirty years a gas!"

"Wisdom!" someone shouts.

"Death is life," says Junior. "We don't like stories that don't resolve themselves clearly, why should we want a life that just poops along? Death is a good way to go. Which is not to say I believe that death is an end. It's an ending, and I hope you know the difference. I've had a good run."

"Is there life after death?" someone asks.

"Tell me when I'm gone," he says, laughing. "If you're still here, yes."

He closes his eyes and takes a deep breath.

"Wait!" says Ken, sobbing.

Junior opens his eyes.

"Can you . . . can you see any of the future?" asks Ken, swallowing his tears.

"Yes," he says, nodding slowly. "That is, I can see up to the next fork in the river. It's a rough ride ahead, but you can make it, and then the river turns and splits. One branch leads to a calm steady stretch of water. The other leads to a deep . . ."

"Do they join up later?" asks the same little boy.

"Always," says Junior, smiling. "That's the ocean, and that's the rain. It's us weirdos in the canoes I'm worried about, but in truth, I'm not worried anymore."

Dominic Kachetti rises from his chair and says, "Good-bye, Junie. As Dominic of this mob, I wish you a good journey. I wish you pleasant dreams and a happy return if we might hope for that."

"Thank you," says Junior, nodding.

The frail old man closes his eyes, takes a deep breath, and exhales for what seems like several minutes. He dies. His old body topples lightly onto its side. He's gone.

We stand here for several minutes, none of us speaking, none of us moving. We're transfixed by the miracle. Ken is sobbing so hard, the room shakes with the vibrations of his sorrow. Suddenly the giant looks up and bellows, "The boy! Where's the boy! The boy!"

I look around frantically. I remember Lily handing him to me, then I handed him to Ken, and Ken gave him to Dominic Kachetti. And then the Dominic gave him to Hilda, and, "I," Hilda says, her voice quivering, "must have given him to Kyle. I didn't look. I was crying and I felt someone take him, and . . ."

We run across the meadow toward Eagle's Nest, but stop dead in our tracks! A coal black jet leaps from the runway into the sky and roars out of the valley, heading south at supersonic speed!

51

Ken runs after the jet, though it's a dot on the sky now. He falls to his knees on the runway and pounds the ground with his fists. Andrew runs after him. Everyone else freezes.

"Get Raz," I say to R.D. "Now."

Lily looks at me as if she's slightly surprised I'm taking charge, but she says nothing.

"Hilda," I say, "stand by to talk to him if necessary. We'll take the call in our room."

I hustle Lily back to the lodge. Hilda and Kachetti and R.D. come with us. A moment later the call comes through. Raz's voice, gruff and angry, barks out at me. "What the hell's going on?"

"The hell," I say, trying to stay calm, "is that Kyle Dobbs has taken Noah and gone south in a fast black jet. To Pearl's. We insist that you do something about it now!"

"I have the disc," he says. "The record. The tape. It is an amazing accomplishment. It will sell billions of copies!"

"Did you hear me?" I scream. "They have taken Noah!"

"Now listen . . ." he says.

"*You* listen, blood buddy," says Lily, grabbing the phone from me and snarling into it, "I don't give a shit about any fuckin' disc, album, video, horseshit! You hear me? I don't care about anything but getting my boy back safe and sound, *now!* If anything happens to him, you've trashed everything, and I won't sleep until you're dead. *You* have the power, Raz. For exactly one revolution of this planet, and then you'll be wishing you *were* dead. End of conversation."

A moment later, John bursts into the room. "You gotta come

quick!" he cries. "Ken's up at Eagle's Nest! He's threatening to jump. I've done some hang gliding off that thing and it's a *long* way down."

We all rush out of the room, charge down the stairs, cross the meadow and run up the mountainside. When we arrive, Ken is sitting on the very edge, Andrew beside him. Lily motions for us to stay where we are. She walks out to them, touches Andrew on the shoulder and says, "Move over, fellas." She sits down and lets her legs dangle over the edge with theirs. I tiptoe up behind them and squat down to listen, ready to make a grab for her if *any*body starts to fall.

"Listen guys, I know you're bummed out," she says, her voice gruff, "but if you kill yourselves, or even if only one of you does, I'm gonna be so pissed off, and I'll tell you why."

"I betrayed him," says Ken, burying his face in his gigantic hands. "I promised him I'd keep him safe as long as I lived."

"You can't promise things like that," says Lily. "You're not God, Ken. Besides, you have to trust that boy, you know. He's young, but he's no dummy. He'll be back tomorrow."

"I let him down," says Ken. "He trusted me. How's he ever gonna be able to trust me again?"

"Noah's not a guilt-tripper," says Lily, shaking her head. "He's a baby. He loves you. He knows you'd never intentionally hurt him. Don't be so ego-whatsit. And besides, he's *my* kid. Where do you get off dying over him if I don't? Quit doing my job, man."

"Some of us aren't so highly evolved, Lily," says Andrew, his voice cracking. "Me, for instance. I'm tired of all the good people I know dying. My lover, my best friend, Rain. My analyst, Junior. My mentor, Juneau. Countless others. Ken, perhaps, who showed me the falls. Lily, I'm so tired of being alone. I am so weak from seeing the babies stolen from their mothers. Why should *I* not die?"

"I had abortions," says Lily, her voice shaking. "Because I didn't want to bring babies into scum. And I gave away a baby I had, because I was unfit to be a mother. And I punished myself for it with drugs and worse for the rest of my life. I sold myself to Pearl because I hated myself so much. But god damnit, Andrew, you know better than anybody, no matter how far down you get, you gotta get up! You can't let the worst failure, the worst pain keep you from trying! Because this is the only chance you get as *you!* I'm not saying we don't come back, I'm saying we don't come back our*selves.* This is the only time you'll ever get to be *exactly* you. So kill yourself if you wanta, but remember you might have found the greatest love! You might have seen the greatest thing! You might have written the greatest song! You might have helped somebody who *really* needed your help, so that it changed her life, and let her come up here, and be with these people, and make a record of her singing. That's what you did for me, Andrew. That's what you both do by not killing yourselves."

She pushes herself back from the edge, gets slowly to her feet, and sings a song. Her voice echoes across the valley and bounces off the trees. It circles around us, picking up power, and chases after Noah, a guardian ray, flowing southward.

And when the moonlight shines
Down upon your baby face
I will sing this song to guide you
All your life
And when the moonlight shines
Down upon your lovely face
I will sing this song to guard you
Through the night.

52

"There is nothing I can do," says Lily, holding on to me. "I feel so sick. I feel so empty. I feel burned out inside. I feel gutted. God! It hurts!"

"It's gonna be okay, Lily," I say, trying as hard as I can to believe it.

"But what can I do?" she asks, her eyes wide with terror. "I don't want to hurt like this anymore, Charlie. I think I'm gonna die. I really do. I can feel my insides breaking, Charlie. I'm breaking! This is too much, too much, this is too much! Hold me, Charlie! Hold me! God! God! How can it hurt like this? It's like knives! It's like there's knives in my stomach and in my chest! I can't breathe! Oh, God, I'm gonna throw up again!"

I get her into the bathroom, but she doesn't throw up. Instead, she turns to me, wild-eyed, and says, "Let's laugh, Charlie. Let's laugh. Wanta try to laugh? Please? I can't cry anymore. I can't throw up anymore. I'm empty. My body is dead. Hold me? Hold me? If you don't hold me, I'll die. I don't have any strength left, Charlie. Hold me."

I help her back to the bed and she lies down on her back, staring up at the ceiling. We can hear Ken moving around in his room. I had him come in and tell Lily he wasn't going to kill himself, but that didn't help much. She was already too far gone.

She starts to gasp for breath. Now she relaxes a little and says, "It's a joke, right? This is a joke. This is some sort of stupid thing they've figured out. Hilda set this up, that bitch. She says she didn't see Kyle take him, but she *gave* Noah to him!

Oh, Charlie! Ken said she was okay. He said she was generous! She's so generous she gave *my* baby to that monster! For what? What weren't they getting? What don't they have? How can they want more than paradise? How can they do this to a little baby? How can they, Charlie? Hold me, please? It's starting again. It's starting to twist in me! Maybe if I get in the tub. Make it really hot? What do you think? Oh, Charlie! God! God, I can't take this again!"

I run her a hot bath, but she won't get up from the bed. She looks at me and cries out, "How can we go on, Charlie? Charlie? How? Can't you do something to *help* me?"

"Lily," I say, putting my arms around her, but she pushes me away.

"Shit!" she screams, her body shaking violently. "Shit! Shit on everything! That's what they do! They just get what *they* want and then they shit on everything else!"

I put my arms around her again and hold her as she sobs.

"Oh Charlie Charlie Charlie Charlie if Charlie if Charlie if he doesn't come back God Charlie I'll die! I'll die! I'll die! I'll die! Oh God! Oh God! Oh God! I can't *take* this! It's too much, *too* much! TOO MUCH PAIN!! Please! No more! No more no more no more no more."

She struggles to get away from me. She claws at the air. She sinks her teeth into my arm. She scratches my chest. She's drooling. She's out of her mind with grief.

"I can see him in her, in her, in her *hands,* Charlie," she says, trying to twist away from me. "I can see her taking, taking, taking him into that that that nursery she built for him, all the toys . . . and stuff . . . and and and shit! Shit! Charlie! Hold me!"

I hold her with all my strength, but I'm afraid it won't be enough.

"But Noah looks at her," says Lily, her words turning sing song, "and he says no no no no no no no no no no no until Pearl goes *insane!* He's no dummy, not my boy, not Noah, you named him saying no no no no no no no no until she gives him to some old lady." Lily nods frantically and whispers urgently, "She would hire a sweet old lady, some sweet old lady so he'll be okay for the night. I know Pearl, that's what she'd do, hire some some some . . ."

"He'll be okay," I say, holding onto her. She calms down and leans limply against me.

"I go to him every way I can, Charlie," she says, sighing heavily. "I go to him in my mind. I fly down there and I hold him until morning and then I bring him back here. But it's not real. I can't really do anything. There's nothing I can do." She explodes again, screaming, "PEARL TOOK MY BABY!!"

I wrestle her down on the bed and pin her under me. She looks me right in the eye and says in a perfectly normal voice, "Are you God? High priority clearance requested. Around the rugged rock the ragged rascal ran. Please? Please save my son? Save him? Save Noah? Don't kill him. Don't hurt him. Do *not* let her have him. Kill me, but save my son. He's my flower. He's my gift to you, not to her. Not to that evil person. Please God? Don't let him die. Not yet. That would be such a waste. He needs to live a long life like Junior. That was good what you did with Junior. That's what I want for my Noah. And a wife. He should have a good wife, because he'll make a terrific husband, I really think he will. I'm not just saying that because I'm his mother. He has a very charming personality. So you'll have to give her a long life, too. And they should have a decent place to live. You know? Good water, clean air, quiet. He likes it quiet. Quiet."

She blanks out. The light starts to fade from her eyes. I shake her and she whispers, "I'll die for him. I'll die for him. Charlie? You be the witness. I'm cutting a deal with God. I'm handling this. I'm cutting this deal myself. I'll die for Noah, in his place."

"No," I say, looking down at her. "You don't need to do that, Lily. He's gonna be okay. I promise."

"Hold me, Charlie. If you don't hold me, I'll disappear," she says, wrapping her arms around me. "I'll just be nothing.

Tighter? Tighter! Hold me tight! Are you holding me? Please? God? Please? Bring back my son. Let me see my son. Then I'll die for him."

I get her sitting up on the edge of the bed. She stares at the floor for several minutes. She gives me a startled look and says, "Charlie? You love him as much as I do, don't you? You love him as much as I do and I haven't let you cry. I haven't let you. I'm sorry. You go on and be crazy now, and I'll hold you. Go on. I've done enough of this shit. It's almost the next day, isn't it? He'll be here soon. He doesn't want all that shit she's got. Kids don't need that shit, they just need a little room to run and lots of love. I can just hear him, can't you? Saying no no no no no no no like he does. He'll drive her crazy and she'll be *happy* to give him back."

"You're right," I say, wiping her face with a towel. "She'll give him back because he'll scream at her until she does."

"She's so sad, Charlie," says Lily, the tears rolling down her cheeks. "She is the saddest, loneliest person. Her whole life has been like this night. This horrible night."

"Oh, man," I say, shaking my head.

"You think it'll ever be day again?" Lily asks, putting her hand on my shoulder. "You think this big ball of shit will ever get all the way around again so we can see what the hell we're doing?"

"Yes," I say, kissing her cheek. "It always has."

"Let's go for a walk, Charlie," she says, smiling weakly at me. "Let's walk down to the river."

"If you want to," I say, helping her to her feet.

"Oh, God, Charlie," she says, shaking her head and closing her eyes. "I'm gonna throw up."

I kneel beside her at the toilet, keeping a hand on her back as she wretches. After a long time, she turns to me and says, "How can I keep doing this? There's nothing in me. I have nothing left. I must just stink. How can you hold me? How can you stand me? I'm horrible. Don't! Don't! I won't let you!"

"Lily," I say suddenly, shocking her into silence. "I love you.

I don't care if you stink. It doesn't matter. You can puke all over me if you want. I'll still want to touch you."

"Yeah," she says, making a face, "but I won't want to touch you."

"So, you have slightly higher standards," I say, shrugging. "You done throwing up for a while? Shall we have a bath?"

"Will you wash me?" she asks, sounding like a little girl. "Will you wash me and then hold me all night long? Until the morning? Until the morning when Noah comes home? Will you?"

"Yes," I say, helping her stand up.

"And will you promise me that Noah will come home? Will you promise?" she asks, holding my hands and staring into my eyes.

"I promise," I say, nodding. "He'll be home."

53

Morning finally comes, and it's a brilliantly clear day. R.D. comes to get us. We follow him across the bridge to the airstrip. Dominic Kachetti, Hilda and Andrew are already here. A white jet slants out of the sky and drops silently onto the runway. I can see Raz's face under the canopy of glass that extends over the long narrow cockpit. He turns to look at us, but his face is expressionless.

A door opens midway along the fuselage. A stairway unfolds itself to the ground. Raz emerges, all in white, save for a black belt and holster in which he carries a revolver. He approaches us quickly, scowls and says, "The boy's on board. With Pearl. She wants to negotiate his release. She wants to do it directly with you, Lily. I tried to avoid this, but she has the kid, and she'll kill him if she has to."

Lily staggers. I catch her in my arms. She lets me hold her for a while. Now she rouses herself and moves away from me, her face calm and determined.

I want to strangle Raz. I want to smash Hilda's face in. I want to charge the jet and murder this Pearl monster, but all I can do is stand here and tremble with rage at the insanity of it all. I try to clear my mind of violent thoughts. I want to give all my strength to Lily, but the anger floods through me and I hear that murderous hum beginning again, filling my brain.

Lily and Raz and I approach the jet. Kachetti, Hilda, R.D., and Andrew walk a few feet behind us. Raz makes a megaphone with his hands and shouts, "Show them the boy, please."

A woman steps into the doorway, Noah in her arms. He stares groggily at us and I can see he's been drugged. I feel sick to my stomach. The woman hands him to someone inside the jet. She comes down the stairs. She's tall and broad-shouldered. She's wearing a gold sequin jumpsuit unzipped down to the tops of her large breasts. She has long fiery red hair, and a fiercely beautiful face. Her eyes are coal black. Her eyelids are painted silver, her cheeks are daubed with blood red rouge. She's wearing black spike heels and her fingers are covered with diamonds. She is easily the most horrifyingly gorgeous woman I have ever seen.

Her voice is deep and husky. She folds her long arms under her breasts and says, "Hello, Lily." She devours me with her fierce eyes and says, "So, this is Charlie. I'm surprised. I expected someone bigger, someone better looking, someone with more character. I just analyzed his puny little ass and he's mostly water."

Lily stares grimly into Pearl's eyes and says, "Name the deal. Quit fuckin' around. I want my boy."

"Can't we visit?" asks Pearl, batting her eyelashes. She seems larger than life. There's something overwhelmingly powerful about her. She glances around the valley and says, "Somehow I knew I'd come back here someday. It's so beautiful, isn't it? But it isn't real. You'll go insane here inside of six months."

"The deal," says Lily, closing her eyes.

"In a moment," says Pearl, running her fingers through her brilliant red hair. She looks over our heads and waves. "Hello, Papa," she purrs. "You look terrible."

Lily and I turn around to see who she's talking to. Dominic Kachetti bows his head. I can't believe it. Pearl has been everywhere we go.

"He didn't tell you?" says Pearl, pretending to pout. "I'm disappointed, Daddy. It used to be your favorite story. About the bad little girl who kept playing with the giant, even when the Dominic said not to. You didn't *tell* them? Why not?"

"Hilda is your *mother?*" asks Lily, her eyes wide with terror.

"No," says Hilda, sneering at Pearl. She puts her arm

around her husband's waist and holds him upright, her face a mask of indignation. "She's from his *first* marriage. If she'd been *my* daughter . . ."

"I would have thought God was a munchkin," says Pearl, sneering, "and I would have spread my legs for all your clean little artist friends instead of poor old Ken. Where is he anyway? Sold him to a zoo or something?"

"No," says R.D., shaking his head. "I locked him in the bunker so you wouldn't kill him when he attacked the jet to save Noah."

"How thoughtful of you," says Pearl, her eyes burning with hatred.

"Why can't you just leave us alone?" cries Kachetti, clenching his fists. "What gives you the right to go around hurting innocent people?"

"Innocent?" says Pearl, smiling sardonically at Lily. "Have you made *me* the villain, Lil? Please, dear, I didn't start this. I got into this game a long time after the rules were set up."

Pearl's eyes meet mine and I shudder at the murder I see in them. I see no remorse, no doubt. She could kill us all and have sex five minutes later. I can *feel* the violence of her thoughts, I can *see* the scenarios of slaughter playing over and over again in her mind.

"It's you," says Andrew, moving past us, stopping a few feet from Pearl. He seems so small next to her, small and fragile. "I didn't recognize you at first," he says, a dazed smile on his face. "Do you remember me?"

"No," says Pearl, giving him a cursory glance. "Should I?"

"Andrew," he says softly, his smile turning to a frown. "We spent a night together in San Francisco. It was a long time ago. But I'm sure you remember. Of course, I didn't even *know* these people then, so I had no idea that you were Ken's lover, that you came from here originally. And I never really described you to anyone here, so they never thought that . . ."

"No," she says dryly, cutting him off. "You're mistaken. I don't know you."

"I'm not mistaken," says Andrew, reaching out and touching her wrist.

She sneers down at his hand and bares her teeth. "Please don't touch me," she growls. "I might have to kill you."

"This is amazing," says Andrew, taking his hand away. "How can this be happening?" He turns to me, incredulous, and says, "Charlie. This is her. The woman I told you about. The woman . . ."

"Who is this *black* man?" asks Pearl, cruelly. "Get rid of him, would you Raz?"

"Come on, Andrew," says Raz, taking him roughly by the arm.

"No!" shouts Andrew, pulling away. "You can't do this to me! It's inhuman! I won't allow it! Kill me if you want to, but at least say that you remember me."

"I fuck *so* many men," says Pearl, snorting. She laughs wearily and says, "All right. If it makes you happy, yes, I remember you. I used the line about wanting you to write my story for me. You were fun, I think. It's all rather vague now. Blends together."

"Was it that I failed to satisfy you?" Andrew asks, bowing his head. "I mean . . . for me it was . . . the best. Just the best. It . . . it . . . changed my life. You wrecked me, Pearl. I've spent *all* these years learning everything *all* over again, and now you're telling me it meant *nothing* to you? How can that be?"

"No, no, it was . . . fine," she says, looking away, annoyed, her face softening slightly.

But I don't want her to soften. I want her to be an inhuman thing, not a woman with feelings. I can't let her be human. I need to hate her to stay strong.

"You were *okay.* All right?" she says, sighing heavily. "Not the worst, but nowhere near the best. Okay? It's all an illusion anyway."

"No," says Andrew, grimacing in pain. "I think that's your error, Pearl. I think that's the mistake in your thinking. Because we *are* real. This is *real.* This is not some existential joke." He turns from her and walks away, taking his place beside R.D.

"Of course," says Pearl, waving away the momentary interruption and glaring at her father. "It makes such perfect sense that he'd end up here. You have this uncanny knack for attracting impotent artists."

"What do you attract?" asks Lily, shaking with rage. Her eyes are slits. Her fists are clenched and trembling.

"I attract little drug addicts," says Pearl, looking into my eyes as she speaks. "Little promiscuous, cocksucking nympho drug addicts, who talk about music and never make it, and talk about helping the world and never do. It's no surprise to me that you took over so fast here, Lily. These are *your* kind of people."

"Okay," says Lily, nodding slowly. "I was all those things, Pearl. I was. But I'm not anymore. I'm making my music now, and I'm trying to raise my boy as well as I can. And I want you *gone* from here. So name the deal."

"Nicely put," says Pearl, viciously. "I always admired your brevity."

"Make it clear," says Raz, his old eyes bleary with rage.

"Don't push me," says Pearl, clenching her fists. "I want those songs, Lily. Those special songs of yours. I want the rights to them forever, and I don't want your voice heard, ever, beyond the confines of this poisonous little valley. For which I will give you Noah. And then as long as you remain silent, I'll leave you alone. Do you understand, Lily? As long as you remain silent, I'll leave you alone. That's a better deal than most people get. Most people get hurt no matter what they do these days."

"You rotten bitch," mutters Raz, his hand moving toward his holster.

"Oh, that's right," says Pearl, running her fingers through her hair again. "You're a saint now, aren't you Raz? I keep forgetting. You use solar power, don't you? You recycle things." She forces a spiteful little laugh. "But you still stab people in the back. That's still your main source of income, isn't it?"

"Listen," says Raz, shaking his head rapidly, "let's just say . . ."

"Did you cut a deal with her?" asks Lily, pointing a shaky finger at him. "Did we sign in blood, or was that just bullshit?"

"You don't understand," he says, glancing nervously at Pearl. "I . . ."

"Okay," says Lily, her lips quivering, the tears dripping from her eyes, "it's a deal! Just give me my boy! Give me my baby! I'll never sing another note! I swear to you! Just give me my baby! Please! Please, Pearl!" She falls on her knees and kisses Pearl's feet and cries, "Have mercy on me, Pearl! I have no more pride! I'm begging you, please give me my baby back! I'll cut my vocal cords! But *give* me my baby!"

"Ah, but that's not the end of it," says Pearl, her voice rich with power, a righteous smile on her face. "I have to get home safely. If I were to simply give you the child, what would stop Raz here from killing me? Nothing. I came here at great risk to myself."

"Name the deal," says Lily, letting me help her up. "I'm not gonna beg anymore, Pearl. Name it."

"A hostage," she says, looking right at me. "Until I'm home safely."

My heart starts to pound. I can feel things closing in. They can talk all they want, but I *knew* it was gonna come down to this. It's either me or Lily or Noah. This is it. This is the moment I've been living for.

"Take me," says Kachetti, stepping forward proudly.

"No," says Pearl, smirking. "You've got martyr written all over your face, Papa. Sorry. You never wanted me, why should I want you?'

"Is that what this is?" asks the old man, shaking his head, "continued retribution because your mother left us? That was nobody's fault! That was just life!"

"You drove her away," snarls Pearl, the waves of hatred pulsing from her body. "Remember? While you whined about artistic freedom, she worked her fucking fingers to the *bone* supporting you! So you could smear paints on canvas and anguish about the hungry and the oppressed! You used her up! You never did a fucking thing to ease *her* pain! Or mine!"

"I did my best," he says, gruffly. "I brought us here, didn't I? We could have had a good life, but she hated me too much already. And I'm sure that if she hadn't hated me, *you* wouldn't have hated me. You would have loved it here. I know you would have."

"Oh, really?" says Pearl, trembling with anger. "I didn't know what hate *was* until you found us at the falls. We were just children! That's all we were! Little children playing with our things, and you beat us! You beat Ken and you beat me! For playing with each other! How could you? How? You're supposedly enlightened, right?"

"I struck you *once!*" cries Kachetti, raising his hands to the sky. "It was a mistake! How many times did I fall on my knees and beg you for forgiveness? A thousand times! The minute I struck you I fell on my knees! Here! I'll do it again!" He falls on his knees in the mud, prostrates himself and sobs, "Please, please forgive me! I'll do anything you say. Anything!"

"And then you bought me off, didn't you?" says Pearl, closing her eyes and swallowing. "You bought me a fancy car and sent me away to school. *Any*thing to keep me away from his big dick."

"It wouldn't have worked," says Hilda, helping her husband to his feet. "Ken isn't . . ."

"Shut up," says Pearl, turning suddenly to Lily. "I want Charlie. He's the only logical choice."

"No," Lily whispers, taking my hand. "You'll just kill him."

"No, she won't," says Raz, putting a hand on his gun. "I'll see to that."

"See to what?" I ask, my body tingling. "You couldn't keep them from getting Noah, how you gonna keep 'em from getting me?" And as I say that, I realize that Raz would love to have me out of the way.

"Don't worry, I cut a very good deal," says Raz, winking at me. "And besides, I'm driving."

"No," says Lily, shaking her head. "No. This stinks. Let her have the boy."

"All the better," says Pearl, laughing at Lily. "Then you can sing your songs and be a big star. And I'll have Noah. Our original deal. Remember? You had him because *I* told you to, *Lily.* You didn't even like his father, did you, *Lily?* It made you sick to do it with him, didn't it, *Lily?* Remember? So why not let me keep the sickening child? Then you can start over fresh with Romeo here."

Lily leaps at Pearl, kicking and biting and clawing at her. But Pearl just keeps on laughing. She punches Lily hard in the forehead, knocking her cold.

"Okay," I say, glancing down at Lily. I can see she'll be up in a minute. This is my only chance. I don't think about it. I just go.

Raz and I walk quickly up the stairs, following Pearl. Kyle appears in the doorway. He has a gun in one hand, Noah in the other. He hands the boy to Pearl, and trains the gun on me. I give Noah a quick kiss, as Pearl hands him down to R.D. I turn and watch him carry my son to my wife. Andrew is kneeling beside Lily, cradling her in his arms. She's just starting to come around.

Now I'm inside the jet. Kyle pushes me into a seat and tells me to buckle myself in. Raz goes up to the cockpit and we start to taxi. I'm sitting in the middle of the cabin, facing forward. Kyle and Pearl sit on either side of me. These are the only seats on the plane. We turn, pick up speed, and lift off. The rockets flare and we're gone.

54

We level off eight miles high. Kyle unbuckles his seatbelt and gets up. His face is gaunt, wolfish. His eyes are bloodshot. His hands are trembling. He smokes some hash and glares out the window. Pearl pushes a button on the arm of her chair and it slides forward on a vacuum rail, turns, and reinserts itself into the floor. Now she's facing me. There's something overwhelmingly warrior-like about her, murderous and single-minded.

"So," I say, my heart pounding. "Uh . . . what's the in-flight movie? Or don't we have time?"

"Not funny," says Pearl coldly. "Try again."

"I don't want to die," I say, but my words feel powerless.

"Yet you came," says Pearl, baring her teeth. "Why shouldn't we kill you? What did you ever do for me?"

"I thought Raz said he'd protect me," I say, knowing that he won't.

"You thought maybe he'd pull a kamikaze on us?" says Kyle, laughing hideously. "Crash the plane? Or come in here shooting? You obviously don't know the man. Blood means nothing to him. He sold me his daughter. He cares so little for you, I can't tell you."

"He said he'd protect me," I say, my words as meaningless as any I've ever spoken.

"Then where is he?" asks Kyle, laughing again. "Listen to what I'm telling you, Charlie. The guy *sold* me his daughter. His *own* daughter. He doesn't die for a piece of shit like you."

"Sit down, Kyle," says Pearl, gesturing to the empty seat.

Kyle lights a cigarette and sits down, turning his chair so it faces me, too. He blows smoke at me and shakes his head in disgust.

"You see," says Pearl, reaching toward me and touching my cheek with a long fingernail, "Raz left you alone with us precisely so that we *would* kill you. He wishes you very dead. He wants Lily all to himself. You see the deal? Lily saw it. *I* get you. *Raz* gets Lily. *She* gets her baby. For now."

"For now," says Kyle, echoing her.

Pearl looks me over from head to toe. She stares into my eyes and says, "I'm gonna kill you, Charlie. But first I'm gonna torture you. Won't that be fun?"

"Can Raz hear us?" I ask, barely able to talk.

"Yes, I can," says Raz, his voice booming over a loudspeaker.

"Turn it down," says Pearl, her eyes burning into mine. "You sound like God."

"This better?" asks Raz, turning down the volume.

"You're at about Moses," I say, trying to make a joke.

"And you're not funny," says Pearl, curling her hand into a fist and punching me in the mouth.

My lips and gums burn with pain! My mouth fills with blood! "Did you deal me, Raz?" I scream at the air!

"It's more complicated than that," says Raz, static in his voice. "You see . . ."

"I'll take that as a yes," I say, licking my bloody lips. Now I say to Pearl, shaking with fear, "Please don't kill me. I don't want to die."

"And yet you came," she says, squinting at me. "*Knowing* you would." She takes my hand in hers, lifts it to her lips, and kisses it. She leans close to me, touching her nose to mine, and whispers, "That's the big mystery, Charlie. Why? This is certain death for you. I don't know whether to puke or applaud. Do you expect me to *admire* you because you're stupid? After all, from a survival point of view, this is incredibly dumb. The little shit isn't even your genetic offspring. He's just some kid from some guy I hired to bang Lily." She sits back and stares at me, her mouth slightly open. She wrinkles her brow and says, "I mean, I said to Raz, and you can ask him, I said, 'Why would a man in good health *volunteer* to die?' And he said he didn't know, but that *you* would."

"How'd you get to know me so well, Raz?" I ask, my voice trembling, my lips aching.

"He knew you the minute he saw you," she sneers, laughing viciously. "You should have seen the way he played you and Lily before your big dome concert. He videotaped it for me. All of it. And you know my favorite part? The way you go for that all-is-lost routine. Now that's funny." She laughs a little, thinking about it. "And then you went out there in front of that audience so triumphant! And you just murdered them, didn't you?" She rears back her head and laughs and laughs, but there's no joy in it. She stops and says, "He fucked you so totally, it's mind boggling. But I still can't figure out one thing. One last little thing."

"What?" I ask, covering my mouth with my hand, feeling my lips puffing out.

"How you survived this long," she says, shaking her head and frowning. "And just what the fuck you think you're doing here."

"Listen," I say, swallowing a mouthful of blood and licking my lips, "could I take a few minutes to think about this? I made the decision sort of spontaneously, in case you're interested."

"I'm not," she says coldly. "But I'll give you a minute. We can spare a minute, can't we Kyle?"

"Barely," he says, leaning close and spitting in my face. He's about to put his cigarette out on my cheek, but Pearl stops him.

"Soon, Kyle," she says, smiling sweetly at him. "Let's give him his minute first."

So I close my eyes and try to calm down enough to think about why I'm in this jet, about to die. Nothing comes to me except that deathly hum. But now, when I'm sure my minute must be up, I see something. It's like a big vivid scene from a movie. I see Noah. He's walking in the valley with Ken. He's about nine years old, and he looks a little like me. I know that's impossible, but he does. I see him laughing and running and diving into the river with Lily. I see him growing beautiful and strong. I see him raising a puppy into a dog. I see him hugging his mother at bedtime. I even hear him sing in that sweet, high voice I know he'll have, and that's enough reason for me. I've had my ride. Noah's just starting. Noah's my boy and I love him. And I love how Lily loves him. "I love them more than I love my own life," I say, opening my eyes.

"Liar!" snarls Kyle, sticking the gun in my face. "You're just stupid, Charlie! Stupid! You made a mistake! Admit it! You got lucky with one shitty song and then you blew it! And now you've blown it again!"

"Put the gun down, Kyle," says Pearl, her voice icy. "And don't pick it up again until I tell you to. Do you understand?"

"Okay," he says, sullenly. He lowers the gun, but keeps it ready in his lap.

Pearl turns to me and asks curtly, "Which song was yours?"

" 'Hey, Baby,' " I say, my whole body shaking.

"*You* wrote 'Hey Baby'?" asks Pearl, her black eyes bugging out of her head. She lurches forward and rakes my face with her sharp nails and screams, "Come on, man! This isn't funny anymore!"

"But I did!" I cry, desperate for her to stop hurting me. "I did! It was a long, long time ago, but it's true. I . . . I wrote it!"

"You didn't *tell* me that," she says to Kyle, furious with him. She looks at me, searching my face for signs of a lie.

"What difference does it make?" says Kyle, laughing nervously, fingering his gun.

"You said he was nothing!" screams Pearl, leaning close to me again, her eyes quivering as she tries to focus on me.

I can smell her sour breath. I can smell her stinking perfume. And I can smell her sweaty body and it sickens me.

"You said he was dirt with a pretty face," whispers Pearl. "Dirt didn't write 'Hey Baby.' "

"He stole it," says Kyle, smirking at me. "Didn't you, Charlie?"

Pearl touches my cheek. Now she puts her bloody fingers in her mouth and tastes me. "Who are you anyway?" she asks, her voice quivering. "How'd you get into my life? I didn't want this. I had this ending a whole different way. I had you toilet waste from the stink dungeon! And now you're telling me you wrote 'Hey Baby'? Lily told you how special that song was to us, didn't she? That was *our* song, you fucker!"

She punches my mouth again and again! She gets out of her chair and stands above me, trembling with rage. I have never felt such horrible pain, such terrible fear. I spit blood and pieces of my teeth, but she doesn't care.

"How dare you pull this shit!" she screams. "How could she *do* this to me?"

I try to curl up into a ball. I cover my head as she showers me with blows!

"Did she tell you we made a tape of it!" screams Pearl. "Did she tell you it was the only song I ever learned to play, and that we made a tape of it and she played lead and did all this other shit so you couldn't hear how bad I was? Did she? Did she tell you how proud I was of it, how I listened to it all the time? You fucker! You stinking piece of shit!" She turns to Kyle and shouts, "Why didn't you tell me about this? Why?"

"He didn't write it," says Kyle, squirming in his seat, looking at his gun. "Lemme kill him for you, Pearl. He stole it. He never wrote anything! He doesn't have an original note in his head. He plays music like a third grader. He couldn't have written it!"

I uncover my face and say, "I produced her record." I can barely speak through my swollen lips. "Have you heard it yet, Pearl?"

"You?" says Pearl, snarling at me. She's turned into a dog-person. Now I know what Lily means. "You?" she says, clawing at me. I put up my hand and she rips the skin. "Kyle said *he* did!"

Kyle raises his gun to shoot. I brace myself, but Pearl grabs the gun from him and slaps his face with the back of her hand.

"That's enough, Kyle!" she says harshly. "I'm running this show." She looks up at the loudspeaker and yells, "Did he, Raz? Did Charlie produce the album?"

"Says so on the liner notes," says Raz, coughing. "Maybe he did. I don't know."

"It's a lie!" screams Kyle, seething with fear. "He ripped me off! Lily wanted me to . . ."

"Shut up," says Pearl, waving him silent. "I don't care about her fucking record. I want to know if this guy wrote 'Hey Baby.' "

"He couldn't have," says Kyle, gripping the arms of his chair. "That's a classic. This guy couldn't write a classic in a million years!"

"Did you?" asks Pearl, turning to me, her face suddenly cool and impassive, her voice barely a whisper.

"Not really," I say, my heart pounding, the hum of death loud in my head.

"What?" she says, moving closer to me, her eyes turning wild. "You lied?"

"It just came to me," I say, swallowing my blood. "But I don't know where it came from."

"I can't even imagine such a thing," says Pearl, deep, deep bitterness in her voice. "I'd give anything to have a song come to me."

"Yeah," I say, nodding. "It didn't happen to me again until I met Lily."

"Were you two gonna get *married?*" asks Pearl, leering at me.

"Are you kidding?" says Kyle, forcing a laugh. "Lily's fucking half the guys in . . ."

I'm out of my chair onto him so fast he's half dead before Pearl can get me off of him. She's unbelievably strong! She picks me up like fluff and throws me across the cabin! I hit the wall and I'm looking out the window at a forty-thousand-foot drop. I move to the center of the room, set myself, and get ready to die.

"Fascinating," says Pearl, training the gun on me, her eyes

wide with a hostile curiosity. "I don't believe you wrote that song. I don't know if I could kill you if I believed that. I probably could, but maybe not. So why don't you sing it for me. And then I'll know if you wrote it or not. I'll be able to tell. And then . . ."

I close my eyes and the hum grows louder. It moves from my head into my throat, and from there it begins to vibrate in my chest, surrounding my heart. I feel dizzy and weak and overwhelmed with pain, and now I know why I'm here. Not to save Noah. Not to save Lily. But to die. Because deep inside I *am* scum. I am.

I open my eyes and look at Pearl. I spit more blood and say, "I killed somebody. I'm a murderer, just like you. And I can't stand it anymore. I thought I could be a hero, but I can't. So let Kyle shoot me, or you do it, but I'm not singing my song for you. Got that? I sold out before, and this is how it feels. So kill me, Pearl. Go on."

"You don't care about Lily?" asks Pearl, taking a step toward me.

"I love her as much as I can," I say, my heart pounding against the hum, "but I'm not worthy of her. I'm a coward next to her."

"Would you sing your song if it would save her life?" asks Pearl, coming closer still, aiming the gun at my heart.

"I would do anything for her!" I cry. "It's myself I can't . . ." I start to sob. My whole body convulses and I double over vomiting, and I keep on crying and crying, but these aren't really tears! It's bile! It's something from so deep in me I didn't even know it was there. I vomit again and feel this horrible twisting pain in my bowels. I open my eyes expecting to see Pearl sticking a knife into me, but she's not. She's just standing there, staring at me, watching my pain. A jagged spasm rocks through my stomach and chest! Another rips me and another rips me and another rips me! I fall to the floor and it feels like she's kicking my ribs in, but she's not. She's just standing there, staring at me, watching me die.

But I remember! I remember! I remember that no matter how far down you get, you gotta get up. I gotta get up and fight my own horrible, stinking, putrid, rotten self!

I struggle to my feet and lean against the wall. I'm breathing hard, but god damnit, I'm breathing. I look at Pearl. She's crazed, completely out of her head. She knows what's happening. She's been here a thousand times before. Kyle gets to his feet and stands beside her. His hands are trembling, his face is white as a sheet.

"You want me to sing the fuckin' song!" I scream. "Okay! You listening, Raz? You listening, Kyle? You ready, Pearl? You listening? 'Cause I'm gonna sing it! And then *I'm* gonna tell *you* if I wrote it! You got that? *I'm* gonna tell *you*. You got nothing to say about it!"

I close my eyes and a memory washes over me, a memory of Lily. She's sitting next to me in my stolen car, her honey brown hair blowing in the wind, and she's singing "Hey Baby," and she's doing it right. But what makes it so good? What makes Lily such a great singer? That's the big question, right? What is it?

I close my eyes and sing it for her, trying to sing it the way she does, wanting more than anything to thank her for resurrecting me, for loving me, for letting me love her, for letting me love her child. And now I sing it for the boy, making it a lullaby. A sweet, forgiving lullaby.

And that's the secret. *That's* the way you do it. You say goodnight. You say good-bye. You say sleep tight. You say . . . don't cry. You say I'll never stop loving you, no matter what you do. I'll never stop loving you.

I keep singing, but I open my eyes, and Pearl is crying. Kyle is sitting in his seat, his face buried in his hands. And that's either a lot of static, or I've gotten through to Raz, too. But I'm not done yet. There's one more person I have to convince.

So I close my eyes again, and say good-bye to my sorrow, to my fear, to my doubt, to myself. I say good-bye, and now I say hello.

Hey Baby, how you been?
Haven't seen you in a while.
Hey Baby, come on in
Give your old daddy a smile.

Wish you hadn't believed those lies.
I swear none of them were true.
Wish you hadn't believed those lies.
I never stopped loving you,
Loving you.

Coda

Dear Charlie,
Here's a poem for you about our wedding.

the perfect moment
the perfect air
all in white
red roses
by the miracle fall of water

we got married
Charlie and me
to everybody that was there
and everybody that wasn't

we got married
and we were always married
before we got married
and after we got married

then the sun set
but it didn't really
the earth spun us into darkness
and will spin us into light
and spin us into darkness
and spin us into light

we mustn't fear the darkness
the darkness is the dawn

Lily

p.s. I see you signed up to cook dinner tonight. Need any help?